KEPT ANIMALS

A NOVEL

KATE MILLIKEN

SCRIBNER

NEW YORK   LONDON   TORONTO   SYDNEY   NEW DELHI

SCRIBNER

An Imprint of Simon & Schuster, Inc.

1230 Avenue of the Americas

New York, NY 10020

First Scribner hardcover edition April 2020

SCRIBNER and design are registered trademarks of The Gale Group, Inc., used under license by Simon & Schuster, Inc., the publisher of this work.

For information about special discounts for bulk purchases, please contact Simon & Schuster Special Sales at 1-866-506-1949 or business@simonandschuster.com.

The Simon & Schuster Speakers Bureau can bring authors to your live event. For more information or to book an event contact the Simon & Schuster Speakers Bureau at 1-866-248-3049 or visit our website at www.simonspeakers.com.

Interior design by Alexis Minieri

Manufactured in the United States of America

1   3   5   7   9   10   8   6   4   2

Library of Congress Control Number: 2019025251

ISBN 978-1-5011-8858-9
ISBN 978-1-5011-8860-2 (ebook)

For my family, all of you

You might think about the people in the burning house, see them trying for the stairs, but mostly you don't give a damn. They are too far away, like everything else.

—Annie Proulx, "A Lonely Coast"

KEPT ANIMALS

ON THE MORNING of November 2, 1993, just a half mile up the road from where my mother was working as a stable hand, a fire started in Topanga Canyon, California. Fueled by Santa Ana winds gusting sixty miles an hour, the flames raced from the canyon's summit—jumping switchbacks, bursting open chaparral, swallowing manzanita whole—and reached the Pacific Ocean in record time. Despite an unprecedented number of firefighters, trucks, and air tankers dropping water from the sky, the fire's path and rate of consumption were dictated solely by the wind. From Calabasas to Malibu, residents fled, circumnavigating bottlenecked roads on foot, by horse, by Rollerblade. Those who had them boarded boats and watched from the water as the coastline burned, a glowing snake cutting through ash-thick air, day turned to night.

Mama once told me that if you cut down a canyon oak, you can see within its rings the marks of the fires it has withstood, wisps of smoke in the shape of half a heart.

Even before I had been told them, I could feel these stories unfurling within me, stories of events that happened before I was born, their heat still palpable.

In the end, the Old Topanga fire consumed over 18,500 acres, nearly four hundred homes, and the lives of countless animals and the people who tried to save them. That area of the Santa Monica Mountains is known as a fire corridor, its topography and ecology inviting such large-scale burns, yet this fire's cause remains listed as arson.

They've never known who to blame.

TOPANGA CANYON, CALIFORNIA

JULY 24, 1993

RORY—SHE WAS then just Rory, not yet anyone's mother—saw it first and thought it was a dog. A small breed, a cairn or a spaniel pup that had snuck beneath a fence seeking food or affection only to get its first pat of the day from the fender of a speeding car.

It was not yet dawn and the canyon walls were denim blue under the moon's soft light. Rory leaned forward to see the animal better and Gus, her stepfather, pulled the truck over. They'd come across roadkill nearly every morning. Deer, rabbits, even a coyote; bodies in the road, noses pointed toward their last intention.

Ever since school let out for the summer, Rory had been rising in the dark, waking Gus, wanting to work her full list of horses before the sun reached its scorching height.

"That's a fox," Gus said.

The rust-hued fur, the blackened lines of its muzzle and tail, were apparent in the beam of the headlights now. Rory sat back, relieved. She'd been imagining looking for a collar, having to call the number on the tag.

"I've lived here twenty-odd years and I've only seen one other. Had eyes the size of plums," Gus said, making rings with his fingers, looking through them at Rory.

"Come on," she said. "Quit playing. Let's move it already."

"I can get this one," Gus said, putting his hand to the roof to lift himself out. He'd put on weight. Rory worried about his heart.

After the deluge of rain the winter before, Governor Pete Wilson had declared an end to six years of drought, but the lawns in the valley were only coming in green now because the rains that had hit the canyon ran down its parched crevices, never sinking in, going on to feed the L.A. River, the reservoir, and all those automatic sprinklers instead. The canyon's creeks were dried to cracking already and Gus said the animals they kept finding had wandered from their beaten paths, hunting water. Burying them was beside the point—taking a vulture's work—but he'd agreed they could stop and move the bodies, sparing them from being speed bumps the canyon's tourists winced over.

Weeks ago, when they'd found the coyote, Rory felt compelled to say something—not a prayer so much as an apology on behalf of mankind—and she'd said a few words for every animal since. Gus obediently lowering his head, then mumbling, "That was good," when Rory was through.

She closed her eyes now, readying words, but Gus was making a racket in the flat bed of the truck—a bucket dumped out, a bridle tossed aside, the metallic clank of bits and buckles. She turned around in time to catch the silken drape of the fox slipping from his hands and into the emptied bucket, the feline liquidity of its fur. She was still fixed on the bucket when Gus closed himself back into the truck.

"Is it alive?" she asked, gooseflesh riding her arms. "If it's still alive we could—" She was imagining spoon-feeding it, warming it beneath saddle pads, nursing it back to health.

Gus tipped his hat off and gave a nearly imperceptible shake of his head.

"But," Rory started. "If it's dead—"

Gus was looking into the well of his hat. "You should say your little prayer—"

"My *little* prayer?" she said. "Why's it in the bucket? Why would you keep it? You're the one—"

She was about to remind him of the vultures, the cycle of life, the notions he'd fed to her, she was realizing, just to keep them moving. She stared hard at him as he pulled the truck back onto the road, the twitch of a secret smile beneath his beard. She put her boots up on the dash, knowing how he hated it. "She won't like this," Rory said.

He rolled down his window and ran his hand through his straw-gray hair. Both of them knew *she* meant Mona, Rory's mother.

Ten years ago, when they moved into Gus's house, Mona insisted he box up all evidence of his old hobby. Rory, just five years old then, had a particular fascination with the birds, sitting motionless on perches, not yet understanding what taxidermy involved. In all these years, she hadn't wondered if he still did it, but he hadn't given her reason to until now.

"Did you hear what I said?" she asked.

They were cresting the mountain, nearing the ranch, the day's first light splintering through the trees, a sandy light.

"I did," he said, and turned the truck down the driveway and under the ranch's iron archway:

LEANING ROCK RANCH

EQUESTRIAN TRAINING AND BOARDING

They weren't the first to arrive. The gold convertible Mercedes belonging to June Fisk, of the Fisk twins, was already pulled in alongside the L barn, the coveted space that stayed shadiest the longest. The other cars, each one dustier than the next, belonged to the men who lived and worked on the ranch; Tomás's was the worst of all, up on cinder blocks, yet to run.

Gus pulled in next to the office and hoisted the parking brake, rocking them back in their seats. Behind them, the bucket tipped over with a fleshy thud.

"Jesus," Rory said. "Can we please just bury it?"

"This place is a tinderbox," Gus said, ignoring her, looking up at the hillside. Rory had heard his theories about the downpours, about the winter rains being what actually ushered in wildfires, by growing the ground fuel. "Just you wait," Gus said. "It'll be one of you." He looked toward June Fisk's Mercedes. "Lazy with your cigarettes, flicking a match out of the car. It won't take much."

"One of us?" Rory asked, with a laugh of disbelief. Each of the Fisk twins, June and her brother, Wade, owned horses more valuable than their cars combined and neither of them ever said more than a half sentence in Rory's direction. She made a stable hand's wage of $3.75 an hour, exercising horses for people like them. People with air-conditioned homes and beach vacations, people who could afford a lack of commitment. Every other day, Rory had to ride Wade's chestnut Hanoverian, Journey. "The Fisks don't even know my name," Rory said. "Besides," she started, "I don't smo—"

"I'll tell you what," Gus interrupted, lifting the toes of her boots and dropping them off the dash. "You don't tell your mother about this"—he tipped his head toward the back of the truck—"and I won't tell her you've been sneaking her cigarettes."

"Seriously?" Rory said. She had taken maybe a dozen, but so carefully, and over weeks.

"Seriously," Gus said, his eyebrows lifting with the challenge.

Beyond the ranch, beyond horses, what they shared most was a fear of Mona.

Rory got out of the truck with an itch to take the bucket from the back, to run with it into the hills and bury the poor animal, but instead she closed the door and leaned back in through the window, mocking his country drawl. "Mighty kind of you, Mr. Scott."

THAT AFTERNOON, THE boy got away from Sarah Price in the market.

She was reading the ingredients on a box of fish sticks—busy hating Everett for requesting such plebeian food—when she looked down and saw the boy was gone. *The boy.* Sarah thought of Charlie as the boy only when they were having a bad day. She could not bring herself to appreciate the dichotomy of the toddler brain: at any given hour of the day he was madly dashing away from her, but in the pitch of night he insisted, repeatedly, incessantly, on having her at his side. And now she wasn't completely sure when she had last seen him. She was exhausted, but not in the mopey, leaden-foot way people tended to be in this heat, rather in a deeper, more hard-wired way: a compulsion to get out and shake loose of something. Everett wished she'd have the nanny, Carmen, do the shopping, but she knew he wasn't being considerate so much as being fearful of some rogue paparazzo taking her picture looking disheveled in this sad little market, then splashing it on the cover of *ET*.: "You'd Never Know She's a Movie Star's Wife." No matter, she liked the sifting and choosing, the mindless accomplishment of it. And this market was never crowded. Sarah loathed crowds, lines, gatherings of any kind, really.

The boy. Charlie. My boy. An emptiness was opening behind her ribs, a sinkhole of space. Charlie was a beautiful boy, unmistakable. His grandfather's copper-red hair and emerald eyes and his father's toothy grin. Even if someone didn't know he was Everett Price's son, she would worry. He stirred a need in people to touch him, to pick him up. To take him?

She heard his laugh—his impish snicker—before she saw him. He was in the produce area, looking up at a man in a white, blood-mottled apron: a butcher, bent over Charlie with a ghoulish grin. It took Sarah another stride, a split second, to see the slice of orange tucked between the butcher's lips. Even as she had him in her arms again, Charlie was still laughing. The butcher pulled the fruit from his mouth. "He's an easy laugh, that one."

Sarah was working to keep ahold of him, the boy pushing and

twisting against her, wanting, as usual, to be down again. She pressed her face to the seashell of his ear: "Be still."

"But they can get away from you sometimes, can't they? I was about to walk him back to you . . . Mrs. Price."

"Of course you were," Sarah said abruptly, turning away, resenting that pause before he said her name. That he'd said her name. He didn't *know* her.

Had she felt liked here at all? They'd moved from Beverly Hills, where they were recognized and respected, to this gauche ogling. She'd been the one who wanted to move. To get away—as away as they could and still be near enough to the studios, the necessary parties; god help her. Though now, of course, Everett had been cast in a film that was shooting in Toronto. And he'd been in Vancouver all of June, and New York the month before that. Did anyone even make movies in Hollywood anymore?

Sarah thought better of how she'd spoken to the butcher. "Of course you were," she said, over her shoulder, with renewed warmth. Charlie was twisting in her arms, still trying to see him.

"Paul," the butcher said. "My name's Paul, Mrs. Price."

"Thank you, Paul," she said, and then for some reason she kept on walking, right past the register, still talking—"Thank you, so very much, thank you, Paul"—she was rambling. "He just needs me, you see. He wanders off and"—she was backing out the door—"I'm his mother. So, we have to be on our way." *Like a crazy person;* this was Everett's voice in her head.

She'd gotten to the car and had Charlie in his seat before realizing that she still had the basket, that she'd set it down on the seat beside him as if it were her purse, the fish sticks there on top.

IF NOT FOR his finding the fox, this had been just another day of work, of resenting the tightness of his boots in this heat, teaching one lethargic jumping lesson after another. Gus's last class was a training-level group of prepubescent girls on an older string of horses, all taking their fences as if weighed down in glue. Into the speaker system, he chided: "Ease up on the reins, ladies. Are you looking to jump these fences or back up over them?"

He'd seen Rory going up the trailhead on her mare not long ago. He needed to get her a ride home. He'd already decided how he wanted to articulate the fox; curled as if sleeping, one eye open above the bush of her tail.

"Okay, that's enough for today," he said into the loudspeaker, and every apple-cheeked kid dropped her reins as the horses turned for the barn.

In the distance, vultures swept black circles above the god-size fist of sandstone that teetered on the westernmost hillside above the ranch. Carlotta Danvers had named the ranch Leaning Rock because of it, back in the seventies, when she first bought the land, being sharp enough then to know naming the threat destigmatized it. It had been three years since her Alzheimer's diagnosis, yet Gus still aimed to please her with the way he ran things.

As soon as the ring emptied, Gus called to Jorge, his head stable hand, who stepped over the fence and began walking out the fire hose. With the water rationing lifted, Gus had the men hosing down the rings and the walkways throughout the day. Twenty years ago, he'd taken a job here exercising horses, same as Rory did now, never anticipating he'd become the manager, let alone the lead trainer, but here he was. There'd been articles written about him: "The Cowboy Equestrian."

Gus briefly considered asking Jorge to take Rory home, but June Fisk was still around. And Gus didn't like what Rory had said, that the Fisks didn't even know her name.

"It shouldn't be much out of your way," Gus said. He'd found June putting her horse up for the night, the sky casting around in pinks and oranges. "I'd sure appreciate it."

"No, I'd be happy to," June said. "For sure."

June didn't always clock so many hours at the barn, but Gus knew she was getting ready for Fresno—conditioning Palmetto in the hills, taking a dressage lesson in the afternoon. And it wasn't unusual for kids to mill around the barn anyway, lingering by the vending machine, watching the men clean up after their horses. Some of the girls flirted with the stable hands, especially Tomás, the youngest, as if practicing for boys at school, but June wasn't that sort. She wasn't so aimless. Not unlike his Rory. Wade was another story, always zipping in and out in that open-sided blue jeep of his, friends in flip-flops piled in the back, whistling to him to hurry up, startling the horses. If Wade had half of his sister's dedication; if they'd had to share a car, he'd at least be here more often, but Gus registered there was some friction there, between the twins. These were vague thoughts: horseshit, forked and tossed. What mattered most was that June was reliable and willing to take Rory home. Maybe they'd become friends.

Rory was back in the L barn, cleaning tack, working lotion into the leather like it was a contest. Her mare, Chap, nickered to Gus from her stall.

"June here's offered to give you a ride home, Rory."

"You're staying, then," Rory said, not looking up.

"Now, Rory." He sighed.

"Now, Gus," she said. For a time after he and Mona had married, she'd called him Dad. He'd been Gus for a long time now, but right then it sounded all wrung out, the same way Mona said it. "I know why you're staying," she told him. Before he could respond, she turned to June, obliging as ever: "Just gimme a minute to wash," she said, displaying the palms of her hands.

"For sure," June said again. Her little gold Mercedes had white leather seats.

JUNE FISK WAS gay. Everyone knew this—everyone except Gus—and they also knew it was the source of a rift in the Fisk family. Despite this or maybe because of it, June wore a necklace with a small charm of two entwined Venus figures, a piece of jewelry that Rory had heard she revealed whenever one of the younger boarders got up the nerve to ask if "it" was true. So, when Gus said June was going to drive her home, Rory hesitated, picturing Mona, a cigarette dangling from her lips, taking in June's car as they pulled up, her expression souring as if June's goddesses of love were entwined on the body of the Mercedes itself. Hay fever kept Mona at a merciful distance from Leaning Rock during the day, and her job took her into the valley every night, usually just as Gus and Rory were getting home. But if she was still at home now, when June pulled up, Rory knew that through some invisible vibration in the air, she would feel Mona's opinion of June, her fancy car, and her orientation. Mona's moods and opinions took up an inordinate amount of space in their house, but lately, Rory had noticed an energy within herself, something spirited, maybe even angry, and she'd been letting this new force make different choices for her.

This was the first time Rory had ridden in a convertible. It was not unlike galloping downhill. Her hair was pulled back in its usual braid and tucked into her shirt, while June's cropped box-dyed blue-black hair danced at the line of her chin.

June said something that Rory couldn't hear, then repeated it: "You work too hard."

Rory shook her head. She could have said the same about June, except she only rode her own horse and didn't have to spend half the day forking out stalls.

"You ever get away? Leave the canyon? Leave the barn?" June asked.

"For school," Rory said.

"Polk High?"

Rory nodded. Polk was in the valley, off the 101, cloaked in smog. She knew June went to a private school, somewhere in Brentwood or Santa Monica, near the ocean's salt-scrubbed air.

June had a broad, plain face with a slightly piggish nose and large white teeth. She was not what Rory thought people considered pretty, but her features were tidy, well-kept, her eyes the wide honest kind, though she often wore large round sunglasses. She always rode in a white cotton button-up shirt, tan britches, and tall polished black boots; dependable as a uniform. The opposite of Wade, who often showed up in swim trunks and a serape, smelling of Banana Boat. But Wade's confidence shone brighter, a luxury in his own body that drew people's attention.

June stuck a cassette into the tape deck.

"Lou Reed?" Rory asked.

"Yeah," June said. "The Velvet Underground, so yeah." She nodded at Rory and turned it up. "How old are you?" June was practically yelling, competing with the wind and the music.

"Fifteen." Rory knew she was small for her age, muscled and flat-chested.

"You ever smoke? Pot, I mean. You ever smoke weed?"

Rory's cheeks flushed.

"Aw, I should get you high sometime. I kinda owe you—all your help with our horses."

It was rare for June not to come work her horse, Palmetto, but when Rory had the chance to ride him she considered it a pleasure. She'd have ridden Pal for free, but she thought better than to say so.

Rory knew that plenty of the *barn brats*—this was a Mona phrase—smoked weed. She knew the wet-skunk smell. It had never interested her before. "Okay," she said, louder than necessary as the car slowed, then stopped, and the wind stilled. Then more softly, "I mean, sure. I'd smoke with you. Whenever."

June smiled at her. They were stuck in a line of traffic now, backed up a half mile from the stop sign at the fork onto the main road, right alongside the gated entrance to the Price estate. One of the two winged gates was standing open, like a beckoning arm. The closed side of the gate read, 521 OLD CAN, the lettering in glinting hot silver.

14

The other half—Rory had driven by a thousand times—completed it: YON ROAD. She'd never seen the gate open this way, never laid eyes on the front doors. They were double wide, heavily varnished wood, with an enormous clay pot of fountain grass on each side. A broad silver plate framed the doorbell, shiny as a mirror.

"You know them? The Prices?" June asked. Everyone knew *of* the Prices.

"No," Rory said. "You?"

"The daughter?" June said, her voice ticking up in a question. "Vivian? She transferred to our school, Merriam Prep, midyear. Seems nice enough, a little arrogant maybe. But it's got to be tough being a movie star's kid."

"Right," Rory chided. But June wasn't laughing. "You're kidding, right?"

"No. Really." June tucked her hair behind her ear. "Wade sure thinks she's *all that*."

"He thinks she's pretty?" Rory asked. "Vivian?" She liked saying her name, the slip of it, like rope untangling.

"You've seen pictures of her, haven't you?"

"Yeah, of course," Rory said. She'd seen Vivian in Mona's magazines, the kind full of gossip and wardrobe imperatives, but also—"Our house looks down on their yard."

"Bullshit," June said, glancing at Rory. "Really?"

It was another two and a half miles and a two-hundred-foot climb up the ridge before they would reach the bridge that led to Rory's driveway. Carlotta's sprawling house was perched above the dilapidated little A-frame they rented from her, and now that house, their house, hovered ironically above the opulent expanse of the Price estate. All the canyon's walls were tiered with houses this way, a result of people putting themselves where they didn't belong. After the winter rains, the pylons of some houses had become exposed, precarious as the legs of a new foal. But the Prices had dug themselves a big flat lot, and from Rory's bedroom window, through a stand of scrub oak, she could see the landscaped gardens, the winding slate paths, the giant sandbox, the blue gem of their pool. "I swear. From my room. I've seen her there. Not a lot, but—" She'd watched Vivian swimming. Often. Countless times. Seen her lying at the edge of the pool, the top to her bikini flung aside. "I can see their pool."

"From your room? Shit, that's something," June said. "Maybe you'll show me?"

"Sure."

When the Prices bought the land, it had been only a hillside consisting of the oaks, a windbreak of eucalyptus, and a small adobe shack. Then orange-vested surveyors came scrambling around like colonizing ants. Bulldozers followed, digging out the slopes. They downed oaks and all the eucalyptus, chain saws buzzing, and set them on truck beds like piles of matchsticks. Rory had watched, hidden up behind the remaining trees, inconsequential as a squirrel. Eight months later, the adobe shack had stretched into a single-story estate, the shape of a flying white crane, with its wings holding—rumor was—eight bedrooms, all spotted with skylights. There'd been grumbling about the bulldozing, more Hollywood types moving in, until a sizable donation was made to the Topanga Historical Society. Rory knew she had a view others would want.

At the fork, Rory directed June left, but they still had to wait for a break in traffic.

"Do you think she's pretty?" Rory asked, amazed by her own boldness.

"Vivian? I think she's pale."

Pickup, car, van, car. Too many people with maps. June gunned it through the smallest break between oncoming cars, saying, "This heat has got to quit."

In the dirt turnaround that served as their driveway, June stopped short, and a net of dust hung in the air. Mona's car was gone, and Rory let out a relieved breath. "She's at work."

"Your mom?"

"She's a bartender," Rory said.

"A bartender," June repeated, nodding.

"In Reseda," Rory said, wishing she hadn't. She untucked her braid from her shirt and gripped the end of it. A nervous habit that Mona was always pointing out.

"Huh. So, nobody's home." June cut the engine.

"You want to come in? There's beer. Some harder stuff, too."

"You drink?" June was running lip gloss over her lips, checking it in the rearview.

"Sometimes." A lie, but the kind with a wish folded up inside, a wish for another version of herself.

"Right," June said, puckering her lips. "For sure."

ON THE PHONE, Sarah's doctor said, "You sound overtired."

Sarah knew by the occasional flare of sound coming from the

east end of the house that Vivian was home. Charlie was in his high chair, painting the tray with the remains of his dinner. She'd given him something green. Eventually, Vivian would come out and make herself food, but not until Sarah had gone to bed—however temporarily. It was a routine, Charlie's calling out for her, again and again, then clinging to her neck as she tried to soothe him, groping for her breasts as she stroked his back, shushing him, until finally she would relent and feed him in the glider. Then, when she was sure he was truly asleep—those heavy-lidded eyes!—she would rise, moving toward the crib as seamlessly as she was able, only to have his eyes inevitably pop open as soon as she bent toward the railing of his bed. His torso would go rigid and he'd thrust his feet to the floor, scrambling away, running from the room, down the hall, flopping onto the carpet. She did not recall Vivian's infancy rendering her so powerless, but surely this forgetting was nature's trickery. She'd anticipated Vivian's teenage years would leave her feeling diminished—and oh, how they did—but this dual attack on her wits . . . "I'm just not myself right now," she said to her doctor.

Ever since Everett had left, yet again, she and Vivian had fallen into a pattern of avoidance. Vivian could simultaneously own a room and not exist in it. She was always stretching out by the pool or putting her feet up on the couch, a Discman tethered to her head, her mind elsewhere while her vanity seemed to pulse, awaiting a spotlight. Her presence was an invitation for Sarah to move to another room. But maybe that was okay. Maybe it was simply Charlie's turn to have her now. The baby she had so feverishly wanted.

On the phone, the doctor asked again, "Are you still breast feeding?" He would refuse to up her dosage if she said that she was. They'd had this discussion before.

GUS WAS IN the back of the main office, the room that had been Carlotta's office; a picture of her son and daughter was still there on the wall. He'd had a drink, maybe three, enough to dull the senses before he cut. It had been a long time, but this was a beautiful animal, a thing to put his mind to, to do right. Mona wouldn't be home for hours. He poured another drink, but then set it aside, a reward for when he was through the hard part.

The fox hung from a ceiling beam, one paw strung with twine. He held the limp paw and drew his knife in a ring around it, scoring the skin, before drawing the blade down the flank, where the fur shifted from red to gray, stopping at the tail.

Outside, the ranch had gone still; a lone mockingbird, a horse's gusty exhale, and the hum of the freezer behind him were the only sounds.

It didn't take much to tug the skin away, separating the hide from the musculature inside, but then there was the odor, that iron tint of blood, enough to overpower the whiskey. He sat down. Every time, this smell did him in. *Sissy Gussie.* His sister, Joy, she never cried when their father hung a deer to drain. And now she was more than just a ranch manager—she had her own land back in Wyoming. *A man can get used to anything,* his father always said, implying Gus wasn't one. It was a phrase Gus still repeated to himself when any complaint took hold. Every jealousy. He knew that wasn't how his father intended it, that he would've never put up with what Gus was dealing with. Not from his wife. But Gus wasn't his father, thank god.

He threw back the reward whiskey and refreshed it, stepping out the back door for air, the smell of the cooling earth. The stars were tipping and swimming around him. So he was drunk. He could admit that. Something to eat, that was what he needed, then he could get back to it. When had he last eaten anyway?

Earlier, he'd seen Jorge sitting with Sonja, his wife, in the shade of the sycamore up against their squat stucco house, speaking in the abbreviated murmur of spouses. Happy spouses. Jorge had been eating from a paper plate—stewed meat, maybe peppers and onions, rolled into a tortilla. That's what Gus needed: home-cooked food.

Sonja was always cooking for Jorge and Tomás, her son, and usually making enough for the three other men who also lived on the grounds, in modest quarters above the school horse tack room. When Mona hadn't wanted to help with Carlotta—despite the fact that she lived directly above them, that they rented their own house from her—Gus had hired Sonja to come and look after her, make her meals, too. After that, he'd been offered a plate of Sonja's food on occasion, but he knew better than to expect it.

Still, he was hungry now. And the light in their house was on, a beckoning orange glow. Leftovers, he'd only ask for leftovers. And tomorrow he would apologize for the disruption.

VIVIAN WAS IN her room, on the phone with McLeod. This was the third time she'd called him since they'd moved, since her transfer from Westerly, where McLeod taught AP English, to Merriam Prep, yet another private school where yet another white man in his early thirties stood before his pupils (half of them hungover) and tried lamely to avoid meeting her eyes only to end up looking at her tits.

"How does it feel to be a stereotype?" Vivian asked. "He even wears the same cologne."

McLeod sighed. Everything on his end was overly loud as his "home office" (she had learned this on their second tele-soirée) was actually his garage, acoustically resonant, but most important (maybe?) it was outside of his wife's domain. "Is this why you're calling, Vivian?" He had given her his number when she'd taken too much "R & R" from classes at Westerly, offering to "be available" to help her catch up, only she never called until she'd started at the new school. "To insult me?"

"Noooo," Vivian crooned. "I'm calling because my dad's been away for so long that he might as well be at war, and I'm desperate for a father figure, but not a real father figure, McLeod, just the figure part, the part that wants my breath in his ear."

"I can't do this, Vivian."

"Yes, you can, McLeod. Play along. I'm bored in my ivory tower. And so hot." Vivian had muted her television: clips of President Bill Clinton in a press conference, followed by various men, Colin

Powell and others, all in uniform, the scroll on the screen: *Gays in the Military?* That fucking question mark.

"Where's your dad now?" McLeod asked.

"Don't ask, don't tell," Vivian intoned.

"It's better than nothing," McLeod said.

"Canada. Is Toronto *in* Canada?" Vivian squeaked, playing dumb. "That's where Daddy is this time." Then her voice went flat again; disappointed. "It's not what he said he'd do. Clinton, I mean."

"It's progress."

"You're all so smitten with him," Vivian said. She clicked over to MTV. From her bed, she could see across the patio and pool to the other wing of the house, to her parents' room (more mausoleum), and to Charlie's room, where Sarah was drawing the curtains, as if this would keep him in bed. "Why don't you tell me about your wife instead? How is Mrs. McLeod?"

WHEN JUNE CAME inside, Rory saw her house as if she too had never seen it before: the trail of crusted dishes, the dripping faucet, the dead flies on the windowsill. June moved past her and pulled a glass from the kitchen cupboard, tearing away the last paper towel on the roll to clean the glass's rim. She ran the water a solid minute before she filled the glass, downed it, then looked at Rory. "So, where's your room?"

Upstairs, June slipped off her sandals, set her sunglasses down on the dresser, and moved into the room. She paused to touch the battered camera that Rory kept on a hook beside the bookshelf. A Canon AE-1 that Mona had given her earlier that year, having unearthed it from the bar's lost and found. Rory had accepted it indifferently until Mona elbowed her, saying, "Come on, I know you wanted one." They were uncomfortable, these moments when Mona knew her like this, though Rory couldn't say why.

June was in the bathroom, looking at the two taxidermied birds Rory kept on a wicker table beside the sink. The ones Rory had snuck off with as a little girl, before Gus could pack them away, believing she was rescuing them from the horror of being sealed up in a dark cardboard box. A red-winged blackbird and a towhee. Each frozen atop mesquite perches, permanently alert.

"Those are weird," June said, brushing off her hands. Then she pulled her britches down and sat on the toilet, the stream of her urine audible. Rory turned, fiddling with the knob of the floor fan, the room suddenly hot. "But it is nice up here," June said.

It was nice up here. It was always a relief, to remember her separateness from Gus and Mona, from how they lived below. Her room had been the attic, long, like a train car with a pitched ceiling, but with three windows that sat above the tree line, letting in a play of light against the unpainted pine walls. Gus had refinished the floors and he'd managed to turn the storage room into a narrow bathroom. *I didn't marry rich, but I sure married handy,* Mona had said, rubbing his neck. Years ago, Rory had begun cutting images from magazines, from *Equine Times, National Geographic, Vanity Fair,* and the more obscure news magazines that Carlotta let her cart away, and tacking them to the walls. She'd chosen some for their faraway destinations, others for their composition, their intimacy. She'd

looked at the faces in these pictures for so long and so often that
she felt she knew them. Otherwise, Rory kept the room spare: her
bed, a rocking chair that Carlotta had given her in one of her manic
unloading of things, the single dresser, a bookshelf, and the industrial
metal fan—its low breeze lifting the corners of the pictures now.
June was holding down the image of two women walking across a
beige wash of desert, each balancing a basket, a shine in their eyes,
aware of the photographer.

"You headed to Kenya, Scott?" June asked, her finger to the
caption.

"Probably not," Rory said. Scott was Gus's last name, but Rory
didn't correct her.

"Sure you are," June said, pulling a bag of weed from her pocket.

GUS KNOCKED AND leaned into the doorframe. He heard the inside of
the house go quiet. He knocked again, and Sonja opened the door.
Her face was blurry, but he registered some antipathy. Behind her,
Tomás stepped into the living room and, seeing Gus, he stopped,
lifting one hand to wave. He had his headphones on, his head bobbing. Gus went to lift his hand to wave back, but he'd been leaning
on that hand and now he was moving into the kitchen, past Sonja,
trying to explain, "I'm not here to make work. I promise. I'm only,
I'm hungry—I couldn't stop thinking about some food. Your cooking, Sonja. I haven't eaten since—"

"Señor, you're here so late," Jorge said. There he was! Sitting at the little kitchen table in the corner of the room, a can of beer perspiring in front of him. The chair opposite him slid back from the table as if by magic. "Siéntate, mi amigo."

Gus got a hand on the chair and sat, feeling welcome now. But there were other voices in the house—a garble of Spanish. There, the radio on the counter, the term *NAFTA* a life raft in an otherwise unrecognizable sea of words. Gus had mostly picked up curse words over the years. "I'm a stray dog, looking for scraps." There were three more cans on the counter, drained and buckled. Mi amigo.

Jorge said something to Sonja and Sonja leaned into the hallway, yelling to Tomás—the boy yelling back, "Claro!" Tomás was taller and ropier than his mother or Jorge—clearly another man's son—but Jorge treated him as his own. Yes, a couple of stepfathers—they had plenty in common.

Sonja put a kettle on and riffled in the fridge, peering into repurposed cottage cheese containers until she found what she was looking for, shaking two rolls onto a paper plate that she set in front of Gus. He brought the cold fist of a roll to his nose. It was one of the cheese-filled rolls she baked in the mornings. "It's frío," he said. His tongue felt thick.

Jorge and Sonja were speaking in rapid-fire Spanish now. What was this warm orange light? The walls were marmalade.

Sonja waved a hand between them at the table. "Those were for Tomás." Rice. He'd have liked rice, maybe chicken or ground turkey, a meal that would stick to his stomach. He found Sonja's face, her narrowed eyes. "Eat," she said. "Then Jorge will make coffee for you."

"Cabrón," Jorge said, not yet getting up.

Gus lifted the roll and forced himself to chew. Sonja took a beer from the fridge and set it in front of Jorge. He had seen them squabble once or twice before, always drawing together again easily enough. Jorge cracked open his beer. Gus wanted one sip. Just one.

"It's the last," Jorge said, sensing Gus's longing, and slid the can toward him.

This—the can across the table—tipped Gus's thoughts to Mona, to the ever-available movie in his mind, her sliding a drink to another man, one of her regulars, leaning over the burnished wood of the bar, her breasts right there, inches from the always faceless man's hands.

"That's a hazard," Gus blurted. He'd found the source of the orange glow: a scarf thrown over a lamp in the living room. "A fire hazard," he said, pointing. His mouth was full, fizzing with beer and dough.

"We're not working now," Sonja said.

The teakettle was whistling, growing louder. Jorge got up.

"If you live here," Gus said, "in this house, on this land—" He took one more sip, to clear his throat. "Then you are always working—"

"Why are you not home, Señor?" Sonja asked. "You need time off, no? You should be home, in *your* kitchen."

Indeed, Gus thought.

Jorge was stirring instant coffee into the mug, the chink of the spoon against the porcelain.

He leaned toward Sonja and whispered to her before setting the mug down in front of Gus. Sonja walked away, cursing under her breath. She pulled the scarf from the lamp and disappeared around the corner.

Gus raised the mug. A door slammed. His hand shook. "Buenas noches," he called to Sonja, his eyes still adjusting to the sudden light.

RORY OPENED THE window and stepped out onto the narrow lip of grating. It was a place for setting plants, not people, but June stepped out, too, sitting on the windowsill, not yet bothering to look down, focused on the rolling paper, the thread of weed she had pinched there, saying, "It's going to be an easy competition, really. And your mare is so fit now. You should totally come." She was quick with her hands, creasing and tightening. She was talking about Ram Tap, the three-day in Fresno that she and Wade, in his half-assed way, were training for. "I mean, why not enter?" she asked, flicking her lighter to the end of the joint.

"Money," Rory said, blurting out the impolite truth, June having seen how they lived.

"Oh," June exhaled. She handed the joint to Rory and then she looked down. "Shit," she said, "That really is some place." She lowered herself in beside Rory.

The half-smoked butts Rory had lifted from Mona's ashtrays, smoking them out here, had her expecting the burn on inhale, but this was better, the taste lusher. They had to pull their knees up to their chests and pass the joint on the outside of the bars. They sat like that, pressed together, until the pool lights came on beneath them, like the opening of a show.

"They really can't see us up here?" June asked.

"Nope." A lightness had come over Rory, as if the iron grating were floating away from the house. June's bare foot was up against hers. "The lights are on a timer," Rory said.

June smiled. "How often do you sit out here, Scott?"

Rory took it for granted that the trees concealed her, though one of the gardeners had looked up once, shielding his eyes from the sun, and Rory had waved to him, a tic of cordiality from working at the ranch. "Our TV was broken for a while," she said.

June laughed, a high shrill laugh that she let roll on too long.

The week before, Rory had watched Mrs. Price overseeing a delivery of succulents, while her diapered son smudged his face against the glass of the sliding doors.

June knocked one knee against Rory's. "Look, look," she said, pointing at the house.

Someone was moving behind the white curtains. "That's the mom," Rory said.

"Mrs. Sarah Price," June announced, trumpeting into the shortened joint.

Mrs. Price came outside in a sleeveless, white, ankle-length nightgown that glowed against the darkened yard. She walked past the pool and June crouched into herself.

"She can't see us," Rory said, though a chill moved through her.

"Can she hear us?"

"I don't know." Rory whispered. "I've never sat out here with anyone, talking."

Mrs. Price and Vivian had the same long, amber hair, the same light-footed gait. She was eyeing a flower bed near the sandbox now, a spade in her hand. She began digging.

"She knows it's like fucking night out, right?" June said. "Does she always do shit like this? Dressed like that?"

Rory shook her head. She thought Mrs. Price looked like the subject of a painting, a photograph.

✢

McLEOD REFUSED TO talk about the missus. "No," he said. "How about you tell me what Merriam Prep has you reading this summer instead?"

"Conrad," Vivian said, rolling away from the view of the garden. "So two years ago . . ." Her mother was outside now, being weird.

"Heart of Darkness?" McLeod asked.

"Hmm. I'll be back in AP next year." She was on top of her comforter, the phone cradled between her ear and her arm. She knew he could hear her breathing.

"Good, so they recognize you're capable. Tell me what you're reading for fun, then."

"I'm not."

"Shame on you," McLeod said. "Well, what are you doing for fun, then?"

She didn't answer. There was power in the pause. She heard the creak of his chair, his settling in, enjoying her. "See, McLeod," she said. "You already know. I'm calling you for fun."

"Don't."

"McLeod, Mickey McLeod, keep talking to me," she sang.

"I can't. And there's our trouble, Vivian. I should go."

29

"Should," she said, "suggests you might not."

"I *am* hanging up."

"Tell me it was good to hear my voice."

"And your breath in my ear," McLeod said.

OUTSIDE THE OFFICE, Gus stood in the light pooling on the ground by the back door, retracing his thoughts. *Your kitchen.* Sonja's admonishment. He knew Rory was most likely home alone, eating cereal for dinner again. He never talked to her about Mona, about the nights when she didn't come home at all. *A man can get used to anything.*

He looked in the window, at the pink ribbons of innards laid across the wood plank; the fox's fur still attached at the ears and muzzle, like a shirt drawn over a head.

Maybe Rory already understood everything about Mona. How there were days that she danced into his arms, when her laughter was contagious, right up against days full of animosity and dissappearing. Maybe Rory didn't need to talk about it. Maybe it was Rory who could teach him a fucking thing or two about getting along in this world. Just rolling with it.

He felt in his pockets for his keys. He did want to be home. Sitting with Rory in *his* kitchen, eating anything at all.

AN ACCORDION OF time had spread open: ten minutes, an hour?

They'd watched Sarah Price go in the house and come out again. June remained quiet, mouth open. Rory felt light and tired, half-steeped in a pleasant dream. She was wishing for her bed, when Vivian Price came out of the house. June covered her mouth as if she'd been about to shout. Vivian was wearing the black one-piece, her hair pulled up in a high bun, a towel slung over her shoulder. Rory straightened, feeling she'd just made good on a promise.

Vivian looked in her mother's direction, but neither of them spoke. She dropped the towel at the pool's edge and stepped onto the first stair, the marbled light of the pool dancing against her skin. Rory let out the grip of her ribs as steadily as she could; she'd been holding her breath. Vivian's dive into the water was silent. She came up, swimming a breaststroke, her face rising and dipping at the water's surface. June began to laugh a scoffing, quiet laugh. She put her hand on Rory's knee, as if to steady herself.

"What?" Rory asked.

"I mean, are they, like, vampires?" Her laughter pealed higher, her hand still on Rory.

"They are pale," Rory said quickly, somewhat worried Sarah Price could hear. It wasn't true. There wasn't anything sickly about the Prices. Vivian Price, especially. She was beautiful. Rory knew this from the magazines, but she knew from this distance, too. It was clear in the way she carried herself, as if leading others behind.

When Vivian stepped out of the pool, she slung her towel over her shoulder without drying off. June's hand loosened. It wasn't until the sliding glass doors closed that Mrs. Price looked up in Vivian's direction, her daughter already inside.

"*You* think she's pretty," June said. "I can tell." She was facing Rory—the proximity of her breath, its disrupting warmth. "I'll light this again," she said, lifting the joint to Rory's mouth. "There's one hit left." Rory inhaled, smelling the lighter's fuel. "Now keep it in," June said. Her hand was back on Rory's knee, the other on Rory's shoulder turning her until June's cropped hair hung like a curtain around their faces. "Now exhale," June said, her mouth already on Rory's mouth as she spoke.

Not a kiss. Rory recognized this was not a kiss. June was inhaling, pulling the smoke up out of Rory's lungs and into her own. Rory started to cough, and June sat back, her lips sealed, her breath held, until she smiled. "I wasn't sure you'd let me do that," she said, a thin ribbon of smoke escaping the side of her mouth.

OUT IN THE yard, in the dark, Sarah was more at ease. The heat more tolerable. Or maybe it *was* hormones. Perhaps she was beginning to menstruate again; she hadn't since Charlie was born. Everett always suggested hormones whenever she complained, so quick to imply that women were mere animals.

Earlier, after she'd gotten Charles to bed, a mockingbird had started up and she'd picked up the phone dimly mistaking the bird's prattle for the phone's ring, overly hopeful, only to hear the monotony of the dial tone. She'd gone ahead and called Everett then, in Toronto. She listened as he answered sleepily, "Hello . . . hello . . . hello." Then, "Sarah, is that you? Sarah, don't let Charles play with the phone. Please, Sarah. Hang up. I've got a four a.m. call, for

Christ's sake. I need sleep, Sarah." Everett needed sleep! When she called again, she found herself incapable of making words, though she wanted to tell him how hot it was, how unbearable, truly, it would be to sleep next to him anyway. Was Toronto nice this time of year? Had he been to the hotel pool? Of course she knew how busy he was, but wasn't there time for dinner with the cast? They talked this way, in her head for a while. When she tried again, it only buzzed, a phone left off its cradle.

Whenever Everett called of his own volition, it was always in the middle of the day, just as everything around her was so bright she couldn't focus. Not that they ever spoke about Charlie. She would have liked to talk about Charlie. She felt if Everett would just remind her that the sleepless nights, the boy's rebelliousness, this heat—it was all normal, hearing that from him would bring some relief. His validation. Why did she always yearn for his validation?

Oddly enough, Charlie had gone down fine that night, even before dark. He'd napped only briefly on the drive back from the market that morning. Perhaps that was the trick, simply wear him out. But he was going to wake up again. He always did, needing her as Vivian and Everett did not. Had Vivian come outside? But of course it was Everett who needed sleep.

Digging in the soil, her nails painfully edged with earth, in the far corner of the garden, she began to worry she would not hear him when he woke. Though the way he could cry, she often heard him long after he had stopped, like a stifled alarm in her own body.

❖

JUNE DROPPED ONTO Rory's bed. "Next time, I'll bring more. Then you won't have to kiss me again," she said, smirking.

Rory was in Carlotta's old rocker, her pulse in her ears. "It's okay," she mumbled.

Only the bathroom light was on. There was a lamp on the bureau, but Rory couldn't will herself up to turn it on. June was looking at the glow-in-the-dark star stickers above the bed, clustered in the pitched peak of the roof.

"Wade says it's Sarah Price who's the rich one. Everett's famous and all, but apparently Sarah's dad left them some ridiculous inheritance when he died."

Rory rocked the chair. "From what?"

"Fuck, I don't know. Whatever people die of."

"I mean, where did his money come from?"

June shrugged. "Where's any of it come from?"

June's father was a doctor and their money seemed otherworldly, yet Rory heard envy in June's voice.

"I hope you'll forgive my lingering, Scott. I don't like driving when I'm high."

"You're not," Rory said, fingers busy at the seam of the chair's cushion. "You're not lingering, I mean. Stay, if you like."

June rolled to her side, her face backlit by the bathroom light, unknowable, but Rory could feel her eyes. "Wanna pass the time over here?" She patted the bed.

"I'm good," Rory said, her mouth, her hands, trembling.

"I'm only teasing," June said. "No need to fear the lesbo, Scott."

"Oh," Rory started. "It's not that. I just—" She stopped, listening to an announcement from the bridge over the creek, the ba-dum, ba-dum of a crossing car.

June was smelling the air. "We should've used a dryer sheet."

Be Gus, please be Gus, Rory thought, but his truck and Mona's car made two distinct sounds, and this was Mona, and because Mona moved with a lizard-like swiftness, she was already inside and hollering, "Rag-Tag! You here? Whose Mercedes is that? Where the hell's the truck?"

Rory jumped up and closed her door. It closed as if a wind had snapped it shut.

Then louder, but muffled: "Rag-Tag? You hear me?" That ludicrous nickname followed by the click of Mona's heels on the stairs. "I came home early. Bar was too slow."

The room had lost all its air. June was feeding the leather strap of her sandal through its buckle, her big round sunglasses already back on.

A CAR KEPT coming up behind Gus and dropping away, making him feel rushed and woozy. He was driving in his socks; it was easier to feel the pedals under his feet, switching back and forth between the gas and the brake, taking the curves—one after another—like the barrel racer he'd briefly been, back in Wyoming, where quarter horses were king. Where the loyalty of one's wife was expected. He pounded his fist to the wheel and felt its bounce.

As soon as he thought the other car was gone altogether, it caught up with him. He recognized that car. Someone he knew. He bumped off the road, thinking to let them pass on the straightaway, but all he saw in his mirror was the ghost of the dust cloud his tires had kicked up.

He pulled back out again with his eyes to the road ahead, thinking of the animals. Coyotes and coons were easy to spot, moving in packs, but the deer. Sometimes they'd come out of nowhere—dumb in rut, heads full of steam, as deadly to a driver as to themselves. Gus had never hit one, but he'd been in the car plenty of times when his father had. His father had said it was better to steer for them when they appeared, that you had to take them with intention. Hitting deer being as common and shruggable an offense as striking your own children.

SARAH KNEW CHARLIE would wake up soon. She felt it. He always woke up three to four times a night.

She wasn't feeling right. The heat, surely. She went through the house opening the French doors, the windows, even the front door, begging for a breeze to come through—something natural. Of nature. She hated the peaty stink of Everett's beloved central air. A cold washcloth, that would help. She lay down and let the water drip over her temples, her neck. Maybe it was another migraine coming. She was worried about the sun, about how soon it might be up. Was it really only 10:32 p.m.? Truly? So she could, she actually could fall asleep, but the sleep that beckoned was a deep, definitive sleep, and knowing this, sensing this, she remained hovering, lying there, so awake, until there he finally was, his little voice. "Mama," he called. "Mama, in."

VIVIAN HEARD CHARLIE, but he wasn't calling to her. Sometimes he did. Sometimes, Vivian thought, she was more comfort to him than their mother. She turned up the television: *Headbangers Ball,* a show she detested (that ass kiss of a host, Riki Rachtman), but the noise drowned out her mother's anxious voice in the hall, pleading with Charlie. What would it be to have this house to themselves? Just her and Charlie. They would color the walls in crayon, sing to one another through the intercom, eat ice cream for breakfast. She'd buy back that blue lounger they'd had two houses ago, the one that reclined with a hand crank, the fabric of its arm worn to a thin velvet where she used to sit beside her father. She'd find it again and she'd sit Charlie in her lap and she would read him all the fairy tales her mother had deemed too scary. She'd get him the bunny he wanted. Two, so they'd have a thousand babies, scurrying and sniffing and flopping all over Charlie's feet.

GUS WAS ONE blind curve from passing the Price family gates. His mind skidded from the possibility of a deer jumping out onto the road to the way Mona had taken to sleeping, curled up and facing him with her hands balled to fists.

The car lights behind him were closing in again. He was aware of the enormous concrete wall of the Price estate, of the impossibility of an animal's dash from behind that eyesore, but then he blinked and there was a boy.

A coppery glint. Then clearly, a boy. In the road.

His body as white and haloed as the moon in fog.

Gus hit the brake. And turned the wheel. He turned the wheel then hit the brake. His high beams lanced a rock wall, a tree trunk. The boy's red hair.

He would remember the boy's red hair as being near enough to touch. If he just reached out his open window, he could have touched him. It was like a roller coaster he'd once ridden, a thing that hurtled people toward one another and then, just as quickly, whipped them away from one another again.

The truck spun and spun, dancing toward a reinforced wall, and then the hood buckled in a metallic roar. Gus was against the wheel, wedged so deeply that he could not see the maroon Honda Civic that had been following him. Or how it had to swerve to avoid the back of his wrecked truck, but he could hear its tires, their shrieking attempt to stop. And the impact. The world was an echo of that impact, followed by a salvo of shattering glass echoing off the canyon walls, before the hiss of escaping air began—a tire, a radiator hose—followed by a woman screaming. Gus's head dropped to the wheel. He was unaware of the multitude of fractures in his left leg, unaware that the boy he had turned to avoid, whose hair he might have touched, was Charles Leon Price, nineteen months old, or that it was Jorge Flores in the maroon Honda Civic. Jorge, who had been following him, hoping to see his boss—*mi amigo,* he had said—safely home, only to be the one who struck and killed the boy. The boy who, two minutes earlier, had gotten away from Sarah Price, just long enough for him to find his way out the front door and through the half-open gates while she ran to answer a phone that wasn't ringing.

LITTLE SNAKE, WYOMING

MAY 3, 2015

MOST OF THE roads around here run straight and flat, no blind spots to speak of, with everything there is to see visible from a half mile out. But when you turn off I-70 and head up Savery North, our place briefly appears as if pressed right up against Battle Mountain; a trick of the eye, a deceitful compression of distance that reveals itself as soon as the pavement stops and you head up our dirt road. The mountain falls away and the house, the two barns, the old homestead cabin, all rise up against the backdrop of the foothills, swelling and spreading as if the land beneath them were taking a big deep breath. That's how Mama describes it, anyway, how it looks to her when she's coming home; returned to us worn out from wherever she's been, but never wanting any help with her bags, each one weighed down with her beloved cameras.

For me the thing most worth noticing about our acreage in the Little Snake River Valley isn't the trickling clear water of the creek to our west or the blooms of lupine that paint the foothills purple all spring, but rather a fact, a fact that—without the balsa wood sign I hand-carved as a twelve-year-old girl—could easily go unnoticed.

My sign sits at the peak of the foothill to our east, and it reads,

Put one foot to the west
and one foot to the east
and
you will be a bridge over
the Great Continental Divide

I remember, back when I staked that sign, I talked my grandad Gus into coming up the hill to see it and he stood there, rubbing at his bad leg, then snorted, "You will be a bridge? Could've just called it what it is. Saved yourself some injuries there." The two of us looked at my bandaged hand. That sign had taken me a year of afternoons and nearly as many bloodied fingers—but I hadn't taken the project on as an easy thing to do so much as something I could do on my own.

It was his sister, my great-aunt Joy, who first told me about the Continental Divide and how it touched the edge of our backyard. And she was the only one that I took up there to see it who followed the sign's instructions to the letter, putting one foot left, her other wide to the right. She set her hands on her hips then, her headscarf snapping in the breeze, her eyes mischievous, but her voice deadly serious. "It's right here, Charlie, that a girl can take a piss in two oceans at once."

Aunt Joy gave me the biggest laughs I ever knew, but she also said it wasn't her place to answer my questions. Everybody says I was born asking questions. Chatty Charlie, Grandad called me.

School was a thirty-minute bus ride into Baggs (population 423), but by the sixth grade not a single teacher had thought to mention the Continental Divide, so what else wasn't I being told? I'd been particularly displeased with school that year. Day one, we'd been assigned a family tree and there was nobody in my house who could help make mine look like anything but a stick. Everyone else had branches like a cottonwood, twiggy with lines back to the earliest homesteaders, the Ute, or the Arapaho, and everyone—everyone except me, that is—turned out to be a fifth fucking cousin to Butch Cassidy or the Sundance Kid.

In all my life, I'd never lived anywhere else, had hardly ever been anywhere else, but that year I understood I was an outsider.

Maybe twelve's just a bad year as years go. But by the time school let out, I had shot up three inches, and when Mama came home she was looking up at me like I was someone she hadn't been expecting. I started slouching, trying to hide my changing chest—its resemblance to the teats of our collie was a daily horror to me. And the worst wasn't even the bleeding, when it began. It was my voice—the new rumble of it in my throat, the way it came out silly from my mouth. I didn't want to know the woman it was inviting in.

We run a breeding barn of seven broodmares, one stallion, and a goat we keep as a comfort animal for the mares when they're in labor. When a broodmare gives birth to a foal, we don't say that foal was born, we say it was thrown. Four to six months after a broodmare throws that foal, we wean it from her milk, making it reliant on us, on the human hand, for feed, and when that trust is well established, when that foal's a yearling, we break it in, making it an animal in our service. I suppose the year I turned twelve was the year I was broken in. I stopped talking so damn much and I gave in to what this ranch needed of me. I rose early and worked late, completing any and all manual labor without complaint, *listening more than whistling*—that was how Aunt Joy put it. I wanted to be of use, to her especially, but I also hoped the work would keep me lean, even sinewy, like she'd always been. I didn't know then that we weren't blood. I wouldn't know that until after she was dead and gone.

I forked stalls in the morning, helped with the feed before feeding myself. And after school, I brought the cattle in from the hills, brushed out the pastured mares. I watched and learned whenever Joy was working with a foal. What time remained, I worked on my balsa wood sign, sitting on the porch of the old homestead cabin, only moving inside when the first frost came. Inside, the sound of my knife scoring that wood mixed with the patter of mice in the rafters, their footpaths a lacework above me, the musk of their feces and Mama's old chemicals for film developing mixing in the air. Aunt Joy would come and look in on me, the same way she'd checked on the foals at night, making sure a wilier animal hadn't come through hungry.

I remember missing Mama more that year than I have any other.

That was ten years ago. I'm no kid anymore. And Mama still travels more often than she is home.

"What're you writing there?" Grandad asked me earlier, standing in the doorway to my room. He's taken to seeking me out. Used to be he thought I talked too much and now he chides me for keeping to myself.

"I'm writing to Mama," I told him.

"It's been too long," he said. He meant since we've heard from her. Her birthday, that was the last time we got a call through.

Some days he asks me to check the papers, like Aunt Joy checking on the foals. But we both know that there'd be a call to us before it ever hit the AP. Least that's what we've heard. Nothing I want to think about.

"Make sure you tell her about Chap," Grandad said, putting a hand to my windowsill to look onto the back pasture, out to where we keep Mama's mare. The goat is with her now, though she hasn't thrown a foal in years.

"I already did," I said, as if I really were writing to Mama, as if that weren't a lie.

"Someday," Grandad said, "you'll get to travel, too."

I licked the tip of my pencil. "Do tell! Where is it you think I ought to go?"

Grandad made a gesture toward my weatherworn sign, as if I only needed to walk up and over the Great Divide to be ushered like the rain into a different set of tributaries, to a new ocean, another life. But he didn't say that. He just made the gesture.

Aunt Joy died three years after we staked that sign, living a dozen years longer than any of the cancer doctors said she would, being the best kind of stubborn. When she died, that was when I knew what it was to really miss somebody, to know they'd never be home again. Mama will be home soon enough, then gone again; more apparition than mother. And Grandad knows as well as I do that even if I wanted to leave, even if I had somewhere to go, I can't. Maybe he could take care of himself, fry his own eggs and wrestle his laundry into the machine, but there are fifteen other heartbeats on this ranch, all relying on me for their feed and clean stalls. With my mother away, I am the only able-bodied person here. So here is where I am for as long as there are places in the world that require my mother's attention.

In all her years of leaving, I have never asked if I could go with her. Not once. And not because I knew she would say no, or because I'd seen the photographs of where she's been, but because long ago I recognized the look that she comes home with. It's the same look a horse has after it's been spooked, eyes alive to the peripheries, to what hides in the shadows, the ghosts beyond my view.

"I'm fine right here," I told Grandad. "Sometimes it's best to keep to what you already know."

TOPANGA CANYON, CALIFORNIA

EARLY AUGUST 1993

IT HAD TAKEN two weeks for all of them to go, the photographers and the newscasters with their microphones and lights; no longer waiting outside the house, no longer feigning a respectful distance while trampling the flowers left at the roadside. Vivian missed the cameramen (and their fucking apathy) least of all. They'd been beastly shouldered men, hoisting their equipment with callused hands. Vivian had spit on one of them and all the others had scrambled to turn their cameras on, too late (ha, ha). She'd swung her hair back, put a solemn smile on her face, and escaped being that night's news clip, to be recycled on the morning shows, a segment loosely structured on Kübler-Ross's stages of grief . . . denial, anger (cue the spitting Price girl), bargaining, depression. *Stage:* a neat little word. But there had been no denial (how could there be?), and anger wasn't right (connoting a logical frustration), or bargaining (for her baby brother?). Charlie, Charles. Vivian had held him the day he was born, and when Mommy had to be whisked away into emergency surgery (hemorrhaging), they had let Vivian keep Charlie, with Carmen beside her in the room, a nurse yelling back, "We're still trying to get ahold of your father." Ha; Daddy had been gone the day Charlie was born *and* the day he died. It was rage. Yes, rage! That was all there was: unwieldy, roving, and thick-as-tar rage, seeping into the cracks of anything else she felt or pretended to feel. Since Daddy had come home there was a whole lot of pretending going on. And a fair amount of dipping into his Klonopin prescription.

Today, for instance.

They'd just gotten back to the house after Charlie's much-delayed funeral, and Vivian was lying on the settee, replaying the brief service, still in the dress that Mommy had deemed too sheer—her sole remark to any of them the entire day. Carmen had cried the loudest, but she was the least medicated of them all. Vivian had yet to see Daddy cry, even once.

"You said I could grow it! You said, reinvent yourself!" Daddy was yelling into the phone, yelling at Bobby Montana, his agent, and rubbing at his offending beard. He'd been growing it since he got home, despite the heat.

After the accident, it had taken Daddy three whole days to get on a plane to LAX and come home, and that was only after Vivian told him about hocking that loogie at the union grunt, narrowly missing being the human-interest story for Connie Chung. Daddy loathed bad PR more than bad reviews. In all fairness, he had tried to bring Vivian to him, sending a limousine and a first-class ticket, arranging for a PA to pick her up at Pearson International. But Vivian had refused the limousine, refused to pull herself up off of

Charlie's bedroom floor. So Daddy lingered in Toronto for another sixty-eight hours, as if not showing up to the set of his own life would halt production, stop the dead son story line. Somehow Bobby had kept this episode to a minimum in the tabloids, demanding the family's grieving process be respected (tear-free absence included).

Daddy was pacing a groove into the living room carpet, listening to Bobby now. Then exclaiming, "Because I like vodka, that's why."

The service had been small, intentionally, with enough security to shoo away the few photographers that showed up, but now that she thought about it, Vivian had felt the eye of a camera lens days before, in the parking lot of the Trancas Market in Malibu, just up the road from the loony bin where Daddy had sent Mommy ("It's a recovery center!" he kept saying). There was a certain sensation to having your picture taken, the bloodletting warmth of a leech on your skin. But she'd let her guard down; they both had. Daddy forgoing a bag in the store, carrying the bottle of vodka out, tucked under his arm. It was true what they said about Daddy, that looking like Gregory Peck almost made up for his lack of complexity (on-screen, anyway).

"Jesus Christ," Everett said. "The cover?" He sat down on the end of the settee, ignoring Vivian's outstretched feet. "*Star? Star* magazine? Was it a slow day in the Menendez trial?" He started picking at the cardboard Carmen had duct-taped over the ragged edges of glass that remained in the sliding door.

The irony was that they'd delayed the funeral long enough to let Mommy's injuries heal, knowing that the bandaging of her hand and wrist would be too open to tabloid conjecture (god forbid it be correct), but now they had an image of Daddy looking like a lush, and so near the upscale sanatorium where Sarah Price was known to be convalescing.

Vivian pictured it: the two of them, Daddy a stride behind her, grappling with the change he'd just been handed, trying to push his sunglasses back up his nose with the hand of the arm awkwardly cradling the vodka. *Reinvent yourself!* Bobby *had* said this when he visited, said it to both of them and then turned to Vivian and cupped her face in his hands and told her, "From great tragedy, springs great talent!" Followed by his hot breath leaning in, "I could have work for you tomorrow, say the word." Her response had been laughter, a wild, barking laugher. Daddy had offered her her first sedative then.

"Can you believe this?" Daddy had his hand over the receiver, talking to Carmen, who had come into the room to say she was making dinner early. "What are we having?"

"Spaghetti," Carmen said, no longer asking what he wanted, but declaring (amen).

"She was fine," Daddy said, talking into the phone again, talking about Mommy, clearly. "No, no. I'm not saying that. Just—just that she held up."

The doorbell chimed and a pot clattered to the floor, water sloshing. Carmen had jumped at the sound of that particular chime, as it meant someone had made it past the gates (how, exactly?). "You okay?" Vivian called to her.

"Sí," Carmen lied. "It's okay."

Again, the chime. Of course Daddy had left the gates open when they drove back in, his new MO of carelessness. "You left the gates open?" Vivian hissed.

But Daddy was listening intently to Bobby, his captain through this newest of PR storms.

Carmen had gone to the door—not opening it but asking what it was they wanted.

Vivian was suddenly very tired, lying back on the stupidly hard settee. She braided her hands atop her chest and closed her eyes. It was a memory of Charlie—they took over like this, holding her in their grip. He was in the garden, running from her, his arms waving, his eyes wet with tears of laughter.

"Señor Price." Carmen was standing on the top step of the sunken living room.

"No, no. I've got to go, Bobby," Everett was saying into the phone. "*I know* we'll get through it. Yes, of course, it could be worse. Thanks a million, Bobby."

"He says it's about the pool, Señor Price," Carmen said, holding her hands in front of her, one tucked into the other, like little spoons. Vivian loved her for tolerating them.

Daddy clicked the cordless off and threw it onto the marble-topped coffee table. As it hit, the back of the phone broke off, the plastic splintering, and the battery dropped to the floor.

"Fuck me," Everett said under his breath, leaving the pieces, and going for the door.

Mommy's bloodied hand was the reason Vivian had dialed 911 that night, not yet knowing about her brother. Mommy standing there with her head thrown back, howling in apparent agony, glass shards at her feet, and blood running down her arm and onto the floor.

She could hear Daddy and the voices of two other men in the

cavernous entryway of their house. And then the front door closed again. This house was an echo chamber.

"The gates!" Vivian yelled. "Make sure you fucking close them!" She was facing the yard, but she saw Daddy's approaching reflection in the glass of the remaining sliding door. "I hate this house," she said now. "I *hate* this house." She sat up, putting her feet against the black plastic fragments on the carpet. "I hated that phone. I fucking hate this white carpet. I hate everything about the way Mommy did this house." She put her hand to the cold marble surface of the table. "I hate this table. This settee is a slab of rock. It's like an airport terminal in here. There's nothing to lean on, nowhere to really sit. No wonder you're never here—"

"No," Everett said weakly.

"You know what I miss? I miss the blue lounger, your armchair, Daddy. An Easter egg blue. You remember." He had to remember (Klonopin and all). As a little girl, she had sat on the arm beside him as he did the crossword. "You remember, don't you?" she asked, but he wasn't there—his eyes the glossy stones of someone gone inward. "Who was that at the door, Daddy?"

"Your mother ordered a fence." He motioned behind him. "They were here to install the fence." He refocused his eyes, dropping back to her, a tired, red-rimmed look. "They apologized for being late."

"A fence?" Vivian said. "But we have a fence. Concrete walls, even."

Everett nodded. "This was for the pool. For around the pool."

"Around the pool?" But he didn't have to clarify. She understood. A fence for the pool, to prevent Charlie from drowning. At last, Daddy began to cry.

THE REGISTRATION FOR the three-day event in Fresno had eaten half of Rory's savings and there was still a long list of things she needed, never mind wanted.

"Don't think you're getting any money out of me," Mona said.

"I'm using my own money," Rory said. Two-thirds of her wages at Leaning Rock went to pay for boarding and care for Chap, and the rest went into a savings account, at Gus's insistence.

"And those are *our* debts," Mona said, waving a potato peeler toward the stack of bills. Not my debt, Rory thought. Those were Gus's medical bills. There were new ones daily, the pile so high it was leaning against the wall, an expectant guest. "And you think you can run off like a barn brat, have a holiday, eatin' out and sleeping in a fancy hotel room?"

"Motel," Rory said. "And I'm competing."

"She'll stay with Robin," Gus groaned from the couch. He was home from the hospital, but lame, his leg held together by a dozen screws and a cast that went to his thigh. Rory could hardly look at him, seeing only the black stitches in his face, the lingering swelling around his eyes. *Eyes the size of plums.* Such a fool.

Robin Sharpe had taken over the management of Leaning Rock and all of the upper-level lessons. She had offered to let Rory share her motel room.

"Right," Mona said. "You don't think she'll be shacking up with her new pothead friend?"

June had taken Rory by the hand that night, pulling her past

Mona on the stairs, and the two of them had gotten out the front door before Mona removed one of her kitten heels and tossed it at them, the shoe hitting the door just as the first sirens came screaming up the canyon.

Gus lifted himself up higher on the couch, looking out the window to see what car was coming over the bridge. He lived in fear of Sonja coming back from Chino, where she'd gone to be nearer to Jorge, whose trial date had still not been set. They were charging him with involuntary manslaughter. Gus hadn't been to the barn since the night of the accident, and if it weren't for June and Robin, if they hadn't talked Rory into training for Fresno, Rory probably wouldn't have been able to show her face again either.

Sometimes June helped Rory with her to-ride list, the two of them just riding up the Leaning Rock Trail or all the way to Calabasas Peak—Rory had to ride other people's horses at the hottest point in the day now, when she didn't have a dressage or jumping class. She always brought a bottle of water from the office freezer, and when they'd reach the peak only a thin core of ice remained. Once, Rory dropped that ice into her mouth and chewed and June had teased her—"Chewing ice is a sign of sexual frustration"—but that was as flirtatious as June had been since that first night.

Gus settled back into the couch. "It's just another nurse," he said, saying it to Rory, as if she'd been worried with him. But she would have been happy to see Sonja. These nurses clearly came from some scattershot care agency that Carlotta's daughter, Bella, had chosen. In the days after the accident, Rory had been the one to check on Carlotta, filling Sonja's absence, but now that these nurses came, and Gus was laid up on the couch and Mona spent half her waking hours prefixing meals and freezing them and the other half trying to talk Gus into an interview with a magazine—"a paid interview," she always corrected—Rory wanted to be anywhere but here.

Most days, after they left the barn, June would pull into the market parking lot, and they'd drop their seats back and stare up into the trees and share a joint. June had stories about acid trips and mushrooms, pills with names like Dancing Shoes, Black Sunshine, Final Daze. In the market, she bought them American Spirits and sandwiches. Sometimes they didn't talk at all, just listened to Morrissey, the Violent Femmes, and other days they were barreled over in laughter about things they couldn't recall later, lost in the black velvet of their high. A few times, Wade had met them, jumping out of his Scout and into June's backseat, lying back there like it was a hammock. June disappeared a little when Wade was around.

"Robin already paid for the room and she asked for a double room, so that I *can* stay with her." Gus hated Robin when Carlotta hired her, believing she'd only been hired for being Bella's friend, having more connections than actual skills. But Robin had been proving him wrong, as only the underappreciated can. *"And,"* Rory went on, venomous, "she's lending me her coat and tails."

"All right, all right—" Gus and Mona said, nearly in unison. They both smirked, amused by this unexpected camaraderie.

"Thanks," Rory said.

In the living room, Gus turned on the television. He'd begun to brave the television again, images of that night finally usurped by new tragedies.

"So that's it," Rory said. "We're done talking about Fresno?"

From the other room, Gus moaned. "A pill, Mona. Are you holding out on me?"

Mona looked at her watch. "Another hour, Cowboy. No sooner."

On the TV, Rush Limbaugh came on, surrounded by copies of his books, his face on every cover.

"Turn that up," Mona said. "I like him."

June's car was coming across the bridge. She took it faster than anyone else. But Gus lifted himself again, craning at the window. "June," he said, matter-of-fact.

Mona lit a cigarette off the burner, beneath the pot of boiling potatoes, squinting at the heat.

"I probably won't be home for dinner," Rory said.

Mona smiled. "You don't say."

"Come on already," June was hollering out the car window. "We can't be late."

Rory was already running for the car, one hand against the bouncing body of her camera. She'd been bringing the Canon with her everywhere, taking pictures at the barn: the lower-level lessons, trail ride views from between Chap's ears, Chap in her stall, June, and Wade, but only because he was always coming at her, grinning at the lens.

It was their dressage lesson June didn't want to be late for, dressage with Ema, the new instructor Robin had poached from L.A. Equestrian. People said Ema looked like Sharon Stone but with dark pixie hair. On Ema's first day, June said, "German women are my new thing," with a salacious lift of her eyebrows. Ema wore black suspenders. And now, apparently, so did June. "You are such a suck-up," Rory said, snapping the elastic at the top of June's shoulder.

"Come on, I really like these," June said. "They're practical and oddly erotic."

"Isn't the box of pastries enough?" Every day, June bought a variety box of pastries and left them in the office for Robin, Ema, and Adriano, who had taken over as head stable hand. Rory reached into the back and took a lemon poppy muffin for herself.

"I believe that if you suck up consistently, it eventually appears sincere. Besides, we aren't all wowing Ema like you are, Scott."

The day before Ema had said, "Rory is a puppeteer," describing the way she and Chap moved together as if connected by invisible strings. Robin was letting Rory ride in the group lessons for free, and everyone's surprise at just how capable Rory was—years of watching everyone and learning at her own pace—made this secret gift feel, somehow, earned.

June pressed the lighter in and drew the American Spirits out of the glove box between Rory's knees. She was smoking a lot, blaming her anxieties about Fresno—about having to beat Wade and what winning would mean for her state ranking. This was their go-to, most urgent topic of discussion. Rory insisted June only open the windows a crack and that she keep a can in the car for ashing. Rory had come to find this car's smell—warm leather, the pong of stored weed and stale cigarettes, and the trace of the White Musk June was always putting behind her ears—comforting.

"Journey's not the galloper Pal is, but he is indestructible over fences, so all Wade needs is a descent dressage test and he could beat me." They were turning up Old Topanga Canyon. "Isn't that ridiculous?"

"He's not indestructible," Rory said, feeling scripted. She took the cigarette from June, inhaling and exhaling. "Robot horses malfunction, too."

"Journey is rather robotic, isn't he?"

"Mm," Rory said, laying her head back, smoking with her eyes closed. There was no escaping this part of the drive, the turn past the Price gates, beside the wall with the long black, then white streak; the punctuation of Gus's truck. She kept her eyes closed, but she always felt June steal a glance at her. Not until they were beyond the shoulder where they'd found the fox, when she felt the rise before the ranch, did Rory open her eyes again. As always, June smiled the same tight, apologetic smile at her. Rory reached into the backseat then and put a hand on the box of pastries, so they didn't overturn as June steered them down the driveway and into the ranch.

"So when you win," Rory asked, "will you snap your suspenders at the ribbon ceremony?"

"For sure," June said. "You know it." She parked in the last empty space, next to the school horse corral.

Sancho was working there, his round frame hunched and pulling away at the cape ivy that had tapped into the water pipe that ran to the school horse trough. He looked up from behind the corral railing, his dispassionate eyes meeting hers. "Fuck," Rory said, remembering. She had said she would help with that, days ago.

"What?" June asked.

"Nothing," Rory said. "I just forgot something."

"You need to go home?"

"No," Rory said. "Not like that. Is today the tenth?"

June nodded. She had said she would help Sancho, but she had also told Adriano that she would come up to the house for the party. The ninth had been Tomás's birthday.

In some ways, right after the accident had been easier, no one expecting anything in particular, her presence enough. She sat with Adriano, held Sonja's hands while she cried, and she leaned into Tomás, his arms strung around her until they both pulled away to wipe their faces dry. She had spent more time with them there, at the barn, then with Gus in the hospital. But as time passed and she needed more hours to train—she hadn't had the time to help in the way she used to, no longer mucking stalls, cleaning tack, or sanding and repainting the jump rails. Robin hadn't seemed to mind; her paychecks hadn't changed.

"Una fiesta pequeña, nada más," Adriano had said sheepishly, either afraid she'd tell Robin or embarrassed they couldn't do more for Tomás; Rory couldn't tell which. He'd handed her a card and she'd signed it, generically, thinking she'd find more words—better words—at the party, but then she'd forgotten about it altogether, going home with June, as usual, leaving everything else behind.

THE PILLS KEPT the pain at bay through the night, but during the day it inserted itself like a boot hook in Gus's back. The bath settled it down some and the bath required Mona's help.

He would position himself on the tub's rim and Mona would

steady him by the elbow, helping him shimmy out of his boxers, the porcelain a cold pain against his bare ass. He'd watch her pull the black trash bag over his cast and he'd hold the end of the tape while she wrapped it around the top of his leg. She'd test the water and pull his shirt from him, stretching the collar away from the stitches. Those threads had spiders that ran off, back and forth over his cheekbone. He'd phoned the hospital, fed up, only to be told that that was what nerve damage was. "A small price to pay," the nurse had said, as if she had his toxicology report right there.

Once he was in the water, Mona sat on the lid of the toilet, flipping through a magazine, sometimes clipping recipes, sometimes reading him an article. When the water finally turned tepid she'd toweled him off. It was the best of her, this Mona, on the other side of the accident. Except when a reporter phoned her back and then she went hungry in her speech, coaxing. She'd already told him a thousand times how the butcher at the market in town had given an interview, recounting how he'd seen Mrs. Price and the boy in the store the afternoon before the accident, how he'd been paid five thousand dollars for answering four questions. "Only four. I asked him myself," she said. "Five thousand. And every word of it true. That boy ran away from her in there more than once. She never had a hold on him. She's the one to blame, you ask me." He hated this most, Mona's admonishing Sarah Price. Sometimes—in the harried space between his waking and sleeping—he heard Sarah Price talking to him, always as if they were old friends who'd just found one another at a party, huddled and whispering against the din around them. "We need the money," Mona said, though the amounts the magazines were offering had dwindled. "I won't," he'd tell her and then she'd always say, "You aren't the one who killed him," because Mona's world was black and white this way.

Tonight, toweling him dry, she was hopped up not about an interview, but about going back to work at Hawkeye's. "He still hasn't covered my shift for tonight." She'd worked at that bar for thirteen years, but now, after two and a half weeks off, there was risk of her being replaced altogether? She was rubbing the towel down his arms in a suppliant way.

"Gimme that," he said. "I can do this myself."

"You know he'll hire some fresh young thing. And that's the last thing we need."

"I told you," Gus said, taking the towel from her. "It's fine. I'll be fine. You can go."

Mona looked at him, then put a hand to his knee and ripped the tape from his leg. The trash bag fell to the tile. "Well, all right, then," she said.

In 1982, when they'd met, Mona had been the fresh new thing at Hawkeye's. Gus was returning from a jumpers' clinic he'd taught in Temecula and he had a hankering to sit in a dark bar, with a basket of fried food, in the company of strangers. He'd never set foot in Hawkeye's before and when he saw Mona behind the bar he'd had a religious kind of feeling. She was wearing a cut-sleeve T-shirt, her strong shoulders exposed, her dark brown hair hanging down her back like a shining cape. When he ordered a ginger ale, she leaned toward him—the twinkle to her eyes same as a calico cat—and said, "Come on, now. I can't trust a man who doesn't drink." He checked her hand for a ring. "That's a funny philosophy," he said. "No, it's not," she said, straightening herself to pull a beer from the tap. "When a man doesn't drink, it tells me his impulses are too dark for him to handle." No man that's not true of, Gus thought, but instead of saying so, he took the beer and asked for a bourbon chaser. He went home with Mona that night, to a one-bedroom apartment in a complex crawling with Cal State Northridge kids. Inside, Rory was asleep in their shared bed, her head buried beneath a pillow. Mona paid and dismissed the sitter and then she let him bend her over the kitchen counter, pans gently rattling on the stove. She fell asleep with her head in his lap, sitting on the couch, and he stayed that way, sitting up all night, stroking her hair and planning the breakfast he would make for her and the girl in the morning. A few months later, as they were walking hand in hand through Topanga State Park, he proposed and, after nodding yes, Mona had said, "Rory likes you. She never likes anybody."

But now Rory was never around and when she was, it was clear she wanted little to do with him. Despite his charitable overlooking of the marijuana smoke that rode in on her at night and his having talked Mona into letting her go to Fresno.

"I haven't been alone in weeks," Gus said to Mona now, realizing.

She was straightening her blouse in the mirror. "Well, it might be nice," she said.

It had been *nice* not to have to think of her at work, of the men who kept tipping higher, ordering chasers, about the cologne they left behind on her clothes.

"Why are you looking at me like that?" she said.

"Nothing," he said. She'd put on a jean skirt and blown her hair out so it shined.

"You're just hungry," she said, and then she was in the kitchen building him a turkey sandwich, dumping chips into a bowl. She set it all on the table beside the couch, handed him a glass of water, then reached into her pocket to retrieve the pill bottle.

"Would you still be going back if I'd answered their questions?" Why had he told her he could do this himself, that he'd be fine? "The magazines?"

She looked at him, mouth sour. "It's a little late for that." She was struggling with the cap to the pills.

"I know," Gus said. He hadn't been fine alone, not a single day since they'd met.

The cap popped free in her hand. "You're still my cowboy, Gus," she said, shaking out a green-and-white pill. "My cowboy on Prozac."

TOMÁS WAS LOADING feed, forking bales and swinging them up onto the tractor bed with hay hooks.

"I brought you these," Rory said. He didn't stop to see. "It's a new pair of gloves."

"They're nice," Tomás said, only stealing a glance. "But they aren't for me."

"Oh, come on," Rory said, "I'm trying to make amends." But it was true, the gloves were far too small for him. They weren't the show gloves, but the tan work gloves Rory had gotten for herself, the tag still attached. She'd been wrong, thinking he'd remember—that he'd recognize the joke. The very first time he'd forked bales, he'd done it without any gloves, Sancho ribbing him the whole time. The soft pads of his hands had blistered and gone slick with pus, but he'd only shown Rory—she was maybe ten—and she'd gotten the first aid kit and helped him wrap his hands. She was gonna say something about how wise he'd grown, believing that that, at least, was old history, a day they could've laughed about.

"How about you get me a pair that fits then?"

"Maybe I will," Rory said. She'd grabbed the gloves on a run to the Feedbin with Robin, charging Carlotta's account, a detail she knew Tomás wouldn't approve of. She lifted her camera up over her head and set it down on the tractor seat, going to help him load. "Or I could take your picture?"

He'd been looking at the camera, but he pulled his baseball hat lower now. "No, thanks."

Of course not. Tomás was reserved, quiet, preferring the music in his Walkman to small talk with the boarders, despite the girls who tried.

Rory ripped the tag that held the gloves together and pulled them on. "You all right?" she asked. He'd barely looked at her.

"I'm fine," he said, his voice betraying him.

Rory scrambled up on top of the loaded hay, reaching down for the next bale, hooking it, then saying, "I'm sorry I didn't come last night."

"It's okay," he said, tossing a second bale fast and high enough that she only had time to step out of the way.

"Did your mom come home?" she asked.

Tomás and Sonja had moved into the house on the grounds six years ago, and Rory recalled being annoyed at Gus's assumption that she and Tomás would be friends, as if the four years between them weren't a lifetime then. Had Gus always been trying to find her friends? Thinking her lonely? Well, she didn't feel lonely anymore.

When Rory turned back for the next bale, Tomás had taken his hat off and was wiping his face dry. "Are we done already?" Rory asked. If Tomás hadn't dropped out his sophomore year, they'd have overlapped for a year at Polk.

He had his hands on his hips. He was gangly, his body boyish, but his face had the angles of a man's—a concave sweep between his cheekbone and jaw, a strong, almost blunt nose—but he only grew a whisper of a mustache and his forehead was often broken out in acne where the band of his baseball cap sat. He had Sonja's deep-set, dark eyes and thick black hair, but in the sun his fairer skin went red. Manuel and Adriano had teased him when he was younger, calling him Rosita or Thomas. Jorge had put a stop to that. "She'll be home tomorrow," Tomás said.

Rory swung down, pulling her gloves away. "I'm sorry she missed it, too."

"I asked her not to come." He reached out and touched the gloves in her hand, pulling away the last of the plastic tab that she'd missed. "I wanted her to stay in Chino. I wanted her to stop him . . ." He had always called Jorge Papi, but his voice slid away now.

"Stop him?"

"He pled no contest," Tomás said, looking at her.

"No contest?"

"It means he won't fight. He won't have a trial. It means he won't have to tell anyone anything else that—"

"Stop," Rory said.

"He'll get seven years, Rory. Then they'll deport him. Nobody is saying this, but I know." His jaw was set, resigned. "That's what will happen."

Rory had known that Sancho and Manuel had no papers, but she had thought that Jorge . . . He had worked for Carlotta longer than Gus. Why hadn't she sponsored him? When Rory had come to the ranch after the accident, the gates had been padlocked shut and Tomás, after opening them to her, had said it was to keep the television crews from coming, trying to interview them, but it was also for INS, she understood now, for fear of them using the opportunity. "No," Rory said. "We won't let it happen. Robin, Carlotta—they can help. He'll work here again."

"Why would he want that?" Tomás said, his voice flat.

"Because," Rory said.

"You know Papi was following him, Rory."

"That night," she said dumbly.

Tomás nodded. "But what I didn't tell you is how he came to our house asking for food. Or that Papi gave him coffee and told him to stay. *Sleep on our couch,* he said. But Gus wouldn't listen, so Papi insisted on following him."

Rory flashed on the red banner that had run across the bottom of the television screen: *Actor's Son Killed by Drunk Driver.* By the time Gus was wheeled back from surgery it had been revised: *Drunk Immigrant Kills Movie Star's Infant Son.*

That was when she'd gone to the barn, June driving her, taking her back through Calabasas, avoiding the floodlights they'd seen on the news, illuminating the crime scene, but casting hard shadows. June had left her at the gate, having to get home, her father already freaking out about her having been in the canyon that night. It wasn't until Robin returned her to the hospital that Rory saw the footage of Gus's truck being towed away, dragged from the retaining wall, the newscaster declaring that the driver of this truck, Gus Scott—"unable to comment at this time"—was a "near hero." She went on to describe how they had learned from crime scene analysis that he had turned, sparing the boy, and subsequently sustained life-threatening injuries himself. "If only this other, this intoxicated, Hispanic man hadn't been speeding down the road behind him." *If only this other* . . . The sun had come up by then and the glare was so great Rory thought everything in the room could blister and melt away like a strip of film exposed too long.

There was no such thing as a near hero.

"Why are you telling me this?" Rory asked, feeling as if her heart were suspended within her by a flimsy string. "What am I supposed to say?"

Tomás tucked his hat back on. "June's calling for you," he said.

Rory heard her, but she couldn't move. She was staring at his Dodgers hat, so tattered and faded she'd never really registered it before. He wasn't looking at her. She looked down at the suede gloves in her hand, still satiny and new.

"Go on, Rory," Tomás said. The horses in the L barn had started stomping the ground, nickering, impatient with the wait. "I can finish here."

Her mouth had gone dry. It was a hundred degrees out, only slightly less insufferable than the day before.

"Rory." Tomás stopped her.

"Yeah?"

"It's good, actually—that you didn't come."

"To your party?" Rory asked, surprised.

"It wouldn't have been the same."

IT WAS A sharp left off PCH and down a narrow road to visit Mommy in Malibu. The shrubbery was densely planted to obscure the estates, but it also hid any view of the water. When at last there was a glinting wedge of Pacific Ocean, they turned, following the stucco wall painted the same golden green as the coastal grass (a brush fire beige). Carmen punched in the visitor's code Daddy had written out for them and the gate retracted. The parking lot was thinly populated: two Mercedes, two BMWs, three Porsches, and a Lexus. On their very first visit, seeing the cars, Everett had said, "I told you it was nice." As if they'd been on a waiting list. The only signage was outside the main door, a demure gold-plated placard that read, CLIFFSIDE REFUGE (it's a spa, a wildlife sanctuary, it's rich folks on the brink!).

Daddy wasn't coming because he had "meetings." Paramount, Sony. Meetings meant calls. But calls at least meant he wasn't out "antiquing" (a.k.a. fumbling through yard sales in a pathetic disguise) but was pacing the halls of the house in his bathrobe, trying to sound like a man wizened by his struggles rather than undone (though undone he was).

Cliffside consisted of a broad green lawn, spotted with single-story "resident bungalows" and two main buildings, all clay brown with Spanish terra-cotta roofs. Down a gentle slope was a man-made pond so clear that it had to be chlorinated, ringed with pearly white Adirondack chairs. The sound of croaking frogs and the titter of birds was ever present, as if looped over a sound system.

After they'd signed in, Carmen sat down on a bench outside the main building and reached into her shoulder bag, withdrawing knitting needles and yarn. Vivian stood, watching her mother's bungalow, waiting for her to be led out.

Click, click—Carmen's needles—click, stitch. "This place, Vivian. I can smell the crazy."

In the days they'd spent alone, Vivian asked Carmen to stop calling her Ms. Vivian, a formality Mommy had grossly insisted on.

"That's just the lilies," Vivian said to Carmen.

An orderly approached and motioned for them, but Carmen did not stop knitting.

"You don't want to come?" Vivian asked, trying to remember if Carmen had spoken to Mommy at the funeral—the first they'd seen of one another in weeks.

"That's right," Carmen said. Of course. She wasn't paid well enough for any of this.

Vivian followed the orderly to the pond, where Mommy must have been sitting all along.

Vivian took a seat in the neighboring Adirondack.

"I was gathering myself," Mommy said. "I'd assumed your father was coming."

"He has meetings," Vivian said. "Well, phone calls."

"He's getting work again, then."

"I suppose," Vivian said, and then, "Honestly, Mommy, he's a mess. He sleeps on the couch and he lives in his bathrobe, except when he's antiquing, that's what he calls it, but he's just buying all this shit—" Vivian stopped. Had she cursed in front of Mommy before? She couldn't remember anything anymore; her memories were all projected underwater, the audio garbled, her eyes stinging. She wanted to tell Mommy about the fence men and Daddy's crying, but that might have been cruel. For Mommy she would tuck her cruelty in a back pocket.

"What kind of shit?" Sarah asked.

"Flea market shit. Yard sales. Old, smelly, mildewed: books, furniture, pillows. Other people's pillows! Lamps and ashtrays? I don't even know. It wasn't what I meant, not at all."

"What you meant?" Mommy kept rubbing the hem of her shirt (her new compulsion?).

"I told him I missed our old furniture. But just the one recliner. The Easter egg blue?"

"I remember it. You spilled something on the seat and it soured—that's why I left it. That was two houses ago, Vivian." Mommy closed her eyes. Vivian hadn't spilled, not once. "That was before your Grandad died."

Grandad. Leon. Leon of the Two Watches, as Vivian thought of him. A wire-thin man who wore a watch on each wrist, one set to local time, the other to China, who never cared for Everett and who treated Mommy like an exotic plant he'd grown to show off. His funeral had been an infinity of limousines, followed by a sudden, incomprehensible wealth. Nearly overnight. It was as if they had been standing beneath a trickle of a spring waterfall—Daddy's steady work, small indulgences here and there, the old chipped dishes replaced with new—and then it was a torrent, the force of it blinding. Two new cars, a new stone set in her mother's ring. Whatever shoes Vivian desired. Get two pair! A new house with a kidney-shaped pool. The Jamaican cook who also cleaned, until Mommy found her wearing one of her necklaces.

"I wasn't ready for all this," Mommy said. Vivian wasn't sure if she meant the money or Charlie's death. "You've always handled things better than I have, Vivian."

"That isn't true," Vivian said.

"Who's the one doing the visiting here?"

Vivian didn't know what to say and Mommy rested her head on the back of the Adirondack, her eyes closing, her face turned up into the sun. The skin of her neck and around her eyes had gone soft, the wilting petals of a flower. Mommy had never been like other Hollywood wives. She didn't like being photographed, the upkeep and injections. She didn't want to be seen. "You like it here, don't you, Mommy?" Vivian was playing back all the previous visits, from the first catatonic, shock-riddled days to her stoic posture and Valium-glossed eyes at the funeral, to now, this—resolution?

"I might as well," Mommy said. "A caged bird and all that. Though this isn't, it could be worse. Do you ever think about the man?" Her eyes were still closed.

"The man?"

"What do you think about letters, Vivian? You know, in the mail?"

The way Mommy spoke sometimes felt as if it required a secret code and Vivian's failure to crack it could result in an explosion. Silence often seemed safer. "Letters?" Vivian braved.

"I wrote one to him, to Jorge Flores."

"The man who killed Charlie?"

"Oh, Vivian," she said, shaking her head the same way she did at the end of laughing. "I killed Charlie, now, didn't I?" Her voice was light and easy.

"You're scaring me, Mommy. You didn't kill Charlie. It was an accident. A horrible accident."

"See. That's why I wrote to him."

"Mommy. Why? He was drunk. Point zero seven. That's basically the limit."

"Yes, basically," Mommy said. "Sleep deprivation is as dangerous. Yet here they're happy to give me drugs to help me sleep. I do feel rested, finally. What were you doing that night, Vivian? Do you remember?"

"Stop, Mommy." Of course she remembered (Mickey McLeod, Bill Clinton, Powell, Rachtman, Charlie calling). "Mommy, someone might read that letter. They might give it—"

"To the press?" Mommy asked. "Perhaps. Let them. But it's divisiveness that sells magazines, don't you think?"

"Yes. I guess. I don't know. Have you sent it already? Does Daddy know?"

"I have. And your father can clutter up that house all he wants. I'm not sure I can ever set foot in it again."

"You want to move us? Again?"

"No," Mommy said.

"No what?" Her mother could induce bewildering panic in her. Vivian only wanted clarity (say what you mean!). One of her earliest memories was of her mother handing her a kite in a city park, her mother's hair blowing in the wind (hence the damn kite) but she carefully, methodically molded Vivian's hand to the kite's handle and then, clear as day, she said, "Now let it go!" and Vivian did. She let go and the entire kite (body, string, tails, and handle) darted into the sky, its bright colors a blurred rainbow and then only a pin-prick against the sky. The sight of it left Vivian breathless, joyful, astounded—she had launched a rocket! But when she looked back at them to share her pleasure, it was Daddy who said, "What the hell did she do that for?" and Mommy's face went pale and woeful. This was them (nuts plus shell).

"No," Mommy said now. "These birds aren't real at all. There isn't a tree anywhere in sight—" She painted her hand across the landscape. "Yet it sounds as if we're in a rain forest."

Vivian closed her eyes. The birds got louder. "Maybe it's meant to be relaxing?"

"Or maybe it's meant to make us all go insane," Mommy said, laughing a laugh that Vivian wished didn't sound so much like her own.

GUS HAD MONA by the wrist, asking her for one more kiss. She was leaving for a double shift this time, but before her lips met his, her eyes went to the window and there were the creaking axles of the van, crossing the bridge. "Who is it?" he asked, already knowing.

"You'll have to talk to her on your own," Mona said, hurrying toward the door. "I'm already late." The screen door slapped shut, the springs gone slack.

Mona's Chrysler started up, her tires spraying back pebbles.

Maybe, he was hoping, she would go up to Carlotta first. But then there she was, obscured behind the screen door, not knocking.

"Sonja," he said, his voice cracking over her name. Her eyes seemed to be adjusting to the darkness of the house, trying to find him inside. "Come in," he said, not getting up, knowing every move he made from then on was only going to confirm his cowardice. "You headed up to see Carlotta?" Like they were neighbors making small talk.

"No," Sonja said, stepping inside. She looked smaller, reduced somehow. She had an envelope in her hand. "She has the help she needs." She was avoiding looking at him.

"I know she prefers your help," Gus tried.

"You've been to see her?"

"Well, no." Only Rory had. "But those nurses—" He'd lost steam, unhooked from any straightforward train of thought. He tried to push himself up on the couch then, to establish some dignity or—more likely—to show her his injuries. Like a dog rolling over to expose its belly, declaring itself harmless. He hadn't meant any harm.

"I didn't want to come here," Sonja said. She was looking at the burls of dust at the edges of the wood floors. "I've never been inside your house before."

"Is that true?" he said, "Well, I would've cleaned if I'd thought you were coming." Had she really never been inside his house? Three years of her going up to Carlotta and he had never offered her a glass of water? He recalled her pulling the scarf from the lamp, the door slamming around the corner from their yellow-tiled kitchen. He hadn't sat with Jorge for very long after that. El Jefe. That was their name for him, just never to his face.

"Sonja, do you still want to be Carlotta's nurse? I'm sure we could figure that out, if you wanted." His neck felt hot and tight.

"You could," Sonja said. "I'm sure."

Robin had called to tell him that Sonja was talking about moving Tomás away with her, that she was considering staying in Chino. Gus had felt a flash of shameful relief, but Robin's concern was about good labor, how long it might take to find new help, the time to train them. "Do you *need* the work—" he asked. If he needed money, they had to need it more.

Sonja threw the envelope at him then. "Jorge wanted you to read that. He says you're suffering, too." Her eyes moved over him. "Are you?" she asked, her face drawing together. "Are you suffering?"

An acrid taste rose into his mouth. He shook his head.

"I didn't think so," she said. "You're a man in *your* home. With *your* family. You're where you should've been all along."

Gus pulled at the skin of his neck, a collar too tightly cinched. He had yet to touch the envelope. It had been folded and refolded, its creases yellowed. "Is he okay? Jorge?"

"You know." Sonja crinkled her nose. "Más o menos." Sarcasm. She stepped abruptly toward him. "Do you remember what you said to me? That we are always working? Or were you too drunk? He was working. He thought it was his job to see you home."

"He *was* drunk, too," Gus said. He could hear his own pulse and the echo of it in his cast.

"No." She had yelled. He had never seen her yell, how her body inflated with it, lifting her. "Don't do that," she said, quieter now. "Papi had three beers. Never more. And only for his sleep, for his shoulder. That was all." She touched her shoulder. "It never healed, not right, because he never told anyone. A caballo kicked him, when he first started with her. He didn't want to complain." All the times he had seen Sonja kneading Jorge's shoulder. "It was probably broken in there, but he didn't want to be trouble. Prison is all trouble." A phantom spider crawled across his cheek, up behind his eye. He put his hand to his face. She turned her back on him. "Go on, open it already," she said.

Gus had driven through Chino. He knew the beige fortress of the prison, the sun-scorched fields, Mount Baldy in the distance.

He lifted his leg and set it down. Sonja moved into the kitchen. The postmark was a week old.

Dear Mr. Flores,

Not from Jorge but *to* him.

Dear Mr. Flores,
I am writing to tell you that I do not blame you for the death of my son, Charles Price.
    I hope that this will bring you some peace.

                                       Sarah

Sarah Price. Gus's pulse went rapid and loud, his leg throbbing. Beneath the long loops of her handwriting were Jorge's stiff, penciled words: *Gus, I want peace for you, too. Jorge.*

RORY SUGGESTED THEY skip the parking lot and get home. She hadn't been feeling right for a few days.

"No way," June said. "You can sleep in tomorrow." The barn was closed Mondays. Never days Rory looked forward to, navigating around Gus, his moods and naps.

They sat in silence, dropped down heavily into their high, until Wade came tearing into the lot, House of Pain's "Jump Around" thumping from his stereo.

"Shit," June said. "I'm too stoned to deal with him."

He parked right up next to Rory's side and leaned out his window, peering into June's convertible like it was a cookie jar. "I knew you two would be here drooling over each other." Without touching the ground he stepped from his truck into June's backseat, smelling of mouthwash and Ivory soap. He'd changed, too, no longer in britches, but a pair of Levi's and clean white T-shirt, a braided leather necklace against his chest. Rory felt itchy with dry sweat.

"I thought you had somewhere to be," June said.

"Patience, Butch. I stopped at Trouble's to have myself a scrub."

"Trouble's mom's house, you mean."

Trouble was their nickname for Johnny Naughton. Sometimes Trouble, sometimes Johnny Naughty. He had a shaved head and skin that freckled and peeled. A more-than-unfortunate complexion for a surfer that left him looking thirtysomething rather than the twentysomething he was. He'd gone to Polk High a decade ago, but Rory had heard the bad-boy folklore, how he ran with the Surf Nazis, believing they owned certain waters, that the ocean was theirs to patrol, and how he'd had to leave the country for six months while "some drama" blew over with a girl. "One minute she liked it. The next minute she didn't." That was how Johnny Naughton talked. When he wasn't surfing, he worked at a classic car shop on the Westside, which was how Wade and June knew him; he'd worked on their cars. He came to the barn sporadically, always eyeballing girls while he waited for Wade. Wade was endlessly amused by him. Gus had called Johnny a railbird, a lowlife, telling him to get lost. Bad for business, Gus said, but now the barn brats just giggled at him encouragingly.

Wade had slipped the joint from Rory's fingers, winking at her. June swapped one tape out for another.

"Lou Reed? Seriously? How about you Wild Side up some Zeppelin or Floyd?"

"For sure," June said, turning Lou Reed up.

"Whatever, Butch. It smells like a bong in here. You oughta get yourself one of those little trees."

He laid his head back and stretched his legs. Rory saw him reach inside his jeans and adjust himself. He blew a smoke ring and broke it open with a lancing finger before it drifted away. June had gone small. Rory reached down and brought her camera to her lap. She fiddled with it, adjusting the aperture, then turned it on Wade, centering his face in the viewfinder. She felt June watching her. Rory had recognized her camera's ability to shift a dynamic, to alter the energy between her and everyone else. Usually she felt she'd gained something, a kind of solidity. Wade blew a smoke ring at the lens. Click. "You like that, Scott? You want me to show you how?"

He was easy to photograph, lithe, handsome, the strong nose with a breathy flare of the nostrils, the ruddy complexion. The same features that presented themselves as cheerful and organized on June's round face were more primal on Wade. Perhaps the difference was his mouth, how it was always a little bit open, revealing his teeth, the points of his canines.

Rory rested the Canon in her lap and took the joint from him, blowing one perfect ring.

"Not bad," Wade said.

"Not bad at all," June said, straightening herself behind the wheel. "In case you haven't noticed, Rory could teach you plenty."

Several times that week, Robin had told Wade he should watch Rory's form over fences. She'd had to steel her mind, refocus herself in the saddle—it was easier to be the one doing the looking.

"Kiss my ass," Wade said to June.

"Get your feet off my leather." June reached back and smacked at his dusty flip-flops.

"I'm cleaner than you two twats."

The tape abruptly ejected itself.

"What the fuck?" June said. "Johnny can't fix shit."

"Thank god," Wade said. "I was ready to bail."

With the music gone, the sound of retching was suddenly audible, coming from the creek bed behind the dumpster. Wade put his hand on the back of Rory's seat, leaning forward to look, and part of Rory's braid caught in his grip. Her eyes went wet. It was a homeless man in dust-caked clothing—his hands were on the dumpster, pulling himself into view. Rory had seen him walking the road before.

"Just what we need, another drunk-ass beaner," Wade said, lying back down.

Rory rubbed the sting at her scalp.

"You got beaner in you, don't you, P.G.?" Wade said.

P.G. A bastardization of the nickname Jorge had given her years ago: Pequeña Guerrera, Little Warrior.

"Wade, shut up. You are *killing* my high," June said.

"Come on, June. You know you've wondered. I always knew you had beaner in you, Rory. Maybe something fancier, some Cherokee or like real Indian?"

"You're an idiot," June said.

"Explains why Tomás has such a hard-on for you," Wade said.

"He does not," Rory blurted.

"I mean, you're cute. Don't get me wrong. Nothing wrong with a little Hispandex. Trouble thinks you're all that. I know he looks like a skinhead, but those guys really just want a piece of spice for themselves."

Rory's face went hot. The homeless man was halfway submerged in the dumpster, riffling for anything edible.

"Trouble would fuck a goat," June said.

"You calling your girlfriend a goat, Butch?"

"You are so vulgar," June said. "Enough."

She knew it was because her skin went an olive brown in the summer and because of her hair—the hair Mona refused to let her cut, that she kept braided back because otherwise it was so dense and wild. She didn't know what she was, except for her mother's side: all black Irish, Mona said. And Rory had no memory of her father and had only braved asking about him once: "Your father wasn't anything," Mona said. Which seemed true enough. He had never been anything to Rory anyway. "I'm Irish," Rory said, looking at June. "Not that it matters."

"It doesn't," June said.

Wade smiled. "Aren't you the sweetest, June. That's what I'll call you two, Sugar and Spice."

Wade left when the parking lot lights snapped on, scrambling into his truck as if he were late. "Don't miss your curfew," June hollered as he spun the truck around.

"He has a curfew?" Rory asked, dimly.

"Nah," June said, a part of her still tucked away, protected from Wade. Rory didn't want to go home just yet. "He's not always such an asshole," June said.

"He didn't get to me," Rory said. "I mean, I'm used to it."

"Yeah," June said, running her hands over the steering wheel. "I know what you mean."

"Trouble's worse, anyway," Rory said. The moon was up, a sharp sickle behind the trees.

"Oh, Johnny's not so bad," June said. "Where'd you think all this weed comes from?"

"Oh," Rory said. "Right." She hadn't wondered before.

"Can I ask you something?" June said. "I mean, will you be honest with me?"

"Of course," Rory said.

She figured this would be about Fresno, and was preparing a flattering response about the likelihood of June's win, but then June asked, "Do you still sit outside? On your balcony? Watching Vivian?"

"What? No." This was true. She hadn't. She couldn't. Not anymore. She had drawn the curtain back, she had looked, yes, but she hadn't seen any of them and even the few times she'd realized she was waiting to, she'd stopped—understanding that she could never look down there in the same way again. The cherished thrill was gone; there was no innocent witnessing. "It's not the same anymore," Rory said. "I wish I'd never looked, that I didn't have that view at all. That we hadn't seen them that night—"

"Hey," June said. "But that's the night we became friends." Her voice was chirpy now, changed. "Just tell me you aren't going to look. I mean, because I just think that would be—"

"Wrong," Rory said. "Yeah, I know."

"Good," June said, almost cutting her off. "Well, come on. Switch seats with me. I've been thinking, I should teach you how to drive."

SONJA CAME BACK in with a glass of water and his pill bottles. "You take these?" she asked.

"Yes," Gus said. Sweet mercy. His mind thrummed with the anticipation of relief. "Just two codeine."

"It says one."

"Please," he said, leaning into his good foot, wanting to take the glass of water and the bottle, too—but that's when she kicked him, with some force, in his good ankle.

"I know you can walk on that thing," she said. She kicked him once more, solidly.

He bit down on his lip, the pain radiating in places he'd forgotten.

He waited, accepting that she might not stop, that she might keep kicking him for some time, but then she sat down on the couch beside him.

"Now you can have two."

She shook the pills into her hand, giving him two and then setting one into her own mouth and swigging from the glass of water before passing it to him.

"She didn't send that letter from here." Sonja touched the top of the letterhead, the blue embossing: CLIFFSIDE, MALIBU. "I looked it up. It's a rehab, for drugs. And suicide. She's suffering, that I know for sure." Sonja looked as if she might cry.

Gus imagined Sarah Price in a white hospital gown, an equally white room, attendants in uniforms. He heard soft instrumental music and remembered fondly the cloud that had encased him on the other side of his morphine drip. Sonja wiped at her face with the sleeve of her shirt, then folded the letter in half and tucked it into the back pocket of her jeans. He had wanted to keep it. Ingrate.

"He could get a hearing in three years, with good behavior. I tell him, 'Be quiet. Keep your head down. Don't bother nobody.' I don't want Tomás in Chino. He belongs here."

Topanga. Gus had heard it was a Shoshone word, meaning, "above place." Heaven.

Outside the window there was a black flash. Gus followed it into the lichen-covered trees: only a crow, but it was holding the slack leather body of a lizard against the branch, drawing its insides out. Same way he'd left that fox in the back room of the office. Someone had to have cleaned up after him. How that body must have turned in this heat.

"I want to help you." The words so readily there Gus hadn't thought them. "I have to help you," he said.

Sonja extended her hand, palm up, welcoming a stack of cash. She was smirking.

"Work alone isn't going to be enough." The motor of him, slow to start, was humming again. "Not for either of us. I don't know what I can do, but I'm going to find a way. I will think—"

Sonja exhaled as if to say it was all hopeless, her posture going limp against the couch.

"Maybe Chaparral," he said. It was a short walk to the realization that the mare was all he owned, all he could sell if money was what they needed. And she might actually be worth something, 'specially if Rory did well in Fresno. Robin had told him how fit Rory had her. A new, real lawyer for Jorge, the payment to the anesthesiologist, the labs, every hand in a latex glove seemed to send a separate bill. The mare wouldn't pay for it all, but—

"Rory's horse?" Sonja said. "Don't you dare."

WHEN SHE FINALLY got through without McLeod's wife answering, Vivian compared herself to Marlow, on a dark slip of river surrounded by savages. She'd known the allusion would garner an appreciative moan, but then his voice turned all syrupy with concern. "Actually, I'm fucking fine, okay?" This was the first time she'd spoken to McLeod since that night and she'd only called to prove to herself that calling him didn't make anyone die, that it wasn't her fault.

Of course she wasn't fucking fine, not really. Everett's sudden hoarding of broken things, Mommy's dive into lunacy, and her friends weren't her friends now, not when she wasn't interested in being seen at the beach or sucking smoothies at the Malibu Country Mart. All of their siblings were still alive, their parents still within the realm of acceptable mental instability, and their worst fears were of unfounded rumors about meaningless things.

"The funny thing is, I never really liked any of them anyway."

"Who?" McLeod asked. She could hear the rising tremor of Mrs. McLeod in the background, calling him.

"Any of them," Vivian said.

"Vivian," he said. "I have to go."

"Of course. Women have a sixth sense about these things."

"Will you call me again?"

"If no one else dies," she said and hung up.

Another chair had been delivered earlier that day. Blue, but a royal blue. The movers had left it in the foyer, wrapped in Saran Wrap just like one of the lasagnas people kept bringing after the accident. But it had been weeks now since the house was filled with meals, steaming in their own juices (culinary dioramas), and the flowers, so many flowers, slowly wilting in their browned water. And now here she was missing all that ripe decay. Maybe, just maybe, she even missed the hulking cameramen and their indifference. What now? What did she need now? She tore at the plastic on the chair (not even a recliner!), shredding it in sheets until the clear spaghetti of it lay all around her on the floor. If the cameramen had stayed, if they were still sitting outside on the hoods of their trucks, breathing heavily, she'd have pushed this chair to the roadside and sat down with them, given an interview, asked questions back (What did they hope to learn? What was it people needed to know? Why did they think her family held some magical key for how to be—even in tragedy? Or did they want to see them suffering?). As if in response, as if she'd answered one of her own questions, the buzzer rang. The buzzer outside the gate.

Sliding over the plastic strewn on the floor, stumbling to depress the intercom, she yelled into it, "Do you want to see me crying? Huh? Is that it?" She hoped whoever this was would give her a reason to go on yelling (it felt so good to yell).

"Oh, I'm sorry," came through the other end, "is this a bad time?" Then static.

"Who is this?" she asked, disarmed. It was an oddly familiar voice, a voice from another life, a voice from school?

"Vivian? It's you, right? I'm sorry for just coming by like this, unannounced, I guess, but, well, could I—come in?"

Yes, this was a boy from her new school, from Merriam Prep.

"It's just me," he said. "Wade Fisk."

LITTLE SNAKE, WYOMING

MAY 21, 2015

GRANDAD'S BEEN WALKING around the house like he forgot something, eyes searching, one hand worrying at his beard. It's not just the house he wanders; he's out in the corrals now. I can see him, from my bedroom window, standing with Mama's mare. He's got a hand on her—out of fondness, but also, I suspect, for balance: two old animals leaning into one another.

He wanted me to write Mama about Chap, about the fact of her still being alive. She's ready to go—every day that's plain—but Mama asked us to try to wait for her to put Chap down.

A thousand times I've been told, that mare is the reason for us living in Little Snake, and for our livelihood. We're the only event horse breeders in all of Southern Wyoming that I know of—as if we needed another thing to set us apart. That mare's a miracle horse, Grandad always says, before looking to me for my reliable eye roll.

Chaparral, a 16.2-hand Andalusian Warmblood cross, heavy-footed over fences, but a quiet, rhythmic galloper and a liquid mover.

Up until now, anyway. Horse is thirty-two years old and it's clear in the way she lists, the give of her back, and that blank fly-stalked stare she's giving Grandad now.

Grandad bought her at a meat auction in '88, looking to buy a new school horse for the ranch he was working then, thinking he'd prove to the ranch's owner how well he could read an animal, registering its soundness of mind and the willingness of its heart even when staring down its final day. When the auctioneer brought Chap to the block, she was so underweight her head looked like an anvil, but her bone structure—apparent as it was—was solid, and there was still interest in her eyes. With no meat on her, Grandad was the only bidder. Hauling her home he was figuring she'd be best for his older students, for the adults, but when he walked her off the trailer, that mare fixed those interested eyes on my mama and the two stepped toward one another until the mare's muzzle was in the cup of Mama's hands and their heads had tipped together, announcing their inseparability.

A school horse paid for itself, but to keep that scrawny mare as her own would come at a cost, so Grandad had Mama start working at the ranch, symbolically at first—she was only ten that year—but soon enough Mama became necessary to the day-to-day operations. Right up until '93, when the fire broke out and they came here. *Never looked back,* that's something else Grandad always says.

He's the only one of the three that got out of that fire without a scar from it. Mama's is a braided line of white flesh, like a whip of flame licked her arm, thinning and disappearing at the base of her neck. Chap's is worse. Almost her whole left flank, from her belly to her ear, was burned—not just singed fur, but skin blistering, falling away down to the angry pink. Grandad says an injury like that can kill a horse from the shock of it alone. But not Chap.

Seven horses died in that fire and everything on that ranch—all but an old house and half of a barn—burned to the ground. It's not something Mama or Grandad talk about much. So I might not know anything about it if not for the scars and the fact that when there's news of a fire elsewhere, a look settles over each of them, their breath stopped in the grip of their memories. I swear, sometimes, I can feel the heat and shine of that fire, but it's no memory. More a sensation, like a scrap from a forgotten dream rising up in the early morning and then, just as swift, gone again.

I was born eight months after that canyon burned, to the day: July 2, 1994. Course I came early. "Early in every way," Grandad says. Mama was only sixteen.

When Grandad came in from the pasture, he stood in the kitchen looking at me like I might ask him a question. "No," he said, finally. "I don't think she's going to wait. I don't think that she wants to wait any longer at all." He meant Chap, of course, because we don't know when Mama's coming back. And he's right, it's been too long since she called. But Grandad's the one who's really grown impatient.

When he isn't walking around like he's mislaid his keys, he is preoccupied with the phone. If he has forgotten anything, it is how to wait. And yet we have always waited. We have always been the mountains and Mama the rain—never predictable, but always, eventually, coming back through.

In 2003, when the Iraq war began and everyone in Carbon County heard that Mama was embedded there, they seemed to believe that all the images we were seeing—the statue of Saddam being pulled to the ground, the actual Saddam dragged from the earth like Hades himself—were Mama's alone. Truth was, she spent the first weeks of bombing in northern Iraq, in Kurdistan, far enough from the "shock and awe" that there was time to ask people if she could take their picture before she did. She was already known for her pictures of people's faces, for getting them to look back. Pictures that let you think you know a person. In Kurdistan it was eager-eyed men ready for America to drop its bombs, wanting regime change, believing their lives could only be made better. But Mama understood her images would exist in a context that wasn't yet known. She's always lived at the flash points—running toward the explosions—the moments when the course of history shifts. Like Grandad says, Mama's just different from the rest of us.

That same year, the boys in school, the ones with older, enlisted brothers, were suddenly talking to me, asking if Mama had been with the 3rd Infantry, the 2nd Marine Brigade. I was nine. I said I didn't know and they shot finger guns at me.

When the pictures changed, when the images were not of a cut-and-dried "victory," but of the actual shit show that was happening, everybody still thought Mama was the messenger. She had made her way through Baghdad and down to Najaf and that was where she still was when a car bomb killed 124. She took pictures of the dead, before their mourners came to lower the lids of their eyes. Mama said she saw their souls leave and that she took those pictures *for the people who killed them, hoping against hope that they could be moved—maybe that's ridiculous. Maybe compassion is weak.* I read that in an interview, knowing Mama would have been looking at her hands, shaking her head, dismissing her own answers as she gave them.

In ninth grade, I heard two boys talking about me in the hallway at school.

"What about Charlie?" one of them said.

I could tell by the way they were walking and talking, the haughtiness of their stride—that I should stay unseen. I was by then the full-chested, broad-hipped woman that I had fought so hard not to become.

"Yeah, Charlie's got great tits, but I heard her daddy's a turban head—"

These were boys, I knew, who'd lost brothers in the war, whose prejudice would only deepen with time. But I can't say I hadn't started wondering about my father by then. In some weird way, I wanted what most girls my age wanted: the approval of strangers. Except my stranger was the father I didn't know. Sometimes he was a face in our photo albums that I didn't recognize. Other times he was every man my mother's age in town. I assumed he was young, that it had been a fling, *an accident*—that's the word I think of most often when I wonder how I got here. I only feel trepidation, even fear, when I imagine asking Mama about him. She has never known her own dad. Why should I need something different?

"A turban head, huh?" Nat Hinkley said. *Mathew Hinkley, Star Footballer, Killed in a Firefight. Casper Star*, front page. "So that's why they breed them silly Arabians out there."

I didn't set those boys straight about anything, but what we actually breed are sport horses—not breed specific, but a mutt of a horse meant to excel at three-day eventing, some inevitably stronger on one day over another. Like any of us.

With its dressage test, cross-country run, and stadium jumping, the three-day started as a cavalry test, checking the readiness of a horse and rider to go into battle, so it kind of makes sense that Mama says it was good training for being a photojournalist, for a life of chasing after catastrophes. Though now winning just looks like coming home alive.

I still haven't told Grandad that I haven't been writing to Mama, that these pages aren't for her at all. But he is right about the mare. She's got that faraway to gone look in her eyes.

Downstairs, just now, the phone has started ringing and Grandad has shoved back from his chair so hard I feel it hit the wall, the vibration coming up through the floor.

Grandad's voice is muffled, but I can hear that quiver he gets. It's the way he always sounds when an animal is sick.

Or when there's been news of someone's dying.

He's calling up to me.

I don't want to go.

TOPANGA CANYON, CALIFORNIA
LATE AUGUST 1993

AFTER THE HORSES were loaded for Fresno, Wade called shotgun, but June edged him out—it was her car, after all, and she was the one letting Rory drive. Rory slid the driver's seat forward, dried her hands on her britches, and tried to shift. June reached over and turned the key in the ignition. Rory dropped her head to the wheel. "Right," she said. "Maybe I *am* nervous."

"For sure," June said. "That's half the fun." Robin and Tomás had already left with the horse trailer, but the haul was heavy, and Rory planned on catching up to them soon enough.

Wade leaned into the front seat. "Dad would fucking kill you for this, Butch."

"Ah, but the beauty in this scenario, Wade, is that Dad's not fucking here."

Rory knew Mrs. Fisk wouldn't be coming to Fresno either, that she'd be busy with the PTA, a bake sale, her book or tennis club—*preoccupied with looking the part of a perfect mother,* as June put it. "Just don't kill me," Wade said. "My life's just begun."

Rory had discovered that driving was not so unlike riding a horse, a matter of thinking two steps ahead, but turning onto the 101, she felt the one significant difference: You had only yourself to trust.

June grabbed Rory's arm. "Shit, not too fast."

"Oh, let her have her fun," Wade said above the wind, laughing. "Dad's not here, right?"

For a while they flew along, from the 101 to the 405, June's hair whipping around her face, and then, just before they met the 5, Rory had to slow to a crawl.

June popped in one cassette after another, the tape deck spitting each of them back out.

"We should have left *your* car with Johnny," Wade said, before putting his headphones on, making stabbing attempts at the lyrics to "Been Caught Stealing." He'd left his Scout with Johnny, for some souping up of the engine.

It was an hour before they'd inched their way onto the Grapevine—a steep stretch of the 5 that nosed over the San Bernardino Mountains—and at the first plateau, there was the beacon of a gas station and a convenience store, and in the lot Robin's black F150, and the ten-horse trailer with the Leaning Rock crest.

"About time," Wade said, ripping off his Walkman. "I'm famished."

"And I've got to pee," June said, already scrambling over Rory, saying, "Don't let Robin see you driving. She'd definitely tell my dad."

"Ouch," Rory said, laughing. "Jesus, okay."

June was scuffing her way inside, knock-kneed, trying to hold it, the backs of her leather huaraches flattened under her heels. Wade ran past her, then beat her to the door in mock slow-motion.

Instead of following them in, Rory stopped at the trailer, stepping up on the fender to reach inside and stroke Chap's head. "Hey, lady." The mare had been sulky all morning, even lethargic. Rory heard Tomás moving around inside the trailer's narrow tack room. She still felt awkward with him, a mix of shame about Gus and embarrassment over her having taken up with the Fisks. She whispered into the silky pocket of Chap's muzzle, "You worried we aren't ready for this, my lady?"

Gus had gotten up to see her off that morning, waking before dawn, like they used to. He had fixed her toast and juice. "You're at home on that horse, Rory. Always have been. Don't let it matter who else is competing." Mona had stayed in bed, impervious. "Bring home a ribbon," Gus had said. It wasn't a real possibility, she knew. She was just glad to be getting away.

The bells on the door jingled as Rory stepped inside the store, but no one turned around. They were all by the magazines, clustered together: Wade, Robin, June, and a few of the younger barn brats whose mothers had come along to groom them: to French-braid their hair, iron their shirts, sweep their tack trunks clean so they'd have somewhere to sit in their Bermuda shorts.

"What are you guys looking at?" Rory asked.

A hand shot up from the midst—Wade's hand, holding a magazine. "I'm in fucking *Entertainment Weekly*!" His hand dropped back down and the huddle around him tightened. Rory had to wedge her way in, as he read aloud, "Wade Fisk, son of prominent Beverly Hills plastic surgeon Dr. Preston Fisk."

"You read that already," June said.

"Spice hadn't heard it. Dad is going to shit," Wade said. "He'll get fifty new patients off this."

One of the mothers reshouldered her purse and led her daughter away, the others following, noses up, their doe-eyed daughters looking back at Wade.

"You're a pig," June said.

"Oink, oink."

June bent, tugging her sandals fully on. "That headline—it's going to crush her."

"No, it's not," Wade said. "How would you know, anyway? You don't know my Viv."

Rory looked at June, but June wasn't looking back. To Wade, June said, "She's got to be more human than you are."

"She's not all dark and brooding, Butch. I mean, look at her. Look at how good she looks! What woman wouldn't love this?" He smacked the splayed pages with his hand. "I'm buying ten of these," he said, pulling them from the rack.

June shook her head, moving to the soda machine. Rory picked up the last magazine.

"Living It Up After Baby Brother's Death. Vivian Price Frolics in Malibu with Son of Doctor to the Stars . . ." They were on a beach, together, sitting in the shade of an empty lifeguard stand, Vivian leaning back against Wade's bare chest. Not just leaning, her head was thrown back—laughing. The teal blue bikini top, her white denim cutoffs, and Wade's fingers across her bare belly, tickling her.

Living it up.

Ice cubes were tumbling from the ice maker into the bucket of June's cup.

"You knew?" Rory asked.

"He always gets what he wants." June shrugged, alternating pumps of Orange Crush and 7UP.

Rory hesitated, then said, "Is this why you asked me if—" She stopped.

"If what?"

"Nothing."

"What, are you jealous?" June asked.

"Don't be ridiculous," Rory said.

On the stillest of nights, lying in bed with the window open, Rory could sometimes hear Vivian swimming. But she only closed her eyes then, just waiting for the lapping of the water to stop. She didn't want to be who she had been on the night of the accident. There had to be a Before and an After Rory. *After Baby Brother's Death*. But this picture— the look on Wade's face, his slavering mouth—woke something new in Rory, a thought that, maybe, she was supposed to protect Vivian Price.

"I just didn't know." She closed the magazine and returned it, nonchalantly, to the rack.

"That Wade's not beneath porking the bereaved? Yeah, well, he's not."

"Does he know about that night?" Rory asked. "About my room?"

"About your view?" June shook her head no. "Even twins keep secrets. Besides, you said you weren't looking anymore—" She sucked on her straw. "And I think I trust you."

Outside, Wade was back in the car, sitting shotgun, looking at himself in the rearview mirror.

"You should," Rory said.

"Good," June said. "Okay, then." She was going for the door.

"Hey!" The woman behind the cash register, dressed in a hot pink muumuu, stood up. "Those sodas aren't free, you know."

"She'll spot me," June said, pointing at Rory, the bells on the door already jingling.

"Right," Rory said. The cashier looked at her now—a deep furrow in her brow, rolls of flesh at her neck—and sat back down. "How much?" Rory asked. The woman held up two fingers, and went back to watching her show on the television above the register.

It wasn't the first time Rory had stolen something. There were the cigarettes from Mona, the work gloves she'd charged to Carlotta's account. Then new spurs, the watch for the cross-country run. But those were things that she needed for Fresno, things that Carlotta, if she'd been lucid, might have gifted her anyway. So this was different. Back by the freezers, out of view, Rory rolled and tucked the magazine into the back of her britches, leaving her shirt hanging loose. Holding herself upright to keep it from jabbing or, worse, sliding out. She put a five on the counter. The woman never took her eyes off the television as she handed Rory her change, saying, "Your friend's a real cheapskate."

SARAH DID NOT want to speak about Charlie anymore.

There was something so messy about continually discussing "her loss." There had to be a cost-benefit equation to it all. Or, rather, she felt she was owed. These last two years, the pregnancy and the first stage of mothering, had cost her a certain self-regard. Could she get that back? What of her son's solid little hand gripping her finger? His warm, snot-stifled breathing against her shoulder? The heft of him in her arms? No, of course not. No. No. No.

"Let us be frank," Sarah said to Shrink. She'd taken to saying this too often, but it elicited a wry inner smile, as if "Frank" were someone she might very well become. "It's been good for me to be here, I can acknowledge this, but what am I gaining now?" What she meant was, did Shrink actually think that she was coming out the other side of this with her mind intact? She'd seen her son's body turned into a wrung-out towel. Charlie, her son. And she'd thought of him as *the boy.* What kind of a mother was she? The bewilderment in that man's eyes as he was led away—it had mirrored her own. He wasn't evil. Or rather, if he was, she was, too. Jorge Flores. Gus Scott. Sarah Price. Her name was inextricably linked to theirs. Sarah Price, no longer just the daughter of Leon and Eleanor, wife of Everett. How was she to attend a cast party again? Raise a glass in honor of her husband? Look her daughter in the eye?

She'd seen the picture of Vivian with her new boyfriend. The woman orderly with the bread loaf feet had brought her a copy of the magazine, believing, it seemed, that it was every mother's dream to see her daughter with a doctor's son. Or maybe this was like the bird sounds, playing on loop, intended to create a confused docility.

Shrink wrote on her pad of paper, nodded, bounced her pointed shoe, her stockings shushing together. Her mother, Eleanor, had worn stockings.

She hadn't spoken much about Eleanor with Shrink. She wasn't sure she knew anything about Eleanor anyway, not really, everything about her having been in accordance with Leon. "Yes, my mother would have done well in a place like this," Sarah said. "Removed from him." Whenever Leon was undergoing an episode—believing himself capable of superhuman feats—he would persuade Eleanor to go with him on one of his reckless drives to nowhere. Drives that always ended in an infraction of some kind, just enough to jolt him back into himself. And Eleanor, knowing exactly what she was in for, just tucked her purse in the crook of her arm and waited for him to hold the door. And every time they returned—the car parked cockeyed on the front lawn—Sarah would be seething. "How could you get in that car with him?"

"And you know what she would say to me?" Sarah was reporting all of this to Shrink. "She said—as calm as one of your orderlies over there—she said, 'How else did you expect me to get home?' Just like that. Ha," Sarah said, "ha," sitting back in her chair.

She waited for Shrink to scribble on her paper, diagnosing her mother: Enabler. Codependent. Unstable. Her father: Bipolar. Clearly bipolar. Wasn't that what they called it now? Not just a rich and entitled drunk, but actually split, divided by extremes. Two sides, no dawn, no dusk, no in-between—no matter how hard Sarah had wished it.

"What do you think she meant?" Shrink asked.

"She meant," Sarah said, "that he was her home, Leon, her husband."

TOPANGA CANYON, CALIFORNIA

"Your father."

"Mm." Sarah hadn't understood this about Eleanor until now, not with the clarity that came from saying it out loud. "No one else mattered to her except him."

Shrink made an unintelligible sound and began scribbling. Sarah had a sinking feeling. Everett, she had always needed his approval.

She let her eyes settle on the painting on the far side of the wall, a remedial bit of landscape with a rudimentarily drawn Cape Cod–style house that reminded her of the summer home of a friend from boarding school. They'd run off there together on the weekends, telling the headmistress they were going home. Surely the house was still there, the street still lined with aspens and maples, probably still in that friend's family. New England wasn't like Los Angeles, always shedding skins like an ever-fattening reptile.

"Do you want to get home, Sarah? You must miss your husband."

Talking to Shrink was like talking into a tin can, her voice distorting down the string. "Yes," Sarah said, resigned. "Yes, of course I do."

"Sarah," Shrink said, "it is my recommendation that you be removed from mandatory watch. In other words, when you feel ready, you are free to go."

Sarah pictured a mattress on a curb for anyone to take, the hand-drawn sign: FREE.

"It means you only have to be here if you choose to be." Shrink removed her glasses and dangled them over her bouncing knee, shush, shush. "It seems to me, Sarah, that you are no longer a threat to yourself or to others." Though this was a statement, Shrink's eyes were questioning. It was too obvious to remind her that we are all always a threat to one another, so Sarah remained silent and Shrink seemed pleased by her lack of response. "Neither I, nor your husband, will have the legal ability to keep you here any longer, Sarah. You can go home now, if that is what you would like to do."

RORY'S DRESSAGE TEST was stiff, lifeless even. Chap was apparently apathetic under the pressure of competition. Still they were sitting in ninth with a score of 58.2, good enough. June's test had been as expected: She was sitting in second with the lower, more desirable score of 42.8—the points being a tally of faults in their ride. June was off with Robin now, walking the cross-country course again, saying she'd see Rory at the upper dressage ring soon, as everyone was going up to watch Mark Adler's test.

Mark Adler was a two-time Olympian who'd flown in his most prized horse: Cosmo's Waltz, a seventeen-hand, dapple-gray Thoroughbred stallion. A horse with bloodlines back to Native Dancer, or some esteemed racehorse, anyway. Without June, Rory wouldn't have known any of this. She was bringing her camera up to the ring.

Wade was already there, still on Journey, still in his coat and tails. "Aren't you gonna ask me my score?" he hollered over to her as she crested the hill.

"Sure," Rory said, steering Chap up beside him. They were the only ones on horseback. The rest of the audience was in the bleachers. "Tell me your score?" Wade made her tired now.

"Forty-one point eight," he said. Journey blew the dust from his nose.

"Really?" One point better than June.

"Don't sound so surprised." Journey's neck was dark with sweat, as if Wade had worked the horse into a frenzy before their test even began. "You more upset that I'm ahead of you? Or more worried about June?"

"Worried? No," she said. "It's great. I'm happy for you."

"Of course you are, Spice. Of course."

Rory ignored his practiced wink. She untwisted the lens cap from her camera, tucking it in the waistband of her britches. In the farthest warm-up ring, Cosmo's Waltz was an ivory silhouette, but unmistakable: his sheer size, Mark Adler's black top hat and tails a thin exclamation mark above him.

"That camera's a wreck," Wade said.

"I know," Rory said. There was a crack in the viewfinder and a light leak she'd yet to diagnose.

"Where is June, anyway?" Wade asked. Rory spun the camera on him: click. "Hey. Warn me first, would you?"

She'd never caught him off guard like that before. "Maybe next time," she said, smiling. Maybe he'd tipped off the photographer— the paparazzo who'd photographed him with Vivian.

"Can you believe people trailer from all over the country to train with this guy?" Wade said, watching Adler in the distance.

"Yeah," Rory said. "I can."

June had said Adler interviewed potential students and only invited a handful to ride in his clinics in Colorado. Rory imagined a log cabin office against the foothill of a mountain, horses in buffalo-checked blankets, and heated, indoor arenas. "June should ride with him," Rory said, knowingly baiting Wade. "She'd get in."

"Not a bad idea. A consolation prize for when I beat her. How's she doing anyway?"

"Doing?" Rory asked.

"I'm planning on winning this one. I've never beaten her before, but it's good to take her temperature. She takes shit hard, you know? She's sensitive."

Rory looked down, adjusting the f-stop on the Canon, willing him to keep talking.

"You know how she can get. All down in the dumps. Shit's brutal for her already, you know?"

Rory didn't know, not really. But there had been a few times in the parking lot, when they weren't talking, and June seemed to have gone somewhere else.

"They say you're born like that," Wade said, pulling his gloves off. "That there's no choice."

"Depressed?" Rory asked.

"No, Spice. Not depressed." He put a finger to one nostril, snuffed up his nose, then spat into the dirt. "Gay," he said. "Born like that. At least that's what I heard, but there's no telling Dad that. He says it's bullshit. Says June needs to stop playing around. She's gotta have some choice, right? People decide not to do shit all the time. Like you, Spice, am I right?"

"What?" Rory said. The camera took on an inordinate weight in her hands. "I don't know what you're talking about."

"Come on," Wade said. "You could go either way, I know it."

His voice had a bite to it. Chap shifted beneath her. "I've seen you looking at me, Rory. At least you got a picture, right? It's too bad I'm already taken."

"You're wrong," Rory said. She wanted to throw the camera at him.

"Figures they were walking the course," Wade said then, standing up in his stirrups. Rory turned to see what he was looking at: June and Robin coming up the hill.

"I swear Robin plays favorites," Wade mumbled. He put his hand to Journey's neck. "I need you to promise me something, Spice." An urgent whispering.

"What?"

"It's crystal clear my sister likes you—so I need to know that you're not going to mess with her. That you're not gonna go and break her heart. Comprende?"

"I'm not," Rory said. "I wouldn't." She was remembering June's mouth, the warmth of her breath, the air pulled out of her own lungs. The question that had been there, between them.

"Keep it friendly, Spice. Just friends. I'd like to win and beyond that I am not a fan of her getting hurt."

"We *are* just friends," Rory said. Robin and June were fifty feet off still, but jogging toward the ring.

"So you promise," Wade said, not asking.

Nothing had happened. June was her friend. "I promise," she said.

And then June was there, looking up at her, wild-eyed, her cheeks shot red, sucking down a bottle of water. "Did we miss it?"

Rory shook her head. "He's still warming up."

"See," Robin said, a consoling squeeze to June's shoulder. "All good."

June turned to Wade. "How was your score?"

Rory watched him, anticipating his shit-eating grin. But then he lied. "I didn't wait to see."

Rory felt an unexpected flash of fondness for him, but just as quickly it was gone.

Adler's number was being called and he was trotting Cosmo toward the ring in front of them. Rory pulled a small clean rag from her pocket, wiping the camera lens clean. "You're such a professional," June said, looking up at her, a gleam in her eyes that—with Wade watching them—Rory found newly embarrassing.

Chap raised her head from the ground, flicking her tail, calling off flies. If Rory was going to take Adler's picture, she needed Chap to be still, to be the sloth she'd been all morning. Adler turned up the ring's centerline and Rory set her focal point on Cosmo's big marbled head and, looking into her viewfinder, a fantasy swam up: she'd sell Adler a photograph, earn back some of what she'd spent being here. Even above the stallion's forceful trot, Adler's hand stayed so quiet he could have carried a glass of water.

The cigarettes, the gloves, the spurs, the magazine—even coming here, to Fresno. These were all things Rory wanted, but that she knew weren't rightfully hers. And every one of them had called to her with the same tugging desire, like thread stitching in and out of her, the needle focused on what she had to have next. And now, watching Adler ride, seeing through the camera's lens the minutiae of signals he was exchanging with his horse—the stallion's hooves hovering in midair before coming down again—what Rory wanted more than anything was to be one of Adler's students. And there was that hard snag of a knot: that could never be, not for her. It wasn't a thing she could steal.

"God damn," June said.

Adler turned up the centerline again—his test nearly complete. Through her lens, Rory saw the stallion's wide dark eye roll toward them. Chap's tail swished again. Rory went to advance the film, but she'd shot the whole roll. She swung the camera behind her, watching now like everyone else. Cosmo halted square: his legs parallel to one another, his neck round, his mouth engaged yet relaxed on the bit. The audience took a collective breath. But then, as Adler went to remove his top hat and give his final salute to the judge, Cosmo reared up, his front hooves boxing the air. Adler lost his balance and his top hat fell from his hand as he tried to collect his reins again, the hat rolling like a tumbleweed to the outer edge of the ring. Chap's body swelled beneath Rory. Cosmo came down hard and bounced right back up again, taking massive backward steps, his haunches flexing. Rory already had a hold on her reins, realizing—as Cosmo raised his upper lip to smell the air, inhaling deeply—what she had failed to recognize earlier: Chap's apathy was a sign of her being in estrus. A fact this stallion was clearly aware of. Adler had dismounted and was trying to assert dominance, to back Cosmo down by raising his hand to the air, but the stallion broke free of him and was charging in their direction, his ears laid flat back. June and Robin ducked toward one another, Robin yelling, "Holy shit." Wade was turning Journey for the barn, but none of them were as fast as Cosmo and he was on them, spinning his haunches around, kicking out, the shining metal of his shoes flashing toward Journey before turning again, his teeth bared: believing Journey was his competition for the mare.

Rory was spurring Chap up the road, her camera behind her, beating out the rhythm of the mare's strides. She heard the audience's screams turn over into relief, then polite applause, signaling Adler had control of his horse again. Rory didn't look back; she didn't need to know. She was swept up in the escape, in the mare's newly awakened gallop, already thinking about the next day of competition.

"DOES SHE KNOW I'm coming?" Gus asked.

Sonja had offered to brave the drive up the incline to Carlotta's house, leaving Gus without an excuse. His cast had been removed, but he was in a brace and using a cane now.

"I didn't tell her, if that's what you mean," Sonja said, pulling the van door closed. Behind the wheel, she locked her elbows and leaned forward, as if to plow the van up on arm strength alone. Gus saw her take one quick glance at the edge: a two-hundred-foot drop. At the top, Sonja parked outside Carlotta's garage, then turned to him, as if they'd been quarreling the whole way up. "Even if I'd told her, she'd never remember anyway."

He hadn't been up to see Carlotta since early July. She'd been lucid enough then, touching his shoulder the way she always did, a love pat that said, Stay the same.

They found her outside, on the porch swing, her chin in her hand, not registering them. Sonja called to her in a high, practiced voice. The nurses hadn't been dyeing her hair and the white was half–grown out and wiry as a mane.

"Will," Carlotta said. Will was her son, Bella's younger brother.

"Not Will." Sonja sighed, helping Gus up the steps, with a hand to his elbow.

"Well, hurry up and come here, sit with your mother," Carlotta said.

"Will isn't coming." Sonja said sternly. To Gus, "She keeps asking for him."

Will was a grown man, forty-something and far more crippled than Gus. As far as Gus knew, it had been decades since Carlotta had seen him. He had lived with Bella ever since he was seventeen. It was one of Carlotta's horses that had left him paralyzed and neither kid had spoken to her since, believing she had been to blame. The story was, Carlotta had raised the fence one morning, hiking it higher than Will had ever jumped a horse before, insisting he could do it. The horse stopped short and Will went flying, soaring through the air like a trapeze artist, only to drop like a stone onto the jump stand, his body bouncing, then twisting; his spine was damaged in three different places. Bella was in her final year of college, but she came home early to take care of him. "They'll love me when I'm gone," Carlotta would say. Bella had never liked horses anyway.

Sonja waited while Gus used his cane to ease himself down into the swing.

"My god, Will, you don't look any better at all," Carlotta said, searching Gus's profile, trying to make sense of him.

A pair of Keds, bleach white, sat beneath the slats of the swing, an identical pair on her feet. Gus had made efforts over the years to keep Bella aware of what was happening to her mother—leaving messages on her answering machine, never answered. As far as Gus knew, Bella's introduction of Robin Sharpe was the only meaningful interaction she'd had with Carlotta in the twenty-odd years since Gus had known her.

Sonja brought out a stool and propped Gus's booted leg on it.

"Isn't she your biggest fan," Carlotta said, turning her nose from him, acting like a scorned girlfriend.

"I don't know about that," Gus said.

His own mother's dementia had come as no real surprise: an inevitable paring down of a life lived up against her husband's hardness. But Carlotta! Gus had had a faith in her ordinarily reserved for the immortal.

"So, how is your sister?" Carlotta asked, in a tone of a practiced formality.

Gus debated answering as Will. He sensed Sonja inside, listening. "If you mean my sister Joy, she's good. Real good."

Truth was, it had been a while since he'd phoned her.

Carlotta looked down at her shoes. "Damn it," she said. She pinched the thin length of her nose. "Joy's the one with the breeding barn, isn't she?"

"That's right. Quarter horses. She and I used to work sheep there, in Wyoming."

Carlotta poked her finger at the Keds beneath her. "I'm obsessed with them," she said. "I have this feeling I'll need them at any minute. I don't know where it is I think I'm going in two pairs of shoes.

Where would you go, Gus? If you could?" She'd emerged from a revolving door, mid-monologue, her voice confident.

"I haven't—I really don't know," he said.

"The bind you've put us all in, I bet you'd like to run away. But I suppose you'd hoped all that had slipped through this rusty sieve." She tapped her temple. "You're not wrong. I did spend a day mourning your death."

Inside, Sonja was stacking dishes. "That might have been better," Gus said.

"Don't be falsely bashful with me, Gus." Carlotta rocked the swing ever so slightly, sending a stab of pain into his hip. "You're here to say your piece. It's taken you long enough."

"I am sorry," he said, "for the mess of all of this." Sonja went still, listening.

Carlotta put her hand to his leg, an eerily light touch. He couldn't help but hope that one of the hidden doors in her mind was swinging open, that he could be Will again. "Of course," she said then. "Jorge isn't blameless," she said this over her shoulder, directing it toward Sonja. "Every man makes his own choices. Most reliable help I ever had, that man. What was the boy's name?"

Gus had not said it before, not out loud. "Charles Price." He saw the flash of his hair.

"Yes, I read that somewhere," Carlotta said. A dragonfly was hovering above the railing of the porch and she gestured at it. "Those bugs can see three hundred and sixty degrees. All the way around themselves. If I come back, it'll be as that bug. Hindsight, foresight, sideways sight." She leaned into him, like a schoolgirl

111

sharing a secret. "It's Robin Sharpe who turned out to be worth her salt. Didn't see that coming, did you?"

"No," Gus said. "I suppose. She's capable enough—"

"Aha. So you're giving up, then?"

He had been ambitious once. He was tired now. "No," Gus said. "Quite the opposite." In the kitchen, Sonja cleared her throat. "I came for your advice."

"Stop," Carlotta barked. "Is that what we're calling money now? Advice?"

The dragonfly lifted from the railing, a helicopter from a battle-field. "It's not like that," Gus tried, sincerity eluding him.

"You're going to have to go back to work, Gus. Reassert yourself. You've still got something to teach those kids. Maybe you better talk to your sister. Like you tried before—"

It had been a decade since Gus had asked Carlotta to let him start a breeding shed at Leaning Rock, suggesting they have Joy come in to consult, but—"You said it was too risky."

"Ah, that's your weakness, Gus: You back down too easy. You're like an insecure Clydesdale. It makes you lazy and on your worst days, it makes you dangerous. Get back to work already."

His ears were full of a tinny ringing, as if she'd struck him. "I can't ride."

"That's got nothing to do with anything." She made a frustrated motion. "You know horses. Besides, I've seen the books and you've been skating. Of course you need money. We all need money." She looked down at her sneakers. "Prove me right about you, Gus. I'd like to be right about bloody something."

"**HE'S SUCH A** crybaby," June said, meaning Wade.

She was talking to Rory through the crack between their stalls, both of them looking at Preston Fisk, who was standing outside Journey's stall on the other side of the walkway. He had arrived in Fresno right after breakfast, which meant he must have left L.A. at 4:00 a.m., a fact that added to the chilly, urgent air about him.

"Of course he wakes up at the ass crack of dawn to come here for Wade," June said. "And not even Wade, really. He's only here because to him that horse is a four-legged pile of cash."

Wade and Tomás were in the stall, tending the wound that Cosmo had left in Journey's side the day before. It was clear, in his tailored suit, that Preston Fisk had once played competitive sports.

Rory was trying to read Robin's lips. "Do you think she's blaming me?" Rory whispered.

"You mean because your mare is one hot mama who makes all the stallions go wild?"

"I'm serious," Rory said. "I never would have brought her up by the ring if I'd—"

"If you'd known what Robin should have realized. She's the trainer, Rory. It would only make her look bad to blame you. Besides, *that's horses—shit happens.*" This was something Gus always said and June's saying it now felt like a kindness, but also true. It wasn't her fault, not completely.

The cross-country course in Fresno consisted of twenty-four fences over three miles of uneven, rolling terrain; grass to sand to leaf-littered woods. Their running order was the opposite of the day before: Wade up first, then June, then Rory. Rory waited for Wade and June to leave for the warm-up ring and then steered Chap to the peak of a hill that looked out over the first six fences, hoping that watching a few other runs would inspire both of them. The first was a girl on a long-legged bay gelding, whose big round stride covered ground as seamlessly as wheels. As they turned toward the water obstacle Rory could see the pair was out of Adler's barn—the kelly green HR insignia on the saddle pad, Heritage Ranch. The girl was a small, tight fit atop the bay, bouncing like a spring up and over each fence, and she took the embankment without any hesitation, relaxing her hold on the reins and inviting the bay's drop into the muddy water. Just like that, Rory thought. She watched each ride as if through her camera's lens, looking for the nearly imperceptible shifts in their bodies. Chap pawed the ground, growing eager. The announcer called Wade Fisk to the starting box and the countdown to his run began: *10, 9, 8.* Chap pricked her ears, and with her calves, Rory said, Not yet. *3, 2, 1.* She checked her watch so she could track Wade's speed, then swung her leg forward, reaching down to tighten Chap's girth.

Someone was yelling. It was Robin's voice. "Get back on!"

Wade was on the ground in front of the falling trees oxer, fence three. Journey's nostrils were flared, a spooked horse, empty stirrups swinging at his sides. Shit. Rory scanned the spectators, finding

Preston Fisk. His expression was stony, unreadable. Wade had his whip in his hand, and he struck his boot with it, Journey's head jerking back, startled by the sound. Rory flashed on Carlotta, the time she'd dismounted one of her horses and started whipping it, repeatedly, lashing the air, until its legs were braided with blood. That was the day they'd known she wasn't well enough to work horses anymore. *Breathe,* Rory thought. In her better days, Carlotta had always told them to breathe in unison with their horses, to try to sync up their heartbeats.

There was low applause from the crowd as Wade remounted.

He steered Journey around and picked up a canter, standing in his stirrups, then dropping down to his saddle abruptly, as if he could launch Journey up and over the fence. Rory knew then that Journey would refuse again. Journey came from a long line of winning sport horses, never having to prove himself, to grow bigger or try harder, a tin man of a horse, an echo chamber for Wade's bravado. On the third approach to the fence, Rory watched Preston Fisk, seeing his shoulders lift ever so slightly, trying to hoist his son up and over the oxer with his will, and then the twitch of defeat when it didn't work. Preston adjusted his shirt cuffs and walked away. This third refusal meant elimination. Rory watched Wade dismount and leave Journey on the course, discarding him. It was Tomás who jogged out to retrieve him while the announcer said, "Ladies and gentlemen, this heat continues to make even our top contenders lose their cool."

"Where the hell have you been?" Robin asked, as Rory trotted into the warm-up ring.

She had only ten minutes to get Chap limber. June was already in the starting box, a single-minded look on her face.

"You've got this," Rory called to her.

"If you've been hiding, avoiding Wade and his dad, don't give it another thought. I can handle Preston Fisk," Robin said.

Rory looked down at her. "Thank you," she said. "I didn't mean—"

"Never mind," Robin barked. "Get moving. You're all falling apart on me."

Rory got in a dozen sprints up and down the warm-up ring. The mare was loosened up, even playful. Rory heard June's score come over the loudspeaker: clean over all the fences, and fast.

"Don't be afraid to use those spurs," Robin said, steering Chap into the starting box. "Now we know why she's been so dull, so get after her, you hear me?" Rory felt the spurs on her heels, but she was sure she wasn't going to need them. Robin smacked Chap's haunches and the mare swung in, bobbing her head against the bit, her hooves prancing in place.

"Ten, nine, eight," the announcer started. Rory ran a hand down Chap's neck, feeling the roiling muscle of her.

"June's moved up with Wade out," Robin said. "No harm in giving her a run."

"Five, four, three, two," Everything went silent, Rory hearing only the beat of her own and Chaparral's hearts. "One."

The two of them leapt onto the open green.

Fences one and two were an easy opening combination. And now, fifteen strides out from the falling trees oxer, Rory realized she'd never started her stopwatch. She wouldn't know her pace, except to sense it, but she was up and over the oxer now and she had a long clear run of the field ahead. She got up in her half seat and brought her whip around, cocking it like a jockey does. She'd never laid a whip to Chap like that, never would, but just having it there created a new current of electricity between them. She gathered the mare up for the ditch and palisade—up and clear—then let her out again. Hooves and pulse and wind. At the embankment into the water, Rory remembered the golden stitching of the HR rider, the poise of her seat, and then she *was* her, sitting deep into her saddle, letting Chap take control of the bit before leaping into the water as easy as a kid to a puddle, the cool of the water spraying up, the hit of swampy stink riding on with them. Chap had never run so fast or jumped so neatly. This was months of galloping in the hills paying off, of secretly jumping her over fallen logs, of trusting one another. Chap jumped higher out here, an arc to her back that Rory levitated above ever so briefly, finding the balls of her feet against the stirrups, her thighs holding on. She scarcely touched the reins and just after the angled combination, her crop fell away. Jump, land, gallop, jump, land, fly. It might not be so easy in the ring tomorrow, but now, she was galloping through the finish line, knowing she had zero faults. Easing Chap back into a trot, she stood in her stirrups, listening for her final time over the loudspeaker: she'd been five seconds faster than June.

Robin came running down the hill, pumping her hands in the air. "I knew, I knew," she was shouting. "I knew you had it in you."

"I forgot to start my watch," Rory said.

Robin was jogging to stay beside her and Chap. "You didn't need it." She laughed. Chap shook and froth flew from her lips. June was coming toward them on Pal. "She's in first," Robin said. "She's pleased. But you should be, too. Do you want to know where that run put you?"

Rory shrugged. "Of course."

"That was impressive," June said, catching them. Pal's sweat was dried to his coat, crisp and white. "You've moved into fifth."

Robin patted Rory's leg. "How about that?" She was in the ribbons. She'd have a ribbon to bring home to Gus, so long as Chap didn't take any rails down the next day.

"What about Journey? Is he okay?" Rory asked.

"Vet checked him," Robin said. "He's sound, wasn't that. It'll all be fine."

"I should say something," Rory said. "I still feel bad."

"Nah, don't bother," June said. "Daddy's taking him over to meet Mark Adler."

VIVIAN WAS STRETCHED out on a towel beside the pool. She'd looked so pale in that picture with Wade. She dropped a straw into the papaya-seltzer-vodka spritzer she'd managed to mix between dinner with Everett and Carmen's cleaning up.

"You're going to burn," Everett said. He'd sat down at the table, under the umbrella, his Watchman TV blaring while he fiddled with the channels.

"That's the point."

She'd stopped thinking of him as Daddy. He was more like a cousin. Cousin Everett. A distant relative who'd gotten stranded here and grown too comfortable after some snafu in his travel arrangements.

"Maybe we should get a tanning bed," he said, settling on the primal ranting of the nightly news (what to dread, who to fear, and the weather never changes!).

Vivian closed her eyes. "Yes, let's buy a tanning bed. It'll be like living in Los Angeles."

"Oh, I see. Very funny."

Howard Stern had been fired and an abortion doctor had been shot in Wichita, Kansas. Vivian couldn't stand it. "Everett," she said, hoping to move him inside. "When will you go see Mommy again?"

"It's only been a week."

"More than two."

"I'll go. I'll go soon." He leaned toward the tiny screen. "Are you hearing this?" NASA had lost communication with the Mars *Observer*. Vivian rolled over and opened her magazine again. "You like him?" Everett asked. "Wade?"

He wasn't looking at her. He didn't really care. Why ask at all? "Yeah," she said. "I like him enough."

Though she wasn't thinking about Wade so much as Theodore LaGrange. Years ago, she'd talked Teddy into driving her up to the lake cabin Everett had bought in Big Bear, telling her parents she was spending the night at a friend's. Everyone called Theodore Teddy. *Big Teddy Bear,* she'd growled at him, pulling the fur rug around them. She'd run her hand over the fur, then onto Teddy, his breath minty with schnapps. They were on swim team together. She was fourteen then and he was seventeen and so frustratingly nice, never trying to take off her shirt, holding her all night long. She'd talked him back to Big Bear a second time, but then they couldn't stay, couldn't even go inside because Everett's BMW was already there when they arrived, the lights inside dimmed, smoke coming from the chimney. "My dad," she said to Teddy, realizing her father wasn't alone and that he wasn't with Mommy either. Like a boulder rolling from the hillside and dropping to the road in front of her, an impasse, crushing whatever innocence had lingered. Teddy drove them back the long way, around the lake, with a consoling hand on her knee. At the first turnout, she'd insisted he stop, and she'd found her way onto his lap, losing her virginity this way, alongside the reflection of the moon and its ladder of light on the surface of the otherwise pitch-black water.

"That's good," Cousin Everett said. "He seems cute enough."

"He rides horses," Vivian said.

"Oh, really?" He still wasn't listening.

"Up here," Vivian said. "Up the road." It had been one of the first things Wade had told her. That he knew Jorge Flores, though he'd not called him by his name. Saying that, knowing him, the man who killed her brother, made him feel particularly—how had he said it, *connected* to what had happened. That he'd needed to tell her, in person, just how sorry he was, that if he'd known about him drinking at work—she'd gone ahead and kissed him then, wanting to taste his pity. Wanting a repository for her anger. *That Mexican* . . . that was how he'd referred to Jorge Flores. She dropped her sunglasses down on her nose so Cousin Everett would feel her stare. "It's probably why he's so good in bed."

Before Cousin Everett could speak—his face had bloomed a primary red—the phone started ringing inside. A muffled, buried ring, a cry for help from beneath the avalanche of rubbish he'd brought home. Vivian strode inside, navigating the three blue armchairs, the clutter of lamps and collectible (?!) clocks, the topographical map of the Hawaiian islands that sat inside a cracked frame, behind which was the ringing replacement for the other portable (x marks the spot), and answered in a high note of fake pleasantry, "Price residence. A small faction of us is still operating in reality. How may I help you?"

"I'm calling on behalf of Sarah Price's doctor." This was a nurse from Cliffside who'd not yet dipped into the meds, such was the speed and agitation in her voice. "We're calling to check how Mrs. Price is adjusting? Because it says here that she missed her required post-discharge appointment. We do not take—"

"I'm sorry?" Vivian asked. "What did you say?"

"Who am I speaking with? May I speak with Mr. Price, please?"

"This is a joke," Vivian said, stepping outside again and handing the phone to Everett.

"This is Everett Price," he said, his eyes questioning Vivian.

She was picturing Mommy just beyond the gates, standing there, locked out.

"Post-discharge?" Daddy asked, then repeated the question with varying deliveries. Then a litany of expletives. Then threats.

Vivian made her way back through the house, to the front doors, opening them to emptiness—the same warm air as by the pool, the white noise of distant traffic. The fountain grasses shifted in their pots. She opened the gates onto the road, just as a car was passing, its music trailing behind.

Ever since the accident, Mommy's BMW had been left alongside the outer wall, right where she had parked it earlier that day.

Out back, Cousin Everett's litany peaked in an exclamation of "Son of a bitch!"

Vivian looked in the car windows: an empty handbasket from the local market beside Charlie's car seat, a pacifier dropped to the floor. All still sealed within, a time capsule. As if there were any going back. As if Mommy hadn't already told her she wasn't coming home.

RORY WAS WATCHING the red bars of the motel clock shudder over—10:12 to 10:13—when someone knocked on the door. She had torn the picture of Vivian and Wade from the *Entertainment Weekly*, throwing the rest of it away. She slid the picture into the drawer of the bedside table before undoing the latch. She assumed Robin had locked herself out, but there was June, in her nightgown and a short matching pink silk robe. She was bouncing on her toes, the motel pool lit up and steaming behind her. "I found pot," she said, then checked the balcony above for eavesdroppers. She'd been asking around all weekend, unwilling to travel so far with weed in the car. "Come on," she said, and took Rory by the wrist.

"Where is everybody?" Rory asked, following.

"They all went for drinks with Adler. Robin, Daddy." June sat down on the lip of the pool and set her feet onto the shallowest step. The rest of the motel was quiet, a few lights flickering in the split between curtains. June pulled a joint from inside her bra and lit it up.

"Is Wade with them?" Rory asked, pulling her sweatpants to her knees, dropping her feet in the water beside June's.

"The favorite child," June exhaled. "Of course. Daddy will have him riding in one of Adler's clinics in Colorado soon enough. I'd put money on it."

"Where'd you get this?" Rory asked, looking at the toothpick of a joint.

"Stable hand."

"Not Tomás?" Rory asked.

"No, a guy from Flying J. Perfect, right?" Rory was coughing. "Yeah, it's dirt weed," June said. "But it's better than nothing."

Rory lay back on the asphalt and they passed the joint back and forth. The sky was darker here, devoid of city lights, the stars sharper, more glittering. "It's kind of beautiful out here," she said.

"Now I know you're high," June said. "It's Fresno. It's kind of a fucking nightmare."

"Wait," Rory said. "Why aren't you with them? With your dad and Robin? I mean, if anyone should get to ride with Mark Adler, it's you."

"Yeah, but Wade's the one with the injured horse that Daddy can hold over Adler's head. That's Daddy. A surgeon in and out of the operating room. His business motto is: There's a fortune to be made in every misfortune. That is *literally* his motto. I'm sure he's making Adler feel like he's saving himself a lawsuit."

"A lawsuit might be preferable," Rory said, still lying down, talking to June's back.

June laughed then, but when she stopped she landed in that melancholy place and Rory thought they'd sit not talking for a while, but then June said, "I asked him if I could bring you."

Rory couldn't see June's face, couldn't read it. But her robe had slipped, revealing one shoulder. "Bring me?" Rory asked.

June turned to look at her. "I wanted to go with them, see if I couldn't get in on all of this, honestly, but then I thought about you and I wanted us both to go. I thought you should at least get to meet Mark Adler, but when I asked—"

"So your dad does blame me? For Journey?"

"No," June said. "It's not that. It's that he—he understands that you aren't just a friend to me."

That phrase. "But I am," Rory said.

"I know, but when a friend is also—you know, someone I—"

"You know?" Rory sat up. "I don't know—" She looked at her hands, squeezing one inside the other, thinking about Wade.

June was assessing her. "You're serious?" she asked. "I mean, I know you're not exactly clear on it, but it's not just going to go away, Rory. You think if you ignore it, it'll just starve and die off? Is that it?"

"I don't know what you're talking about."

"Really? What about Vivian? Sitting out there, watching her? Because your television was broken? Come on, Rory. We're the same."

"You're wrong," Rory said. "I was bored. She's—they're famous. Anyone would want to look."

"I know you better than that," June said. "You don't care about famous."

The water at Rory's feet had gone cold. "You're wrong," she said again. This weed was no good, her teeth chattering, her body rife with anxiety. She wanted to talk about anything else, anything but herself. "Maybe you can still meet with Adler. Maybe even ride with him—"

"Rory, that's never going to happen," June said. "My brother might be a C student while I go premed, but Daddy will always prop Wade up, however he has to, because Wade is the legacy he prefers to this. To me." She fanned her hand at herself.

"I bet you win tomorrow," Rory said, grasping.

"For sure," June said. "I have to win. That's all I have." She took a long drag on the last sliver of joint then flicked it into the pool.

"And you'll snap those suspenders, right?" Rory said, letting herself smile.

June looked at her. "You know, it took me a while to get up the nerve to knock on your door tonight." She was looking at Rory's lips, at her mouth. "Because I knew I had to tell you how I felt and that it was going to be awkward for you, but . . ." Her hand was turning Rory's face toward her, the same as when they'd sat on her window ledge, the curtain of June's cropped hair falling around them, the tips of their noses touching. Rory anticipated June's mouth on hers and she held her breath as if this would stop time, giving her the nerve she needed to brush June back, but then June's leg crossed over, straddling her. Rory tried to back away, dragging herself back on her elbows, the skin scraping the pocked pavement. "Stop," June said. "You'll hurt yourself." Her breath was laced with smoke, her skin with the White Musk she always wore. "Just relax."

If she shoved June, she would fall backward into the pool, and what a commotion that would make. Rory didn't want anyone to come outside. "You're wrong," Rory said. "You're wrong."

"For sure," June said, her lips against Rory's. "I'm wrong," she said, the words pouring into Rory's mouth and then the wetness of June's tongue was traveling over her lips and the silk of her robe was brushing against Rory's arms. "Lie back," June said, pushing her hips into her.

Rory hadn't kissed anyone since Martin Jarvis in sixth grade, a dare at a party. It had not felt like this. He had been hesitant and clammy where June's mouth was warm and her hands roving. From Rory's neck, down her chest, and then her knee slid between Rory's legs, right up against her, relieving a kind of ache, a soreness, that Rory hadn't yet registered as being there. "It's okay," June said, tugging at the string of Rory's sweatpants, a new chill in the air hitting Rory's skin, before June's hand slipped between her thighs and Rory was twisting against it, like an animal folding into a net, but June didn't stop, didn't pause her hand from rocking until Rory was having the sensation that she had been dropped, that she was falling, plummeting, as if down a hillside—the same sensation as in the dream she had been having, almost every night since the accident, a dream about her house endlessly falling—but here, now, distantly, was the possibility of relief, even comfort, and Rory gasped, released, reaching the ground, her whole body springing awake. She pushed June away, startled to find her still on top of her, the weight and warmth of her. Suddenly, she could barely breathe. And June was giggling. "It's okay," June said. "That was so—"

A door above them was opening and June had turned to look.

It was Tomás. And Rory saw them from his point of view, how she was halfway out from under June, June's pink robe falling off, Rory's sweatpants undone. "Stop fucking smiling," Rory said, catching June's smirk, knowing that from that angle Tomás could see everything.

COUSIN EVERETT HAD left the house as if wearing a cape and mask, dead set on finding his wife.

Vivian turned on the television, wanting its noise now. NASA was continuing to send out communications to the *Observer* every twenty minutes, hoping to regain contact.

"It's out there somewhere. It has to be. It's trapped in heliocentric orbit," McLeod said.

Vivian had called him without wanting to talk really, just wanting the warmth of the phone to her ear. She certainly wasn't going to mention Mommy's running away. "We keep this quiet," Cousin Everett said, tripping over a box of VHS tapes on his way to the door.

"Heliocentric orbit," Vivian repeated. The night was an eerily still one, not even a whisper of a breeze, no sound of birds or leaves to fill in the sense of vastness all around her, but holding ever so still, rooting herself to the slate of the pool, she could feel the day's heat seeping up out of the earth around her. She'd taken a Klonopin, had a few sips of vodka.

"You're awfully quiet tonight, Vivian Price," McLeod said. "Do you want to talk about it? Any of it? We've yet to talk about your brother and I was wondering if that article, if the headline—"

"What, bothered me? But I am *living it up.* Did that make you jealous, Mickey? My picture with *the son of a doctor to the stars*? I thought I looked a little pasty, no?"

"Have you been drinking?" McLeod asked.

"I *am* drinking."

"I've never heard you drunk before."

"I've never heard *you* drunk before."

"Is this a game, Vivian?"

"No, Mickey McLeod. This is, very much, not a game."

"Do you need me to come over?"

"Yes, need," she moaned.

"Jesus, Vivian."

A drawer opened and closed. The snap of a lighter, the hiss of escaping fuel (oh, this was new!). "Have you taken up smoking, McLeod?"

"I shouldn't have asked that. I want to be clear with you. I can't come there."

"But I'm all alone," she said. In the space between his voice and hers came the chatter of coyotes. No pups, all full-grown animals. "No one would ever know."

"These calls are in my capacity as your former teacher–turned-friend." She knew the flush of his cheeks, the way he was shaking his hair back from his eyes, how he probably held his cigarette too delicately. "I can be here for you as a friend, but that is all."

"Friendly friends," Vivian said. "Does your wife know you smoke, Mickey McLeod?"

He sighed. "No."

"Good. Let's keep it that way," she said. Everything had gone quiet again. The quiet was the worst reminder of Charlie being gone; everything she couldn't hear anymore, everything that would never be as boisterous as it once was. Bunnies, she'd wanted to get him bunnies (they'd have been eaten by the coyotes—facts were facts). "McLeod," she said.

"I'm here."

"No," she said. "You're not. You're way over there. As lost as any of us."

"Trapped in heliocentric orbit," McLeod said.

IN THE MOTEL lobby, Robin said, "Keep your head in the game today, Rory." She was signing the bill, sliding the keys across the counter to the clerk. She'd not come back to the room until midnight, tiptoeing in, assuming Rory was asleep. "You can stay in the ribbons, I know it. You're the most tenacious rider I've got."

"I think you mean June," Rory said.

Robin smirked. "She's focused, but she's also used to winning."

"Right," Rory said. She was tugging at the sleeves of the button-down she had to wear for the final day of competition, feeling they were too short. "Wade left, right?" she asked, hoping.

"No, just Preston," Robin said. "Wade wanted to stay and cheer June on. He's got plenty to look forward to now anyway."

"A clinic with Adler," Rory said, not doubting this had worked out for him.

"Yeah," Robin said. "How'd you know?"

The night before, when June had followed after her, knocking on the door again, Rory had refused to answer. "Come on. That wasn't so bad," June had whispered into the doorframe. "It was just for fun, okay?" The clock had read 11:12 then. Not even an hour had passed. She found she was holding June's lighter, her fingers stiff around it. "We can forget that ever happened, okay? It'll be our secret." June was saying this outside the door. Tomás had gone back into his room. When June finally left, Rory pulled the picture of Wade and Vivian from the drawer and under the rattle of the bathroom fan, she held it over the toilet, clicking the lighter until the glossy image lit, dropping it as soon as it got too hot to hold.

The jumping phase didn't require Chap's mane to be braided, but Rory was braiding it all the same, standing on a bucket, her fingers still tight, folding one plait of hair over another.

"How is she?" Tomás asked, startling Rory. "Sorry," he said. "I scared you."

Rory only glanced at him, worried what his face would reveal of the night before. "No, you surprised me, that's all," she said, steadying herself on the bucket, her eyes back down.

"I heard you moved up," Tomás said, pulling on the brim of his cap. "You're in fifth?"

"Doesn't matter," Rory said, unraveling the braid she'd messed up. "Chap's bound to pull a rail."

"Okay. Well, I just wanted to wish you good luck."

She looked at him now. His face was changed, softer somehow. Like he knew, like he understood—that hadn't been her. "Thanks," she said. "That means a lot."

Wade and June were down the barn aisle; June's voice rising up, full of irritation: "I'm in first and he leaves, Wade. He'd have thrown a party for you and you know it."

"Hey," Wade said. "I stayed. Doesn't that mean anything to you?"

"Whatever," June said.

And then June wasn't in first anymore. On the second fence, she hesitated, and Pal added a hopping stride, leaving them no room to get off the ground, his front hooves taking a rail down on ascent and then his back hooves taking down another. Eight faults, four for each downed rail.

Rory was still trotting Chap around the warm-up ring, relieved the mare felt as supple and relaxed as she had after yesterday's hard run. She kept her head down, but she saw June cursing as she exited the ring.

Robin called her over. "That's the deal with this sport, each test matters as much as all the others. Nothing is ever cut-and-dried, Rory. You have a real shot at this now."

June was out of the ribbons, Rory realized, doing the math. "I can't beat June," she said, understanding that there had been this unspoken contract.

"You *are* beating June," Robin said. "You just have to keep beating her now. Pick up a canter and let's keep Chap spry until your number's called."

Don't let it matter who else is competing. That's what Gus had said to her as she was leaving, as if he'd hoped this for her. Rory slowed her breathing, matching Chap's. She was aware of being watched from the stands, of Wade sitting up there.

"The next bell is yours," Robin said as Rory passed.

Twelve fences inside a ring at 9:00 a.m., with shadows slanting across ground her mare had never run over before. The first fence was a four-foot-three oxer. Chap was up and over, clean. A left turn to a triple combination: up and over, two strides, up and over, one stride, up and over. And then on fence five, she felt Chap's back left hoof touch a rail. She was cresting fence six when she looked back for the rail on the ground; she was so sure that it would be lying there, but it was still in its metal cradle, barely rolling. She was over fence eight when she saw June, no longer on Pal, but up alongside the judges' box, her arms crossed, wiping at her face, her skin splotched. Chap kicked out between fences, a kick of frustration, and Rory heard Robin outside the ring. "Let her out, Rory. She wants more freedom."

Fence ten, eleven, twelve were a blur, but she was done. Finished. And exhausted. She'd hardly slept.

"Do you hear that?" Robin asked.

Rory shook her head, but she was looking into the bleachers, to where Wade was coming down the steps, heading for June, and she realized then that everyone else was clapping. The raucous sound of it turned on. "You're the first clear ride that course has had all day, Rory. You've won, Rory. You've fucking won."

"But I didn't—" Rory started.

"I know," Robin said, smacking Rory on the knee. "I told you."

By the time the ribbon ceremony was over, and Rory had walked Chap back to the stalls, only Tomás was there, bent down beside Pal, wrapping his legs for trailering home.

"Where did they go?" Rory asked.

"You can ride with us," Tomás said, and Rory followed his gaze, to where June's Mercedes was pulling out of the event grounds, making a dust bloom on the horizon line.

"Did she say anything?" Rory asked.

Tomás shook his head no, but Rory could tell he was embarrassed for her.

"Shit," Rory said.

In the truck, wedged between Tomás and Robin, Rory kept her ribbon on her lap.

Tomás watched the passing fields outside his window—the neat corduroy of almond trees, then orange trees. Robin turned on the radio, fiddling with the knob to get around the static, eventually finding a Tracy Chapman song, humming along, lost in self-congratulatory thoughts.

Suddenly, the land outside was a blackened swath, from the roadside back to a line of fencing in the distance. "A fire," Rory said.

Tomás nodded. "It's the fastest way to prepare the ground."

Gus had told her fire was nature's great decomposer, how it enriched the ground, allowing seeds to take root. That sometimes it was necessary.

Tomás turned toward her, and she saw how tired he was, how long the three days had been for him. "I grew up on fields like these," he said. "Before we moved." He looked across to Robin, who smiled back at them, not listening. He touched the long silks of Rory's ribbon, sliding them through his fingers. "You're not happy you won, are you?"

"I am," Rory said, "I *am*." Neither way sounded true. "It's everyone else who's not."

"They're not everyone," Tomás said.

THE WEATHER WAS shifting, cirrus clouds streaking the sky. There was Mercury, no, Venus, but Vivian wanted to find some sign of the Mars *Observer,* though she'd heard that required a telescope (one of the few things Cousin Everett hadn't brought home). She was trying to find the switch to turn the pool lights off when Johnny Naughton came around the corner with Wade leaning into him, walking like he was wearing high heels, knees dancing, head tipped onto Johnny's shoulder.

"How the hell did you get in here?"

"I have my ways," Johnny said, shrugging, his round face crinkling like paper in a fist.

She knew well enough not to press Johnny. She understood how he fit into Wade's life—a pit bull kind of friend, the type you have around if you're unsure of where you stand in the world.

"Whatever," Vivian said to Johnny. "What's wrong with him anyway? I thought he was in Fresno." She stepped toward Wade. His breath was vinegar.

"Got home today. He came to pick up his car and we took some pills."

"Brilliant," Vivian said.

Johnny dismissed her with a paw to the air. "It's nothing. For real. He'll sleep it off."

"Here?"

"Unless you got another boyfriend coming," Johnny said.

"Can't you take him home? Where's June?"

"She went home hours ago. Besides, he told me he wanted to see you."

"This was before he lost control of his face?" Wade's head sagged, a guttural sound escaping, his mop of hair hiding his eyes. "Why can't he stay with you?"

"Because," Johnny said, his face scrunching up again.

Vivian smiled. "You still live with your mom, don't you?"

"So what," Johnny said, his red eyes on her. "You do, too."

"Funny that," Vivian said, almost ready to have a laugh over Mommy's disappearance (but no, too soon). "Except I'm seventeen," she said. "What're you, thirty?"

"Just wait. It's never gonna be this good again, girl." He gestured to the other wing of the house and then up the hillside. "Plus I hear you've got a real fan club up here."

Vivian sighed. "Whatever. Just put him in there." She gestured at the chaise just inside the sliding doors to her room.

Steering Wade inside, Johnny kicked over a jar of sea glass, but otherwise successfully arranged Wade in a seated position, while Wade kept blubbering, "Ehm so tyrd. I hay her." Johnny propped Wade's elbow, so his hand held up his head, then he saw himself out.

"You make no sense, Wade Fisk. But I'm somewhat glad you're here."

There was something graceful about Wade, even obliterated as he was, his long arms draped along the chair. Like a Kennedy. She put a wastebasket next to him and a glass of water on the table, before getting in her own bed. Sometimes they had sex at the house, sometimes they'd drive somewhere, doing it in the back of his Scout. He was more tactical than the other boys she'd been with, as if dialing in the numbers of a combination lock. He'd laughed when she'd told him that, asking if he ought to be offended. "No," she said. "I just mean you know what you're doing." And he'd come back with "Maybe you've just never been properly fucked."

She woke up once to the sound of him vomiting in the bathroom. Then, again, to him kneeling on the floor beside her, whispering, "I'm so sorry," toothpaste on his breath. She drew the sheets back then, letting him curl behind her, and slip her shorts down, and pull her onto him. Maybe she preferred the backseat of the Scout. Though even there, sometimes, she cried afterward, trying to explain through deep breaths that she was fine—it had gotten easier to piece herself back together, to hide the fissures that sex unearthed. She wasn't going to tell him about Mommy running away or how Cousin Everett had brought home so much shit there was now one room in the house so full of stuff that they could no longer open the door.

When she woke again, it was to daylight-dappled sheets and a breeze on her skin.

She found Wade outside, leaning against the house. "Feel okay?" she asked. He brought his arm around her. His shirt was off, his skin damp and fragrant. "You showered," she said.

"I couldn't get back to sleep." He kissed her forehead. "Johnny shouldn't have brought me here."

"I dunno," she said, biting her lower lip. "Johnny said you wanted to see me."

He looked at her. "Who doesn't want to see Vivian Price?"

"Did you like the picture of us? In *ET*?"

"Of course," Wade said. "Did you? June said you'd think—"

"She's wrong," Vivian said, stopping him, not wanting to hear about their bickering. She slipped a hand into his jeans thinking that would call him back, but he was staring into the trees. Mommy had wanted those trees removed until the surveyor explained that their roots were all that was holding the hillside together. "What are you looking for?" she asked.

"Not what. Who," he said, looking down at her. "You've got neighbors up there. A real fan club, it turns out." The same thing Johnny had said.

"I can't see," she said. "It's someone you know?"

"Nah," he said, looking up again. "Forget I said anything. It's nothing for you to worry your pretty little head about."

LITTLE SNAKE, WYOMING

MAY 22, 2015

I HANDED THE phone back to Grandad and I went into town. I left Grandad standing there, with the phone in his hand and that look on his face, all the color drained out of him. I drove through Savery and all the way into Baggs. I'd listened on the line and then I'd handed the phone back and all I'd said was "I'm going to town." I didn't wait for a response because I couldn't be there, not one second more. Soon as I turned onto I 70, I saw the storm in the distance. A dark gray cloud and its skirt of rain. I drove past my old school—one school, K through 12, enrollment never topping two hundred—and I kept driving, turning down Route 13, watching in my rearview as the storm turned with me, following me like an apparition. We were the mountains, Mama the rain.

It's only two miles down the 13 before you hit the Colorado border, but I didn't get that far. I knew I'd have to go back and when I did I ought to have something for the two of us to eat. I'd say I just went for groceries.

The Passwater General Store is the only thing between Baggs
and the Colorado border. It's a one-room place with a single freezer
and a rack of candy bars and another of chips. I used to hoof it there
after school, buying ice cream, gum, packets of hot cocoa powder
that I ate off the tips of my licked fingers. Like most good things,
Aunt Joy had turned me on to it, seeing how I wanted to kick up
dust someplace else. Andy Passwater—the owner—had always
been at the register. But today he wasn't there.

"Well, look who's here," Mrs. Traden said when I stepped inside.

I'd never seen Mrs. Traden in the Passwater, let alone working
the register, and the incongruity of her being there stopped me just
inside the door. When my aunt Joy was alive, Mrs. Traden was
someone we had over for meals once a week.

"And soaked all the way through!" She was rocked back on the
stool and she let the front feet of it clap down like a gavel then and
I jumped at the sound. "You okay there?"

The rain had caught up to me as I pulled into the lot, coming
down hard as hose water, but I couldn't make my legs do anything
like running, so water was pooling around my shoes. I felt embarrassed, but I couldn't place about what.

"Charlotte? I asked, are you okay, then?"

Mrs. Traden has called me Charlotte for as long as I can remember and no one, not Mama, not Grandad, not even Aunt Joy, ever
corrected her.

"I just got stuck in the rain is all." My socks sloshed as I tried
to escape down the aisle, past the thermoses of coffee, the Doritos.
My pulse had kicked in again. Soup, I was thinking. Bread. Get
these things and go.

Mrs. Traden and her husband used to own the land our ranch sits on. They'd given Aunt Joy and Grandad their first jobs, raised them up to adults, as Aunt Joy told it. Then Mr. Traden passed and Grandad followed his dreams to California. Mrs. Traden sold the land to Aunt Joy then, for an amount far less than it was worth, out of respect, I guess, for a woman going it on her own. But that bargain left Aunt Joy owing Mrs. Traden meals for all eternity and when she was over, she moved around the kitchen like it still belonged to her, touching the tops of things like we'd done less than a decent job dusting.

"Didn't think I'd see anyone in here today," Mrs. Traden called down the aisle. "I was just about to call Andy and tell him I was closing up—he's out with a bronchitis that'll probably be the death of him. He's ninety years old, you know? Leave it to Rory's kid to show up on a day like today. Where is your momma this week, anyway?"

Two cans of soup. The loaf of bread. A bag of coffee beans. I stepped back to the counter. "I'm not a kid anymore," I said. "I'm twenty-two now."

When I was a kid, I rode my bike in rain like this, taking the turns as fast and hard as I could, sending water off my tires in a fan, wanting it to be visible to the planes overhead. Mama always flew out of Cheyenne, and in the bitter pit of my thinking about her then, I believed she flew out more often than she flew home, the logic of the math irrelevant.

Until now, until it was true.

"You know your momma's a hero," Mrs. Traden said. "She's probably in Syria, don't you think? There's fighting there, I hear."

141

"No," I said to Mrs. Traden. "She was in Ramadi." I was realizing I had never been alone in a room with Mrs. Traden before. She had always sat opposite me in our kitchen nook, looking at me like she was a decorator making a decision about wallpaper, unsure of my pattern, my quality. "She was supposed to be in Syria. She had been in Syria; that's where the bureau thought she was. But she took a lead. The fighting was so bad, nobody was going in. I don't know how they found her, but there was a bomb and she was there. She's been dead for days."

Mrs. Traden stood up as quickly as if I'd sunk my teeth into her ankle. "I don't understand," she said.

"They called us. Just now. They told us she wasn't where she was supposed to be. She left her translator and her driver behind. She trusted a bad lead. There were no other American journalists there. Of course, that's probably why she went, to be the one. The only one. It'll be in the news. Not until tomorrow. She always put herself in danger. So fucking stupid." I heard this, the hatred in my voice, and saw the way my hands were shaking, from somewhere outside myself. Mrs. Traden got so quiet I thought she was going to cry. "My name isn't Charlotte. My name is Charlie," I said.

"Oh, Charlie," Mrs. Traden said. "I know. I've always known your name is Charlie. I just didn't—I never cared for the reason why. There's so many things your momma didn't get to tell you." Beyond the excessive makeup Mrs. Traden has always worn, I could see there were things she knew about Mama, things Aunt Joy or Grandad must have said, things that neither of them had ever told me. "You have to ask more questions," Mrs. Traden said, like some kind of clairvoyant. "You've always been such a quiet kid."

"No," I said. "Not always."

If Mama's camera had been found, if her final pictures could be seen, I know they would be a rapid series of faces, throngs of people trying to go about their lives, and that among them there'd be that person who saw her back, who sensed her looking. A person who desperately wanted their agonies known, desperately enough to strap a bomb to their own body and walk out into a crowded street.

"I have to go," I told Mrs. Traden. The rain had stopped and pulled up into a dark ceiling, a flash of clear blue sky between here and home. "I've been gone too long."

TOPANGA CANYON, CALIFORNIA

EARLY SEPTEMBER 1993

ON THE FIRST day of school, Rory dropped woodshop and went to claim the last open seat in Photo II. She'd heard the teacher loaned a camera to any student who could take apart, thoroughly clean, and reassemble one. The Canon she'd taken to Fresno had proven impossible to fix.

When she'd gotten home from Fresno that night, Gus was waiting up and his eyes went big, seeing her blue ribbon. "Don't look too surprised," she'd said. He embraced her—the first time since the accident—but then he started right in about breeding Chap, that he'd thought he would have to sell her, but now! He was a man newly obsessed with an idea. Going on about Carlotta suggesting it, how they'd find an affordable stallion, and in less than a year's time there'd be a foal. Rory imagined this spindly limbed foal yoked and struggling, dragging them all up out of the hole he'd put them in. She told him that Chap had been in estrus there, but she stopped short of telling him about Cosmo's Waltz and Journey getting hurt and how she'd been left behind. She recognized he was in need of a certain enthusiasm for this new plan, but what she felt for him, for herself, even for Chap, was a mix of pity and regret. "But you're okay with it?" he asked, reading her. "It'll be great," she said. In ten years, she'd never wanted time away from the barn, but now she was relieved school had begun.

The photo teacher, Mr. Foster, stopped to sign her yellow slip, then returned to clicking through a series of slides on the overhead projector: earth from outer space, Kate Moss in Calvin Klein, Elizabeth Taylor laughing at a party, landscapes that went from the sublime—a mountain's peak splintering the sun, a stately saguaro cactus—to violent—rice paddies from an open-sided helicopter, bodies strewn on the ground. Foster hesitated, scrutinizing these last few images, before he shut the projector down. Pete Leonard, a green-bean-shaped boy with a lopsided nose that made it impossible for him to say anything without it sounding nasal, asked, "Were you in the army? Did you kill people?"

Foster was potbellied and short with a turnout to his right foot and a gait that suggested he favored one hip. He had not been in the army, he told Pete; he had not killed anyone. But from her seat in the middle row, Rory understood that he *had* been an embedded journalist in the Korean, no, maybe Vietnam War. Why are you teaching here now, in this crud factory of a school, Rory wanted to know, but she stayed silent.

"Now, what *I* wanted to talk about," Foster went on, "is why bother? Why take pictures? What's the point?"

There was the sound of bodies slinking down in their seats, a pencil drummed a desk. Only Pete Leonard raised his hand. Foster ignored him, looking at Rory, eyebrows raised, clearly wondering would she—the new student—be participating? "Rory?" he asked. "Is that right?"

"Sorry. Yeah, that's me." She didn't ordinarily volunteer anything. "Photographs show us," she said, her voice low, "I don't know . . . where we are."

At the barn, she'd gone back to her old routines, working horses, forking stalls; whatever friendship—or whatever that was—she'd had with June was over. The few times she had seen Wade there, she'd set her attention that much more intently on the horse she was working. She was returned to who she had been, only now she knew the difference. Just yesterday, Wade had left his saddle in her tack room, on her hobby horse, meaning it was hers to clean.

"And—" Foster was pressing her.

"How we fit in?"

"Interesting," Foster said, his cheeks drawing down. "Meaning?"

"Meaning . . ." The front row turned around, their eyes on her. "Meaning how we fit in *our* lives versus someone else's life? They can show us how other people live, other ways of being. Photography lets us travel. Kind of." She was thinking of the images on her bedroom wall, the children in the Bayuda Desert, the bus station in Brussels, but also the newspaper clippings after the Trade Center bomb, the riots in South Central, the old man lying in the street, beaten for being Mexican. "Pictures wake us up. They give us perspective. How we compare." She flashed on Vivian and Wade on the beach in Malibu, the shiny blue spark of magazine paper. "Of course, plenty of it's just bull—" She stopped herself, her face going hot.

One of the Goth girls—weighted down with spiked bracelets and a raccoon's mask of mascara—made a hissing sound, an approving one, Rory realized.

"Yes," Foster said, "plenty of pictures are just bullshit." There was snickering and Foster smiled. "In this class, however, we will aim to take pictures that aren't. Glad to have a live one in here, Rory—"

"It's Ramos," Rory said. "Rory Ramos."

THE PRIVATE DETECTIVE discovered that Sarah Price had gotten into a town car in the parking lot of Cliffside Refuge and had the driver ferry her forty-five minutes down PCH to Marina del Rey. Marina del Rey being the nexus for all forms of departure (boats slipping from their docks, planes taking off from LAX, and car dealerships glimmering on every corner).

"So she drove right past here," Vivian said, not so much speaking to the detective as she was realizing it out loud. Mommy in the back of a Lincoln Town Car, in her favorite yellow summer dress, her sunglasses on, sitting at the traffic light at the base of the canyon, avoiding looking up the road toward home.

"That's correct," the detective said, not looking at her. He was seated on the opposite side of the kitchen bar, his eyes never leaving Everett, as if he were being paid to look only at him. He'd introduced himself as Detective Gregg, quickly clarifying, "Gregg is my last name."

Everett was having vodka, olives buried under the ice, and still wearing the blue-and-yellow Hawaiian shirt he'd worn for the table read of the action movie that morning where he'd had to reassure the producer that his stretch of bad PR was behind him (like chicken pox). "Go on," Everett said, sounding as scripted as ever.

In Marina del Rey, Sarah told her driver to wait and went into the bank and made a cash withdrawal that was *luckily* (Gregg's word) large enough to require the branch manager's approval. She paid the driver, "tipped him one hundred dollars," Gregg said, missing the point. "And at the first car dealership in the line of them there, she bought"—Vivian was thinking, used, beige Ford (innocuous, average)—"a used, tan Toyota Camry." (Damn, so close.) "She spent the night in the house in Big Bear before going northerly. That's what we know."

"*Northerly*? We? That's what *we* know? I've known *all* of that for a week," Everett said, downing his drink. "You're fucking useless." He picked the *L.A. Times* up off the counter and threw it at Gregg, who stumbled backward off his stool. "I'm paying you to find where she is *now*. Don't you understand?"

Gregg adjusted his suit and rearranged himself back on the stool.

"I'm sorry," Everett said to the detective. "I'm upset."

"It's part of the job," Gregg said, growing calm. He stole a look at Vivian.

"You've had other things thrown at you before?" She leaned over, letting her breasts touch the counter.

"I can't wait around here forever," Everett said, uncapping the vodka.

"It's your turn now," Vivian said to Gregg. "Did you forget your line?"

"I can find out more," Gregg said, his Labrador eyes back on the ball.

"Well done," Vivian said. Everett was looking at her sideways.

"I have work, damn it. She's supposed to be here." Everett brought the bottle of vodka down too hard against the counter. Gregg flinched. Vivian slid her empty water glass toward Everett, and he mindlessly poured her a drink as she knew he would.

"Yes," Vivian said, nodding. "Mommy disappearing is so inconvenient." Gregg's eyes followed her glass as Vivian reeled it in, raised it and drank. "But Detective Gregg is on it," she said, wiping the vodka from her mouth with the back of her hand before winking, just to give him a little scare.

AT THE END of the day, Robin Sharpe called a meeting on Gus's behalf, asking the men to gather in the office. Only Manuel and Tomás had spoken to him since his return to the ranch, and gruffly at that, while Sancho and Adriano refused to greet him, let alone take work orders.

Sancho came in first, flicked on the air conditioner—a second-hand box that kicked on and rattled—then sat down, dropping his head back as if to take a nap. Manuel and Tomás came in together. Tomás removed his hat and sat down on the arm of the couch, leaving Manuel the seat. Manuel crossed one leg over the other and began pulling at a nail stuck in the sole of his boot.

"Adriano's not coming," Tomás said.

Was there any way to win them over? He'd put this question to Sonja on the drive in that morning and she'd said, "Let them kick you." He'd have preferred it.

"Okay, then," Gus said. Robin was at the desk behind him. She'd offered him that chair, but he explained to her that that might not look right, that he'd been going about this all wrong. That he should sit with them, but now that meant leaning against the desk, his cane hooked beside him. His eyes drifted to the clock.

"We don't want to be here either," Manuel said.

"I'm sorry," Gus said.

"Good," Sancho said, his eyes still closed. "Can we go now?"

Gus wanted to say that Sonja and Tomás, even Jorge, had forgiven him, but that wasn't the road in; their forgiveness wasn't a bargaining chip. He didn't know where to look. He suspected Sancho, reliably dispassionate, was the one who'd cleaned up the back room, disposing of the fox, clearing the bucket of brine. He was who they called whenever the vet came, when there was blood or bone involved. But Gus wasn't going to ask, knowing the reminder of it would only validate the extent of his idiocy that night.

"Gus?" Robin. "You were going to speak, yes?"

"Yes, I am." He took his hat off and ran his hand through his hair. "I've made a mess of things, I know. And I'm not asking for your forgiveness, though some of you"—he looked to Tomás on reflex—"you've offered it. But we *all* need to be back to work. I know you've been doing that without me just fine, but—well, I can't do it without you."

Manuel said something under his breath, about Tomás.

"I'm sorry?" Gus said.

"Basta!" Tomás said to Manuel.

"No," Gus said. "I want to know." He looked at Manuel, still fighting the nail. "I want to come clean here."

Manuel laughed. Sancho was smiling, too, his head back, eyes closed.

"What's so funny?" Gus asked, the thinnest effervescence of hope rising in him.

Sancho lifted his head. "He said you can't come clean without Tomás." He was looking at the door to the back room of the office. "Because Tomás is the one who cleaned up after you."

Tomás was adjusting his baseball cap with both hands, his eyes pinched in annoyance.

"He wasn't alone," Sancho said.

"You helped?" Gus asked. "I figured you—"

"Not me," Sancho said. "Rory. Tomás and Rory cleaned up in there. She—"

"No más," Tomás said, standing up. "Stop." He turned to face Sancho. "Papi wants us to move on. If you won't listen to me or him"—he threw his arm toward Gus—"then will you listen to Papi? Can we please get back to work now?"

He said this last to Gus, supplication in his voice. Gus imagined Tomás coming at him, fists flying. He wished for it.

"Okay, then," Manuel said. He had dislodged the nail from his boot, a farrier's nail, and he dropped it to the floor, standing up to go.

"I am sorry," Gus said. "I understand—" Manuel stood up and Sancho got up, too, following him out. Tomás hesitated at the door.

"Is it true?" Gus asked. "Rory was with you?"

"She came here on her own." Tomás said. "Yes. I followed her in here. She was upset."

"Tomás," Gus said, shaking his head. "I was dumb. You're too young to have regrets, but if they come, I hope—"

"I asked Mami to let me go," he interrupted. "To let me take the car and follow—"

"Thank you, Tomás," Robin said.

Gus had lost track of her. He put his hand on the boy's shoulder.

"I should go," Tomás said.

Gus watched him leave, the thin drawn line of him disappearing into the big barn. Since Fresno, Tomás had taken on extra hours, acting as personal groom for the Fisk twins, work and money that Gus assumed had to please Sonja.

"That wasn't what I expected; that was—" Gus paused, easing himself down to the couch.

"*That was* a step in the right direction." Robin put her hands behind her head, revealing the yellow stains in the underarms of her shirt. Gus still wasn't sure what to make of Robin, but he was trying not to be so suspicious of everyone, to give people the benefit of the doubt. Even Mona, especially Mona. "How've the hot lights been working on Chap?" she asked.

"Not sure," Gus said. "Hard to know." Robin knew Carlotta had offered him some help with a stud fee, but it wasn't much, and finding a sire that complemented Chap and that he could afford was proving difficult. The hot lights were an attempt to trick the mare's natural cycle, to make her body believe that the days were as long as they were in spring, when the internal clock of her still-wild system told her to breed so she could rear her young in the most temperate months. Here it was September and the days were still hot as a lizard's back, but the nights were coming in cooler, stretching longer. "This is all feeling like a helluva crapshoot." He scratched beneath his hat.

"I must admit I'm fascinated," Robin said. "I'd like to help, if you're game, that is."

So she understood he wasn't her biggest fan. "Well, there is a stallion in Canoga Park. He's long in the tooth, but the price is right. And he's close—"

"You want a live cover, then?"

"Always preferable to insemination if you ask me, but desperate times—"

"Did Rory not mention Mark Adler? The stallion he had in Fresno?"

"No," Gus said. "I don't think she did."

"But you know who he is, don't you?"

"Of course."

"Rory," Robin said, some admonishment to her tone. "I'm sure she was still feeling bad about what happened . . ." Robin described the dustup Chap had caused outside the dressage ring and as she went on, Gus watched Rory walking down the driveway on Mrs. Keating's big sorrel sport horse, her camera strapped to her, as always. "Of course I took the blame with Preston," Robin was saying. "I should've known, should've considered the possibility at least. But man, how Preston handled Mark Adler. I learned a thing or two there."

Preston Fisk. Preston Fisk had a personalized license plate that said GR8FACE and a plate frame that gave the number to his plastic surgery office. "What are you getting at, Robin?"

"Well, I don't know about the timing with Chap, but the clinic's the first two weeks of October and Journey's going to need a haul out there and—"

"And what?" Gus laughed. "I don't think you're understanding; I haven't got Mark Adler money—not that much. I have to be real here. The horse in Canoga—"

"You have to spend money to make it in the breeding game, do you not?"

Do you not? Who the hell was she? What kinda *game* was she playing at? She'd started sifting papers on the desk, where innumerable stacks had accumulated. He would tell Carlotta just how disorganized new management was. Robin stood up, nodding to herself, some thinking finalized. "The thing is, Gus, Mr. and Mrs. Fisk have taken a greater interest in the ranch lately. Not the horses exactly, but the investment that they can be. They see how good it is for the twins." She had an envelope in her hand, the thing she'd apparently been hunting, and was tapping it against the desk now.

"So?"

"So I know you didn't get to say everything you wanted to say to the men—"

"Is that right?" Gus crossed his arms.

"That's right. I think you wanted to tell them that you know things will never be the same again, but that you don't *only* want to get back to work, you want to make Leaning Rock a better place to work. You want to improve it. And so do I. Any association with

Adler is an opportunity for us. I can't make any promises, but having a foal out of Heritage, starting off like that, well, I'd be willing to talk to Preston—"

"Where is Adler in Colorado?"

"Craig. Craig, Colorado."

Gus knew it. Just over the border, maybe forty-five minutes from his sister's place in Wyoming. "How much would Preston pay?"

"I can't say, I was just thinking out loud, really." She extended the envelope in her hand. "This came for you," she said. Yet another bill, Gus was sure. "If you decide you're interested, you'll let me know."

She left the Dutch doors open, the AC still spitting out what cold air it could. He looked down at the envelope. It wasn't a bill. It was a letter, hand addressed. From the barn came the chatter of girls between lessons. He knew this handwriting, the long, high arc of each letter. He'd seen it once before. *I do not blame you . . .* He heard the rattling slide of a barn door opening. And then he heard her voice, the whisper of it as if at his bedside in the hospital. The voices in the breezeway of the barn became the voices in the hallway, the nurses at their station, and Sarah Price was sitting in that off-white room with him. The paper of the envelope as pale and crisp as her hospital gown. She *had* sat with him. He knew this with a sudden clarity. She had spoken to him the night of the accident. They had met.

September 3, 1993
Dear Mr. Scott, Have you ever slept in a car? It is oddly invigorating . . .

THERE. STANDING BACK up, Vivian saw the window again—a perfect rectangular shimmer, deep within the trees, catching the sun, but the sun was setting, her chance fading.

"I have to go," she said into the phone, pulling her shorts over her still-damp suit.

"Go where?" McLeod asked.

"I'm not actually sure," she said. She was drifting around the pool on an inflated raft when she first saw the window and had been sipping vodka by the pool ever since, waiting, as if it might pop out again (à la Whac-A-Mole). Calling McLeod had been the end result of giving up, but now there it was, undeniably so.

"You *just* called me, you know?"

"A convenience," she said, the whip of her words slicing the air (hiya!). The window was winking at her through the trees; there was no time for playing footsie over the telephone. She hung up.

The lines of their property made a shape like a large wedge of cake. The curved edge followed Old Canyon Road, the angled northern line was carved into the hillside and shored up by a concrete wall, twenty feet high, while the third line was defined only by a short, hip-high wall. Back here, this was where she'd played tag with Charlie, shuffle running, letting him catch her on the back of the leg—"Ah, you got me"—turning around to his squealing laughter. *You got me.*

The hip-high wall and the hillside of obscuring scrub oak beyond didn't seem any real deterrent, but her nerves were slippery with vodka. She hoisted herself up onto the wall (in swimmer form) and looked down at the dry creek bed. It was a steeper drop down the other side, onto the witch-fingered roots of the trees scratching into the red clay ground. Her house almost looked inviting from here, through the whiskery blur of overgrown grass. If it weren't for the mess inside—it was a beautiful house.

A lizard dashed beneath the carpet of fallen leaves and Vivian dropped over the wall. She wrapped a hand around a low, lichen-cloaked branch, wedged her foot against the trunk of the tree, and considered the incline, realizing if she was going to gain any ground it was going to have to be on her hands and knees.

"YOU OKAY?" TOMÁS asked. "Sit down. I'll bring water."

Gus had read the letter in the office, then again in the barn, like touching a hot pan twice, plain dumb. Tomás had him sit on a tack trunk, then jogged off toward the office. Gus touched his back pocket, the letter there, folded and tucked away.

Tomás returned with a nearly frozen bottle of water. "Was it your leg?" he asked.

"No, no," Gus said. He was considering telling him. Surely Tomás knew about the letter Sarah Price had written to Jorge, but in this letter, there was no mention of forgiveness. He took the bottle of water down in breathy gulps, until the plastic contracted in his hand, empty. "A bit of heatstroke maybe," he said. The humidity of the summer months was gone, replaced by a dry static charge that left the pollen of the jacaranda trees clinging to the walls of the barn. "Maybe allergies, but I'll be fine."

Tomás spotted Rory coming down the hill on Chap and waved for her to hurry. The sky was rolling over into dusk. He'd given her a hard time earlier, telling her to put the camera away and ride her list; take your damn time with Mrs. Keating's horse, he'd said, because the likes of Mrs. Keating mattered, and she should be riding Chap only after her work was done. And she'd listened. For what inexplicable reason did she still listen to him?

"He was sick," Tomás was saying above Chap's clip-clopping across the asphalt. "I found him, white as a sheet."

"What's wrong?" Rory asked, pulling Chap up.

"No, no, I'm like new again," Gus said, raising the empty water. "Heatstroke."

Rory dismounted with a hand to the straps of her camera, an aptitude to the way she did this, a suggestion of the woman she might become: methodical, quietly bold. Why hadn't she told him about the fox? Why had he had to hear it from Tomás? They were both eyeing him with a mix of suspicion and concern. When he'd come home from the hospital, he'd found every store of whiskey had been poured out.

"Quit looking at me like that. I said, I'm fine." He stood up as if to prove them wrong.

"All right," Rory said, handing him Chap's reins, a sign she was satisfied he was okay.

He ran his hand down Chap's neck, admiring the liquid shine of her coat. She was as fit as she'd ever been, and Rory had done that while he was wearing a groove in the end of their couch. The mare leaned her head into him, as if propping him up. He heard Rory click off a photo. "Please, don't," he said.

In the upper ring, the floodlights blinked on. Robin had added a seven o'clock class, geared toward adult novices, one of her more lucrative changes. The PA system crackled alive, Robin's voice echoing against the hillside. "Maybe I'll stick around a little while," Gus said.

"I want to get home," Rory said, irritated.

"I have things to discuss with Robin, when she's done." He didn't want to tell Rory about the possibility of going to Colorado. Not until it was a sure thing.

"I can take you," Tomás said to Rory.

"You got your car up and running?" Gus asked.

Tomás shook his head. "No. But—" He looked at Rory. "June asked me to grab her something to eat, from the market and—" He pulled the keys to the Mercedes from his pocket. "She's riding with Ema."

"Of course she is," Rory said.

Gus heard some poison in her voice. He answered for her. "That's very nice of you, Tomás."

VIVIAN'S PALMS WERE scored with scratches, her knees caked in dirt, but she could see the house above, the lip of the roof anyway. She dug her toes into the shifting ground, her hands grasping the ivy, the grass, all of it coming up by the roots, but moving her along. She was twenty feet from the crest of the hillside and then she'd be there and—and then what? Exactly what was she going to do? And how was she going to get back down? The climb in reverse was impossible, comical even; she'd be turned into a rock bouncing down the hillside. Then, as if this thought had propelled her, she started to fall (son of a bitch). She threw her arm back, hoping for a branch, but as soon as she had a hold on one it came away in her hand and she spun sideways, only one hand free to break her fall. She heard a tearing sound and her breath was knocked free of her body. She landed in a fetal ball, curled as a new fern against the forest floor (but drunk and pissed off). The tearing sound had been her shorts and the skin of her thigh was also open, weeping blood.

She was still closer to the house above than to her own.

THE TOP WAS up on the Mercedes and even with his body bent toward the wheel, Tomás's head was touching the fabric. Rory set her camera and backpack at her feet. June's Grrrls mixtape was playing so low she could hardly hear, some Hole song. "What the hell is this?" she asked, as if she hadn't been in this car, tolerating this screeching enough already.

"I don't know," Tomás said, pressing eject repeatedly. "It's just stuck." He turned the volume all the way down. "June said something about Johnny Naughton fixing it soon."

"Right," Rory said.

"Actually, I've been thinking I'd ask him to take a look at my Supra."

"You know that guy's a racist, right?"

"They all are," Tomás said. "But he's a racist who knows cars."

Rory pressed one hand into the dash and hit eject fast with her other hand, and the tape spat out.

"Okay," Tomás said. "But do you know about timing belts?"

"No," Rory said. She went fishing in the glove box for the cigarettes she knew she'd find. "Least this still works," she said, pushing the dash lighter in. She felt Tomás watching her. "You want one?"

"I shouldn't," he said.

"You worried June's gonna reprimand you or something?"

Tomás adjusted his hands on the wheel.

"Fuck, I'm sorry. That was shitty." The dash lighter popped, and Rory took it, holding the cherry-red end to the cigarette. "You can tell her I took this one."

"Oh," Tomás said. "I wasn't exactly planning on telling her I took you home."

"Yeah, this she wouldn't approve of, would she?" Rory said. "Does she talk about me?"

Tomás shook his head, but he also sniffed—a tell, Rory thought. Now he had new loyalties.

"All right, then," Rory said. "It doesn't matter to me anyway."

"It's just a job," Tomás said. "It's more money, that's all."

"I know," Rory said. She couldn't fault him for taking the work. "She won't notice the cigarette missing," Rory said. "I promise. With money like that you don't have to keep track of anything, really. She never noticed when I took joints from her anyway."

Tomás looked at her. "You two sure were a funny kind of friends."

Maybe he was only talking about the joints, this small deceit, but what sprang to her mind was him stepping to the railing of the motel balcony, seeing them together. She had sealed that night away, pressed her shoulder up against the door to it, but Tomás saying this—unlocking it all again—her whole body blushed. The heat behind her eyes was like a sudden fever. "I never wanted her touching me," she said. "Whatever you think you saw, it isn't true."

"Oh," Tomás said. "I wasn't talking about that."

She closed her eyes just in time then, pinching off the world that was about to flash by—the Price gates, the possibility of the gate being open. It occurred to her then with an unwanted clarity that driving this road had to be even harder for Tomás.

"I hate this," Rory said, drawing hard on the cigarette.

"It's okay," he said. "I mean, I didn't know, I thought that you and June—"

"Not like that!" Her body was so tense it had wrung from her a voice that was not her own. "I'm not like June. I'm not gay, okay?"

Tomás rolled through the stop sign and out onto the main road. "Shit," he said, checking the rearview. "I didn't mean to do that. Fuck."

They drove on in silence, Tomás continually checking the mirror to be sure no patrol car was coming. Rory dropped her half-smoked cigarette into an empty soda can.

When they neared Greenleaf Road, Rory said, "Turn here," just to have something else to say. He already knew the way. He pulled over the bridge and in behind the two-horse trailer. A cobweb was strung in its back window, a sparkling lace in the headlights of the Mercedes.

"Well," Rory said, "thanks."

She gathered up her camera and bag and had her hand on the door when Tomás said, "Are your pictures any good?"

Rory let herself smile, relaxing. "I don't know yet. I hope so." She had shot rolls and rolls of film, but she had yet to finish Foster's first assignment, a self-portrait, which she had to do before he'd let her into the darkroom.

"If you ever want to show someone, I'd like to see," Tomás said.

"Okay," she said, opening the car door. "I definitely will, one of these days," she said. *"For sure,"* she said, knowing he'd get the joke.

VIVIAN HEARD A car cross the bridge and in the illumination of its headlights she saw a dirt driveway, crescents of tire tracks, the hitch of a trailer that was tucked out of view. The house was right up against the ridge, so near that she had to press herself against its chipped brown siding. The car engine was purring. She got to her knees and crawled to the corner, craning her neck, still unable to see the car itself, only the moths dancing in its lights. The blood on her leg was tacky, matted with dirt and broken leaves. If she stepped out now she could startle whoever it was ("Movie Star's Daughter Induces Heart Attack in Old Pervert." Ha). She heard the voice of a young girl, words she could not decipher, then the car door shut, followed by the squeak of a screen door opening and its closing clap. As the car pulled away, she scrambled to see it, catching the cat eyes of its brake lights, but the color of the car itself was unmistakable, a car she knew. June Fisk's.

RORY'S ROOM WAS still holding the day's heat. She turned the fan on low and opened all the windows, stopping to look down to the Price pool below. The lights were on, the surface of the water rippling, bougainvillea tumbling across the stone patio and into the water. All the curtains were drawn, the gardens dark and still. Rory had yet to see Mrs. Price. She had been looking. Ever since Fresno, she had let herself look again. Not every day, but sporadically. Out of concern, never amusement, not anymore. She was sure no one was really *living it up*. Though she had seen Wade there, Wade and Johnny actually. They were parasites, using Vivian for her house and pool. Once, she saw Wade shove Vivian into the pool and—though she might have imagined it—she thought she'd heard Vivian's shrill scream, its mix of delight and terror.

She hit play on the tape deck by her bed, prompting the unnervingly quiet first chords of Pink Floyd's album *Wish You Were Here*. In the bathroom, she felt behind the mirror, finding and lighting one of the joints she'd lifted from June.

THERE WERE NO other cars in the front of the house, just the horse trailer, its wheel wells trimmed in rust. The front door had been left open and only the screen remained between her and the inside.

"Hello," Vivian said quietly. Beneath the porch light, the gash in her leg was beastly. "Just me out here," she said, cupping her hands to see beyond the screen. "Bleeding out."

Whoever this girl was, this friend of June's, there was no sign of her now.

Out of habit, Vivian slipped her shoes off just inside the door.

GUS HAD ANGLED the bathroom mirror when he'd built the bathroom, saying it would make the room feel bigger, but instead it reflected the umber tiles of the counter beneath and the wood floor, blackened with water damage over the years—a room folding in on itself. Gus's red-winged blackbird was on the counter, a bird he'd told her could be found anywhere grass grew in the continental United States, as if to say it wasn't all that special, but she still saw it as she had at five years old, a creature full of unknown potential. She exhaled into the paper tube she kept stuffed with a dryer sheet, damping the smell, just in case anyone came home early.

She set the joint on the rim of the sink and pulled the rubber band from her braid, shaking out the plaits of her hair. She turned the bird on its mesquite perch toward the mirror, so that they would be looking at one another there. She wanted to disappear in the billow of her hair, to be just another object in the frame. She picked up the camera and sought her focal point: a self-portrait, since she had to.

THE HOUSE OPENED into the living room, a threadbare couch facing a small television atop a buckling shelf. On the coffee table was an ashtray, thick with ash, soda cans, and magazines. Maybe she'd just find a washcloth and go. Find the road back down.

In the kitchen, she leaned into the sink and guzzled water from the faucet, watching fruit flies lift from a bowl of mold-speckled oranges. She cupped water onto her face. A dirty white stove, dotted with toast crumbs and a gray slick of grease. She pulled the dish towel from the oven handle and wiped at her neck and face. The digital clock incorrectly read 2:02 a.m. (time clearly not of the essence). She peered into a cabinet, hoping for an easy swig of something, maybe a box of Band-Aids. She tied the dish towel around her wounded leg (G.I. Jane here).

In the living room, there were only a few framed photographs: a woman with fine wrinkles around almond-shaped eyes; a man, jowly, but handsome in a jovial way, always in a cowboy hat, his smile—shit. *Him.* She knew him. The corset of her ribs pulled taut. This was *that* man's house. The man who'd swerved. *Nothing for you to worry your pretty little head about.* Why had June been here? She spun around to the door, the window. The stairs. There was a backpack sitting on the bottom step. Of course, the girl's voice. She searched the photographs again: the man, Gus Scott, with his foot up on the railing of a fence, his face in shadow beneath his hat, and a girl with him (ten or eleven) with the same dark hair and eyes as the woman.

She could hear the music now, the acoustic guitar. Pink Floyd. She stepped onto the bottom stair, as silently as she could, and lifted the backpack to her shoulder like it was her own.

RORY WAS CHANGING the focal point in the mirror—from the bird back to herself, snapping one picture after another—until, mid-click of the shutter, she heard her door opening. She would later find that her body had become a blur in the frame, though the eyes of the bird remained in focus.

"Vivian," she gasped. The camera nearly fell from her hand. "Shit," she blurted. "You're Vivian Price."

"You were expecting me?" Vivian said, stepping into the room, indicating the barely righted camera in Rory's hand.

"No," Rory stammered. "I was—" The camera, the joint between her fingers, the mane of her hair, all felt electrified. She set the camera down and flicked the joint into the toilet. "Fuck," she said, instantly regretting its extinguishing hiss. She ran her hands over her hair.

"You look different," Vivian said.

"It's my hair," Rory said. She was stoned. "Wait, from when?" Vivian's eyes grazed over her. She was holding Rory's backpack. A dish towel was tied around her leg. Rory saw these things but Vivian, the fact of her, was still too hard to comprehend.

"There's a picture of you on the mantel," Vivian said. "Downstairs."

Rory had not left the bathroom doorway, feeling the bedroom no longer belonged to her.

"With the man who swerved," Vivian said.

Rory's pulse became a watery thrum in her ears. She looked at her hands.

"And clearly you're a friend of June's."

"No," Rory said, too quietly to be heard. "Not anymore."

"And you're a photographer?" Vivian went on, not waiting for a response. "But that's all I know about you. Well, that and your view—" She turned toward Rory's window and Rory watched her T-shirt shift at the curve of her shoulder, the tied strings of her bathing suit at the back of her neck revealed. The teal bikini.

"How are you here?" Rory asked.

"I climbed the hill," Vivian said, pulling a leaf from her hair.

"Jesus," Rory said. "And you're hurt." The dish towel around her leg was darkening with blood.

"I'm fine," Vivian said blithely. "It's not so bad."

"No," Rory said, considering the climb she had made. "It—we should get it clean."

Vivian slid the backpack from her shoulder and lifted her foot to the end of Rory's bed to get a better look at her leg. Her foot was clean, but in stark contrast her ankles were scratched and smudged with dirt. "Maybe you're right," she said. "Do you have anything—"

In the bathroom, Rory opened drawers, digging out bandages, gauze, and tape. She found Betadine and ran water on a washcloth. She heard the give of her bedsprings: Vivian Price sitting down on her bed.

"I assume you know Wade and June from that barn?"

Rory brought the washcloth, dripping water down her arms. "Yes," Rory said, standing in front of Vivian now. "But we aren't friends." Who had told her? June? Or had June told Wade—of course, of course she had. After Fresno. And now Vivian knew.

"But just now, I saw you," Vivian said. "June just dropped you off here." She was untying the dish towel from her leg. An abrasion, raw and still bleeding, but not deep.

"You were outside?" Rory said.

Vivian nodded. "I wanted to know who my fan club was."

This phrase, she could hear Wade saying it. "It doesn't look like you need stitches," she said, clearing her throat. "Anyway, that was June's car, but she wasn't driving."

"Oh," Vivian said.

Rory extended the washcloth, but Vivian had leaned back on the bed, a clear suggestion that she wanted Rory to clean the wound. And Rory kneeled beside the bed. "It was Wade, wasn't it? Who told you about my room?" Rory set the washcloth to the side of the scraped skin and Vivian winced.

"Just do it quick," Vivian said. "So it doesn't hurt so much."

Rory folded the washcloth over and held it there until she felt the muscle of Vivian's leg relax. "This house was here long before yours. I mean, it's not like I meant to be able to see your yard." Vivian's eyes were closed, her eyelashes golden against her cheeks. "It's just a coincidence, I guess."

Rory moved the washcloth, trying to take as much dirt as she could in one motion.

"Shit," Vivian said.

"This might sting more," Rory said, showing her the bottle of

Betadine. At Vivian's nod, she squirted it across the wound, the dish towel catching most of what slid down her leg, some leaking past, staining the blanket beneath. Rory tore open the package of gauze.

"You don't like Wade very much, do you?" Vivian asked.

"Hold that there," Rory said. Vivian was searching her face as she put her finger to the corner of the gauze. Rory unspooled the tape, tearing it with her teeth. "He doesn't like me either." She pressed the tape into place and looked at what she'd done, feeling briefly dizzy again—she'd just bandaged up Vivian Price's leg.

"Thanks," Vivian said.

Rory looked up at her. "Of course," she said. "I try to help everyone who breaks in."

Vivian laughed. She had made Vivian laugh.

"Well, I'm sure you want to go now," Rory said. "Whatever Wade told you about me, it isn't true. And I won't—I don't look at your house or anything."

"Actually, I was just realizing that I don't even know your name."

"Rory," she said. "Wade didn't tell you?"

"Just Rory." Vivian smiled. "Like Cher?"

"Rory Ramos."

"Rory Ramos," Vivian repeated. "Alliteration. That's always fun. You know, you have really beautiful hair." Rory had started to braid it back, but Vivian put her hand to Rory's wrist, stopping her.

"I do?" Rory asked, looking at Vivian. There was something about her that required a narrowing of attention, like a distant shoreline.

"Leave it down," Vivian said. "I like it."

Rory let go of what braid she'd finished.

"So, what's with the birds?" Vivian asked, looking behind her now, to the dresser.

The towhee was there, on its side, having fallen off its perch weeks ago. The wooden base and twig of mesquite stood separately. "Here." Rory picked it up and handed it to her. "I don't know what glue to use to glue it back on."

Vivian took the bird gingerly, turning it over in her hand before bringing it to her nose, as if this were a perfectly normal thing to do. Rory laughed.

"What?" Vivian asked, running her finger down the bird's rust-hued feathers.

"Nothing," Rory said. "I mean—you smelled it."

Vivian shrugged. "When else can you get this close to a bird?"

"Gus makes them," Rory said, bringing the blackbird from the bathroom counter. "He doesn't shoot them or anything. He finds them. They're animals he's found—already dead."

Behind Vivian, the window curtain luffed on a shallow wind.

"Gus," Vivian said, looking at the bird's leaden eyes. She'd said his name with the same tinge of bitterness Rory used in her own thoughts about him now.

Vivian turned the towhee over again, its beak trained up. *"Already dead."*

"Because they were sick," Rory clarified. "Or dehydrated—" She flashed on Gus pulling the truck over, bumping onto the dirt shoulder, the shine of the fox's fur in his high beams.

"Or hit by a car," Vivian said, a sharp glint of pain crossing her face.

Rory had gone back to the barn that night, needing to hold the fox in her hands, to do what she wished she'd done in the first place, take it from him—that might have altered everything that came afterward. It wasn't until now that she wondered who had struck the fox, how far back the blame might lie.

"I didn't mean to frighten you," Vivian said, still cradling the towhee in her hands. "Coming here like this."

"You didn't," Rory said. "I understand why you came. I really do." She was going to the window. "You want to see?" she asked. "I want you to see." She was holding the curtain open, waiting for Vivian, sensing that showing her the view was an opportunity, a new chance to make everything a little more right.

LITTLE SNAKE, WYOMING

MAY 29, 2015

THE HILLS HAVE gone purple with lupine and the air is thick with the stiff smell of fresh-cut alfalfa. We have four foals in the pasture, still young enough that they keep tightly to their mares. The trees and the underbrush are bustling with new hatchlings: magpie, meadowlark, mourning doves. All of this made Mama's funeral feel that much more peculiar.

There are people in New York, her friends, I was told, having a service for her there, a celebration of her life. The part of her life that I did not know. These friends are her colleagues, all people who run toward danger. We didn't invite them here, but this is where Mama asked to be buried. A thirty-seven-year-old woman who'd already prepared a will.

Our friends from neighboring ranches came in their coveralls, their jeans and bandannas, leaving cold pasta salads and casseroles in the kitchen, before standing with us as she was lowered down into a plot beside my great-aunt Joy, who rests beside Mr. Traden. I guess it's a family funeral ground, of a sort.

We called Mona to let her know what had happened. Grandad had kept up with her some over the years, updating her on Mama and me, I guess, but when she said she wasn't well enough to travel, Gus hung up and looked at me, disappointed. "I'm a creature of habit," he said.

A month from now, the four foals will have to be weaned from their mothers. Grandad was dreading putting Chap down without Mama, but I realize now it is the wean that I don't want to do on my own. Maybe I've always stretched it out, every year, every herd, always waiting the extra days or weeks, however long it took for Mama to come home. Mama always did it gradually, patiently, easing the foals into their independence. First, moving them to a neighboring corral, just in the daytime, so that they could see their mares, but only touch noses. A day or two gone by this way, she'd separate them into neighboring stalls at night, so that they could still smell one another. Then two stalls apart. And so on. There is irony in this, of course. This consideration from a mother who herself would up and leave me, sometimes in the dead of the night.

After everyone left the house, Grandad, in his suit and tie, lumbered up the stairs, still in his boots, still caked with the softened earth from around her grave. I heard him rooting around and I was figuring he'd come unraveled, that he was finally going to break twenty-two years of sobriety. Mama had warned me, saying I had to tell her the minute I smelled alcohol on him. But then there he was, taking his slow, snap-pop steps back down the stairs, one knee doing the bending for two, and balancing a box in his arms. "She wanted you to have this," he said. It was an ordinary filing box. The kind with a handled lid that lifts off easily, that suggests the contents are artfully arranged in lateral files, but when I lifted the top away, it was a jumble of negatives and empty negative sleeves, black-and-white proofs, dodging and burning tools, newspaper clippings. Mama shot most of her work digitally, but she had made a darkroom out of the kitchen in the old homestead cabin, and she'd carried a little black Leica with her wherever she went.

I pushed the box back toward him. "I don't want it," I said, assuming I'd be looking through more images of famine and war.

"No, no," Grandad said, understanding. "These are from before you were born." He held the handles of the box and rocked it back and forth like he was panning for gold, and the piles of negatives shifted, revealing more clippings, pages of handwritten notes—some folded up, some torn from notebooks. "All of it's from 1993."

I let myself have the thought, *My father,* and picked up a black-and-white proof sheet, searching the tiny images, nearly all faces I didn't know. "This is you?" I asked Grandad. A man heavier than Grandad is now, his face fuller, younger, and a horse leaning into him, the white star on her head unmistakable. "And Chap," I said.

"Yes."

I knew it was the fire of 1993 that made them leave, that they'd gone before it was even contained. And that only a week later, as Mama and Grandad were settling in with my great-aunt Joy, rains hit the canyon, washing away the burn-loosened earth, destabilizing the hillsides and the houses only barely spared by the fire. All that

and then the Northridge quake in January of '94. So they considered themselves lucky, despite Mama's and Chap's burns, despite
the loss of their home, even as Mama realized I was with her then,
that she was pregnant at fifteen.

"Why would she have wanted me to have this?"

Grandad took off his hat and ran his hand over his head. "I know
she was meaning to give it to you, to show it all to you, at some
point—" He stopped. Something in the box had caught his eye.
"Sarah Price," he said, picking up an envelope, a letter addressed
to him.

"Sarah Price?" I asked. His face blanched white. "Price?" I
repeated.

Price. I had heard this name, whispered between them, easily
misunderstood as the cost of a thing.

After Grandad went to bed, I walked out to Chap's corral and I
started in on the hole we will need for her. She is too uncomfortable
for us to move her any closer to Mama and she is wasting, refusing
feed. I dug just outside the corral so that we'll only have to take
down the fence between where she stands and where she ought to
fall. Once the ground was opened, I lay down on the slip of earth
between the hole and the fence. Chap's eyes are gray, blind in the
night, but she smelled the air, knowing I was there. Eventually her
breath grew even beside me, her body slacking into sleep, and the
earth, turning, folded us into the darkest embrace of night.

Before you shoot a horse, you have to draw an X across their forehead with your eyes. Two lines, each running from one ear to the

opposite eye. But when you fire, you aim just slightly above center, to get around the bony ridge of the forehead. When the shot rings out it will echo through the valley, the birds will scatter from the trees, the neighbors pause their work, and the caribou and the coyotes will freeze, ears pricked. It is a silence that is equal parts shock and hope. I've been living in that kind of silence for a long time.

Our family has always had secrets: that Mama smoked, that she hid her packs behind the darkroom door, that Grandad took antidepressants, that we sometimes bred grade mares. Even Aunt Joy's cancer was a kind of secret, another thing we didn't discuss. The same brand of silence there was about Mama's being gay and the fact of my father having had to have been someone, once upon a time, somewhere. There'd never been reason for me to suspect that I was named for a dead boy, never any kind of clue, but as Grandad spoke and my eyes grew tired reading the clippings from the newspapers, the magazines, that same uncanny feeling was coming over me, the sense of having known all along.

"I always assumed," Grandad said, refolding the crease-thinned pages of Sarah Price's letter, "that this had burned up in the fire, same as everything else."

TOPANGA CANYON, CALIFORNIA
LATE SEPTEMBER 1993

Dear Mr. Scott,

Have you ever slept in a car? It is oddly invigorating.

I have been thinking about you, about our brief time together in your hospital room. Do you remember? There are certain memories of that night that are alarmingly clear, but my memory of sitting with you has a haziness that I fear might be lending me a fondness for you I should not possess. You were asleep when I came in—your leg in a system of pulleys that I spent some time trying to figure out how, if at all, it was attached to your bed. When you woke, you started pressing the morphine button and you kept looking toward the door. They told me that you had been taken to a different hospital. I hadn't asked, so I knew they were lying. I sensed, even before I read your chart—before I knew that you had been drinking—that you and I had something in common, a shared culpability for my son's death, at the very least. I have never enjoyed alcohol, but I think I have been living my life with the same kind of willful passivity that is brought on by drinking. Do you remember what I told you that night? How I put Charlie down and ran to answer the phone, thinking it was Everett, that everything else could wait if he was finally returning my calls. . . .

Mr. Flores was trying to follow you home that night, wasn't he? He knew how drunk you were and felt duty bound, didn't he? Subservience will be the death of each and every one of us. It has not gone unnoticed that you have refused all interviews. You, too, are uncomfortable with this kind of freedom we've been left, aren't you? Tell me, Mr. Scott, what hurt was it that you were trying to numb?

Five days ago now, it was decided that I am no longer a danger to myself or others and I was set free, dismissed back into society. Maybe you heard about my suicide attempt? In actuality, I only put my hand through a glass door. A perfectly logical response, but Everett saw an opportunity. Maybe I have only ever been an opportunity to him, a means to an end, my own needs— my Charlie—an inconvenience. This is to say, I am not going home. Not now.

I can see my car from inside this diner where I sit, writing to you. It's a good car. Japanese, I believe. I drove it on empty for nearly twenty miles and it never gave out, despite my invitation. I am full of precarious desires, but beneath them all is a wish for distance.

Do you think it is possible to leave one's hurt behind? I want to leave it, bit by bit: a little beside this bowl of untouched soup, more in the mailbox with this letter. Tomorrow, I will wake up

somewhere in Illinois and hope that my burden will be lighter still.
What do you think New Hampshire is like this time of year?
I hope this finds you moving on—Gus, if I may.

S.

In the past week, he had read Sarah Price's letter a dozen times, but it wasn't the letter that had him dry. He had remembered telling her, in the hospital, that she should go, that she didn't want to be sitting there with him, and she had answered, "you're absolutely right," but then not moved, the two of them silently staring at one another as if through a glass partition. He wished she had been a product of the morphine.

No, he was sober now because of the drive ahead, his livelihood trailing behind him, meeting Mark Adler in Craig, Colorado, and having to make a good impression. He'd gotten Rory on board with taking Chap there, after her initially lackluster response, which he chalked up to childish squeamishness over the actual breeding. With his bum leg, he would need good help to haul two horses that far. Wade, of course, would be flying separately. A fact that had given Rory visible relief.

All week long, Gus had been sleeping on the couch, thinking that if he stayed there he'd hear Mona come home, that she'd jostle him awake and the two of them would pad back to the bedroom together. But it was always Rory waking him, on her way out the door for school, morning light cutting under the curtains. Tonight he'd called the bar and gotten a busy signal. No matter, he would just wait up for her. He cracked open a Coke. He'd know when she got home.

He turned on the nightly news: Lakers down by ten, temperatures spiking in the valley. He called the bar again and a man answered, a voice Gus didn't know. "Mona's not on tonight."

"She hasn't been in at all?" He dropped a painkiller on his tongue.

"Who's asking?" the man said.

"Her husband," Gus said, choking back the pill.

VIVIAN HEARD McLEOD push the bolt on the garage door as soon as he'd heard her voice (the missus clearly home). "Go on," he said.

She recounted her climb up the hill that night, telling McLeod about the girl she'd found, the view from her window onto her pool and patio. She told him everything without mentioning the stepfather's involvement in the accident, unsure of why she was withholding it. "She walked me home," she said. "In the dark."

They'd shared a joint, Rory steering her over paths that led to the main road, only dimly spotted by streetlights.

"But what can she see?" McLeod asked. An envy in his voice that amused Vivian.

It hadn't been such a spectacular view, no way to see inside unless the curtains were open, but through the branches of the trees there was a clear view of the pool, the surrounding gardens, the sliding glass doors off her room. She stepped outside, talking to McLeod, hoping Rory was looking now.

Along the main road, they'd had to walk single file each time a car came whizzing past, the headlights barely a warning around the blind curves. After a Ford Mustang had whipped their hair back with its speed, Vivian had said, "Wouldn't this be a hell of a way to die?" Rory had turned around, her face knit in concern. But Vivian had actually come to think that Charlie must have been the most alive anyone can possibly be in the moment before he died. He had to have been so unaware of the finality facing him; pure animal mechanism must have filled his body with adrenaline, his child mind thrilling at the sight of one automobile after another careening toward him. That was the kind of kid he was. Her brother. Vivian said none of this to Rory, taking her hand instead. Rory didn't pull away until they were outside the gates of her house. "I should go back now," she said, turning, fully intending to walk those same roads, over the same coyote-thick paths, alone. "You're pretty brave." Vivian smiled. Asking her to come inside seemed too easy, leaving no lingering mystery. She wanted to see her again. "I'm not afraid of the dark," Rory said. "If that's what you mean."

"I drove her home," Vivian said to McLeod. He knew that her Land Cruiser had been taken, an added insult to her academic probation the year before. "I took my mom's BMW." The time capsule of Mommy's car no longer felt necessary.

"And?" McLeod pressed. "Have you seen this Rory since?"

"Of course," Vivian said, stopping there. She wasn't going to give it all away.

Wade was a determining factor for when she and Rory saw one another. But she'd come to recognize whether or not he'd be stopping by from the way he said goodbye at the end of school each day (a slap on the ass: *see you later,* a kiss on the mouth: *that'll tide you over for a day*). Rory would call from the barn, then hike out Zuniga Road, where they'd meet at the bottom of the trail. She had taken Charlie's car seat out of the BMW, but she'd left the shopping basket to skid across the backseat as they took the canyon's turns, Rory jumping every time it hit the door.

"I bet you make her nervous," McLeod said.

One night they drove down to the beach, after the sun had set, the sand still warm on the surface, then cool as their toes slipped deeper. The opal moon rose up, dropping its luminescence down the water toward them. Rory told her how she'd found out that she was seeing Wade, how she'd taken a magazine from the convenience store. "Why'd you steal it?" Vivian asked and Rory shrugged. She told her about a recurring dream she'd been having about her house being the flash point of a landslide. Your typical falling dream, except that Vivian's house was in their path.

Rory was a puzzle, yet Vivian felt no pressure to sort her out. Her presence was comforting, undemanding, quietly adoring.

"But she doesn't even drink," Vivian said. "I told her she just hasn't found her poison of choice, but she flat-out refuses anything I offer."

"You sound impressed by this."

"I'm not used to being refused."

Nearly three weeks had passed since Mommy had been missing. A fact Vivian had not told to anyone. "Not even a word to Carmen," Cousin Everett had hissed, carting more junk (collectibles!) into the house, poor Carmen trailing after him, his shit-sorting assistant now.

"McLeod," Vivian said, stretching out a silence, growing his restlessness, "do you think it's possible to love two people at once?"

There was the spark of McLeod's lighter, the thin inhale and huff of his exhale. This new habit pleased her so.

At the end of the month, Everett was leaving, starting production on the film in Mexico. He'd joked, when he told Vivian, that maybe he'd run into Mommy there (ha, ha, fucking ha). And Wade, she'd since learned, was going away soon after that. "Two weeks," he said, an apology in his voice. Fact was he had been of use to her, especially since school started; a necessary distraction from a year that began with timid condolences and teachers letting her out of assignments before they'd even been assigned. She preferred that the whispery speculations be about what she had let him do to her in the back of his Scout rather than how her family was faring (D-minus, thank you very much).

"I suppose I'd need more clarity in terms of the scenario," McLeod said. "But my gut response is yes."

"McLeod," she said, swaying her feet in the pool. "I didn't mean it as a hypothetical."

"Oh, Vivian," he said. "I think about you, I do. I hope you're going to call—" He stopped.

"I know you do."

"But there are rules," he said.

"Too many rules," Vivian mused.

Wade was coming by today, but she would keep him inside, out of view. Tomorrow, though, tomorrow she would see Rory and she was sure Rory wasn't going to refuse her anything.

✦

RORY HAD MADE two sandwiches, packed water, and her camera, out of habit—nothing else—and left without waking Gus.

"Wade won't wonder where you are?" she asked, closing herself into the black BMW. She'd been surprised Vivian didn't have her own car, but Vivian just smiled and said, "Bad girls don't get to keep their cars." Today they were both skipping school.

"I told him I wasn't feeling well," Vivian said, driving away from where Rory's bus would soon pull in. "Last night, on the phone."

Rory knew that wasn't true, that it hadn't been on the phone. She was aware of these small flourishes of Vivian's. Vivian didn't know she could see a car's headlights when they left, illuminating the gates and then the road beyond.

"Where should we go?" Vivian asked. Meeting at the bus stop, before the bus had even arrived, had been Vivian's idea, but apparently the plan stopped there.

"I know most of the trails," Rory said, pointing to the sign for the state park.

"How well?" Vivian asked. "I've had my share of off the beaten path already."

"It's not like that," Rory said, smiling.

Vivian pulled the car into the shade and Rory stole a look at her, how the light broke through the trees, dancing on her cheeks. She still experienced, semiregularly, the purest disbelief that she was with Vivian Price at all.

She kept them on the narrowest portion of trail, the single track, where bikes weren't supposed to go, where at this early hour on a weekday they were least likely to encounter anyone. And in a half mile or so they'd come to a clearing with a view.

Vivian ran her hands over the patches of wild horsetail grass. And this was sagebrush, mugwort, saltbush, chamise. "How do you know all this?" Vivian asked. She was wearing sandals, her toes skimmed in dust.

"Gus," Rory said.

He used to bring Rory here, before Mona had moved them in with him, telling her the names of the flowers and trees. They'd named Chaparral after this canyon's foliage, *its biome,* Gus used to correct her. Not a single plant, but a whole tier of drought-tolerant and dogged gray-green shrubs. An underappreciated wonder, like her mare, but most people just saw this chaparral as a fire hazard. It was hard to clear and as combustible as old newspaper. "The core of it dries out, saving the moisture for its outer leaves," Rory said. "So, that outer layer, the stuff that the sun can reach, is all that grows green. It's kind of like a beautiful lie and it only grows on the California coast."

"Of course," Vivian said.

"We're going to breed my mare," Rory said. "In Colorado. Gus is hauling Wade's horse out there—I assume he told you—but we're taking my mare along cause this guy, he has a stallion and he's really something, honestly, and—"

"Wait," Vivian said. They'd just arrived at the clearing, but the ocean was shrouded beneath a low-lying fog that had yet to burn off. "You're leaving, too?"

"Well, Gus can't go alone. It's work for me, in a way. I mean, if it goes well, there will be a foal worth a lot to somebody—"

"It isn't even for you?"

"We need the money," Rory said. She sat on an outcropping of sandstone, letting her backpack down. Her camera was inside, wrapped in an old saddle pad. She'd yet to bring it out in front of Vivian, sensing it would be an intrusion. Vivian had told her about the cameramen, the way they ate their meals sitting on the road outside her house. "Like vultures," Rory had said.

"Do you want to go?" Vivian asked. "I mean, Wade is gone for two weeks—"

"He's flying," Rory said. "I probably won't even see him. This barn, it's supposed to be enormous—" She stopped, remembering June, how she'd asked if Rory could come to dinner with Mark Adler. Rory dug the water from her bag and drank.

"That's not what I mean," Vivian said. She sat directly on the dirt, her legs stretched out in front of her, her toes turned in. "I don't care if you see Wade," she said. "I just—"

"I won't say anything to him," Rory said. There existed an unspoken understanding that their friendship was a secret. That Wade, in particular, could never know. Rory was aware of enjoying a clandestine competition with him.

"Can I have some of that?" Vivian asked, reaching for the water.

The sun was lifting behind them, shadows unrolling at their feet. Vivian drank, then put the cap back and wiped her face with the back of her hand. There was a roughness to her gestures that Rory hadn't been able to see from her window, a humanity. "I'm going to tell you something and you can't repeat it, because you can't know," Vivian said. "Because no one can know it."

"We've never even met," Rory said, smiling.

"Sit next to me?" Vivian said, patting the ground.

Rory got up and came closer. The scratch on Vivian's leg had scabbed, looking like a lion's scratch. She was hesitating, waging a debate with herself. "You *can* tell me," Rory said. "For real."

Two hawks were riding a thermal above them and Vivian looked up, watching. She tucked her hair back, revealing the small freckles that dotted the edges of her ears. Then she said, "My mom is missing."

"Like kidnapped?" Rory asked, her hand going to the concave of her throat.

Vivian shook her head. "Not like that. She bought a car and she drove off into the sunset."

"When?"

"It's been twenty-two days since she checked out of Cliffside."

"What? Are the police looking?" Rory asked. "Why isn't this in the news?"

"Why is anything the way it is?" Vivian shrugged. "Money. My dad's agent, Bobby, he's good at managing this kind of thing. And he hired a private detective. My dad knows that if it got out that his wife's missing, he'd look like a fool. She's embarrassing to him." Vivian paused, lifting the silty earth and letting it fall back down, a dust waterfall. "And he's embarrassing to her. Which leaves me . . ."

"Alone," Rory said, realizing. She knew Everett Price was leaving for Mexico, making a movie there.

Vivian was pressing her hands to her face, leaving dirt on her cheeks and around her eyes. Rory took the cloth from her pocket, the one she kept ready for her lens. Vivian opened her eyes, blinking back tears, then looking at her hands, covered in gray dirt, laughing. "Oh my god, I'm a mess."

Rory showed her the cloth and Vivian nodded, her eyelashes wet and clumped together.

"Maybe I don't have to go," Rory said, pouring water onto the cloth and wringing it out before bringing it to Vivian's face.

"Seriously?" Vivian asked.

Gus was staking everything on this foal steering them back around, but here was Vivian Price, telling her things that no one else knew, looking at her with eyes that were now bright and clean and suddenly hopeful. "I mean, I won't go," Rory said, feeling the sun on her back. "If you don't want me to."

Vivian tipped toward her, putting her head to Rory's shoulder, saying, "I don't. I really don't want you to go."

FROM OUTSIDE THE screen door, Gus watched Mona at the stove. She was stirring a wooden spoon around a steaming pot, while Stevie Wonder's "Superstition" played from the living room stereo. Her hips were swinging, her mouth moving over the words. He could still see her the way he had seen her the first time, from across the room. He still loved her. There was sage burning on the mantel, its smoke drawn between them. To the music, she spun from the stove, past the sink, over to the kitchen cabinet, drawing out bowls, dancing them to the table, then shimmying backward to the counter, rattling open the silverware drawer. Exactly what was she so pleased about? He cracked the door. "Hey, my lady," he said, and she turned, surprised to see him.

"You're home early," she said.

His cane preceded him inside. "Rory hasn't been to the barn," he said. "This morning she said she'd get a ride and then she didn't show, so I thought I ought to—"

"Track her down," Mona said. "The inseparable horse-loving duo."

Gus didn't want trouble, not today. Not ever. "You're making dinner already?" He'd wanted to come inside with her good mood, feel the sway of her hips against him, like he used to, a tower of quarters for the jukebox. "What is it?" he asked, hooking his cane over a kitchen chair.

"This chicken thing Becky told me about. Curry something—you just buy this—"

"Becky?"

"New girl at the bar," she said dryly.

He liked this idea, that she'd just been busying herself with a new girlfriend. He put his hands on her hips and smelled her hair. "So, he hired a fresh young thing after all?" She shrank from his touch. "Hey now, things are looking up here, aren't they?"

She stepped down the counter, picked up the salad bowl, and slung it onto the table.

"Hey," he said. "Easy."

"You stopped taking the Prozac," she said.

"You're counting my pills?"

"I do look out for you, Gus. I know you don't think so, but—"

"I was kind of stepping down. It's been weeks since we've been together, Mona. And I thought maybe, well, I wanted to be—"

"What, depressed?"

"No. I *miss* you," he said. "I sleep on the couch, hoping I'll hear you come in or that you'll wake me, that you still *want* me. And now we're leaving the day after tomorrow and we haven't been together in months—"

She touched his arm, telling him with lowered eyes and a jut of her head that he ought to turn around. Of course Rory was standing there, in the doorway.

She adjusted the strap of her backpack and stepped into the kitchen.

"Where have you been?" Mona asked, without any real concern.

"I stayed late at school," Rory said. She was avoiding looking at him.

"You had a list to ride today, Rory. People were expecting you. And Mrs. Keating told me you put her gelding away wet *again* yesterday. You know that doesn't just look bad on you?"

"Right," Rory said, dropping into the kitchen booth. "I'm sorry," she said. "I just, I have a lot more schoolwork this year." She was embarrassed, he thought briefly, because of what she'd overheard. "And, well, it's why I can't go with you, to Colorado, I mean. I just, I really can't be gone for so long."

Gus turned to Mona, wondering if she knew what Rory was talking about, but Mona seemed amused.

"School, huh?" Mona said. "Well, how do you like that?" She went back to the stove, shaking her head.

"Rory, what are you talking about?" Gus said.

Rory picked up a piece of lettuce that had been thrown from the bowl. "I can't go with you. I want to. I know you need the help, but—school is way more serious this year. I was thinking you could take—"

"Rory." He pulled out a chair. "I need *your* help. She's *your* mare."

Rory shrugged. "No, not for this. Not for this she's not."

"So you don't want me to breed her? Is that it? You just want me to drive Wade out and wait around? I can't do that, Rory. We need this break. If Wade can take the time off from school—"

"I'm not Wade," Rory said. "Besides, he's a senior. Junior year matters more."

Mona was setting the chicken concoction down on the table, murmuring out of the side of her mouth, "Thinks she's a college girl now."

"What was that?" Gus said. "If you've got some opinion, Mona, come out and say it." He dropped his fist to the table. "God damn it. Did you know about this? Is *this* why you're so worried about me being on the Prozac?" He waited, expecting the two of them to share a look, but Rory just looked at her hands. They weren't that mother and daughter. He'd forgotten.

"I want you to stay on the Prozac because I don't want some sad sack on the couch. And if I have any opinion at all about either of you, it's that I find it funny as all hell that she's invested in school now and maybe seeing past the dead end of that fucking ranch."

"Nice," Gus said.

Rory hadn't looked up, but he saw the disappointment in her shoulders. Did Mona understand her better than he did now? Why had he always assumed she'd work the ranch with him? "College?" he asked.

Rory shrugged. Of course she was thinking about it, at least wishing she could.

"You take your trip, Gus, and Rory and I will look after ourselves just fine. Right, Rag-Tag?" Mona had put plates in front of each of them and she sat down now, motioning for him to help himself. He couldn't remember the last time they'd all sat down for dinner together. The music had stopped.

"I'm sorry," Rory said to him, then, reaching for a roll, "Thanks, Mom."

TOMORROW, CHAP WOULD be gone.

It wasn't yet dark, but the warming lights had already ticked on, a wash of amber light. Rory had taken her on a trail ride, nothing strenuous.

"How's she doing?" Tomás asked, pulling open the stall door. "It's like a sauna in here." Preston Fisk had already asked Tomás to go to Craig as Wade's groom, so now he was going to make the drive out with Gus, at Gus's request. Rory knew it might be uncomfortable for each of them, but Gus needed good help and she was relieved Tomás would be with Chap.

"Crazy to think she's coming back pregnant," Rory said, running her hand down the mare's belly. "I suppose I should knock on wood or something. I mean, there's no sure thing."

"Yeah," Tomás said. "I bet she wishes you were going."

"I know. Just promise me you'll be there. I mean, I know you've got to look after Journey, but if you can help out, when it's time, promise me you will?"

"I'll do whatever I can." Tomás stuck his hands in his jeans then, sheepish."So why *aren't* you going?"

It was hard not to tell him. She'd come to trust him, to realize that he was one of her oldest friends and that their friendship had a resiliency others clearly didn't. But she lied. "Just school," she said. "Honestly—mostly because of my photography class," she heard herself say, recognizing the absurdity; driving over four state lines, through a thousand miles of vistas and open skies, was far more picture worthy than staying home.

"Oh," Tomás said. "I'm glad. I'd assumed it was Wade."

"No," Rory said. "I don't care about him." It felt true enough.

"Well, he's driving out with us now." There was pride in Tomás's voice. "Mr. Fisk heard Gus needed help on the drive and he said"— Tomás dropped his voice into a baritone—" 'if there is work to be done then Wade ought to learn how to do it.' " Tomás smiled. "So he's making him go with us. Wade's not happy."

"Of course not," Rory said, thinking that had to please Tomás, too, not having to be alone with Gus. "Is Wade still here now?" Rory asked.

"Nah," Tomás said. "He went home to pack up a while ago. We're leaving at dawn."

So she could see Vivian *tonight*. Whichever Vivian it might be. There seemed, each time they met, to be a new facet, an unexpected angle to her.

"Oh," Tomás said, bouncing on the balls of his feet. "I want to show you something." He was waving her out of the stall and up the path toward his house.

It was his car, finally down off its cinder blocks. Tires, taillights, washed, maybe even waxed. "It's amazing," Rory said.

Tomás held the door open for her to get in. The interior was upholstered in a pomegranate velour, the dash, the wheel, the gearshift all in a darker ruby. Sitting behind the wheel now, Tomás wiped his pocket rag over the speedometer. "Isn't it amazing? I wish I could show Papi."

"How did you finish it so fast?" He'd been finding parts here and there, but . . .

"I got help."

Before Rory could even think *Johnny Naughton,* he came out the front door of Tomás's house in his blue jumpsuit and six strides later his pocked moon face was hanging outside her window, and he was rapping a knuckle on the glass. "You had *him* help?" Rory grumbled to Tomás, who was cranking an invisible handle in the air, telling her to roll the window down. "Fuck," Rory said, complying.

"What do you think, Spice?" Johnny said, onion on his breath. "She's a beaut, ain't she?" He had a shine of grease all around his lips. She drew her finger around her own mouth, suggesting he wipe his face. "Your mom makes one hell of a pozole," Johnny said to Tomás, drawing the collar of his coveralls over his mouth, unfazed.

Rory looked at Tomás, disbelieving; Sonja had fed Trouble.

"Johnny's been helping me all week," Tomás said, a hint of apology in his voice.

"He was never gonna find the parts to this baby without me,"

Johnny said. He leaned into the car and dropped open the glove box in front of Rory and there, inside, was a gun.

It's a toy, Rory thought.

But then Johnny dragged it out, the barrel barely avoiding her knees, and Rory saw the heft of it, the muscles in Johnny's forearm flexing. "Honestly, if I had the dinero I'd make an offer to take her off your hands, give her the drive she deserves." Rory heard the uneasy laughter falling out of Tomás and she was sure that the gun was no toy at all. "Sorry about that, Spice," Johnny said, his face bunched up, grinning. "Didn't take you for the nervous type."

"Why do you have a gun?" Her voice was thin, dry.

"It's just something we keep for the shop," Johnny said. "We had a few break-ins over the summer—that kinda heat, man, it makes people do stupid shit. But I wasn't gonna bring it in"—he winked at Tomás—"outta respect for his mom's house."

"Yeah, thanks for that," Tomás said.

"What's this I heard about you not going to Colorado, Spice? Wade was looking forward to having you there. I know you weren't thinking you'd stay to hang around with June."

Rory's hands had gone clammy with sweat.

Tomás answered for her. "She's got school. Can't miss, that's all."

Johnny grunted. "Polk. Nothing to be learned there. Except the girls are so easy. I do miss high school, man." He had one grease-streaked hand clapped on the open window.

"She's taking photography," Tomás tried again. "She's got assignments, that's all."

Why did Tomás keep saying *that's all*? It had to make Johnny think that *wasn't* all. "That right?" Johnny said.

199

"Tomás is going to drive me home now," Rory said.

"I am?" Tomás asked.

Rory turned to him. "Yes, please. I'd like to go."

"Well, all righty, then," Johnny said. He knocked the barrel of the gun against the frame of the door, a deep-gutted clap of metal against metal. "I'll let you two lovebirds go. Gotta christen these wheels, am I right?"

Rory kept her eyes on Tomás, willing him to put the damn key in the ignition already. Through gritted teeth, she said, "This car has an engine, doesn't it?"

"Okay, okay," Tomás said, getting the car started and putting it in reverse.

"Adios," Johnny said, waving the gun in the air like a handkerchief.

THE FRONT OF Hawkeye's Tavern had been repainted cactus green, and a makeshift patio, with plastic chairs and tables stuck with orange umbrellas, was now eating up part of the parking lot. Sitting inside his truck, Gus remembered Mona having said that Hawkeye was putting more money into the place on account of the new condominiums that were going up across the street.

Hawkeye had been Hawkeye ever since losing an eye as a boy, and supposedly as compensation his remaining eye was exceedingly strong. He was a mean pool player, a loyal friend and boss, and had a sense of humor, too, wearing a flesh-colored patch with a bigger eye painted on every Halloween. But Gus had also seen Hawkeye swat a customer's hand away when he tried to take his change. If it weren't for his small stature—he was a pony of a man—Gus might have even been intimidated. When he'd started dating Mona, Hawkeye took him to lunch, letting Gus know that Mona was like a daughter to him, though they were roughly the same age.

Mona's Chrysler was two cars over, with its dented fender. Maybe Mona was here covering for Becky. Maybe everything was right with the world. But if he went in and he saw Mona playing pool, her body focused down the length of the cue with another man's hand at her hip, breathing instructions in her ear, some chump she'd fooled into believing this was her first game of 9 Ball, well, what then? Was he gonna beat the guy with his cane? Was that, maybe, what she wanted? Was she even thinking of him at all? Or just hoping he'd fall prey to a bone infection and drop dead, leaving her . . . leaving her what? A horse. One fucking horse, which wouldn't even come close to covering their debt.

What hurt were you trying to numb, Mr. Scott?

A man can get used to anything.

He slouched in his seat and there was Mona, appearing in his rearview mirror. She was wearing a paisley dress he'd bought her years ago. It still fit, still hugged her breasts. She had raised her arms, squeezing herself between the fenders of parked cars, her stomach sucked in, shimmying toward the parking lot. Gus turned around to wave, ready to get out and go in for a ginger ale, when he saw the flash of her smile as she turned back, taking the hand of the man coming behind her. It was Hawkeye. Gus shut his eyes, meaning to change the picture, but when he opened them again the energy between Mona and this man was as overwhelming as a swarm of bees. Not a manager and an employee, not an old friend, or a father figure, but two people who'd just had a fuck.

THE SUPRA MADE an uneasy noise through a few turns, but it seemed to be running well enough. Tomás had the driver's seat all the way back, so his grasshopper legs would fit. "I'm really sorry about all that," he said.

"I just wish you'd told me before I got in the car," Rory said.

"About Johnny?" Tomás asked. "Or the gun?"

"Jesus," Rory said. "Do you hear yourself? Either one, honestly." As relieved as she was to be away from Johnny, from the maddening feeling of that gun, there was an added exhilaration in driving toward Vivian's house. Even if she couldn't exactly ask Tomás to drop her off outside.

"He got me parts for cost," Tomás said in a voice intended to make her laugh, a singsongy voice that was part question.

"Still not worth it." Rory smiled. It was nice to see Tomás out in his car.

"You know, I've never been invited in for pozole." The wind was pulling hair loose from her braid and she wiped it from her face.

Tomás feigned surprise. "I didn't know you liked pozole."

Rory shrugged. "I guess Johnny's just a better friend."

"Well . . ." Tomás stole a look at her backpack. "You still haven't taken my picture, so . . ."

Rory unzipped her bag. "You want me to?" She hadn't taken a picture in days. The sun had yet to set, a heavy orange slipping from the cupped hands of the canyon walls. "I don't have the best lens for light this low, but . . ." She adjusted her f-stop to 2.8, as wide as it would go and brought the camera to her eye.

Tomás took his hat off and turned himself in the seat, pressing his hair back, keeping his eyes on the road, but smiling. "Can you get a little bit of the car in it? For Papi?"

"I'll have a shallow depth of field." She was looking at him through the lens now, seeing him the way she thought he would want Jorge to see him. Click. "Hold as still as you can," she said. "But keep smiling." Click. For the last six years, they had grown up together, but some days she felt as if she barely knew him. Click. Wind. "I think I got a good one," she said.

"You'll print it for me? So I can give it to him?"

"Of course." She wondered about Jorge often, but asking about him risked shattering the veneer of normalcy everyone had worked so hard to polish. "How is he?" They were on the curve of road that was framed by enormous outcroppings of white sandstone, as if they were driving into the jaws of a mythical creature. Seven more curves and they would be just beyond the gates of Vivian's house. Rory didn't want to get all the way home.

Tomás shook his head. "I don't know how he does it, living like that." Tomás and Sonja went to see Jorge on Sundays, visiting day, but only when Tomás could spare the hours. "But he's upbeat. Or at least he acts that way for us. He told me to go on this trip, you know? He said we have to be open to new experiences, take the chances he can't. He's been going to services is what I think. You know, he never left this canyon, not since 1970, when Mrs. Danvers hired him."

"Really? Why?" Tomás had put his hat back on, its brim putting his eyes in deep shadow. "Because he felt safe here," Rory said, realizing. "How did he meet your mom, then?"

"Oh, they knew each other when they were kids. In Veracruz."

"Really?" Rory asked. "I didn't know, but—"

"They lost track of one another for a while," Tomás said, answering her confusion. "I think it's kind of romantic," he said, shrugging. "He's my Papi. Only one I need."

They had already passed the Price gates, the wall scored with the mark of that night, and Rory had not looked; she was just listening to Tomás, thinking of this, two people finding each other in another country, after a lifetime. It was romantic. Rory was starting to understand how much this road had taken from everyone and what it wasn't ever going to give back. Except maybe to her? Was that possible? She had a sideways thought then about Mona and Gus, how Gus was her only father, but if they ever split up—as they should—Rory wouldn't be able to stay with him; Mona wouldn't give her that choice. Mona made her feel like she didn't have a choice about anything; she was like a bell jar—not protective, just suffocating.

"Stop," Rory heard herself say. "Stop the car."

Tomás turned, his new tires spinning onto the dirt shoulder, the Supra coming to a jerky halt.

"What's going on?" Tomás asked. "What is it?

"I'm sorry," Rory said, turning to look through the rear window. The house was well out of sight.

"You scared me," Tomás said. "Are you all right?" He put a hand on the back of her seat, studying her face.

She wanted to tell him, she wanted to tell somebody, because just thinking about Vivian—about the way she had pressed her nose and mouth against Rory's neck, about how Rory was comforting her by staying behind—it felt worth telling. "There's just, there's something. . . ." She was pointing vaguely toward a sycamore, a balloon listing there, its helium depleted. She raised the camera, suggesting she wanted a picture.

"Oh," he said. "Okay. I'll wait, then."

"No," she said. "I can walk from here. I've done it before. I want the walk. Tomorrow, wrap Chap's legs for me? For the trailer? Don't let Wade or Gus do it, okay?" Tomás was nodding, but in the last scrap of daylight, she could see how confusing she was to him, yet he had already understood her better than she had herself—she was in love, and with a girl. She touched his arm, and when he looked down at her hand she leaned over and kissed him on the cheek, saying, "Thanks," before getting out of the car. She waited until he was gone before she crossed the road.

GUS REFUSED TO leave for Colorado without talking to Rory one more time.

He came home from Hawkeye's with this one thing decided and

he climbed the stairs, believing that the sight of her sleeping—he was imagining the little knot of a girl he'd first seen, sound asleep on her mother's bed, under the flicker of a television—would release him from this fury in his head.

The lights were on in Rory's room, the bed made, the room's vacancy made worse by the rotation of a metal fan blowing the heat and emptiness around, the pictures tacked up on her walls lifting and dropping. "Rory," he said, as if he'd found at least some piece of her, seeing these photographs on the wall: a black-and-white of two small children in Guangzhou. Protests in Liverpool. A Walker Evans. He put his hand—the knuckles already swelling—to a portrait of a woman with dark hair, hair like Rory's, and the same knowing seriousness to her eyes. The caption: "Mary Ellen Mark, on the Set of *Apocalypse Now,* 1979." Maybe she'd be a film major, he thought. They had no money for that. "You are a fool," Mona had said to him when he was still in the hospital, before the story makers had twisted the narrative of what he'd done. She never let him forget that Rory wasn't his daughter, but she *was* family to him. He knew her, he understood her, they shared commonalities, beliefs, in that entrenched way one does with real family. "Rory," he said again, still believing he would find her.

"YOU'RE HERE!" VIVIAN shrieked, vodka breaching the martini glass she was holding. "At last," she said. Rory had heard the slur in her voice through the intercom outside the gates. She was wearing a T-shirt with a green silk screen of pine trees framing a waterfall and the words CAMP WASHITA written in log-shaped letters. She wore only the threadbare yellow shirt and teal bikini bottoms, despite the sun having gone down. "Come in already, come in! I really need to sit down . . ."

As impressive as the outside of the house was, there was nothing orderly to the inside. It was as if the whole estate had been picked up and shaken: things everywhere, tipped over, clustering together, haphazard islands of things, picture frames, a table on its side, as if floating in the expanse of the foyer. The ceilings were so high, so clear and open, that they begged Rory to look up and through the skylights. And then, with some alarm, Rory registered cardboard boxes throughout the mess—packing boxes. "Are you moving?" she asked, knowing this made perfect sense. Of course people as rich as the Prices could build a house and then turn on their heels as soon as circumstances became less than favorable.

"Moving?" Vivian said, looking around. "We probably should, given this mess, but then you and I wouldn't be neighbors."

"I saw the boxes and I thought—"

"Whatever you do, do *not* try to think in this house. Trust me, leave logic at the door."

There were three chairs in the foyer, all of them blue.

"I'll give you a tour," Vivian said, her mouth loose around the words.

Vivian pulled Rory through the chaos, steering her past an open bathroom, an office, and an alcove with waxen plants clustered on the floor. The door handles, the windows, the art on the walls, all shone as if polished, and there were hints of expensive furniture, flashes of marble and leather. But it was all buried beneath a flow of yard-sale rubbish. Vivian was rambling on about the symptoms of hoarding, how Everett had not grown up with money and they'd not really been well off until her grandfather died, and that this mess he'd created was the manifestation of a kind of long-term panic. "He even stopped paying the pool cleaners. But no matter, Carmen and Bobby and me, we're planning this divine intervention. Eventually," Vivian said, going quiet as she turned down another hallway and ran a finger over one of the doors, the letter *C* embossed there, in the wood.

And then they were in Vivian's room, a room predominantly pink and white, the furniture of a girl smitten with fairies and princesses: a white four-poster bed, a matching desk with curved wooden legs, matching gingham cushions and duvet, but then there were Tibetan prayer flags strung behind the bed and a poster of a shirtless Jim Morrison. Tucked between a side table and the bed was a hookah.

"You ever use one of those?" Vivian asked, flouncing down on her mattress. Rory shook her head. "No? Well, Everett brought it home and I told him it was a crazy cool vase, so he let me keep it." She laughed and sipped her martini again.

The desk sat on a shaggy rug and atop the desk was a lava lamp and a small statue of a Hindu god. Shiva, Rory thought. "I'm so glad you aren't leaving," Vivian said. She'd stretched out on top of the checkered duvet. "Enough with the leaving."

"Have you heard anything?" Rory asked. "About your mom?"

Vivian hiccuped. "I'm pretty sure that PI is just another aspiring actor."

"Has he called?" Rory was leaning over the desk, looking at the Polaroids tacked to the corkboard there, finding Vivian in a few, her arm slung around . . . people Rory didn't know.

"Oh, he called. Thinks she's in Illinois."

"So now what?" Rory asked.

"Now nothing. She's an adult. Walkaway mothers are apparently on the rise—that's what they call them, moms who abandon their kids, though I hardly qualify as a child, right? I mean, here I am drunk on a Tuesday," she said, adding a moment later, "I have the spins."

Rory came and took her by the hand, helping her sit. "I'll get you water." Vivian gestured to a door opposite the blue chair. "Walk away," Vivian said in a near-shout. "Because of course women are expected to be cool, calm, and collected about everything they do."

The bathroom was white marble and mirrors, a Jacuzzi tub, a separate glass shower stall. There was a crystal drinking glass beside the faucet. Running the water, Rory avoided seeing herself in the mirror—she didn't belong here.

"Of course it certainly seems like she was calm and collected about it. It's just, I don't know." Vivian paused, drinking the water Rory had brought her. "It would be nice if she'd said something, sent me a letter, or . . ." Vivian trailed off.

"Not left," Rory said.

Vivian nodded. "Can we go outside?"

The pool was larger than Rory had understood from her room

and now she could see the green moss gathering at the bottom. The yard beyond the pool's dull glow was dark, as if everything else had fallen away.

"It's there," Vivian said. She was on one of the oversize lounge chairs, an Aztec-patterned blanket pulled up to her chin. "Can you see it?" Her eyes were on the tree line.

"My window," Rory said, turning to look. "No," she said. "Where?"

"It's there, right there. It's easiest to find when the sun is setting. It catches the light."

Rory kept looking, trying to orient herself.

"Did you bring that camera of yours?" Vivian asked.

Her words were less elastic, as if she were sobering up, and the question felt like a test, suddenly, as if Rory's response would drop her into one box or another. She thought of the images she had seen of the Prices over the years: the posed kind, with automatic smiles, chins at unnatural angles, and then those that revealed their annoyance, their expressions of disbelief. "I did," Rory said, a tremble in her voice that worsened when she tried to get some control. "I always have my camera."

"Come," Vivian said, moving over and patting the space beside her. "You're cold."

The lounge chairs were wider than Rory's bed and the cushions nearly as thick. "Okay," she said, sitting down beside Vivian.

"Come on, come on," Vivian said. "Lie down."

Rory did and Vivian tossed the blanket out again so that it fell over both of them, then she rolled to her side, so that she was facing Rory, her knees up against the side of Rory's thigh. "That's where it happened," Vivian said, gesturing over Rory's shoulder to the sliding glass doors, the one boarded up in cardboard. Vivian had described the way the blood had pooled around her mother's foot, the faint brown stain that remained. "That door is the first thing I'm going to get fixed," Vivian said, dropping her head to Rory's shoulder.

"How long will your dad be gone?" Rory asked.

"A month," Vivian said. "A one-month shoot isn't that long at all, really. And now the world is my oyster!" She swung a grandiose arm toward the shadowy yard, the dark stand of trees, then brought it back down to Rory's arm. Her hand was warm. "What about you?" Vivian asked. "Is anyone going to wonder where you are?"

Rory shook her head. She was sure Gus was asleep, given how early they were leaving, and if Mona came home at all, she wasn't going to check on her.

"So you can stay here, then? Tonight?"

Rory didn't respond except to sink deeper into the cushion. All she meant, Rory thought, was spend the night, but there was a thinness to the air. It seemed hard to catch her breath.

"This is strange, isn't it? Me and you," Vivian said, her voice against Rory's neck.

"I don't know," Rory said, "Is it?" The bold new beat in her chest was vibrating throughout her body, threatening to become an uncontrollable shuddering.

"You have pretty hands," Vivian said and drew her finger up Rory's arm. "I keep noticing that." Rory was shivering. Her arms. Her shoulders. "You're not cold," Vivian said. "I just make you nervous, don't I?"

"No, no. I'm fine," Rory said. Then, "Maybe a little."

Vivian moved closer as if to comfort her, but then she took Rory's hand and brought it to the curve of her own waist and the thread of Rory's wanting suddenly cinched. "I can't," she said.

"Can't what?" Vivian asked. "You don't like this?"

"What about Wade?" Rory said.

"He's just a boy," Vivian said. The faint pleasure in the corners of Vivian's mouth, the way she was looking up into Rory's face, it was almost dismissal enough. And then she said, "I like you, Rory Ramos. I like that you've been watching me. That you stole that magazine. That I catch you staring at me sometimes."

Rory was searching Vivian's face. "I don't want to get hurt."

Vivian smiled. "Nobody does." She ran her hand down the length of Rory's braid, pulling away the elastic band, then running her fingers through her hair.

Rory put her hand back on the curve of Vivian's hip. "This is okay?" she asked.

Vivian touched her lips to the end of Rory's nose, then to her cheeks, brushing over Rory's skin as if her mouth were a feather. Then kissing her. Rory kissing back. Her eyes were closed and her body was untethering from the earth, not falling, but rising, lifting into the trees, a bird, surrounded by rustling leaves—an up kick of wind—and against her body, Rory felt, as if it were her own, the pronounced pounding of Vivian's heart. She focused on it, steadying her breath, and there, between the beats, was the smallest of murmurs. An imperfection. A fragility. These were the things that made Vivian Price so beautiful, the things no one else knew.

"Tomorrow, I want you to take my picture," Vivian said, as if reading Rory's mind.

GUS WAS STEPPING toward the door, about to give up, when the curtains blew back, lifting into the room, and he thought, Of course she's sitting out there, sneaking a cigarette. He moved in heavy deliberate steps, ready to reprimand her, to remind her how parched and brittle everything had become and here were the first winds of fall—not the Santa Anas, not yet, but the cooler, whispery ones, the winds that tricked everyone, lulling them into complacency. "Hey, kid," he started. "You know as well as I do—"

She wasn't there. Only a jam jar on the corner of the grating, full of damp cigarette butts—good girl—and the dark hillside. And beyond the branches was the lit rectangle of the Price family pool. Sarah, he thought.

At any moment, he told himself, she would step outside and take in the night air. She was there. She had to be. He could sense her. There, on the chaise, there was a woman—yes. No, a girl. The feline apathy of her movements, the teenager. The teen version of Sarah Price. And another girl he saw now, lying down beside her. Who was this? He leaned out over the railing, trying to be sure. The grating beneath him went unstable. It was Rory. Rory and Vivian Price, who was pulling Rory's hair through her fingers. He knocked the jar of butts over and it fell between the railings, dropping and cracking open on the hillside. He looked back. They hadn't heard it fall, hadn't heard it break. He was that far away. And they were turning toward one another, one disappearing into the other, a twisting embrace. Kissing. Rory was kissing Vivian Price? *His* Rory. *No,* Mona used to say. *She's just your little tagalong. Rag-tag-tagalong.*

He had lost all hold on his life.

LITTLE SNAKE, WYOMING

JUNE 7, 2015

IN THE BOX of Mama's things, I found a description of a dream—not exactly a journal entry, but a scribbling on pages torn from a notebook. There's an urgency to the handwriting, like she had to get out from under the memory of the dream. A nightmare, really.

I dreamt it again, same as always. Me and Mona moving around the house, cleaning up, straightening the magazines on the table, refolding blankets on the couch. We haven't been arguing. There's no tension in the air. There's even this soft music playing in the background and then Mona smiles at me, like she's satisfied with what we've done, like she likes me, and she goes to sit in the chair under the window and opens a book. I can't see what she's reading, but I know it's a Bible—which Mona doesn't read, but in the dream, I know she believes what it says, that she'd like me to listen to her read it. Outside it's night and I can see myself reflected in the window above her head and my hair has come undone and I know if she looks up

*and sees this, everything will change. I move closer to the glass to
watch myself rebraid it and it's then that I can see past my reflection
and into the darkness—what should just be the dirt turnaround, the
trailer there—but instead everything is moving past the glass like a
landslide. We are sliding down the hill. I feel it under my feet then.
The bounce and roll of the floorboards. We're plummeting. I look
at Mona, terrified, and she just looks up at me with this slapped-on
smile, like a doll, stupidly content.*

When I told Grandad about the dream, asking if Mama ever
told it to him, he just shook his head. "They never got along."
Meaning Mama and Mona, as everyone has always called her. She
lives in Lancaster, California, now, on her own. I told Grandad
that what Mona meant when she told him she wasn't well enough
to travel alone is that she wasn't well enough to mourn alone, that
she is sad about Mama, in her own way. But he said it was just her
emphysema.

We had a broodmare once who wouldn't let her first thrown
colt suckle, so we had to coax her into letting him latch, keeping
watch, so she didn't get hostile. First-time mothers do this sometimes, insecure, their instincts slow to kick in. Usually, eventually,
they settle in and grow fond, trotting off with their babies at their
sides, but I have heard stories of mares who turn their teeth on
each and every foal they throw, their babies having to be reared by
adoptive moms, broodmares who can't help but love on whatever
gangly legged foal you throw in the pasture with them. Still, a first
rejection like that, it lingers.

"She was hard on your mama. Calling her Rag-Tag, for always

tagging along with me. Never a compliment. Told her she looked like a boy so she wouldn't let her cut her hair. Wasn't about her hair, of course—" Grandad bats his palm at the air.

"It was about Mama's being gay," I said, no longer having the strength to play along.

I can feel the boulders rumbling against the house and outside the windows whole trees are being ripped from the ground, and I am suddenly certain of one thing—the kind of certainty only given to us in dreams—that I cannot let Mona know what is happening. That if I keep her from knowing anything, then we will be saved from the impact, allowed to continuously fall.

I asked Grandad if he wanted me to be the one to put Chap down, but he said it was his to do and I didn't disagree with him.

I don't care for the computer much, the way it sends you down rabbit holes you never intended to find, but I turned it on today and went through Mama's old emails, reading them through the lens of what I've learned since she died. In a message from Baghdad, the year I went into the ninth grade, she wrote to me, *I don't talk about you very much. I can't. Not here. No one else has children—none of the journalists, I mean. The soldiers do. But not the rest of us. Yesterday, I slipped, talking to a writer from Reuters. We were talking about home, about what we were going back to and I was explaining how things ran there now, with Joy gone, and I said, "my daughter," and she looked at me as if I'd told her I was a spy. I don't usually talk about home. These things weaken me. I have to forget in order to be here and I have to be here. So sometimes I have to forget about you. Please forgive me, Charlie.*

I heard the shot from the field, felt my body lurch, and only after the silence had begun to fill in again—the chitter of a nuthatch, a magpie chiming in—did I inhale, as if not breathing were going to keep her here with us. When Grandad came back the shot came back in with him, his body like a tuning fork. He sat down hard, not looking at me. He wiped his brow and bent to unlace his boots.

"You want help, Grandad?" I asked. Sometimes the bad leg makes even small things harder than they need to be, but he didn't respond. Surely his ears were still ringing.

Mama won awards for her pictures. Sierra Leone, Syria, the Congo. She captured shots of abandoned storefronts and children playing jacks in vacant streets, postapocalypse, but the images that she was known for are images of people looking back at her. "She was a portraitist," they wrote of her in *The New York Times,* "within a sea tide of commotion." They honored her "unjustly short career" with three images. From Aleppo, Syria, September 2012: amid the aftermath of a barrel bomb, a child, nine or ten, the soot on his face marked by the dried rivulets of old tears, and what you think—at first glance—is a bag under his arm, what is left of his possessions, is actually the body of a dust-covered dog. From the Kunduz province of Afghanistan, 2010: a group of villagers are gathered around sheet-wrapped bodies, men killed in a clash between the Taliban and Afghan forces. Their backs are to the camera, except for a woman in hijab who is looking at Mama's lens with a mix of contempt, helplessness, and resolve. The last is from Istanbul, 2013. She wasn't on assignment but had gone to the U.S. Embassy just before a suicide bomb detonated. Of course, she had her camera and she started shooting. A yellow taxi came speeding past, fleeing, and in the back window a woman is gripping the driver's headrest, her eyes forcefully shut by the guttural determination of her own screaming. "I got lucky," Mama told me when that image was first published, not referring to the fact that she had survived the blast, but that she'd accidentally captured this woman inside the car.

The only thing that ever changes in this dream is the animal that wakes me—a deer or a coyote, once a horse, all hoof and struggle— desperate to get out of the path of our falling house, and it turns to me watching in the window, looking at me with these pleading eyes, yet I know there's nothing I can do, that one of us is going to die and that's when I wake up, heart racing, as if I were the one trapped in the path of my own home.

When Grandad finally spoke, he said, "She called for you this morning." He hung his hat on the arm of the chair, raked his fingers over his sweat-shined head. "She left her number—if you wanted to call her back."

"Mona?" I asked, though we had her number already. "Who are you talking about?"

"Vivian Price," Grandad said. "She heard about your mother."

TOPANGA CANYON, CALIFORNIA
EARLY OCTOBER 1993

BEFORE RORY WAS even inside the screen door, Mona was yelling, "Where the hell have you been? I've been worried out of my mind, Rag. You can't just disappear—"

Rory had stayed two nights at Vivian's, but Vivian had dropped her at the mouth of Greenleaf Road this morning, because Carmen was coming. Rory hadn't expected Mona to be awake, let alone up and making breakfast. She was gesticulating with her cigarette in one hand, the other forking bacon over into popping grease, morning light cutting across the kitchen. A Nan Goldin image, sad and tough all at once.

"Well?" Mona pressed, wiping her face with the back of her arm. The weather had turned static-dry. The two-horse trailer was gone, as expected, but there was a motorcycle pulled in where it had been. "You gonna say something?"

"I—I stayed with a friend."

"For two nights?" Mona had yet to turn to Rory, yet to look at her.

"I left a message. I didn't think that—"

"That I'd be worried? Well, I've been worried out of my fucking mind."

Mona's face was usually readable—her diamond-cut eyes, the jut of her chin, the shift of her high-boned cheeks—but Rory saw now that one eye was pinched small by swelling. "Mom, what happened?" Rory stepped toward her, unconsciously raising her hand to touch the bruise.

"He hit me." Mona turned away, her own fingers going to her face, as if she'd just remembered. "That's what happened."

"Gus?" Rory asked, disbelieving. She stepped back, her backpack sliding down her arm.

"Obviously," Mona said.

I'll kill him—the thought like a struck match, a flash of blue heat. She'd never seen Gus hurt anyone, not like this, not intentionally. He never even raised his voice. It was Mona who got loud, who threw things. Rory watched her crack one egg, then another, into a hot buttered pan.

The bedroom door opened and Rory turned to see Hawkeye stepping into the living room, rubbing sleep from his one good eye.

"Ask him," Mona said. "He was there—"

A hard, short laugh escaped Rory's throat. Hawkeye was wearing Mona's green satin robe, the length of it dusting the floor. Of course, the motorcycle was his.

"Morning, Rory," Hawkeye said. His hair was sticking up at the back of his head, white as dandelion fluff, his forehead red with sheet creases.

"This is how fucking worried you were?" Rory asked. "So worried you couldn't sleep alone, is that it?"

Mona was edging the spatula under the eggs, setting them sunny side up onto a plate, a sour embarrassment visible on her face.

"Now, now." Hawkeye tsked at Rory. "Don't speak to your mother like that. I think she's been shown quite enough disrespect already." He came and sat at their table and Mona poured him coffee and put the eggs and bacon in front of him.

"Is this a joke?" Rory asked.

"I'm not laughing," Mona said, folding a piece of bacon into her mouth.

"He saw the two of you together," Rory said. "That's what happened, isn't it?"

"That's no reason to hit your mother, is it?" Hawkeye said. He blew on his coffee. He had dry, ashy hands. Rory had some understanding of what had gone through Gus, how rage held the potential to breach the edges of all that you believed yourself to be. But why not hit him, hit Hawkeye?

And then Mona said, "School called."

"Fuck," Rory said. Not even under her breath.

"They said you've been out the last three days. They wanted to know if you had mono."

Rory looked at her hands. "I don't. Obviously."

"No shit," Mona said. "You gotta kiss somebody to get mono, don't you?'" But then Mona stopped, looking Rory up and down now. "Or am I wrong? Is that what's going on with you? You actually found yourself some boy trouble. Is that where you've been?"

"Wear protection, kid," Hawkeye said, raising his fork as punctuation.

"It's—no," Rory said. "I was with a friend."

"Is that whose clothes you've got on?" Mona came toward her and pulled at the hem of Rory's shirt. It was Sarah Price's old camp shirt, with the cracking silk screen of green trees, and a pair of Vivian's denim cutoffs, the hems hand-stitched in a rainbow pattern of thread. "And your hair," Mona said. Rory could see the black beach stone shine to the round of Mona's cheek now.

"Yes," Rory said, still feeling Vivian's hands weaving the one thin braid down the side of her face, saying, *This is better.* "This is better," Rory repeated, touching the strand. "I like it like this."

JOY HAD GREETED them on the cattle-crossing grate, waving them in like they were the Macy's Day parade. She had hung an impressive eight-point elk antler on the line of birch-log fencing, but otherwise the barns, the house, the homestead cabin along the river's bend, all appeared unchanged. It had been twenty years since Gus had visited, twenty-five since he'd worked sheep there. "You are a little worse for the wear," Joy said, watching him limp around to open up the trailer. Beyond this he was hoping she'd spare him any real mention of the accident. He'd said all that needed to be said on the phone the week before.

Inside she had stew waiting for them, the table set with mismatched bowls.

"How far is Adler's place from here?" Wade asked, poking around his food. He'd been unable to mask his distaste at hearing the meat he'd been enjoying was oxtail.

"With a trailer it's a little over an hour. Down 13 and over to 40," Joy said. She'd gone for a third helping, always whip thin, no matter what she ate.

"You call that *neighbors*," Wade said, turning to Gus, incredulous.

They were crammed around Joy's little round table, pressed up against the windowsill in the kitchen. Tomás, who'd spent the drive in the backseat, headphones glued to his ears, was staring out the window watching a grouse hen's short-burst flight, the grasses parting as she erupted then dropped down again.

"That is neighbors around here," Joy said.

"We'll be down there first thing in the morning," Gus said. He was eager to be rid of Wade. Tomás, too, not out of annoyance, but more a need to allay his own guilt. How different this might have been with Rory. Staying home for school, what a load of bullshit.

Tomás got up and started stacking everyone's bowls, despite Joy's miming protests.

Gus turned to Joy. "If the mare's ready in the morning, could you make the trip down with us?"

Wade interrupted, "Whaddya mean, if she's ready?"

"Temperature," Gus said. "If it's changed." He'd explained it a thousand times.

"Not always accurate," Joy said, her mouth full. "I say we tease her. I've got a good old stallion, real gentle, and reliable as the sunrise, always knows which girls are ready."

"That'd be fine, I guess."

"Tease?" Wade asked. It was almost amusing how green he was.

Joy wiped at the corners of her mouth. "If he takes an interest in her and she's amenable to that interest, you know, shows him her backside, then she's ready to go meet Adler's boy. If not, we wait."

"So, like, *tease* tease—" Wade said, a hook to his smile.

"Ain't much difference between them and us," Joy said. "She's interested or she's not."

"But we'll go down first thing, either way? I am only staying *here* one night."

"Unless you'd prefer three?" Gus said, sharing a look with Joy.

"No, I know why this boy's so eager," Joy said. "I've seen Adler's commercials. Heritage Ranch, where the best bloodlines are bred." She stopped to pick a string of meat from her teeth, sucking it off the end of her finger.

"Commercials?" Wade asked. "Like, on TV?"

Joy nodded. "Place has got heated stalls, breezeways padded in rubber, a farrier on staff. And of course, you'll have your stable boy here, waiting on your every need."

Tomás stopped moving the sponge over the bowls. Joy was mocking Wade, but Gus couldn't see his way to making that clear.

Joy was seven years Gus's senior and she'd always been a reliable comfort to him. But she'd lived alone for twenty-five years, time that had left the filter between her thoughts and her speech porous.

"You two sure do look alike," Wade said then. An insult, Gus realized. An allusion to Joy's jowly cheeks and thin-lipped smile, which Gus wore more easily as a fifty-three-year-old man.

"Not as much as you and your sister," Gus said. He had figured out a thing or two in their time on the road, the sore spot that June seemed to be. "Wade's a twin," he told Joy. "Sister named June."

Wade stood up abruptly, flattening his shirtfront and swinging his hair back from his face. "Speaking of which, I think it's time for me to call home."

"Phone's that way," Joy said. "There's just the one."

When Gus did talk to Rory again, he would ask her, point-blank, about everything that went on outside his purview.

Tomás turned around, drying his hands. "It's so quiet here. I thought our canyon was quiet, but this. There's only the animals. I like it," he said.

"See," Joy said, throwing a thumb in Tomás's direction. "There's a boy who's not afraid to sit with his own thoughts."

"It's okay if I take a walk?" Tomás asked, looking toward the rise beyond the barns.

Gus and Joy sat quiet in the kitchen as Tomás cut across the pasture, Chap following him down the fence line, lifting her upper lip to the high plains air, inhaling.

"Seems like a real good kid," Joy said. "That one, I mean."

Gus nodded. He hadn't told her much about Tomás. But he had admitted that he was coming with an aim at a fresh start.

"This visit took you too long, Gussie," she said now. "Shouldn't take a spoilt marriage to get you to come see me."

"Who said anything about—" He was going to object, but Wade's chortling laughter broke in from the other room and that was enough to shut him up.

WADE'S VOICE WAS falsely gruff, like he believed he'd grown chest hair crossing the Rockies. "Don't you miss me?" he asked.

"Not so much," Vivian said, looking at her fingernails (chipping from hours in the pool). Rory was still in the water, still trying to swim two lengths without needing to breathe. Carmen had had the men come to clean it, finally.

"Oh, come on," Wade said. "Don't be such a tease." His tongue slithering around on the last word. "I wish you were here. You'd look good in a pair of chaps."

Rory came down to the end of the pool and paused, folding her arms on the edge, watching Vivian (with her Mona Lisa eyes). *Rory,* her name always came to Vivian like an answer to a question. Sometimes she thought of Teddy LaGrange as Rory was touching her, sometimes she was Teddy. She had never been with a girl before (a small white lie she'd told), but more than anything she liked the way it felt when Rory photographed her afterward. She felt briefly powerful then, cunning, like she had everything going for her.

Wade was going on, whining about staying in Wyoming and how he had to sleep on a futon (poor baby). She was waiting for him to say something about Gus, something she could tell Rory.

When she'd told Vivian about going home to Mona and this little one-eyed man (Columbo in a floral robe, eating eggs in the breakfast nook), Rory seemed as disturbed by Gus's broken heart as she was by Mona's black eye.

"There's a fucking buffalo skin on this chair I'm sitting on and it smells like cow shit everywhere," Wade said.

"Patties," Vivian corrected him. "They call them *patties*."

Wade laughed. "You're such a smart girl, Vivian Price."

"No," Vivian said, grinning. "I'm just a pretty little head." She hung up on him and stepped back outside. "How's the water?" she asked in a come-hither voice.

"Was that Wade?" Rory asked. "Did he say anything about Gus?"

"No," Vivian said. "An old friend from school." Vivian could hold her breath for two lengths of the pool and still come up looking refreshed.

THE MARE HADN'T been ready, so Gus had dropped Wade and Tomás at Heritage Ranch alone.

Every day since, he and Joy had trotted Chap out, taken her temperature, and no matter what the number, they showed her to Joy's aging stallion, Buck. So far, the two horses had looked at one another like animals of a different species. "You sure he still knows which end is what?" Gus said.

"You're out of season. You oughta come back in February, March, try again when this thing's meant to be done."

"You think I don't know that?" Gus said. "But this one's paid for, the wheels in motion. I've got this shot or I'm just more in debt. She'll come around," he said, though he no longer felt sure and he tossed every night, hearing the clock tick.

After more than a week had passed, Joy woke him early and dragged him down to the river to fish—seven trout in two hours, a bounty that bordered on offensive. Walking back toward the house, Gus felt a new linen stiffness to the air, the Wyoming winter approaching.

"You know you've missed it here," Joy said.

Gus smiled vaguely. He'd swooped out of himself just then, had seen the picture the two of them painted, how old they'd grown.

Mark Adler's property had been a study in greens: the barns hunter green, the covered ring gray-green and flanked by dark green shrubbery. In the office—a chalet-style building, just as the commercial advertised—Gus had sat hat in hand, while Wade eyeballed the trophy cases. Finally, a spry young woman with at-attention breasts, in a polo shirt two sizes too small, came in, greeted Wade and Tomás, and took them away. Without even so much as a question when Gus said he'd have to come back with the mare. "Yeah, okay, sure" was all she'd said, clearly not paid by the syllable. He'd found himself saying half-baked prayers ever since, aware of the nightmare it would be to return to Adler's ranch to pick up Wade and Tomás in a week, with the mare never having cycled again. Wade Fisk's equestrian taxi, at your service. Fucking hell.

"You know you've missed that mountain," Joy said, still trying to reel him in.

"Of course," he said. "Of course. Just not the sheep." He tried to smile.

They used to work Jack and Janet Traden's sheep up the river and over Battle Mountain, grazing them at Fletcher's Peak. They'd slept under the stars and he'd always woken to Joy's stirring, her deep breaths, checking the air for the iron tint of blood, seeing if they'd lost one in the night. Now all of her breathing seemed labored to him. Every night, she turned in earlier than he did. She'd confessed to him that she didn't have the revenue to warrant full-time help, having to share labor with the Crace family up the road.

"Shit," Joy said now, stopping him with a hand to his chest. Gus scanned the hill, thinking she'd seen a bear.

He did envy Joy her staying power here. Keeping things up and running, with a hound and a collie that took turns lacing themselves around her feet, being pleasure enough. He hadn't called home once, hadn't called the barn. He couldn't bring himself to without having news, good news. Yes, he missed this place, but same as he missed Mona when she was right beside him—just another thing that was not his own.

"No," Joy said. "Over there. It's your mare."

They'd left Buck and Chap in neighboring pastures and they were both at the fence line, that pulse to the air between them, Chap doing the dance that horses do—swishing her tail, showing Buck her face, then her rear. October 13, and she had come around.

"God damn," he said.

"You're taking me with you this time." Joy always had a way of sounding proud of him, even if he'd only fallen into dumb luck.

EIGHTH PERIOD. PHOTOGRAPHY. She was late.

"Well, well," Foster said. "She lives and breathes."

Everyone else was in the darkroom, printing, but Rory had yet to develop new negatives.

She'd missed five days of school since Gus left, but Vivian had been calling the attendance office at Polk, doing a reasonable impression of someone's mother, saying her daughter, Rory, would be absent for a dental appointment, a sinus infection, a stomach bug, knowing this would at least circumvent the school calling Mona again. To keep up appearances, Rory slept at home and rose as if to make the bus, Vivian waiting around the corner in the black BMW wagon. She'd called Rory an addiction, a new kind of drug. She had, Vivian said, made her stop caring about other people's opinions. Rory found it hard to believe Vivian ever had.

"You know what you're doing?" Foster asked, motioning to the table where the changing bags and development spools sat.

"Playing catch-up," Rory said.

She had shot twenty-seven rolls of film, all safely wound in the metal fists of their canisters. Most of them she'd shot in the last two weeks, but a few were from Fresno and before. There were images she remembered taking, holding the memory of them like talismans in her mind, but she had no certainty of their exposure, no confidence in her calibration of film speed and f-stop, let alone which roll had been shot when. She hadn't thought to label them and now there was no way of knowing what, or who, was going to swim up on these plastic ribbons of gelatin and silver halide. There was nothing to do but crack them all open and develop each and every one. Foster was still standing there, waiting.

"I'm okay," Rory said. "I know what I'm doing."

"That remains to be seen," Foster said, turning, and closing the door behind him.

Light-safe bag. Can opener. She slid her hands into the bag and wedged the can opener under the lip of the cartridge until it gave. One after another. She closed her eyes, focusing, feeding one ribbon into the circular teeth of the plastic spool. Only Carmen had seen them together, finding them asleep, holding one another in the guest bedroom. Now they locked doors, even if Carmen wasn't coming. She was thinking of the way Vivian took her hand and moved it for her, as if Rory's hands were just a way for Vivian to know the outlines of her own body.

"How's it going in here?" Foster asked, head popped in the doorway.

He had startled her, but she'd managed not to jerk her hands from the changing bag.

"Fine," Rory said.

"It's even hotter in the darkroom," Foster said.

"Right," Rory said, uninterested in making conversation.

"Are you planning on printing at all today?"

She'd found canisters that would hold three negatives at once, but she wanted to process and dry them all and that was going to take—"No, maybe next time?" she said. If she appeared the right amount of withdrawn, teachers usually didn't push her, but she sensed that the pile of film on the counter and her absences had piqued Foster's curiosity.

"Glad to know you'll be returning," Foster said and left again.

Measure developer, add water, agitate, wait, agitate, wait again.

Rory homo. She thought she had heard this, earlier, in the lunch line. Another girl, saying it under her breath. Rory told herself it was paranoia, that she hadn't changed, that no one knew. How could they? She and Vivian, they existed in a separate realm, a light-safe bag, a world of locked doors and absent parents. Far away from Polk High. But it had been one of the senior girls. Part of the gaggle that always wore baby doll dresses and Doc Martens. Yes, someone had said it. And the giggling that had followed, from that menagerie of hair-tossing friends, was echoing in her ears. With each watery shake of the canister, there was laughter. Was this how she'd always been seen? Wind, wind, mix, agitate, wait, agitate. *Rory homo,* that girl had said. So sure, so knowing. What had changed? *You think if you ignore it, it'll just starve and die off?* June. Nothing had changed, except the girl.

When Foster came back in, he looked surprised to see her still there. The clock: 4:34. She'd missed the last bus, but she started pulling her negatives from the drying line as if she still had a chance to catch it.

"Hey now," Foster said. "You might as well leave me something to grade."

✦

A MAN IN blue coveralls motioned for them to pull the trailer up to a slope-roofed Dutch barn. The aspen trees at Heritage were still green, leaves holding tight thanks to irrigation.

Chap's eyes were roving, her nostrils flared, as Gus eased her off the trailer. He put his hand to the silky skin of her clipped snout. "I know it," he said. "This place is a lot." He'd cleaned her up, top to bottom, helping her look the part. Adler still had to approve of her, so this was a catwalk kind of a day.

Two more men in blue coveralls were coming toward them. "I've seen more men than horses here. Oh, thank heavens," Joy said, recognizing one of them was Tomás.

"Look at you," Gus said. Tomás put his hand out to Chap, and she rested her muzzle in the cradle of it. His coveralls were too small, revealing the tops of his muck boots, but his head was high, the new member of an exclusive club.

"She's sure glad to see you," Gus said.

"I came to fetch her. And Billy here will show you to the breeding shed."

Billy, a white boy with the head of a mule, tipped his big face toward the road.

"Like a cult round here," Joy muttered. Gus had said nothing of what he'd already seen of Heritage, knowing Joy would find it as overly manicured and pretentious as the commercials, if not more so. He hadn't wanted her detecting the covetousness in his voice.

Gus lingered, watching Tomás and Chap move down the breeze-way, until they were threaded into the emerald fabric of the grass on the other side of the barn. "Come on already," Joy was hollering after him.

The breeding shed was a covered ring with wood-paneled walls, and a door at each end, his and hers entryways. Billy gestured them toward a bench behind a padded wall, the only place to sit, it seemed, and left them there to wait.

"I don't see why we couldn't stay with her," Joy said.

"Because Adler doesn't want to have to say no to our faces." With no history of her bloodlines, no papers, Chap had a one-in-fifty shot of Adler letting this all happen.

"Ridiculous. As if an animal's made outta paper."

The deal Preston Fisk had struck on Gus's behalf was that Cosmo's Waltz would cover the mare once and only with Adler's approval of Chap. There would be no guarantee of a live foal, as a papered broodmare in the proper breeding season would have received, but Adler's compromise was that if, in eleven months, there was no foal, Gus would only have to pay the first half of the fee, five thousand dollars. And if there *was* a standing foal, only after Adler's approval via video could Gus register Cosmo as the sire. Papers might not make an animal, but they were what made one worth any real money.

They didn't have to wait long. By the time they'd assessed the construction and general layout of the breeding shed, what Joy would have done differently, et cetera, et cetera, Adler was striding in with Wade Fisk following behind—of course. Men and boys in this echelon always made quick comrades.

Joy stood up, muttering, "Well, will you look at that. They're multiplying."

Gus extended his hand to Adler. There was still no sign of Chap being brought around, and the possibility that Adler had only come to tell him it wasn't going to happen had his bad leg aching. "Gus Scott," he said.

"Call me Mark," Adler said. His hand was as smooth as beach glass. A man with corporate sponsors. "Sit down, sit down. Wade here told me you're recovering from a bit of a car accident. There's no need for you to put yourself out today."

"So that's a no?" Joy asked. "Just like that?"

Adler laughed. "How do you do? You must be"—here Adler looked at Wade—"the sister I heard about. I understand you run your own breeding barn, up north, is that right?"

"Quarter horses," Joy said. Not meeting his offered hand. "Papered or not, I only care how they cut a cow. None of this cousin with cousins crap."

"Joy, quit," Gus said. "I'm sorry," he said to Adler. "Joy, let the man speak."

He shouldn't have brought her. Wade was smiling.

Adler cleared his throat. "Well, you'll be pleased to know your mare's temp is up and my men are bringing Cosmo over. They'll put him in the pen around the way, until we've got Chap readied here. Boy's going to be eager. Hasn't seen a mare since end of May."

The light streaming in the opposite door went dark and Gus turned to see it was Tomás and Chaparral filling the doorway, then the light flashed bright again, filling back in around them, Chap's coat glinting like a penny in a wishing well, and Gus had a flickering memory of the boy's red hair.

"I'd like to offer my help," Joy said abruptly.

"No, no," Adler said. "I don't ordinarily allow women in the shed, so let's just have you two stay back here." At this Adler moved toward the mare.

"Fucking hell," Gus said. "What a prick."

Tomás was still holding Chap. Adler pulled a leather strap from the wall and handed it to big-headed Billy, who brought the strap round Chap's right front leg, cinching it so her hoof was held aloft. Chap looked relaxed enough, her neck and ears slack.

"That ain't necessary," Joy said, her words tucked into his shoulder.

"Let it be," Gus said.

This was no longer about making-ends-meet money for Sonja or even for himself. This foal and its imaginary destiny—its future on the event circuit, its ribbons, maybe even its subsequent offspring— were a matter of pride. Gus needed a new legacy, a better reason to make the news. Even if, right now, it meant he had to sit all stupid-like behind this padded wall with his sister seething beside him.

Wade wrapped the top of Chap's tail, showing he'd at least been taught something about the process beforehand.

Adler came with a twitch then, not speaking to Tomás, but just moving in, silently telling him to hand over Chap's lead and step aside. He pinched the mare's top lip and looped the chain around it, turning, the metal gripping her freshly clipped mouth, but the mare didn't flinch. Even with Cosmo bellowing in the paddock outside now, his hooves scoring the walls.

"He's got skill there," Gus said.

"No," Joy said. "He sedated her."

Gus looked the mare over again. "He'd have said something. Don't you think?"

Joy shook her head, rolling her eyes at him.

The mare was relieving herself, her hind legs spread, her urine falling in a great gush to the rubberized floor. Her instincts were functioning well enough, anyway.

"We're ready," Adler said, hollering toward the holding pen. Then he motioned for Wade, handing him Chap's lead, showing him where to stand to keep ahold of her—her lead *and* her twitch.

"Un-fucking-believable," Joy said. "You're not gonna say nothing?"

"Tomás is nearby," Gus said.

And then Cosmo's Waltz was coming in, a thunderstorm, changing the air around them, his neck coiled with rolling muscles.

"He ain't real," Joy said.

Joy hadn't seen the videos Gus had watched, hadn't understood how much horse he was. And yet Gus's thoughts had also been reduced to windblown scraps: *That horse. This foal. Hot damn.* Adler gestured to Tomás to pull Chap's tail aside and Tomás did, as Adler steered Cosmo to the back of her and everything beyond the stallion and the mare seemed arrested in time. Cosmo reared back and came down onto Chap, one of his front hooves on each of her shoulders. Tomás stepped back. Billy dropped her hobbled front leg to the ground, so she could bear the weight on top of her. There was some alarm in the round bowl of the mare's eye now, wanting to know what stallion was on her. He hadn't nuzzled her neck or put his head to her face, the way horses will in the wild. He hadn't asked. He was thrusting into her. Joy grabbed hold of Gus's wrist and Gus saw the stallion's teeth were bared at the crest of the mare's shoulders, with no neck leather on her, no one stopping him, the stallion still rocking over her, until, finally, he cried out. Wade jumped back, scared.

"It's all right," Adler said, smiling. "Means he's done."

Cosmo went rag doll limp on top of her. Adler clucked at him, and in his own sweet time Cosmo eased himself back down and off her again. Tomás looked at Gus and he felt the relief billowing between them. They'd done it. They'd bred Chap and there was a perfectly good chance of it taking. Sonja. He wanted Sonja to know.

Adler started walking Cosmo toward the door they'd brought him from, passing Chaparral. And Wade released the twitch. Too soon. The mare craned her head and took a hank of the stallion's salt-white tail in her teeth. Of course, the stallion spun around then, shaking Adler off like water from a wet dog's coat. Free, the stallion reared back and his front hooves came down—shining silver: his shoes had been left on. One hoof striking the mare's right eye, the other drawing a slanted line of flesh from her shoulder. Adler and Billy had their hands waving in the stallion's face. Tomás had thrown an arm in front of Wade, protecting him, pushing him into the wall.

"What the fuck," Wade said, looking at Tomás's hand on him. "Don't touch me."

"Why the hell did you let her go?" Tomás said.

"You left shoes on him!" Joy was hollering.

They'd cornered the stallion. His nostrils blowing misty puffs that hung in the air then dissipated. The mare was furiously blinking, her eye flooding with blood.

"She's a piece-of-shit horse," Wade said. "Fucking inbred piece-of-shit horse."

Gus hadn't moved. Joy was tending to the mare and Gus was

held fast to the bench, as if his steering wheel were still smashed against his chest.

"I'll get the vet," Adler said.

VIVIAN DROPPED INTO the pleather booth and set her feet up on the table. She hadn't just barged in, though Rory had her back pressed up against the counter like Vivian was a cat burglar come to take something (meow). "You got anything to drink? I'm parched."

"Like, water?" Rory asked.

"Um, no, like vodka."

Carmen was at the house with an army-size cleaning team, indiscriminately clearing out Everett's debris, Windexing away the ghosts (worth a try anyway). Besides, it was Monday and Rory didn't have to work and here, Vivian was figuring, they could hang out until whenever it was a bar shift ended. Vivian had thoughtfully waited, walking the bridge only after Mona's Chrysler had pulled away. But there was a van parked at the end of the driveway, an old dry-cleaning van with a faded logo that had been painted over.

"There isn't a lot left," Rory said, pulling the bottle of vodka from the freezer.

"I'll refill it, promise. Come on. Just one drink."

It was the first day that felt like fall, a crisp biting wind blowing off the ocean, tossing through the canyon pass, dancing leaves around. It seemed a betrayal of Charlie. The seasons carrying on without him. And now the longer Vivian sat in this house the colder she got. The walls were paper thin, the windows single pane, the floors without automatic heating coils (what an asshole she was). Rory was dropping ice cubes into her glass.

Vivian went and pulled a crocheted blanket from the living room couch. "This okay? Just a little chilly in here." She wanted to cry. It had been building all day long. A wind threw a branch against the kitchen window and Rory's head snapped around to see it. "Are you nervous about me being here?" Vivian asked. "That your mom might come home early?"

"No," Rory said. "I mean, that was just the wind—" She held out the glass of vodka and Vivian drank it (cheap as paint thinner).

"Even if your mom did walk in, wouldn't she just lose her mind to see *me* sitting here? *You* taking *my* picture? Now, that would be an interview the tabloid magazines would pay for."

Rory wasn't laughing. She was pouring a second glass of vodka (a plot twist!). She took a tentative sip and disgust rucked her face.

"Are you okay?" Vivian asked.

Rory nodded "Yeah, fine."

Vivian stepped closer until she was pressing up against Rory. She took her glass and ran it up the inside of Rory's arm. Vivian often did this with just her fingers before she kissed her. Like opening the petals of a flower. But now Rory was turning away. "What's wrong? Do you want me to go?"

"No," Rory said. "It's not that—"

"Well, spit it out." Vivian stepped back.

"This girl at school—she called me a homo. *Rory homo.*" She took a shaky sip.

"You need ice," Vivian said. "The colder it is, the easier it goes down."

"Am I a homo?" Rory asked.

Vivian went to the freezer, which smelled of celery somehow, the walls thick with frost. "That girl's an idiot," she said, twisting the ice tray, cracking out the last two cubes. Rory was staring out the window, at the trees, contorted in the wind. "Hey," Vivian said, dropping the ice into Rory's glass. "You with me?"

Rory drank. "That is better," she said. She had been futzing with her camera when Vivian walked in and she'd abandoned it on the kitchen counter, the strap hanging precariously over the edge (easily snagged and dropped to the floor). She was looking at Vivian, expectantly, her lips still wet. Sometimes Rory was awkward when aiming at provocative, but Vivian kissed her. She kept kissing her, sliding her hand into the waistband of her jeans, waiting for that catch in her throat, the change in the color of her cheeks. Vivian wasn't thinking of Teddy again. "Have you ever been with a boy?" she asked. How odd that she'd not thought to ask this before.

Rory's eyes snapped open. "A boy?"

"Yeah," Vivian said, stepping back. She picked up the bottle of vodka and topped off her glass.

"Um, no," Rory said, wiping strands of her hair out of her face. "I mean, not yet."

"You're lucky," Vivian said. "Boys are trouble. You never know what they're thinking, not really, not beyond sex." She was biting down on the last of her ice. "Besides, boys can get you pregnant, too. So there's that."

"Right," Rory said.

"I got pregnant," Vivian said. "Once. Have I told you that?" She hadn't meant to; she'd never told anyone. But that pressure she'd been feeling all day, this brisk fall air that seemed to be taking Charlie further and further away from her, and now this, a nick in the hide of her.

"Really?" Rory asked. "When?"

"I was fourteen, going on fifteen." She'd never even told Teddy and now here she was telling Rory. "My mom figured it out. I'd barely realized it myself when she put her hand on my stomach and tipped my chin up and said, 'This is going away.' Just like that."

Vivian was crying. Not sobbing, but the memory itself seemed slicked with tears, a family on the inside of a rain-splattered window. That scene in *Caleb's Honor,* the role that got Daddy his supporting Oscar nomination, where the camera is on the outside of the house and all you can hear is the thunder but through the wobbly streaks of the rain-drenched windowpane you see him yelling at his teenage son (and the Oscar goes to . . . the rain machine).

"My mom had been trying to get pregnant. Injecting herself with all these shots, throwing up half of everything she ate. And then there I was, knocked up, without even realizing. Do you have cigarettes? I'd actually smoke one." And more to drink. There must be more.

Rory was already in the living room, lifting and dropping cushions, digging in a handbag.

"Here!" she shouted, coming back into the room, a half-crushed pack of Lucky Strikes in her hand.

She shook one out, lit it, and handed it to Vivian. Rory seemed newly cautious, having glimpsed the wiring of Vivian, the internal explosives (boom!). "I shouldn't have told you any of that," Vivian said.

"But you trust me," Rory said.

There was white wine, a half bottle left, in the door of the fridge. A metal twist cap. She drank all of it, standing in the light of the fridge, then, realizing what she really wanted, she turned to Rory. "Take my picture," she said.

"Are you sure?"

"Never more," Vivian said.

Rory removed her lens cap, adjusted the exposure. She lifted the camera to her eye.

Vivian never needed direction from Rory. She never needed to be told how to pose. She tipped the wine bottle back, showing her profile, bending her knee. Always, Mommy had told her, bend one knee. Click. She turned toward Rory, one arm across the refrigerator's open door, the wine bottle between her fingers, the blanket draped over her arms, the lit cigarette dangling from her mouth. She had no idea if any of Rory's pictures had even turned out. She didn't care. It wasn't about the finished product, but about these moments, with this girl seeing her. This girl after all those leering men, hoping, scrambling to catch her in a moment of weakness, and now, even now, she got to feel strong. "My dad doesn't know," Vivian said, stepping toward Rory's lens. "My mom made me promise. She said that Daddy didn't need to know. I thought she was worried about bad press, about Bobby—"

"Why Bobby?" Rory asked from behind the camera, shooting one after another.

"He used to say I was Daddy's best asset, that I kept people interested in us. Anyway, I thought she didn't want Daddy knowing because he tells Bobby everything, but then she said she didn't

245

want Daddy thinking any less of me." Vivian stopped, looking at the end of the cigarette. "Why do people do this?" She dropped the cigarette into the emptied wine bottle. "My mom got pregnant with Charlie a month after that."

"I'm sorry," Rory said, putting the camera down.

"About which part?" Vivian asked.

"All of it," Rory said.

"Why'd you stop taking my picture?" Vivian asked, sniffling behind the blanket.

"I thought you wanted me to."

Vivian shook her head. She turned and ran the water in the sink, lifting palmfuls to her face. Standing back up, the sun having dipped below the canyon wall, she could see herself in the window glass, her transparent self. Click. "I think I wanted Charlie even more than my mother did. I'd been alone with my parents for so long." She turned back to Rory, what she could see of her. Click. "I held him the day he was born and he opened his eyes and they were these dark pools. Carmen says he was a new soul, that he'd never been here before. That he'll come back. Do you believe in that?" Rory was nodding behind the body of the camera. "I was glad when we moved here. I wanted the quiet, to be home with my mom. With Charlie—" Someone was screaming. Somewhere behind Rory. Click. "There's a woman," Vivian said. She was running down the driveway from the house above.

"Sonja," Rory said.

"Sonja?" Vivian knew the pitch of this scream, the look in this woman's eyes. Someone was hurt.

Then this Sonja was in the house, having swung through the screen door, panting, coming up short at the sight of Vivian there. "Dios mio," Sonja said.

"Call an ambulance," Rory said. Then she was gone.

THE WOUND ABOVE Chap's eye was down to the bone. The vet had Chap on her side, sedated, and had stanched the bleeding. The wound to her shoulder wasn't as deep, but the hair was likely to grow back white, an untrue suggestion about her temperament and care to any future judge. Tomás applied the ointment. Joy was at the mare's neck, ready to pin her still if she started to toss against the vet's suturing. Gus had fallen back against the stall wall. He'd tried to squat down and help, only to end up with his head in his hands. They weren't going to be able to transport her, not today, not with this tranquilizer in her system and this trauma. The vet kept shaking his head. "Please quit doing that," Gus finally said. "You're giving me heart palpitations, for crying out loud."

The vet laughed. Gus hadn't meant to amuse him. "Now, now," the vet said. "I've seen worse." He was a pear-shaped man with a set of bifocals at the end of his nose and a pair of sunglasses hanging from a beaded chain against his chest. "Cosmo hasn't stood for a mare in months. Only natural he'd be as worked up as he was."

"So might you have recommended removing his shoes?" Joy demanded.

The vet looked over his glasses at her; he'd never call out his meal ticket.

"Course," Joy said, and spat into the shavings.

The drugs had Chap's eye rolled back, revealing the milky gray beneath the iris. The stall they'd laid her out in was breathtakingly big. A running water system in the trough, a polished copper grain dispenser, and rubber matting even here, beneath the shavings.

"Wasn't Cosmo who started the trouble anyway," Wade said.

When Adler had gone for the vet, Wade had followed after him, a meek shadow, but here he was again, renewed, his head held up like a rooster's.

"That how you remember it?" Gus said.

"The bandage here is gonna limit her sight, of course," the vet said, as if trying to distract from the tension. Dust motes hovered in the shafts of light, equally useless.

"Was *you*," Joy said, not taking her eyes off the mare's head. "Letting go the twitch."

"Has she ever worn blinders?" The vet tried again. Tomás shook his head, no. He would know. "Well, some horses travel best with blinders, but if you can give her a week's rest before you hit the road again—"

"He can," Wade said.

Gus turned to Wade. "I can, can I? Were you fixing to move in here?"

"Well, then," the vet went on. "The bandage and the sutures can be removed in three weeks' time. I'll trust you have someone decent in Los Angeles who can do this." He said Los Angeles like he was ordering in a foreign restaurant.

TOPANGA CANYON, CALIFORNIA

"Not really," Wade said. "But our barn will be hiring a staff vet soon enough."

"*Our* barn?" Gus was tired of whatever this was. He leaned into his cane and shifted his shoulder against the wall, fixing to get up.

Joy stood then, too, and Tomás scooted around the other side of the mare, knowing someone had to stay ready to pin her.

Wade threw his hair back from his face. "Change of plans. Adler's got a horse going west and he's putting Journey on that trailer, so you don't have to hurry back. You can let Chap rest, visit with your sister."

Gus looked back at Tomás. He had his head down, staying focused with the vet, but he was listening, that much was clear. "Such a nice offer," Gus said. "Kind of you and Adler to make that plan so quick."

"Well, actually, Dad bought me and Tomás flights days ago. I've learned enough on this trip, at Heritage anyway. Plenty of ideas to bring back for Leaning Rock. Who knows, maybe my dad will let you stay on—"

"Let me?" Gus asked.

"Did I forget to tell you?" Wade said. "Tomás, you didn't mention it?"

The mare was waking up. Tomás was stroking her neck. "Easy now," the vet said.

"Out with it, kid," Joy said.

Wade snorted at her. Gus felt his hands go tight.

"My dad's made an offer on Leaning Rock and—"

"Carlotta isn't selling," Gus said. He could feel the turn of the earth under his feet.

"No," Wade said. "I guess she's not. But with power of attorney—"

"Bella," Gus said. "Of course." Bella and Robin . . . *You know things will never be the same again.* . . . Robin had said that and he hadn't heard.

"Funny," Wade said. "I thought you'd be happy. June and I've been riding there our entire lives. Place has to go to someone either way. Might as well be someone you like, right?"

Gus closed his eyes.

"I mean, any other buyer would be twice as likely to let you go."

"Watch yourself, young man," Joy said.

The vet took his bifocals off, letting them drop on their own beaded chain. "Yep, I've seen better days in the shed." He was shaking an enormous pill bottle. "In a bran mash," he said. "For discomfort. Shouldn't affect her odds."

"Thank you," Joy said.

"Oh, I'll be sending a bill," the vet said, opening the stall door. He looked back at the mare. "Keep an eye on her when she goes to stand. Leave her room." The mare groaned.

Adler was coming up now, Wade laying his arm onto Adler's shoulder. Adler gave Gus an apologetic smile and turned to Wade. "Everything all right here?"

Whatever fortitude Gus had mustered was draining from him like sand. A red-hot neediness filling in the empty spaces. "All right, then," he said. The door stood open between him and Wade. The mare blew a blustery breath.

"It's gonna be fine," Wade said, sweeping his hand as if at a fly.

"She's waking up," Adler said.

The mare was taking to her feet, pulling herself up behind him. He heard Joy say, "Gussy," but he was looking at Wade.

"See there," Wade said. "No harm done. She's good as new."

And then Gus said, "Wade," so he'd be facing him, so he'd see it coming, clean and straight: the bridge of Gus's fist meeting the bridge of his nose, the bone breaking like clay, the blood coming like water.

IT WASN'T A choice so much as a cellular dictation, to go up the hill to Carlotta. She was like a grandmother, or what Rory imagined a grandmother could be. It wasn't until Rory had reached the top and saw the front door slapping back and forth on the wind that she was filled with trepidation. But she had left Vivian below, with Sonja. Stepping inside seemed easier suddenly.

Carlotta was in the dining room, on the floor, her leg turned oddly out, eyelids half-drawn, the rug around her darkened, the stench of urine woven into the rotting milk and mothball smells that had come to haunt the house in the last few years. "Carlotta? It's Rory." No response. The room was lit only by the chandelier casting a web of light around the table, leaving the corners of the room dark. Rory felt as if something or someone were watching her from there. "Can you hear me? We're getting help." As soon as she said this, she hoped it was true. Surely one of them had called for an ambulance, however baffled they'd been by the other one being there; Sonja's taking in the emptied bottle of vodka, the wine, too. The cigarettes on the counter. Rory felt like such a child. Maybe Sonja wouldn't say how she knew who Vivian was, maybe—

Was Carlotta even breathing?

Rory lowered her palm in front of Carlotta's mouth, finding a subtle but steady breath. "Help is coming," Rory said, the light of the chandelier breaking into prisms. She was crying for Carlotta, but also for Vivian, for that story, and for herself. Here was Carlotta, the woman who had hugged her as a little girl, and—was she dying? Was this what the end of a life looked like? She wanted to move her, to bring her to dry carpet. She put her hand to Carlotta's arm, but it was so cold and so heavy. And what if she hurt her? "They're coming," she exhaled. "Someone is coming. I can hear sirens." She let the lie of this briefly pad her from the truth, that she didn't know what was going to happen next.

Just then a draft of wind came through the house, sending papers from the dining table scattering to the floor. Rory wiped her face dry. Her eyes had adjusted to the dim light and she saw then what she had felt watching her: The curio cabinets that had always lined the walls of this room were no longer full of only trophies and photographs, but now held animals. The animals that Gus had boxed up all those years ago. The taxidermied raccoon, the crow, the owl—she had wanted to keep the owl, as well, but she had realized the bird was too big to go unnoticed, how disgusted Mona would be. *Gus.* She felt a sudden duty to him. She started gathering the papers that had fallen, as if more order, tidiness, would help keep Carlotta alive. In the dim light, on these papers, she saw Carlotta's full name and that of her daughter and the words *power of attorney shall be granted . . .*

Carlotta's spine was visible beneath her shirt, a string of pearls lifting and falling. "Do you want me to keep talking?" Rory asked, her voice low. "I'm not going anywhere. I'll stay right here."

Her camera was still strapped to her back. She'd grown so used to having it there; putting her hands on it again now calmed her. Though Foster, looking at her negatives, had not been encouraging: *lacking technical precision, overly precise in composition.* She'd shown him Gus with Chap, the two of them a centaur. *Cute,* he'd said. Then the few she could show of Vivian, the more abstract: the curve of her shoulder framing the pool in the background, her feet dangling from the end of the lounge chair. *Safe,* he'd said. *Kind of commercial.* In other words, bullshit.

Carlotta did not register the first click of Rory's shutter. Or the next. The wind through the trees was so loud, a disarming sound. But by the fifth frame, the sirens had grown near and Rory felt her purpose in taking these photographs solidifying. *How do you feel in the world, Rory Ramos?* Foster had asked. *Show me.*

She wasn't taking pictures of Carlotta, but of the empty space around her, her hand at the edge of the frame, the netting of light across the chairs, pictures of the room itself, a room that seemed full of morbid anticipation and she was taking pictures as objection, firing against the unspoken assumption that this was all going to end horribly wrong.

LITTLE SNAKE, WYOMING

JUNE 9, 2015

"DID YOU LOVE her?" I asked Vivian Price.

"That was twenty-two plus years ago," she said. We had only been on the phone for a short time, but there was an urgency to our conversation. Like one of Mama's photographs: the two strangers running toward one another after a blast. "I was just a kid. I wasn't capable of love." She laughs, melancholy. "Not like that. Certainly didn't love myself."

"She loved you," I said.

"Did she?"

She doubts this, even now, coming from the girl who bears her dead brother's name.

There is a picture of me as a baby, framed, on the living room wall. I am sitting on the floor in Grandad's old cowboy hat. My eyes are concealed beneath the brim, but my smile is obvious. Mama is sitting to one side of me and on the other side is Vivian. I had not recognized her before, had apparently never thought to ask who she was, just someone in a four-by-five in the corner, but now I know from going through Mama's old negatives that Vivian has always been here, in our living room.

"She was only here for a few months," Grandad said. "She came for your birth and she stayed for a stretch then."

Given everything I've heard, I assumed something must have pulled Vivian's attention elsewhere.

"Are there others?" I asked. "Other pictures from then?"

Grandad shook his head. "I took that one."

"But Mama took others, didn't she? When I was a baby?"

"After the fire, she didn't pick up a camera for a long time. Not until you were four or five, I think."

In the framed photograph on our wall, Vivian's attention is on my smile, her pleasure clear. But Mama's eyes are on Vivian, unsmiling, unmoved, her expression one of defeat.

"Your mama asked her to go," Grandad said, touching the picture so it hung straight.

"Mama asked her to leave? But—wasn't Mama in love with her?"

"Being in love with somebody doesn't mean you can trust 'em."

"One day you have a mother," Vivian said on the phone. "And the next you do not. I should know." I could hear the bitter way she held her mouth.

"Where is your mother now?" I asked.

There was a long pause. Ice slid the length of her glass, rattled against her teeth. "She lives in New Hampshire. She bought this old house there, very quaint. She lives with a nobody, some guy who runs a garden nursery, but she refuses to divorce Everett. She's gone but won't go away. Her retribution, I guess. He lives in Italy with this French actress. A half-decent one at least."

I was picturing Vivian, alone in her apartment in New York, sitting in an overstuffed chair, still slender, but hunched from years of self-abuses, flipping through the pages of a glossy magazine that deemed her irrelevant long ago. I know from Gus that Sarah Price called Vivian, but only after the fire, wanting to know if the house had burned down—it hadn't. Vivian retrieved the incoming number from the operator. New Hampshire, and not far from where her mother had gone to boarding school. Vivian lived with her a little while, after staying here with us. "You and your mother," I asked. "You aren't in touch?"

"She left me," Vivian said. "She walked away."

Talking to Vivian, I realized how endlessly forgiving Mama was, how she never believed one bad decision, even five, was all a person was. With everything she witnessed, she still believed people are inherently good.

I watched the films that Vivian went on to act in, and there were moments when I saw the same raw beauty Mama captured in her photographs, but I'd hoped to like her more.

"I'm sorry," Vivian said. "About your mom. I'm sorry it happened how it did."

"Were you there?" I asked her then. I had been waiting for an opening to ask what Grandad couldn't answer. "When the fire started? Were you there, at the ranch with her?"

Whenever I ask Grandad how the fire started, he gets this look on his face, like I slapped him gently, like he isn't surprised so much as embarrassed for us both. Like I had something to do with it. So I tried this out on Vivian. "My grandad told me *you* had something to do with it."

She laughed. "I had everything to do with it, didn't I? Go on," she said. "Ask away, Charlie. I'm the one who can answer your questions. Right up until I stole Wade's car, anyway."

TOPANGA CANYON, CALIFORNIA

LATE OCTOBER 1993

INDIAN SUMMER HAD arrived and the windows in Foster's classroom were so high up they required a pole to open, a pole that had gone missing. Not that there was any sign of a breeze. This was the stillness that preceded the Santa Ana winds.

Foster kept grinding his knuckles against his temples as the slides rotated: Arbus, Shore, Cartier-Bresson. They were studying portraiture. Mary Ellen Mark.

Waving the class into the darkroom, Foster announced, as he always did, the next week's assignment, "a portrait of someone who's not your best damn friend. Somebody you have to do a little work to put at ease." Rory thought of Gus, who had still not called. A portrait of Robin, maybe?

In the red-lit room, beneath her enlarger, Rory lined her negatives up on the photo paper, making a proof sheet of the last roll she'd shot: Vivian in her kitchen, posing, tears on her face, then the dining room of Carlotta's house; the progression of that night made plain, right up until the ambulance arrived. Vivian had already left by then. The paramedics said only one person could go to the hospital with Carlotta and Sonja had gotten in. Later, Vivian didn't answer the phone. And hadn't since. When Rory asked Sonja what had happened, she kept walking, only shaking her head, saying, "That girl can't be your friend."

Rory moved her proof from the developer to the stop bath.

Instead of his usual hands-behind-his-back pacing, Foster pulled up a stool in the corner nearest the curtained door, fanning himself with a discarded print. Rory looked at him and he said, "Fighting a headache."

"Can I get you anything?"

Foster shook her off. "Leonard," he said. "Go find me a fan."

Pete Leonard drooped, but went off to do it.

Rory made a series of proof sheets, feeling safe enough with nosy Pete Leonard gone. And the proofs were all small enough that it would take looking through a magnifier to know it was Vivian Price.

"A print of your self-portrait today, Ramos?" Foster said.

"Right," Rory said. He'd let her into the darkroom because she was so behind, but then she hadn't printed that very first assignment, now weeks late. She held her negatives up to the red bulb. One of these strips held the pictures she'd been shooting in the mirror the night Vivian had walked in. There. Found. She had time to print this and another, from Carlotta's dining room: the rug, its gradation of stains, bisected by Carlotta's awkwardly twisted leg—her hip had been broken.

Rory was watching her self-portrait materialize in the developer when Leonard returned with what he clearly hoped would be an enthusiastically received table fan. But Foster only said, "Put it there," indicating the floor. He was standing next to Rory, inspecting her process.

"Take it out now," he said, and she lifted the paper with the tongs and dropped it into the fix. "I like this," Foster said, following its progress to the stop bath. "I like it very much."

"How so?" Leonard said, leaning in. "It's blurry," he said, challenging their teacher. "There's nothing in focus."

"Except the bird," Foster said. He pinched the bridge of his nose, then he lifted his head to the room. "Okay. I heard the bell."

"We have twenty more minutes," Leonard whined. "I brought the fan."

"Ring-ring-ring," Foster said. "Yep. That's the bell. Class is dismissed. Leonard. Go."

Everyone stowed their materials and started out, the narrowness of the room herding them single file, then one by one, through the velvet curtains to the door.

Rory was dawdling, wanting more time, one more print. She was looking at the blur of her own face, wanting to print the images that she'd shot just before, too. Thinking about sequencing, images as stories.

"Ms. Ramos," Foster said.

"Yes, I'm sorry," she said, gathering her things, the filters, the paper. She wanted to offer to close up.

"It's fine if *you'd* like to stay," Foster said, without her having to ask. "If you've got more like that one, I'd like to see them. I'd like you to get caught up."

"I hadn't realized how far behind I was." She was speaking by rote, a sentence she'd said a dozen times to a half dozen teachers already.

"Let's have a look at these proofs that you're so secretive about." He was already pulling them from the drying line. She'd intentionally hung them backward, but he'd been watching.

"You've shot so many rolls of film," he said. And all of them, every single strip, held images of Vivian. "Ms. Ramos," he said.

She was woozy; the chemicals had gotten to her, the possibility of him recognizing Vivian. "Yeah?"

"Those negatives that you showed me last week, I'm not sure I fully appreciated them."

"How so?" Rory said.

"I mean, here, seeing them, like this." His expression shifted. "Are these all the same girl?"

"I don't know," she said. "I guess." She wasn't making any sense.

"Yes. She's quite comfortable with you, isn't she?"

Of course. Of course, he didn't recognize Vivian. He didn't know who she was. He cared about the larger world, about the variations of light, about how to make art. Rory envied him.

"Is she a model? I ask because, well, she's so posed in these here." He pointed at a series from Vivian's house, a roll they'd shot in the garden. "Are you directing her?"

Rory shook her head. "She's, yes, I think she's modeled some."

"Interesting," he said. "But then there are these . . ." He was looking at the images from inside the kitchen. Vivian in the crochet blanket, her red-rimmed eyes. "Much more vulnerable," he said. He wiped a bead of sweat from his temple. He had narrow-set eyes and thin lips that he covered with his palm when he was thinking, his forehead always furrowed. A face that had spent decades pressed up against a viewfinder, trying to make sense of the world.

"What is it?" Rory asked. She was halfway worried he'd understood how intimately she and Vivian knew one another, why she'd gotten the kinds of images she had.

"I can't teach this," he said, running his eyes back over the tiny boxes of her images. The exposures, she'd nailed nearly all of them. Was that what was impressing him? She had an urge to rip them from his hands, to go back to doing this on her own, in secrecy, but first she wanted to hear why they were good. "Having an eye—that expression we're always leaning on," he said. "It's the difference between taking pictures and being a photographer."

When he looked at her again, she felt a magnetic drawing together inside of herself, an annealing of who she was, or who she wanted to be. "And . . . ?" she asked.

Foster smiled. "And now you need to learn to trust it."

CARMEN TRIED TO insist on driving Vivian to school, but Vivian dangled the keys to the BMW in front of her, promising that she wouldn't go anywhere but school, if for no other reason than she pitied Carmen, her having to play parent like this.

"They'll fire me, Ms. Vivian."

"The irony," Vivian said. She'd told Carmen not to call her Ms. Vivian. "You're my auntie, Carmen. Mi tía. Please stop."

"Claro, Ms. Vivian."

Vivian pulled onto PCH. She was plagued by a desire she could not name. She turned on the radio, trying to distract herself with the news—Orange County skinhead pleads guilty to plot against synagogues, Russian cosmonaut makes ninth space walk—but it all spun off without reaching her. How had she become this way? Her inner monologue . . . (gone).

The beach was empty and still, the line between the water and the slate gray sky sharp as a knife's edge. Fire weather. That's what this was. She drove on to school, but only because she was incapable of thinking beyond Carmen's direction.

On campus, she moved through the halls. She heaped herself into a desk. She watched the teacher, his mouth moving, a fish in his tank. At the bell, maybe a little before or after, she drifted toward her locker. And there was Wade.

He had one hand in the pocket of his Dickies and his head cocked like a toddler who'd done something wrong. What had happened to his nose?

Was it Wade she was hungering for? Or had she been bracing for his return? Did it matter? She hadn't seen Rory in days. But here he was, the game of him. She started to walk the other way, as if she didn't know him at all. She heard him jogging after her.

"No, no, no," he was saying. "You can't get away from me." That brass, the audacity of his voice. Mommy would have called it *cheek*. "I know you missed me," he said.

"No," Vivian said, not turning, but walking toward the library. She wasn't answering his question so much as stating a general feeling. No. No. No. She wasn't going to cry anymore.

He got his hand on her shoulder and turned her around, just

outside the library doors. He didn't pull her in or try to kiss her, but leaned against the wall, as if she had shoved him backward. His eyes, the dark contrast of them above the white bandage, were darting over her face, looking for her betrayals (ha). There she was. She'd felt this before, at the end of long-distance swims, this emptiness, a kind of inner collapsing right as the shore arrives at your fingertips (catch me, please). She could write that down, repeat it later to McLeod (*oh, McLeod*).

"What's wrong with you?" she asked.

"You mean my nose?"

Vivian nodded.

"You know you look like hell," he said.

She pushed him then, her fingers to his sternum, feeling the flex of her arms. Some strength. She turned into the library (fucking asshole).

She would disappear into this church of books, fall in between the mahogany carrels, and never be found again. How bad did she look? She *had* changed and for the worse. She'd let everything spiral out of control, telling people she hardly knew things about herself, the very core of her being—ripping it out and handing it over to Rory. And then Rory (who the hell was she?) had left her. It was as alone as she'd ever felt. Standing there, listening to the ramblings of the wife of the man who'd killed her brother. She had had the pleasure of never having to think about her. Or him. Until Rory.

"Hey, hey. Come on." Wade again. His voice a breathy whisper. "Don't run away from me." There was the faint crack of a book's spine, someone turning pages on the other side of the carrel. "You don't look so bad," he said. He tipped his forehead toward her.

Disarming, that's what he was. She lost some piece of herself every time he touched her.

"You're the one with the broken nose," she said.

He'd stopped looking at her face. His hands were on her hips, eyes lowered there.

"How did it happen?" She touched the bandage.

"This guy. Gus Scott." He pulled her toward him. "He's a trainer, from the ranch. *Was* a trainer there, anyway." He winked above the bandage.

"He hit you—" She'd almost said, *He hit you, too?* She'd almost said, *I know who he is. I know, I know, he's Rory's stepfather.* She'd barely gotten a finger over the leak of it in time.

"I might have had it coming." Wade shrugged.

"He really hit you?" Vivian blurted. A freshman passing at the mouth of the aisle—wearing knee-high socks—stopped and stared at Wade too hard. Vivian's face burned.

"Hey, hey. I'm all right." He swung his hair back from his eyes in that way that he did and the smell of his shampoo reached her. "We're all right," he said, smiling. "Me and you, we're good." He brought his mouth down to hers, not fully kissing her, but letting his lips linger along hers. "When my dad buys the place, I get to fire the guy myself." He cupped his hand to her butt and tucked her against his waist. She felt the grommets of his jeans. "I'll be his boss."

"Your dad's buying Leaning Rock?"

He looked at her uneasily. What had he heard in her voice (play the tape back, please)?

"Yeah," he said. "I thought you'd be into that."

"I am," she said. "I'd like to watch you fire everyone." That woman Sonja, she had called the ambulance and then she'd gone rigid, judgmental, gathering their glasses, the empty bottles, explaining who she was, but saying in the very next sentence that *Vivian* should go. No apology. Just protective of Rory. Everyone loved Rory.

"And you?" Wade asked. "What have you been up to?" Underneath his eyes were two fading blue moons. "Did you stay out of trouble?" he asked.

"Not at all," she said, not thinking of Rory, but of how these three words would sound to him (game back on). He put his hands on her arms, slid them to her wrists, and held her against the books. "Not at all," she repeated.

"So you missed me then," he said (so sure).

She gave him a particular kind of smile, thin and quick. Like the flash just before a star's collapse (something like that).

MONA DROPPED RORY off at the top of the driveway, and U-turned, saying, "Find a ride home."

Rory scanned the parking lot, as usual. Robin's truck was there, parked over the lines like she'd pulled in in a rush. It was already four o'clock and the late afternoon light was watery gold, the air arid and shifty, eddies of dust stirred up. At night it was hard to sleep. Rory tossed in and out of the same dream, waking less panicked and more itchy and irritated. In the office it was crisp and cool, the air conditioner properly working. The room had been cleaned, too. The competition photos dusted, the floor swept, the skin of dust wiped from the shelves and ribbons. Rory sat down at the desk and put her head back, enjoying the cool air before looking for her list, hoping it would be short.

"Comfortable?"

Rory snapped to. "June." She was standing in the doorway to the back room, drying her hands on a paper towel. "I didn't see your car," Rory said, instantly regretting she had.

"You look for my car," June said, with a diminutive smile. Her shirt was buttoned up to the top, her Venus necklace hidden. "I drove in with Daddy today." She brought her hand to her mouth, nibbling at her nails. Rory had never seen her do this before. "I quit smoking," she said. "Horrible habit for a future doctor, right?"

"I guess," Rory said.

"Daddy's out walking the property lines with Robin right now. I got impatient, all the waiting for Bella Danvers to catch up. You'd think she was the invalid."

"She's here?" Rory asked.

"Mm, yeah." She was thinner, her shoulders blunt within her clothes, her elbows sharper. "I heard you were really helpful with Carlotta the other day. That you stayed with her."

"I guess," Rory said.

"Well, she's been moved to hospice, so I guess it wasn't so helpful, was it?" She was making a joke, Rory sensed that, but even June was unamused. "She had a kidney infection. And her hip was broken."

"I heard," Rory said.

"Those are not easy things for an already sick woman to heal from. Sonja should've been paying more attention. She's out of a job now."

"She was there every day," Rory said. "What was she supposed to do?"

"Sonja?" June said, glib. "That's who you're worried about? Gus is out of a job, too, you know." Her nails were chewed to the quick.

"Gus? What are you talking about?"

"He broke Wade's nose. Daddy had to reset it, says he can't ride for a month."

"Wade's home?"

June nodded. "Gus hasn't called you?"

Rory got up, looking for her list. Robin always left it—a little piece of notebook paper—tossed in the Silver Cup trophy on the corner of the desk. With school back in session, she'd only been giving Rory three or four horses a day, always Mrs. Keating's geldings, at least. Those horses needed the hills, they needed to run.

"Jesus," June said. "You don't know about Chap either, do you?"

Rory looked at June. "What about Chap?"

"It wasn't so bad. It could've been worse, I guess. She went after Cosmo and he spun on her. Same way he did to Journey. A cut over her eye though. She got stitches."

There was a catch in Rory's throat, the snag of a knot. She should have gone. She'd caused this. She had been so selfish to stay.

Outside, a rush of wind sent the cypress trees along the front ring swaying, nearly bowing. One of Mrs. Keating's geldings—someone had already gotten him out—went spinning, bucking with excitement, across the turnout corral.

"Bella's taking power of attorney," Rory said.

"How'd you know?" June said.

"That's why your dad's out there with her. Walking the property lines of the ranch." There it all was, like a turn in the road coming at her all too fast. "He's going to buy Leaning Rock, isn't he? Because Gus laid into Wade?"

A bead of blood had sprung up at the edge of June's cuticle and she stopped to look at it before sucking it away. "Actually, you're close. But that's not why Daddy is buying the place. It was after Fresno, Daddy told Robin that he'd be interested, that he recognized the investment, the potential of this place. You know the barn in Fernwood has Shannen Doherty boarding her horse there? Well, Robin talked to Bella. And Bella talked to Sonja, just asking her questions. It's been a long time since Carlotta was right in the head."

In the dream that Rory had been having there was always a moment when she was looking at herself in the dark reflection of the glass, her hair wildly undone, and in the soft flesh of her clavicle she would feel a slipping sensation, the meaning of which now seemed so obvious: It was everything that held her together coming undone. She brought her hand to her throat, feeling that blithe tug—as easy as a shoelace drawn clear from its hole. The Santa Anas, they say, can make you feel as if you've been skinned, every inch of you a raw nerve ending. Gus, she thought. Wade. Vivian. Her mare. The edges of her vision were pricked with light.

"Rory?" June asked. "Are you going to faint?"

June had her hand on Rory's knee. She'd sat her down on the couch and now she was crouching in front of her.

"Are you okay? Should I get someone?"

"No," Rory said.

"I'm sorry," June said. Her familiar smells: the White Musk, the weed. "I'm sorry I was the one to tell you. Shit—" She was looking out the window.

Robin and Preston Fisk were outside now, looking at Mrs. Keating's gelding in the turnout. Preston had his suit jacket hanging from one finger, his shirtsleeves rolled up beyond his melon-size forearms, his foot up on the railing as if posing for an ad. A disgusting display of health and grooming. Robin pointed toward Leaning Rock, then turned to the hillside behind the office, beyond Sonja and Jorge's house. A fresh dust cloud whirled, and they shielded themselves.

Another woman was coming up the driveway in a sleeveless blouse and an ill-fitted skirt that was blustering about her legs, her arms thick and soft as custard. Bella Danvers. A watercolor version of Carlotta, in wide, washed-out strokes. Her hair was gray and unkempt, the look of someone assigned to worry over things that might never happen.

And then all three of them were coming into the office and June was up and bouncing on the heels of her boots. "Well, Daddy? What did you think?"

Rory stood. Preston's mouth was the same crude shape as Wade's, and Rory knew, feeling his aloofness, his icy formality, that he hadn't bothered to touch the horses.

"Rory," Robin said, sidetracked by her being there.

"I came for my list," Rory said.

Bella came in and sat, disappearing into a corner of the old leather couch.

"Bella," June said, "this is Rory. My friend that waited with your mother." Her voice an upticked question, though there wasn't one.

271

My friend. Rory looked at Preston. He was rearranging himself to accommodate June's proximity, looking everywhere but at her.

Bella lifted her hand from her lap in a motion that registered more annoyance than thanks. Of course she wasn't grateful. Gus had always said she would sell the ranch off as soon as she inherited it.

"We'll have to redo the office, won't we?" Preston had his eyes on the ceiling fan. "Maybe tear it all down."

"Be my guest," Bella grumbled.

"Rory, I'm sorry," Robin said. "We actually have some paperwork ahead of us here, if you don't mind?"

She was being excused. "But—is there a list for me?"

"Well, no," Robin said. "I guess—not today. But there's plenty of tack to clean."

"Awful," Bella Danvers said. "This wind."

THE MARE WAS back at Joy's. Gus wasn't sure when she'd returned. That morning or maybe the morning before. Who fucking knew anymore?

From where he was lying on the couch, he could see her in the pasture. The bandage over her eye was gone. He remembered Joy saying something about her having been hard to load. He saw Adler's men coming at her with a whip, finding a new use for their hobbling straps.

He smelled coffee and when he rolled over, Joy was setting a mug down on the table. "It's three o'clock," she said. "You're going to get up and help me feed."

She gave him a look, then went back to the kitchen, talking over her shoulder. She'd been doing this all week, talking, almost constantly, and he hadn't heard a word. Like the river over rocks, a near-persistent gurgling.

"I gave her supplements again and the vet is coming to check her sutures day after tomorrow. Mighty generous of him," Joy said. There was real water running. In the sink, he realized. She shut it off. "Stay another week and we could check her here, Gus."

"I'm not staying," he said. Another week? It was sixteen days from cover to ultrasound before you could know. He'd been sleeping too much. "And you shouldn't be wasting supplements. Won't be a foal."

"You don't know that," Joy said.

"Season's wrong. You said it yourself." He'd daydreamed up this scenario where back in the canyon, everybody was standing outside her stall, the vet inside with her would turn to Gus so he could be the one who broke the news, who saw their faces, the cheers going up. He'd pictured cheering. His hand was shaking; his knuckles still smarted. If he could change anything, he'd only change the fact that no one had hit him back. "This is just coffee," he said. No whiskey yet. This was the twinge behind his eyes. He hadn't had a drink.

"Nope," Joy said. "And you're not going to. Not today, sir."

He'd said all of that out loud. Christ.

A memory of the previous night: He'd been talking about Mona, talking, and trying to chew a sandwich at the same time. Or maybe he'd been crying, a mouth full of phlegm. His face was still puffy.

"He should've hit me back!"

"Agreed," Joy said. "But he didn't, so now you're the fool."

He'd told Joy about Hawkeye. He remembered that now. And

he'd told her he'd stay sober today. He'd fallen into a hole, and holes were dark and narrow and hard to crawl out of; some backsliding was understandable, maybe even impossible to avoid.

Joy dropped a dish, cursing as it hit and shattered in the sink.

"You a' right?" Gus asked.

"Yeah," Joy said, looking at her palm. "I'm fine."

She grabbed a rag and wrapped it around her hand.

"Mare looks better," he said, feeling generous, like this balanced out her hand, maybe.

Joy went to a kitchen chair and sat down backward, propping her arm on the back rail. He felt her fixing to talk to him, that she had something to say and she was going to be right, whatever it was. A way to move on with his life, advice on how to be a better man. She was a lonely, two-bit horse breeder, making three bills per foal—four if she got a sucker—and now she was gonna tell him how to run his life and she was gonna be right.

"I got cancer, Gus."

He put the mug of coffee down. It was as if a rat had run right across the floor, sending his thoughts scuttling after it.

"Ain't you gonna say nothing?"

"That would be the same as not talking, so—"

"Asshole," Joy said, standing back up. "I got a year. That's what they tell me."

"Doctors out here don't know shit," Gus said, feeling sure about this.

"I went into Cheyenne, Gus. I got a year, I told you. Maybe two, with the drugs." She unwrapped her hand and tossed the rag into the kitchen, just missing the counter. "It's in my ovaries. Never used the damn things and they got mad, I guess. Spread it around to the rest of me. They say that's what has me feeling so tired now. That I gotta start living like I mean to live. No more chew. Eatin' right. I hate eatin' right."

"What do you want me to do about it?"

She looked at him with an ache in her eyes. Jesus fuck. "Don't do that, Joy. I just, I didn't mean it like that."

"I wanted you to know. That's all. I'm not asking you to stay. I've been doing this on my own plenty long. It's just that—"

"What?" She'd saved him. That was the truth of it. When they were kids. She used to get in between him and their father, hurry him into her closet, and then act like he wasn't there when their old man came in asking, *Where is that little sissy?* He'd watch her, from behind the slatted doors, how she stared their father down. She was a killer in a dress, playing with dolls on the floor, and he could see Dad registering that she was bigger than him. Lionhearted. And now she was fucking dying.

"Do you want me here?" He watched her pull a tin of tobacco from her pocket and thwack it against her palm. "Do you want me to stay?"

"Nah," she said, pinching chew into her lip, pushing it down with her tongue. "I'm just telling you because we both have to quit our bullshit. Quit swinging at people, Gus. You don't have to turn into Dad, you know."

"I already did."

"I don't see it like that," Joy said. "Way I see it is we all got a cancer of some kind. Some are easier to curb than others, some of us get choices. Which feelings, which memories we want to feed. You got choices, Gus, and you get to make 'em every damn day."

"I'M LEAVING," SONJA said. They were hurtling down the hill. Rory couldn't read her face; the interior of the van was so dark, and the windows tinted.

Rory had gone up to the house looking for Tomás, hoping he would drive her home and tell her everything that happened in Colorado, but Sonja had answered and picked up her keys.

"I *have* to leave," Sonja repeated.

"*Have* to leave?" Were the Fisks taking the house from her? Already?

"Jorge's lawyer—he said la migra are looking into my status."

"Immigration?"

"They could come tomorrow. A month from now. I can't know."

"Where are you going to go?"

Sonja sighed. "I can't tell you that."

"You don't know?" No, she knew. Rory saw this on her face, a steeling around her mouth. "You think they'll get it out of me?" Rory asked.

Sonja smiled. "No, but you might tell Tomás."

"He isn't going with you?"

"He is a grown boy." Sonja's eyes fell. "And a citizen."

"Did Bella give you money?" Rory wanted to know this. Bella had asked Sonja questions, that's what June had said. And the fact of the paperwork there the night Carlotta fell . . .

"Don't look at me like that, Rory. I've bathed that woman for three years. I cleaned her sheets after she was sick. I dyed her hair and cut her nails. I bleached her pinche shoes. They had to be white. Blanco, blanco, blanco, she was always yelling at me. Bella didn't *give me* money . . ." There was knowing in Sonja's voice. "But I know Mrs. Danvers gave you a few things, didn't she?"

Rory looked at her hands. Of course, Sonja knew. Two pairs of gloves, a set of spurs, the whip, the sport watch. There might have been more. Rory couldn't remember. The world outside was a yellow pall of smog and dust.

"It's okay," Sonja said.

They'd passed two new signs, handmade with black paint on neon yellow poster board, both of them flapping in the wind, their demand, SLOW DOWN.

"Gus," Rory said, realizing. "He's not coming back, is he?"

"Rory, you don't know that. Don't talk like that. He loves you."

"You love Tomás."

Sonja gave her a look, like she'd underestimated an opponent.

"I told you, he's grown," Sonja said. "He has an opportunity here. The Fisks need him."

Rory thought of Sarah Price, of that term, *walkaway mother*.

"What did you say to Vivian?"

They were driving past the drag mark along the wall, past the gates, where a new rash of flowers had been left outside, their petals plucked away by the wind.

Sonja fanned her fingers on the wheel. "I asked her not to hurt you. I told her—"

"You said what?"

"I told her you were good people, Rory. You are. You're young, but you'll know soon—that girl can't take care of you. She's not your friend. I don't know how you got so mixed up in all of this, Rory, but I know you can't give that girl what she needs."

"You're wrong."

Sonja stopped at the stop sign. There were no cars behind and no cars coming up the main road, but Sonja wasn't going. She was looking at Rory. The same deep-set eyes as Tomás, the same high cheekbones and sallow cheeks. Then she closed her eyes as if trying to locate a pain in her body, willing it to pass. "Tomás had a brother, too."

"Tomás?"

Sonja nodded. "Enrique. He died before Tomás was born."

"They never met," Rory said stupidly. "Does Tomás know?"

Sonja shook her head. "I am telling you because I know what it's like to lose a son. And to believe that it is your fault. It makes you want to run away from everything."

"Vivian told you about her mother," Rory said, saying it as quickly as she'd understood it.

"Yes," Sonja said. "She knew that her mother had written to Jorge. She wanted to know what she said, if she had written to him again." Sonja shook her head. "Sarah Price thinks she loves wrong and now her daughter will take any love at all."

"You think I am any love?"

"I think she does not know the difference."

Behind them someone leaned on an old shrill horn. Sonja turned onto the main road.

The streetlights snapped on, orbs of light on the dusk gray turns, flashing in the car as they drove on, one after another. "What happened to him? Enrique? How old was he?"

"¿Quieres saber?"

Rory nodded. There was the soft pluck of an insect striking the windshield.

"Okay," Sonja said. "I will tell you. Maybe one day you'll tell Tomás."

"He doesn't know?"

"In his bones, sí. But not from me. I've never even said Enrique's name."

"Why not?" Rory asked.

"Because you want your children to feel proud." Sonja cracked her window ever so slightly, as if ensuring she would be able to breathe, and air whistled in, dry as ash. "I waited until Enrique was ten, until I had the money for the coyote, and I thought Enrique was strong enough to cross. We had family and friends who had made it before us, so I trusted we would be okay. I had heard the bad stories, too, but they weren't as bad as not going. But Enrique walked twice as far as I did. Getting ahead, coming back to me. I told him to stop, take it easy. Eventually he did."

"Where was the coyote?"

Sonja snorted. "He got us across, eleven of us, said we would sleep and then go on, but when we woke, he was gone. There was a family with younger girls—they could carry them so they didn't get so tired." She paused. "Maybe I waited too long. First, we ran out of food. When Enrique got this look in his eyes, I tried to pick him up. A hundred pounds of him." Sonja wiped at her face. "Then we ran out of water. The others were gone by then. It was only us, and I had to carry him across my shoulders. My feet bled. My nose bled. Six miles. Seven miles. He weighed so much. And then I saw the lights. It was a whole city of lights. I had to run. I had to get

279

the help he needed as fast as I could, so I put him down." Sonja had pulled the van over. The same dirt shoulder where Vivian met Rory before her bus.

"It wasn't a city, was it?"

Sonja leaned her head back on the seat. "It was one bulb—splitting up—" She danced her fingers in the air. "One pinche bulb outside of a barn, but the doors of the barn were open and inside were pigs. Rooting pigs, everywhere. Last thing I remember was a chicken flying up, fat and squawking, and then—no light."

"You passed out," Rory said, understanding.

"I don't forgive myself. I want to believe he was already gone. That he died while I was carrying him. I felt him get heavy, like grain. But then the farmer came. It was the sun that woke me, not him. I heard him throwing buckets of corn down. And then he was standing over me. He was an old man. I called him viejito, meaning to be kind. Viejito, please, I said. I had some English to use, but he didn't like my *please*. He was old like gringos go, face like a ratty bag. He didn't smile. And then he—" Sonja made a motion with her hands and swallowed, her head nodding. "He—"

"I understand," Rory said.

"I tried to scratch his face and kick, like I was told. I had been warned. But I had not eaten or had water for days. And those pigs everywhere. Snorting. A man ever does that to you—" Sonja lowered her head and Rory saw the anger crawling under her skin. "When he finished, he said, 'I could have used good help. Not a woman. If you'd had a muchacho with you,' he said and I remembered Enrique." Sonja's voice caught. "I shot up and started running, but I was hurting, and I fell. He dragged me back in the barn. I told him where I had left Enrique, as best I could, and he took off on his tractor. It felt like an entire day he was gone. I drank from the pig water and I picked through their slop. I wanted strength. When he came back without Enrique, he said that the animals had already gotten to him."

"That man," Rory said, afraid, but knowing.

"I lost my son," Sonja said. "But, then, Tomás. I was given Tomás."

Rory thought of Tomás's long legs, his thick-knuckled hands. How when Jorge had him laughing, Tomás would smack his own knee, saying, "Papi," his eyes tearing up.

"Tell me where you're going?" Rory asked again. "Give Tomás the choice?"

"Lo siento, Rory. Sometimes we can only take care of ourselves."

IT TOOK CALLING five times in a row before he answered, and when he did Vivian could hear that he was on the other side of laughing, the lingering champagne in his voice.

"Everett Price here."

"Daddy?"

"Vivi, how are you, baby?"

"I want to come see you, for a visit. I thought maybe this weekend, for the holiday. Halloween? Día de los Muertos. We could dress up, you know, celebrate." Turn all this upside down, on its head (acceptance, that was the final stage).

Silence.

She wanted to believe it was a long-distance delay, but she could hear, in the background, the titter of a small group of people, a gathering in his trailer that she could picture all too well: There was the young makeup artist with a side ponytail, smacking her fruit-flavored gum; the male costar, taking mental notes on how Everett held the room; a cutely nervous PA who'd come with more Evian but had been told to sit, stay, relax.

"Oh, well, Vivi . . ." Everett said, his voice trailing off.

"I'll arrange all of it, Daddy. You don't have to do anything. I'll—"

"Production is really ramping up here. How about you have Carmen come on the weekends, too? And here I thought you must be loving having the place to yourself."

"I'm not, Daddy. Not at all. It's miserable here."

Fires had sprung up in Ojai and Altadena, and the sky was choked with the residual heat and smog that the Santa Anas had swept from the valley into the mountains.

"How about you throw a party? I won't tell if you don't." She could hear him winking at the minions, their nods of approval (the coolest dad in town!). "I'll have Bobby help with a guest list."

"I don't want a party. I want to know when my mom is coming home."

"Vivian."

"Everett," she said. "Twenty-three down." It was the first cross-word clue she'd ever figured out on her own.

"You're breaking up, sweetheart."

"You don't remember, do you?"

"We don't always have the best connection down here."

"What Ricky says to Lucy, eight spaces, twenty-three down," Vivian said. "You were so proud of me, Daddy. You used to say that to me, Twenty-three down! Twenty-three down!" She was screaming.

"It really is hard to hear you, Viv. Please give my love to your mother. Let her know I'm thinking maybe Italy for Christmas." (This. This was why Mommy had gone crazy.)

The actress shouted, "You *must* go to Naples. Capri is so fabulous."

"Yes, yes, I've been there," Everett said. "I shot *Otto's Fortune* in the castle by—"

"Is this real? Are you really saying these things, Daddy? Give your love to Mommy? Naples? Can you be real?"

There was a hum on the line. Vivian held the phone away, looking at the little holes in the ear- and mouthpieces.

"Everett," Vivian said. "I want you to listen very carefully. You have one week to either come home or find Mommy, otherwise I'm calling the press and I will tell them that Mommy has been missing for a month. And that you've kept it secret because you're embarrassed. Embarrassed she's unwell or that you don't know how to help. Whatever it is, I might even skip the usual rags and go straight to the *L.A. Times*. No, *The Hollywood Reporter*!"

"Vivian. Stop it. Stop this now." He had no trouble hearing her suddenly. (Int. Studio Trailer: all eyes trained on the Actor) "I'll talk to Bobby. I'll see what he says. I'll get back to you."

"You do that."

"Twenty-three down, Vivi. I hadn't forgotten. And I *am* still proud of you."

"We'll see," she said, hanging up. Maybe too abruptly (but the scene seemed to call for it).

She pulled a Zima from the fridge. How did one go about tipping off the press? *This is Vivian Price, and I'd like you to do a story on my family?* Oh, how the tables had turned in the last three months. The glass in the sliding door had finally been replaced.

When the phone started ringing, she assumed it was Everett calling back (lemmings ushered off).

"Vivian Price," she answered. "Have I got a story for you."

"Do you? I could use a good story." It was Rory. Not Everett, not Cousin Everett, not Daddy at all. "I have an idea," Rory said. "Somewhere I want to go with you."

And Vivian felt the armor she'd barely pulled back on fall to the floor.

AT THE TOP, Rory tried the door. It was locked. She fished inside the Keds still sitting there; Sonja had kept a spare key in one, but it was gone. "Shit," she said.

"Don't give up so easily," Vivian said. She pulled a Swiss Army knife from her pocket, flicked open the blade, and slipped it between the door and its frame. The lock gave with a click. The wind had died down but its earlier gusting was clear in the strung cotton of the clouds.

"Clearly I called the right person," Rory said.

"I'm the only person," Vivian said, going in first, her eyes moving over everything as if Carlotta's house were a cave, alive with potential wonders. Or threats.

Ordinarily Rory understood Vivian's various moods and how best to respond to them. But now, now her thoughts seemed in some unknowable stratosphere. Still, she had agreed to come. All was not lost, she was here. And this was somewhere they could be, without the intrusion of Wade or June.

June had started swinging by Rory's house uninvited, offering her rides to the barn again. The look on Mona's face turning from irritation to gratitude, glad not to have to take Rory herself. And each time Rory had gotten into the convertible she felt she was betraying Vivian. Though that was ridiculous. Vivian had taken right back up with Wade; Rory knew this.

"Kind of gloomy in here," Vivian said, wandering down the hallway.

Carlotta's house was big Spanish tile floors, then high-pile, maroon carpet in the other rooms, a mix of wood-paneled walls and wallpaper, blown-glass chandeliers. There were carvings made from burls of wood, wrought-iron wind chimes in the shape of galloping horses, and, of course, her trophies. Not gloomy, but luxurious, that was how Rory thought of it.

"So where are all these animals?" Vivian said from the living room.

Rory had told her about finding more of Gus's animals here, in Carlotta's curio cabinet. How Carlotta must have unearthed them from the boxes, arranging them like dolls in a dollhouse.

"Hold on," Rory called down the hall. "I'll show you." She was in the kitchen, rummaging through the cabinets. The refrigerator had been emptied, but the dish cabinets and the pantry were full. Aha, rum. And tequila! Rory slung her camera back around her neck.

There was the sound of curtain rings sliding on their iron railings.

"That's a little better," Vivian said, standing in the light.

Rory felt traces of all the afternoons she'd spent up here, listening to Gus and Carlotta talk horses, gossip about the boarders, Carlotta telling Rory with a wink that this was all between them.

"Do you like either of these?" Rory asked, a bottle in each hand.

"I like everything," Vivian said. "But I'm not drinking alone."

"All right, then." Rory set the bottles on the coffee table, opened both, and took a half swig from the tequila, saying, "That's not so bad."

Vivian eyed her suspiciously. Rory drank again.

"Look at that," Vivian said.

Between the two heavily draped windows was a dark outline on the wall, where a love seat had been, the surrounding wallpaper faded by sun and time.

"There used to be a love seat there," Rory said. "A little sofa," she said, wondering if *love seat* was the right word. Vivian, the Fisks, they had different ways of talking about furniture. "I used to sit there, looking through Carlotta's photo albums."

"Her daughter came and took it," Vivian said, as if she'd seen the moving van herself.

Rory looked around. "That's all she took?"

"Not everything means the same thing to everyone else." She took a pulling swallow off the bottle of rum.

"You still want to see?" Rory asked. "The animals?"

Vivian followed her into the dining room. Rory flicked on the chandelier, and the webbing of light fell onto the table again. Rory drew the curtains open, but only partway—Mona was gone, but just to the market, and this was the room that faced their house.

"Oh," Vivian said, seeing now. "These are incredible," she said. She took out the raccoon with its raised paw and the fur lifted, electric, the air was so dry. "Whoa," Vivian said. "Like it's alive. Feel it, though—it hardly weighs a thing."

"No, that's okay," Rory said. "Actually, I was hoping that I could photograph you? Maybe with them?"

Vivian's expression turned amused. Smug, even. This was a Vivian Rory recognized. "So how do you want me?" Vivian asked.

"Like you're one of them," Rory said. "Another wild thing but trapped inside this house."

"Sure," Vivian said. She set the raccoon on the table and took another long pull on the rum, then hopped up onto the table, too. Click. "Maybe like this?" She turned and lay back on her elbows, knees bent, toes pointed. Posing. Like the photo in the magazine, on the beach with Wade.

Click. "No," Rory said. "Different." Vivian rolled to her stomach, staring the raccoon in the face. Click. She reached into its mouth to clear a cobweb. "Leave that," Rory said. "The web. I like all that imperfect stuff."

"And me?" Vivian asked, cocking her head. "How do you like me?"

"Oh," Rory said. "I have a joint, too." She'd almost forgotten. She pulled it from her bra, and the lighter from her cigarettes, and handed it to Vivian. One small benefit of riding with June again, having a joint to share. She drew the curtains closed, only a crack of light, right down the center of the table. She changed the aperture, adjusting for the dim light.

Vivian was blowing smoke into the raccoon's face. Click.

"I want you to move more. To feel, like, more free?"

They smoked the joint. Vivian drank more. Click. Click. Click.

The love seat wasn't the only piece of furniture missing after all. An end table, a wardrobe, and framed photographs from the walls, the same dark ghosts left behind.

Vivian went around the house tossing the blankets to the floor, sweeping papers off of tabletops, throwing a bowl of potpourri into the air. Rory had to load a new roll of film.

The owl. She brought it into the living room and set it on the floor beside the fireplace. "Come in here," she called to Vivian.

"I feel like you want something very specific from me," Vivian said.

"No," Rory said. "Not really." But what she wanted was for Vivian to be as roving in the frame as she felt to Rory in life. Falling, twisting, all a blur. This was how she seemed to Rory—like fragments, pieces she couldn't hold. The animals, the owl, the raccoon—they were focal points, frozen in time, in death. A suggestion of a feeling, an emptiness. But Rory didn't explain this to Vivian; she couldn't have.

"Should I take these off?" Vivian asked.

Rory nodded and Vivian removed her shorts, leaving her underwear and white T-shirt.

"These are good," Rory said. Click.

She wanted Vivian as vulnerable as she'd been in her kitchen, but she also didn't want to bring any of that up.

Vivian fitted into the largest opening of the curio cabinet—her legs and waist within it, Rory had her begin to crawl across the floor. She stepped toward her and moved her hair in front of her eyes, concealing her face, asking her not to look into the lens.

She asked Vivian to remove her shirt. What about her bra? One, then the other.

They gathered the raccoon, the blue jays, the crow, a ferret, the owl, an acorn-eating chipmunk, and set them on the dining room chairs with stacks of books beneath them, until they were of equal height. Rory arranged the camera on a stool. The tabletop bisected the lower third of the frame. She had Vivian step up onto the table and run across it. It wobbled beneath her. "It's okay," Rory said. "Lighter steps, but just as quick." Her bare torso, her legs; a pale streak across the frame. A girl, fleeing. Not wanting to be the feast.

The wind had shifted, and the smoke from Altadena was blowing west; Rory could smell it.

They set the owl against the wall. A peeling floral wallpaper print. She had Vivian roll herself within the curtains and then twist out of them. The owl was wrong. No more animals. Only Vivian. The curtains center frame and Vivian's unraveling escape. Click. Click.

And then Vivian sat down. An energy had left her. Sometimes a certain quiet happened after their fevered pitch of taking pictures, but this was a new roll, still more frames to shoot.

"I want a cigarette," Vivian said.

Rory had an entire pack. "Here, here," she said.

Vivian was against the wall, hunched where the love seat had been. The dark outlines a parenthesis on each side. A burrow. A flash would make the contrast starker, but Rory didn't have one. She drew the curtain open further. Vivian was talking, but Rory had found a light, a frosted bulb that she adjusted until faint shadows fluttered against the wall and the smoke of Vivian's cigarette was sparkling. Her body was curled and still now, but the flex of her neck over her knees, her breasts against her thighs, her fingers playing at her toes was movement enough. Click. Vivian looked up at Rory then and Rory felt a slight constriction to the air.

"You haven't heard anything I've said, have you?" Vivian's chin was resting on her knee now, her eyes imploring. Click. "Stop," Vivian shouted. "I said, stop." She raised her hand, as if Rory were paparazzi.

"Okay," Rory said. "I stopped. I'm sorry. Are you all right?"

"No," Vivian said. "I'm not all right. I haven't been all right for the last twenty minutes. Or the last three years, if you want to know the truth, but I thought—" She was pulling her T-shirt back on, her shorts, stuffing her bra into her back pocket.

Rory went to the window, realizing Vivian was about to go.

"You're checking to see if your mom is home?" Vivian asked.

"I just didn't want—she's not."

"Oh, good," Vivian said. "Because I wouldn't want to make you suffer any undue stress, Rory Ramos. We wouldn't want to put *you* in an uncomfortable situation." She picked up a blue jay from the table and said, "I was wrong. These are all completely vile."

Gus was in the bedroom, lying on the floor—six whole days sober. As hard-won as a bull ride, sore from toe to skull. No pain pills, no booze, no Prozac. The floor felt right to his back and late afternoon naps were making him better company.

The fires in San Diego, Ojai, Altadena, Chatsworth, and the worst of them in Laguna Beach, had made the local news in Little Snake, of all places. But they were saying the winds were dying down and that all these fires—over a dozen had flared in the last few days—would be contained soon; it was just a matter of time. Gus picked up the phone then, finally calling home, but the line rang and rang. Mona never remembered that you had to turn the machine on.

That morning Joy had woken him early and they'd gone to fish again. She had caught him staring at the reflection of the pines at the edge of the river and she told him that was all the Prozac he needed to take home with him. He knew he had to go home, but he'd lost the urgency. Shame thickened time. Made it hard to move. To make choices, let alone own them. Still, he had to get the mare back to Rory. That was what was right. And right, he was finding, was a thing you could feel in your body, if you got quiet—and sober—enough to listen.

Lying this way, he could see under Joy's bed, the floorboards littered with burls of dust and animal hair. She was downstairs, some country station on the radio, talking to her dogs as sincere as ever. Mona hated dogs, claimed she was allergic, same as with the horses.

He closed his eyes, remembering when—not so long after she and Rory had moved in with him—Mona came home one night with the smallest plastic bag he'd ever seen. "Cocaine," she said. Up on her knees on the edge of their bed, her jean skirt riding up her thighs. "Shall we try it?"

Back then, he had had no suspicions; there'd been no suggestion of duplicity. They were, he believed, in love. She used her magnifying mirror and a dollar bill rolled up, talking as if a friend had shown her what to do. He'd have done anything for her, tried almost anything. Before he even lifted his head up and felt the cool drip down his throat, her clothes had come away. On top of him, he saw her go to a half-exhilarated, half-angry place, while he became anxious, doubting he was pleasing her, overly aware of the contrast of his skin against hers, ten years younger. Afterward, she got up and opened the windows, then lay back down beside him, her skin shiny with sweat. His heart was still racing, a frantic sensation at the end of his fingertips that had him wondering about death. She reached over and touched his face, smiling at him so big, like she'd just won a game of chance, and he'd laughed, exhilarated for the first time that night. Then she said, "You liked it," and he didn't disagree. A lie of omission. They watched a movie, one with Wayne or Eastwood. They'd always agreed on Westerns. She got up once and went to where she'd left the mirror, licking her fingers and rubbing the last of the powder on her gums. By the time the film was over, she was asleep. He gathered her hair and laid it against her back. He wrapped his arm around her and fitted his legs up against hers. How warm she was. "Please," he said, his mouth grazing the china rim of her ear. "Let's never do this again."

The door opened. The room had darkened around him, a cobalt blue. The hallway light had Joy in silhouette and ever so briefly Gus remembered Sarah Price coming into his hospital room. He had left her letter on his dresser at home. Some part of him maybe hoping Mona would find it, that it might make her jealous. He'd been stupid with spite. "You okay, Gussie?"

"What time is it?" He pulled himself up to rest against the bed-frame.

Joy snapped on the bedside light: the room, the floor, the contrast of everything sharpened. "Just six now," she said. "You slept awhile. Still feels better on the floor?"

"Mostly," he said.

"I'm making meat loaf and those instant potatoes," she said, sitting down on the cane rush chair by the bed. "With milk instead of water. Lots of butter. That's the secret." She started to dig for the tin of chew that was no longer in her pocket. "Right," she said. "Keep forgetting." They'd made an agreement, both of them choosing health.

"Did I hear the phone ringing?" he asked, remembering the staccato of it under his dreaming. "Was it Mona?" he asked, rubbing at his knee. "Is everything okay?"

"No, not Mona." Joy's voice went far away. "They left pins in there, didn't they?" she asked, looking at his leg.

He reminded himself, she was the sick one, the one who'd been told she had only a year to live. He nodded. "You've got more bad news for me, haven't you?"

She nodded. "It was Rory," she said. "She wants you to call back."

"The fires," Gus said.

"No, not that. It's Carlotta, Gus. She's gone."

"WELL, HELLO, STRANGER."

"It hasn't been that long," Vivian said, dropping her feet into the water. "A week, maybe."

The sky was pink and thick, unmoving, a child's chalky scribbling.

"Actually, it's been three weeks and four days," McLeod said.

"But who's counting?" Vivian said. It was October 28, three days and three months since Charlie had died. And three months exactly before what would have been his second birthday. Lou Reed's "Perfect Day" was playing from the speakers in her room (for irony's sake). She was lying on the patio, feeling sweat pool in her navel. "I'm glad you missed me."

"Did you abandon me just to make sure that I would?"

Vivian could hear Carmen inside, counting the empty beer bottles before carrying them to the trash. She would scold Vivian with her eyes, but she wouldn't say anything. Vivian had worn her down.

"No, McLeod. My mother went missing, actually," Vivian said. "If we want to talk about abandoning. She's gone for a cross-country drive. And I've been alone for nearly a month."

She heard McLeod's lighter drop and rattle against the table before he started to cough. "Oh god, truly?" he said.

"I'm home alone now," she said.

"Where *is* your mother? You can't be serious, Vivian."

"Let's not traffic in the obvious, Mickey. If I knew where she was, I wouldn't be here."

"You'd go find her?"

"If you've a better offer I want to know. I *would* love to see your eyes again, McLeod. I think people need to see one another, to really know what it means—"

"It would be nice to see your eyes." She heard his breath shortening.

"I know it would, McLeod. I know you wouldn't be taking my calls if it weren't for my eyes, right? Or is it the way I used to *forget* to button the top of my blouse. Remember the time I wore those ripped jean shorts—with the little cuts at the top of my thigh."

"Vivian—"

"I know you remember those. I'd finger the little denim strings. I could see you getting hard. That's why you take my calls, isn't it? Why you wanted to help me catch up in school? I always hear the door locking behind you. I'm why you have that stash of cigarettes in your garage. And is that a sodden towel in your hand? Or do you wait until we're off the phone?"

"Vivian, stop—"

"Yes, let's stop pretending that this has anything to do with what you saw in me. I'm not judging you. I just don't want any more lies—no more lies, no more secrets."

"Who has secrets?" Wade was there. Standing over her, his legs in the skintight wrap of his britches, elongated by the wet-looking leather of his riding boots. Like a soldier. "Who's been telling lies here, Vivian?"

"Hey, baby," she said, patting the concrete beside her thighs.

Johnny Naughton was nearby, his Drakkar cologne riding the smoke-thickened air.

"Who *is* that?" Wade jutted his chin toward the phone.

"Nobody," Vivian said, the patter of her heart quickening. "Just my dad."

Wade bent down beside her, his face—that mouth, his nose with its lingering purple. The sky was bruised too, almost mauve. She heard, inside her head, the word *surrender.* "You win," she said.

Wade had the phone against his ear now, asking, "Who is this?" She heard the phone turn over into a dial tone.

"I told you, brah." Naughton's Surf Nazi attempt at English.

Vivian sat up. "You told him what? What exactly have you got to say about me, Trouble?"

"That you're a fucking whore."

RORY TOOK THE cordless upstairs, hoping Gus would call back before Mona turned the blow dryer off, but she was already stomping around the way she did when she was late, that angry energy, her belief that the house was playing tricks on her, hiding her keys.

When it finally rang, Rory answered, "Gus."

"Hi, there, Rory."

Mona picked up downstairs. "Oh, you got it, Rag-Tag? Sure picked up awful fast. Is this *the* boyfriend? Can I introduce myself now?"

"Mom." Rory tried to stop her.

"Mona, it's me—" Gus said.

"Of course."

"How are you?"

"How *am* I? Let's not play nice. You two have your trip down memory lane about the old bat, but Gus Scott, you better hope she left you something good, because otherwise you've got nothing to come home to, you understand?"

"I know it," Gus said. "I've realized that."

"Fuck you. I'm leaving for work."

She missed the base, trying to hang up the phone, and Rory and Gus waited, quiet, listening to the rustle of her handbag, then the clink of her keys, and finally the screen door slamming shut.

"The spring's all gone," Rory said, about the door. "Broke right off."

"Plenty of things that I shoulda fixed around there," he said. "About your mom, Rory—"

"I don't want to talk about that right now."

"I understand."

"You saw the news?" Earlier, Rory had seen Vivian lying by the pool, but now she was gone.

"Yeah," Gus said. "But they said the winds are dying down?"

"Seems like it," Rory said. "Is Chap okay? I should've gone with you."

"She's fine. The stitches are coming out tomorrow."

"And then you'll bring her home? You can come back for the funeral, can't you?"

"When is it?"

"Monday. Day after Halloween."

"I suppose that's fitting," Gus said. Carlotta used to put on a Halloween horse show for the barn's youngest riders, letting them dress up school horses and giving out prizes for best costume, scariest, funniest. A tradition Gus had failed to maintain.

"Can you be back by then?"

"That's soon—"

"But if you left tomorrow?"

"Yeah," Gus said, and Rory saw him taking off his hat and running his hand through his hair like he always did. "Rory, there's something I need to tell you."

She waited. She didn't want any confessions, not about his drinking, or his having hit Mona, certainly not about hitting Wade.

"The night before I left, I went to your room to talk to you. I'm telling you this, Rory, because I want to be better—however you need me to be. Honesty, for starters. So, I want you to know that I saw you."

"From my window," Rory said.

"With the daughter, yes."

"Vivian," Rory said. "Does Wade know?" A sudden clutching at her heart. "Tell me you didn't say anything to him."

"I wouldn't tell that kid my middle name, Rory."

The trees outside began to shift, knocking against the house.

"I didn't mean for it to happen." Rory wasn't sure how to explain, but she started, "But her dad was leaving and her mom, Sarah, she just took—"

Gus interrupted. "I know," he said. "She wrote me a letter—"

"Sarah Price? She wrote you? From where? You have to tell me."

"She was in Nebraska, but she said something about Illinois, too. I didn't believe it completely. Not at first. I left it there, the letter—"

"Where?" Rory was running down the stairs.

"In the bedroom, on the dresser. Just on the top there, I think."

Rory was riffling through belt buckles, loose business cards, receipts, random keys, and pins. There. It wasn't in an envelope. It was folded over three times, so creased and worn it looked like a treasured note from a grade school friend. "When did she send it? September third—"

"She hasn't come home, then?" Gus asked.

"No," Rory said, drifting into the living room, looking at the high, pointed slant of Sarah's writing. Like rushing waves.

Mona had left the television on: *Eye to Eye with Connie Chung*. They were covering the fires, talking about the devil winds, that one hundred thousand acres had burned, how you could see embers in the air all the way from Malibu. Rory looked out the window. It was pitch-dark now.

"Vivian—" Rory was hearing, for the first time, entire days later, what it was that Vivian had been saying while she was taking her picture in Carlotta's: that she wanted to call journalists, magazines, that she was going to find a way to bring her mother home, because that was what she really needed. More than anything or anyone. That love.

Upstairs, the curtains were luffing back and forth, in and out of the room. Rory stood at the window, remembering Sarah Price on the night of the accident, the way she'd walked out into the yard in her white nightgown, digging in the dirt, not even noticing when Vivian was there. "I have to give this to Vivian."

"I understand," Gus said. "Whatever you need to do. I'm just not sure she wants to be found."

The pool lights came on down below and Rory got quiet, waiting, until she saw Wade. He was leaning against the house outside Vivian's room. The mop of his hair, his stooped shoulders, the length of his legs. How long had he been standing there?

"Honestly, Rory. I thought you would hate me by now," Gus was saying. "You have every right to hate me."

Wade stepped toward the pool, and it was clear he was looking up at her, that he saw her there in the window.

"I can't hate you," Rory said. "You're who I've got."

LITTLE SNAKE, WYOMING

JUNE 12, 2015

"JUNE," I SAID to Vivian on the phone. "Tell me what happened to her."

Vivian's voice was thick with amusement. "Oh, she moved to Malibu. She *married* a doctor. A man." She snorted. "Isn't that something? Did just what her daddy wanted her to do."

"She's still there?" I wasn't sure if I could trust any of what Vivian said.

"Mm. Probably has sets of twins, a mouth full of veneers, and an OxyContin addiction. Don't bother with her, Charlie. She wouldn't even remember how she got home that night."

"She'd know where her brother is, though."

"Maybe." Then she said, "You know, that canyon's set to burn again real soon."

Last summer, the last time Mama oversaw the wean, a bald-faced roan, his coloring split perfectly down the middle of him—one limpid blue eye, one nut brown—went and tried to make a ladder out of the paddock gate, aiming to reach his mare on the other side. He snapped his tibia, the hoof separated from the fetlock, dangly as an earring. I was the one to fetch the rifle, but Mama, having the best aim, took the shot. I remember looking at the white side of that colt's face, thinking that blue eye was as close as I'd seen a horse come to crying. I hated Mama then for thinking she was doing right by any of them.

We were sitting on the front porch when I told Grandad I was going to be leaving for California. I didn't cry, I didn't show him my limpid blue eye, but I felt as divided as that colt's markings.

"Of course you'll go," he said. Almost a demand. "But, Charlie, don't expect it to solve anything. There won't be any signs of that fire there now." I already know this. "No great swaths of ore-black earth or darkened, shriveled trees. No evidence left. What Vivian and I can't answer for you, that place surely won't. Those mountains, that land, it's supposed to burn." He took his hat off and looked out at our herd picking their way through the wheatgrass, the foals still moving in lockstep, thin-legged shadows of their mares. "But it's calling you," he said. "I understand that."

The washboard song of the crickets was rising from the grass around us.

"I'll miss your voice, Charlie," Grandad said. "I'll miss you while you're gone."

This softening between us, it makes it that much harder for me to go.

Mrs. Traden has agreed to come and stay in the downstairs

bedroom. She'll cook for him and walk with him to check on the foals. The Craces are sending their sons to help with feedings. And I will come back, I promised him that.

We have five foals right now: two bay colts, one blue roan, and a chestnut filly with the same milk-white star as Chaparral.

"That star," Grandad said, "has shown up in every foal from her line."

More dominant than Cosmo's genes, I think.

"You know the foal, the first one Chap ever threw," he said, reading my thoughts. "Your mother refused to have her registered. I had Adler's approval and everything."

"She was punishing you?"

"No," Grandad said, shaking his head. "Well, maybe some. But she said she wanted that foal to prove itself, like Chap had done. Your mama broke that filly herself. We didn't sell her until she was five years old and running fences clean. An event horse, just like I'd planned. But for a hell of a lot less money than if she'd had papers with Cosmo Waltz's name."

When I was born, Mama gave me the surname of Scott. It wasn't until I learned that Joy's cancer was a hereditary type that any of them told me we weren't blood, that we were family of a different kind. Charlie Scott. That's who I've always been.

"But did she win?" I asked Grandad.

"Of course she did."

I loaded the broodmares and drove them through Savery and up Cherry Grove to the Craces's farm, leaving the foals behind.

Tonight they are screaming, screaming from their bellies out, and refusing any feed. But tomorrow it'll be only half as bad, and by the end of the third day their minds will have spiraled out and spun clean, willing to take grain from a human hand. I've moved them into the main barn, where the walls are solid wood and their stick legs stand a chance.

From upstairs, I have a view into the breezeway of the barn. The moon's so big and high it's casting shadows and I can see our collie, Lulu, drawn large against the walking path. She is tender-footing her way toward the foals, pressing her nose to the cracks between the stalls, as if to reassure them that they are not alone.

Every animal, Mama used to tell me, *knows the sound of another animal's suffering.*

I thought I had gone through everything there was to be gone through in Mama's keepsake box—the photos, the negatives, the newspaper and magazine clippings, the thin strap of a handmade necklace, the few, brief journal entries—but when I went to put the lid back on there was an envelope taped to its underside, and it was addressed to me. *Charlie,* in Mama's handwriting, followed by a long dark dash of her pen, a blank space, but also a kind of dividing line.

TOPANGA CANYON, CALIFORNIA

NOVEMBER 1, 1993

"FOSTER?" RORY ASKED. She was in the darkroom and had heard the door opening behind the blackout curtains.

"How did you get in here, Rory?" It was Foster.

She'd jimmied the lock first thing that morning, sliding a kitchen knife between the frame and the door, the way Vivian had done, but she wasn't about to admit this to him. She'd been working since the first bell, developing what she'd shot at Carlotta's house. She looked at the clock: It was third period now. She was supposed to be in Biology. "It was open," she lied. "And I had a free period, I mean, study hall. I have to leave early today actually."

"I see," Foster said, skeptical. "Well, show me what you've got, since you're here."

The Santa Anas had blown themselves out, leaving behind a dry, pressurized heat. The Sunday evening news, which Rory had watched sitting on the floor, with Mona and Hawkeye eating fried chicken on the couch behind her, had reported all the fires contained, then showed the smoldering remains of homes. They interviewed the parents of trick-or-treaters, each of them saying some variation of how they just wanted to give their kids a normal night, but their eyes were itchy, the air still sooty. One of the kids looked up and said the candy tasted funny. "That's the saddest thing I ever heard," Hawkeye had said.

Rory had printed almost everything she wanted to give to Vivian. She was going to find a way to get these pictures and Sarah's letter to her. She followed Foster into the camera room, where they could look through her prints in real light.

Vivian running across the table. Uncurling from the curio cabinet. Crawling across the floor. Unraveling from the curtains. She had even printed the images of Vivian up against the darkened shadow on the wall, but she meant to keep those for herself. The picture of Tomás, the one he'd wanted for Jorge, she was going to bring to Carlotta's funeral that afternoon, give it to him then.

"Were your negatives flat?" Foster asked.

"Oh, I wanted that. I overprocessed a few seconds because I wanted them a little gray. I wanted the motion to not be so separated from the space, from the background, but the shadows stronger at the same time—and I wanted this grain—like a newspaper clipping."

He kept leafing back and forth between the prints. "I see," he said, his forehead lifting. "These are that girl again, then? The same friend?"

Rory nodded.

"There's something different about her. And the animals—"

"Are they bad?" Rory asked, deflating.

"No, no." He looked up, but not at her, toward the ceiling. His ruminating face. "These are different," he said, looking down again. "Would you mind, Rory, if I showed them to a friend of mine?"

"Yes," Rory blurted. "I would. I mean—I would mind."

"What if I told you the friend is a photo editor? She works with a few different magazines, mostly art magazines, and I think she'd be—"

"No," Rory said. "I can't. I haven't even shown these to Vivian. I mean, an editor, really?"

"Yes," Foster said, smiling. "Would it make you feel better to show them to this Vivian first? Let her see what you've done? They're quite evocative. You have a viewpoint, Rory. Show her the prints, all of these. But leave your negatives behind—every photographer has to learn that lesson."

"But you'll wait?" Rory asked. "Before you show your friend?" Beneath the panic, there was elation: *an editor, a magazine.*

"Of course," Foster said. "I'll wait. But you need to understand that these photographs"—he put his hand on her shoulder—"they have the potential to change your life."

June pulled in with the top up, her windows rolled down, and Red Hot Chili Peppers blaring from the stereo. "Johnny finally fixed it," she said. "And whaddya think of these?" She wanted Rory to admire her new, bigger, blacker sunglasses. "Daddy said I look like Hepburn in *Breakfast at Tiffany's.*" She slid the glasses down her nose. "And look what you've got on?"

Rory had borrowed a dress from Mona, a thinning black rayon

wrap dress, because it seemed like what she was supposed to wear. Carlotta had wanted everyone to gather at the ranch, for there to be food served, music played, and stories told, but Bella wouldn't hear of it, and now Carlotta was getting a church funeral. Rory hadn't worn a dress since she was a little girl—a fact that Mona pointed out as reason why it was hopeless to make it look right—and now, as Rory got into the Mercedes, wrestling the skirt from a sudden hot updraft, she said, "I don't know. It was probably a mistake."

"No, you look great," June said, turning the music down. "It's hers, I take it?"

They looked toward the window where Mona stood, a cigarette held to her lips. "Yeah," Rory said. "The bag, too." It was an old black handbag Mona never used. Rory only had the photo for Tomás inside, no camera or lenses. What Rory really wished she'd taken was a pack of Mona's Lucky Strikes, though this wasn't the time to go driving around with a lit cigarette. Red flag warnings had been posted all over the canyon.

As they dropped into the valley, June said, "What a lovely day for a funeral." In the distance, the sky was smudged with the dark specters of the suppressed fires. "You heard about River Phoenix?" June asked.

Rory nodded. He'd died outside the Viper Room on Sunset Boulevard the night before. "A drug overdose?" Rory said.

"It's like we're living through the apocalypse."

After they'd circled the block a few times, a space opened up right in front of the church. Neither of them was in a hurry to get out.

The church was on a block of apartment buildings, all stucco and lath and muted pastels. Halloween decorations still hung on doors and railings, oddly somber in daylight. The church had a surprisingly large lawn and tables had been set up there—trying to fulfill some part of Carlotta's wishes. The wind was raspy, starting and stopping with the sudden force of a coughing fit, and the tablecloths lifted and dropped, a folding chair falling over. Only Robin was sitting there with Mrs. Keating, and her newest husband, Harold, all leaning over clasped hands, deep in discussion.

"Is that the Leaning Rock crest?" Rory asked, looking at the stitching on the hems of the tablecloths.

"Something Wade saw at Adler's ranch," June said. "My mother had them made."

"Is she coming today?" Rory asked.

"Recovering from the stomach flu. A.k.a. a tummy tuck."

Wade and Preston were walking up the sidewalk in matching gray suits, their hands thrust in their pockets, each of them with that elongated stride that suggested the motion of their legs was what kept the world spinning. Wade was no longer wearing the bandage on his nose, sporting his bruises like a badge. People greeted him and Preston with vigorous handshakes, consoling claps on the back, clearly confused as to who was bereaved and who was benefiting from Carlotta's death. Mrs. Keating and her husband had gotten up from the table and were squeezing between people, toward Preston. "She doesn't want Daddy buying the place," June said, watching out Rory's window with her.

"Really?" Rory asked. She hadn't known there was any opposition beyond her own. Mrs. Keating was in her fifties, overly tan, but muscled and fit as a teenager. She'd always struck Rory as reserved and prissy, because of the cut of her clothes and the fact that she never tried to make conversation, despite Rory's riding her two horses regularly. Gus had said she was old money, that she kept horses longer than she kept husbands, but there was Harold, by her side, animatedly nodding along to whatever she was saying. Preston Fisk grew taller, as if to escape her through better posture. "What do you think they're talking about?" Rory asked, but June was looking up the street.

"Wow," she said, "I didn't believe him. I thought she'd had enough of funerals by now."

It was Vivian. She was walking with Johnny Naughton. Johnny had tucked a black T-shirt into a pair of blue jeans. Vivian's outfit seemed more appropriate for a school dance: a white dress dotted with yellow flowers, Converse high-tops, and a gray sweatshirt, three sizes too big, her face concealed inside its hood. "Who is it?" Rory asked.

"Oh, come on," June said. "Don't play dumb. It's Vivian."

Rory looked at Mona's ratty old handbag, wishing she had brought the letter.

The wind lifted and outside the church, people clapped their hands to their hats. Vivian and Johnny crossed the street.

"Should we go in?" Rory asked.

"You want to meet her, don't you?" June said.

"No, it's not that . . ." Rory started. "I want to see Tomás."

There was some commotion near the door, people stepping aside: Bella Danvers had arrived, pushing her brother, Will, in his wheelchair. Wade coasted over and took the handles from her, playing hero, steering him inside the side door of the church.

"Tomás isn't coming," June said. "You heard what happened? With Sonja? She took off in the middle of the night. None of them are coming, too spooked about INS. I don't suppose you know where she went, do you?" June said, peering over the frame of her glasses.

Rory shook her head. June was wearing a different necklace: a chain connected by a horse's snaffle bit.

"Daddy gave it to me," June said, seeing Rory noticing. "It's from Tiffany's." She fiddled with the charm. "Well, it's good Gus isn't here, right?" The main doors to the church had yet to be opened. "I mean, it's good you're here on your own. Get a fresh start."

"With who?" Rory asked.

June shrugged. "Well, Daddy, for one."

"I'm here for Carlotta," Rory said. "That's all."

"Don't be crabby. I miss her, too." At this June opened her door. She had on black tapered pants and a spaghetti-strap blouse around which she drew a black shawl as she stepped out of the car. She crossed without waiting for Rory, waving to Ema, who'd just arrived.

The barn brats, the housewives, everyone whose horses Rory rode regularly, gave her half frowns and tight waves that seemed less on account of Carlotta and more about the fact that Gus was out of a job.

June and Ema were laughing. And Vivian, Rory saw, in some cruel twist, had been drawn in under the arm of Preston Fisk. She heard him introducing her as Wade's *new* girlfriend, like a newly purchased car. Mrs. Keating was talking to Robin again, Harold checking his watch.

Ema turned to Rory, pity brimming in her eyes. "How *is* Gus?" She was wearing a tailored white linen shirt, teal suspenders on top, her dark hair freshly cut.

"He's fine," Rory said. Wade was coming toward them. "He has impeccable aim."

Ema smiled uncomfortably.

"Well, well, so you two have reunited, eh?" Wade said, only looking at June. "I guess there's no talking sense into either one of you."

"She needed a ride," June said. This wasn't true; June had insisted.

"Well, Spice," Wade said to Rory. "It's been a while. You look different, too. What is this, a costume?"

June swatted him. "She looks fabulous."

A barn brat grabbed June's shoulder and she turned toward her, falling into conversation. Wade angled himself toward Rory. "We need to talk," he said.

"Okay," Rory said, flattening her skirt against her legs. "What now?" He was less threatening here, when he wasn't staring up at her through the darkness.

"It's about Vivian," he said, and his voice snagged into her like a hook. "I think she's been fucking around. And I know you can see, that you look, so I need to know, like—if you've seen anything?"

Rory shook her head. "I haven't."

He sized her up. "Nothing? I don't believe you," he said. "You know I know about your little preoccupation with my girlfriend, Rory. June told me everything." Rory was blushing. "At first I was pissed, but it's cool. I get it. Who wouldn't want to look? She's basically famous—or soon to be, anyway. Look, what if I invite you

312

over? I realize it's not like you know our friends, but if you came tonight—if you recognized—"

"Tonight," Rory repeated.

June turned back toward them. "Would you leave her alone already, Wade. She's my date to this prom."

"Actually I was just inviting Rory to Vivian's tonight."

The church doors opened, and the sonorous chords of the organ started up.

"To *that* party?" June said, clearly annoyed.

"It's a party?" Rory asked.

"Yeah," June said. "Kind of. It was supposed to be a photo shoot. Her dad's agent planned it? Something to do with the movie he's wrapping in Mexico. But Wade here keeps inviting people." June rolled her eyes. "So now it's a party."

People were passing them, filing into the church. Rory saw Vivian, Johnny's hand steering her inside, like she was his pet.

"So, you'll come," Wade said. "Maybe there'll be a familiar face." He winked at Rory. "You'll point him out."

SOMEWHERE JUST INSIDE the Colorado border, Gus was pulled over for rolling through a stop sign. License and registration. The truck wasn't his and the woman on the registration was actually dead, but that was where he was heading—back to California, returning the truck and the horse in the trailer to their proper owners.

"You got a lot on your mind, don't you, mister?" the officer said, letting Gus go with only a warning. Dumb luck had been following him, offering up small mercies that he was only beginning to recognize.

He could've left a day earlier or driven eighteen hours straight, and been back in time for the funeral, showing up as disheveled and remorseful as he felt, but the road was proving grueling on his leg. He kept pulling over and getting out to stretch, checking on Chap. Finally, he pulled in for the night, just outside of Vegas, bringing Chap to the only overnight barn he'd found with a free stall.

When the barn watchman started talking to Gus about the fires in California, how they'd probably been started by gangs, Gus tried to explain about land management and old-growth vegetation, but the watchman just scrunched his nose. "You one of them from the Sierra Club?"

In the motel, Gus spread the comforter onto the floor and watched the light of the television sputtering on the ceiling, the voices of newscasters interviewing evacuees, one of them saying the money that went to AIDS victims should've gone to fire prevention. Twenty-four fires in the course of three days, and arson was the rallying cry around all of them. The spark in Eaton Canyon had been traced back to a transient man trying to keep warm in the middle of the night, and people were calling for the death penalty.

Gus drove back to the barn, mistrustful of that watchman, but he had in fact put Chap's blanket on and she was lying on a bed of fresh straw. She lifted her head as Gus drew the stall door open, but she didn't rise. He eased himself down beside her and leaned back on her shoulder.

He regretted not trying harder to make it back for the funeral, but in this dismal plywood stall, he felt Carlotta's hand to his cheek, teasingly telling him, "It's not like I was there anyway."

Gus steadied his breath until he felt the steady thump of Chap's heart within the barrel of her ribs. How deeply she slept. No more lamps, no more counterfeit days. Just a cool high desert night.

He'd always believed horses could, in some small way, hear your thoughts. Silently now, he asked the mare for her forgiveness, realizing as he did that this was much the same prayer Rory had been saying to the animals, releasing them from mankind's sins. Of course she had gone back to the barn for the fox that night. Not to clean up after him, but to give that animal some kind of peace.

Gus drove back to the motel, looking at every beige car like it might be Sarah Price's. In the room, he lay back down on the floor, still picturing Sarah, but up above him now, sound asleep on the bed, her copper hair, her arm hanging down toward him. He touched the ends of her imagined fingers with his own and told her he'd never take another drink again, so long as he lived.

MONA WAS STILL home, the TV flickering in the window, Hawkeye's motorcycle parked in the shade of the magnolia tree.

June said she'd wait in the Mercedes. Rory hurried, gathering her camera, her backpack, Sarah's letter, and the prints that Foster liked the most. Even the one Rory meant to keep for herself, Vivian naked in the shadow of the love seat.

"Where do you think you're going?" Mona said. She and Hawkeye were sitting on the couch, watching *The Lost Boys*.

"Out," Rory said. She was at the front door. She'd told June she
was running inside to change, the one thing she hadn't remembered
to do. She kicked off her sandals and pulled her riding boots on,
feeling edgier, tougher in them, at least more like herself. "I'll be
back late."

"You're not missing any more school," Hawkeye tried out.

Rory pulled the rubber band from her braid, shaking out her
hair, and swiped Mona's pack of cigarettes from the table behind
the couch. As she ran for the car, she heard Mona stand up and
Hawkeye say, "Aw, cut her some slack."

"She just stole my fucking cigarettes."

The stands of eucalyptus along the main road were shining
white, their gray-paper bark stripped by the wind. Store awnings
flapped like flags of surrender.

"You sure you want to go?" June asked. "I mean, we really don't
have to. We could just, I don't know, take a drive."

"No, no, it's cool," Rory said.

"I'm sorry I told him about your window," June said. "I shouldn't
have."

Rory shrugged and slid the pack of Lucky Strikes into the side
of her boot.

"He's so worked up about this guy he caught her being sleazy
with on the phone," June said. "Like he's some saint."

"He heard Vivian on the phone? With a guy?"

"Yeah," June said. "Like real sleazy stuff."

They had to park up the road and walk down—there were that many cars. The gates were open, even the front doors.

"Oh, this is even more nuts then I thought," June said. There were two beefy men in black suits with their hands clasped behind their backs on each side of the doors. Bouncers, Rory realized, though they didn't say anything to June or Rory as they stepped inside. "They always let girls in," June said.

The blue recliners were still there, but they'd been organized into a row, as if the foyer were a waiting room. Everything else, all of Everett's collecting, was gone. The divine intervention, Rory thought. And now the house was teeming with bodies, half of them with painted faces. Skeletons.

"Oh my god," June said. "It's that Day of the Dead shit. Of course." There was the flash of a bulb, then another. All the furniture was pushed up against the walls, making a dance floor of the central room. Johnny was there, his face painted white, with deep black raccoon eyes and teeth drawn around his Joker-size mouth. "Wade said the movie was like a heist flick, drug cartels, or some shit, but the big scene happens—"

"On Día de los Muertos," Rory said. "Is Everett Price here?"

"June-baby," Johnny was calling.

"No," June said, moving into the sunken living room, toward Johnny. "Vivian is just helping promote it. No way!" June shrieked, admiring Johnny's makeup.

And there she was, Vivian, dancing among the other girls, her hips swaying, her arms waving in the air, her hair swinging against her back, eyes closed. Another flashbulb. She was in a T-shirt and jean shorts. The same outfit Rory had once borrowed. A silent communication? It had to be. Rory needed it to be. She would be patient. There couldn't have been anyone else, no guy on the phone. Only her. Only them.

There were several photographers roving around the house. One was stationed in the library, just off the living room. He had a white backdrop set up in front of the floor-to-ceiling bookcase and assistants were holding bounce cards, directing light. There was a line of girls waiting to have their picture taken, their makeup done, flowers pinned into their hair. Another flash. Outside, the pool was newly covered, but the lights were on underneath, a sapphire in the darkness.

June was dancing with Vivian and Johnny and all these girls that Rory had never seen before. Dancing to a Nirvana song Rory hated, "Smells Like Teen Spirit."

In the kitchen, a woman was at the sink, her hands plunged in soapy water, a white apron on her waist. Where was Carmen? Best that she wasn't here; she would have recognized Rory. An older man with dyed black hair was speaking to this woman in broken Spanish. He had the air of a restaurant manager: fake smiles and a barely contained hostility. Rory met eyes with the woman, silently asking if she was okay. She just rolled her eyes.

On a stool at the back of the kitchen, a makeup artist was painting someone's face, cheeks convincingly sunken, blackened sockets haloed in rhinestones. The makeup artist turned on Rory, barking, "She's my last. I wasn't hired for this. Only models!"

"Hey, Bobby." Wade came in and clapped hands with the black-haired manager. *Bobby.* So this was Everett's agent, Bobby Montana. "You're still here," Wade said. "I thought you guys were packing up soon."

"Hi, Wade," Rory said, adjusting her backpack on her shoulder.

Bobby Montana looked at Rory, unimpressed, and turned back to Wade.

"Hey," Wade said, as if she were an annoying younger sister. "Go ahead and have a look around, okay?"

The hallway bathroom was locked and behind the door grunting and a cabinet banging back and forth. Then a girl's high-pitched squeal, a deeper groan, followed by the sound of glassware breaking on the tile floor. "Shit," the guy said.

The poured concrete hallway looked polished. The alcoves cleared, the tables waxed. In a way, Rory had never seen this house before; a different Vivian lived here. A Vivian who'd been sleazy on the phone with some guy. Rory had lost grasp of why she'd come. Why had she brought her camera?

The door to Vivian's bedroom was closed. Rory tried the handle, locked. She was considering finding something to shimmy into the frame, but there was the click of a shutter behind her. She turned around to see the couple stumbling out of the bathroom, a photographer capturing their blushing fumble. Another light bulb flashed and Rory heard someone say, "That's a wrap." There was the sound of collapsing light stands, the white paper crumpling to the floor. Vivian was laughing, a laugh loosened by liquor. Rory could tell. Maybe something else.

Half the party was leaving. The makeup artist was closing her compacts, two dozen girls streaming out of the house, the woman who'd rolled her eyes at Rory, the photographers following, hefting camera bags, sweat dotting their brows. Wade was standing with Bobby Montana at the front door. Rory stopped, waiting around the corner out of view.

"I appreciate you keeping the rest of tonight . . . mellow? Everett would die if he knew I wasn't staying, but we've got the pictures—it'll be an amazing spread, *The Comeback Kid*. Perfect publicity tie-in with the movie, and Vivian will be booking her own jobs in no time. It's time to move on, am I right? Life goes on. But the fucking traffic! I mean, the 101 was a clusterfuck *before* these fires."

"I totally get it, man," Wade said. "I got your back. Small crowd now."

Vivian was a model? Becoming an actress? What had happened?

"Just don't let her do anything stupid. Everett needs to focus. He's had enough trouble."

"You can count on me," Wade said.

For a brief moment Rory could hear helicopters in the distance, then the front door closed. And ska music started blaring from the stereo.

"Ugh," June said, coming up behind Rory. "I hate this mosh-pit shit."

And here was Wade, putting his arm around both of them. "Well?" he asked. "Anybody look familiar? I got this bad feeling it's one of my friends."

Johnny Naughton was moving from person to person with the cavalier air of a retriever, tail wagging. He stopped in front of girls longer, whispering in their ears, leaving white streaks of paint on the unpainted faces, and sure enough, like baby birds, each one opened her mouth and Trouble dropped a tablet—acid or Ecstasy—onto her extended tongue.

"Not Johnny?" June asked.

"Hell no," Wade said. "Guy's as loyal as a parasite."

"He brought all kinds of weird shit," June said. "He gave me these." She held out her palm. A little white square and a blue pill, a *K* stamped across its center.

"Enjoy," Wade said, moving toward the living room. He stopped and turned back toward Rory. "Take your backpack off, would you? You're making me nervous."

"Yeah," June said. "Let's just stay. I'm actually glad we came."

A tall brunette leaned in and kissed Johnny on the cheek. When she pulled away, he grabbed the back of her head and kissed her on the mouth. When he moved on, the girl turned to her friends, wiping her mouth, wide-eyed but laughing.

Wade and Vivian were walking down the hall, his arm around her, her head tipped onto his shoulder.

It was a sickness, this jealousy. Compounded now by someone she didn't know.

"Here," June said, sliding Rory's backpack from her arm. "Let's just put this in here. They've got all the pictures they needed for tonight anyway."

There was time; there had to be. She would wait. And then she would turn a corner and Vivian would be standing there, alone.

"Well," June said, holding open her palm again. "Shall we?"

TOPANGA CANYON, CALIFORNIA

JULY 2, 2015

THERE IS ONE main road through the canyon, a switchback line cut into the mountainside that skirts the edge of the cliff for seven miles. A funnel-like road made narrower by scrub oak and outcroppings of rock. I cannot imagine anyone walking these roads, yet as soon as I think this, there is a hitchhiker, his grin bright against his sun-worn face, holding a hand-scrawled sign: THIS WAY TO HEAVEN?

Soon after the road widens, small shops with hand-painted signs come into view. One-story places with porches and chimes, peace flags strung from their overhangs. There is the market, the parking lot alongside it, the creek bed, all visible from the main road. Outside the market, men shift from foot to foot, beating dust from their hats, waiting for a car to slow, someone to wave them over—the possibility of a meal.

No one heard from Sonja again. Grandad said she likely went to Tucson, that he remembered her having family there. Or maybe she went back to Veracruz. Jorge was deported after serving five years. "I hope they found each other again," Grandad said.

"Did you ever visit him?" I asked.

"Christ, Charlie." He got up and walked around the room. Running his hand over his head. He kicked the end of the kitchen cabinet. "If I was proud of who I'd been, don't you think we'd have told you all this sooner?"

Dear Charlie, Mama's letter read.

> *I'm not sure where I should begin.*
>
> *In some way every life is the result of a chain reaction of various incidents, but your life, your conception, really, it hinged on rather tragic events. And I feel responsible for most of them.*
>
> *The fire in 1993, the one that Grandad and I have always said is why we left California, started on the morning of November 2, 1993. The same day you were conceived.*
>
> *I was only fifteen. But I already considered myself a photographer and I was already dreaming that I would one day have the life that I have been lucky enough to have. A home among horses, our collies, and sweet Jo-jo goat. I didn't know what kind of photographer I would be, but I knew I wanted to travel, to see the world through the lens of a camera. What I didn't expect, of course, was you.*

Up ahead, I see the fork in the road, the turn onto Old Topanga. There's a fancy restaurant on the corner there, its patio strung in fairy lights. Grandad said they never went there, that it was a place for tourists, but there's nothing gimmicky about it and now I think he meant it wasn't somewhere they could afford.

There is still no gas station. No hospital. A two-room post office and only one fire station off the main road.

The first call came in from a home up above Calabasas Peak. A man pouring himself a second cup of coffee who yelled for his wife, pointing at the white genie of smoke rising just beyond the summit. There's smoke, he told the operator. And then, with the phone still in his hand, there was ignition; a flash of brightness, the flare so strong and high that he and his wife looked skyward, imagining a plane or a bomb had fallen from above. Power lines were tossing in the wind like jump ropes strung from hill to hill, but no, as far as he could see, none of the poles had come down. It looks like it's near the water towers, he said, yes, off Old Topanga Road. Far from any homes, but definitely a threat to the ranch nearby. First there was the crackling sound of brush, then came a whistling gust of wind, followed by a stampede of flames.

I made choices in the weeks, the days, even the hours before that fire began that were the equivalent of lighting a match in the underbrush—selfish and risky—and I didn't stop there.

TOPANGA CANYON, CALIFORNIA

NOVEMBER 2, 1993

"RORY RAMOS, THERE you are. We were just talking about you," June said. She was sitting up against the house, on the ground, her elbows on her knees, the stem of a wine bottle between her fingers, and the same wild saucer-size pupils she'd had for hours. Vivian was beside her, on a lounger that had been pulled under the eave of the house, protected from the wind. The pool cover had been removed and bodies were tucked up against the pool stairs, moving against one another, waves undulating around them. "I was telling Vivian how we were sitting out on your balcony that night. How we saw her here, swimming. She didn't know about your view." June was squinting down the barrel of her finger, pointed into the trees. "Your mom was out here," June went on. "We watched her out here, digging in the dirt—"

"June," Rory said. "Shut up. You don't know what you're talking about."

Vivian laughed. "Oh, no. She most certainly does. It's a pretty amusing story, really, how the two of you hung out that very night. It's pretty romantic. Such serendipity."

June laughed stupidly, then wiped her mouth. "What I wouldn't give to have a cigarette."

"I have them," Rory said, pulling them from her boot. "Maybe you can go inside, smoke in there. Here, take them."

"No, no," June said, swatting the pack away. "Daddy would smell it on me."

It was nearing dawn, maybe 4:00 a.m. The trees were outlined in a turquoise glow. Rory was playing back the night, trying to remember where her backpack had gone. "Where's Wade?" she asked, looking at both of them.

"That's kind of funny," Vivian said, rolling to her side. "You asking me that." She was clearly stoned. But also angry.

In the living room, people were sleeping on the settee, against the walls, on the floor under the table. The hookah had been dragged out of Vivian's room and was on its side in the foyer. One of Johnny's surfer friends was snoring loudly in a blue chaise, his head back, mouth open toward the skylights. Rory started picking up chairs, righting spilled glasses. She had played along, dancing with June, talking to the man-boys and the girls who hung from their arms about surf conditions, blackouts at frat parties, and how the Santa Anas ruin everyone's mood. The man-boys were friends of Naughton, Surf Nazis, the girls apparently impressed. "They don't let just anyone surf their beaches, unless they're known, you know? One of *them*. It's not racist. It's just no riffraff, you know?"

She'd tried to find Vivian alone, saw her moving through rooms, but someone else was always there. And now it was June.

"Well, look who's still up." Johnny's voice. "And look at that," he said, seeing the people in the pool. "That's when you know your Ecstasy is good." He pressed his hands to the new glass and made a humping motion against it. He was wearing Rory's backpack.

"Hey," Rory blurted. "That's mine."

"Oh," Johnny said, turning around. He'd wiped his face paint off, but there were shadows of the dark sockets for his eyes and a white line of makeup left at his jaw. "This is yours?" He swung the backpack off and looked at it.

Rory's mind was racing. "Yes." She took it from him.

"Hey, sorry," he said. "I swear I wasn't gonna steal it." He hadn't looked inside. At least not in the binder. What would happen, she could not fathom, if he'd seen inside.

"Fucking sweating, man, fucking sweating." Wade was coming around the corner, apparently continuing a conversation with Johnny that Rory hadn't heard. "I just spent six fucking hours terrified of my old man. That was the worst fucking ride, Trouble. The worst."

The house's intercom crackled, and someone slurred nonsense into the microphone.

Vivian came in the sliding glass doors. "I need to get out of here," she said.

"Hey, there's my model girlfriend." Wade stepped up and pulled her toward him again.

"I need to go somewhere else," Vivian said.

"Hey, now, I promised Bobby I'd keep you out of trouble tonight."

"Well, it's almost fucking morning, Wade, so job's all done."

"I'm with her, man," Johnny said, wiping at his nose. "Where should we go?"

Rory unzipped her backpack and carefully pulled the camera out.

"You want to go to the beach?" Wade asked.

Vivian was glaring at her. Rory sensed she wasn't wanted along now, not after June's anecdote. Maybe even before that. Vivian had avoided her all night.

"How about the ranch?" Rory asked. "I mean, it's going to be yours soon, right, Wade? Maybe Vivian wants to see it?"

"You're weird, Spice. I'd think you'd be just as pissed as your old man, but no, you're just gonna kiss my ass, huh?"

Rory raised her camera at Wade then. He smiled and she took a picture of all three of them.

"Does she have to come?" Vivian asked.

"She's like my sister's girlfriend, so yeah. Where is June anyway?"

Rory rubbed the back of her neck, feeling the weight of the camera strap.

"She took two Klonopin," Vivian said. "She's snoring on the chaise."

"Fuck it. Come on, Rory, maybe your old man will have actually braved coming home. Robin said he was on his way back with your little mare."

"Oh, yeah," Vivian said. "Your dad." She gestured at Wade's nose. "He's a real slugger."

"At least Spice doesn't hold a grudge, am I right? I mean, it's not like I wanted your horse to get hurt. It just happened." Vivian pulled a half-empty bottle of vodka off the counter and went out the front door. "We can call it even for Fresno," Wade said, following after her.

I worry that you will read this and think how naïve I was. But going to the barn had always felt like a solution to me; it was the place where I felt the most useful in the world, that gave me purpose. I had power there. I wasn't thinking any of this, of course, not so explicitly, but I felt like going there would solve something. Barns are good for hiding, as you know. For secrets and daydreams. Mostly I was excited. I wanted Vivian to see the ranch I loved. I wanted Chaparral to be home, in her stall. The sun was going to rise soon and with it, possibilities. I had only a vague concern about the fact that we had left June.

Outside the house, Wade handed Johnny his keys, saying he still had trails in his vision. He held the front door open for Vivian, giving her shotgun. "Such a gentleman," she said. Then he got in back with Rory.

Johnny pulled out of the gates and Vivian handed him the vodka. "What we should've brought was a bottle of champagne. Christen the place," he said, taking a slug before passing it back.

"Let's not get ahead of ourselves. That one old lady is trying to pull some bullshit on my dad. I'm not worried, but it's gonna take a little longer to finalize the deal."

Mrs. Keating, Rory thought. There was still some hope.

"So, we're going to see the ranch you *might* own," Vivian said.

Rory could only see the very tip of her nose and lips.

"Down, girl," Johnny said. "I think you're in enough hot water as it is."

"Speaking of which, Rory, did anybody at that party look familiar? I invited everybody in Vivian's little black planner."

"Except for a few," Vivian said. She wasn't afraid of them.

"Maybe it's Bobby," Johnny said.

"He wishes," Vivian said, tipping the bottle back again. "And I fucking told you, it was my English teacher from Westerly. He's kind of a friend."

"He's *kind of* a fucking pervert," Wade said. "If that's true. But I am calling your bluff."

Rory's mind was scrambling, trying to get a grip, like an animal's claws against a smooth surface; did she know anything about Vivian at all?

The ranch was still sunk in a pocket of night and the gates were locked shut. Johnny leaned on the horn and there was the sound of horses startling, their bodies rushing back against the paddock walls. Rory could see down to Chap's stall. The door was still open, the stall still empty.

"Jesus," Wade said. "A little decorum, would ya, Johnny?"

"Why?" Johnny smiled. "Don't your spics get up at the ass crack of dawn anyway?"

Maybe Gus would pull in soon. Maybe he had driven all night.

The lights in Sonja and Jorge's house flicked on, then off, and the beam of a flashlight came bouncing down the path. Tomás's house, Rory corrected herself. It was his alone now.

He was running to the gate. "He thinks it's an emergency,"

Rory said. His face was lit up and washed white in Wade's high beams.

"Now *he* looks like a skeleton." Johnny laughed.

Tomás unlocked the padlock and swung the gate open, stepping back to let them pull in, before hunching over, his hands on his knees, trying to catch his breath.

"Ha, ha," Johnny said, pulling into the first space outside the office. "We scared the fucking tamales off you, didn't we?"

Rory got out and started toward Tomás. The wind had begun blowing again, the cypress trees swaying rhythmically, the halters hanging on the railing of the corral making a fitful clanking.

Johnny slammed the door to the Scout. "He thought la migra was coming for his ass!"

The school horses were huddled together under the shed, seeking solace. The lights over the tack room had not gone on—they hadn't woken the others. "It isn't even five in the morning. Of course I was scared . . ." Tomás said, to Rory. Sonja had warned him; INS might come for her, but in her absence, they would ask about everyone else.

Vivian yelled, "Can we all just get the fuck out of this wind?"

"Yeah, let's go," Johnny said, adjusting his belt buckle. "He's got beer up there," he said, with a fist to Tomás's shoulder. "I know that for a fact."

"No," Tomás said. "I mean, only a few."

"Tequila, too, no doubt," Wade said. "We'll have a drink, then I'll give you the tour." He put his arm around Vivian, but this time she pushed at him, walking away on her own. She didn't look back at Rory.

Rory started to follow, but Tomás touched her arm, stopping her. "Are you all right? That's Vivian Price, isn't it?"

"Yeah," Rory said. "I'm sorry about this. I didn't think Johnny was going to wake you."

"I'm just surprised you're with them—" Then Sonja hadn't told him about Vivian, about them.

"Well," Rory said. "I—you weren't at Carlotta's funeral. And then there was this thing at Vivian's house. A party, I guess. I got invited. Wait," she said, remembering. "I have something for you." She took his hand, leading him into the office, out of the wind.

Inside, she flipped on the desk lamp, a banker's lamp, the sort that threw a soft yellow glow onto the surface beneath it. She lifted her backpack to the desk and started riffling through. "It was in here." She pulled the binder out—it wasn't in there—it was in its own sleeve, she'd made sure. "The picture I took of you," she said. "I printed it. Oh, here."

She'd zipped it into the exterior pocket. It was dark and grainy, with little definition, not like the others, but the lines of the car were clear, and the abandon on his face, his independence. She held it out to him, but he was holding the binder.

"Can I? You said you would show me one day, remember?" She *had* said this. He laid the binder down and began turning the pages, seeing the prints of Vivian.

"I don't know about photography, but these are really crazy."

"Because they're of her?" Rory asked.

"No," Tomás said. "I mean, honestly, I didn't even realize that, not until this one . . ." The picture of Vivian staring at the lens from above her knees. That was her. That was what Rory loved about that image most; she had captured the Vivian she knew. "How did you do this?" Tomás was asking. "They're really, really cool—I mean, they're haunting."

She started telling him about Foster and the photo editor he knew and how he'd agreed to wait to show her the negatives until Rory had shown Vivian. "She still hasn't seen them," Rory said. "Honestly, I only went to the party to show her and then we were never alone. No one else knows." Rory looked at Tomás, seeing that he understood, grateful she could read that on his face, that she knew him that well. That he wasn't judging her. She had an urge to thank him, but the Dutch doors slammed open and Vivian walked in and on the wind that rode in behind her the sleeves of the binder fanned over like a flip-book. She was alone.

"You have to see these," Tomás said to her. "Are they coming?" He went to the door, closing it, but there was no view of his house from the front of the office.

"Hi" was all Rory managed to say.

Vivian pulled the binder across the table, bringing it closer to her, directly under the lamp. Rory couldn't see her face, couldn't read it.

"I've been wanting to talk to you all night," Rory said finally. "I have—"

"Lemme guess," Vivian said. "An opportunity?" She smacked the back of her hand against the image in front of her—the one Rory had intended to keep. "Were you thinking maybe you'd sell these? Make yourself a little bit famous? I don't know if you heard all that nonsense with Bobby, but I'm about to become a model, maybe even an actress? Something to transform myself—an opportunity on the heels of Everett's new feature. Did you know, Rory, there's *an opportunity in every tragedy?* It's true. Bobby Montana said so. In fact, did you know my brother wasn't even two years old when he died?" She was still flipping through the pictures. "And here I am getting to chill out and smoke a joint in the house of the guy that fucking killed him? So by all means, sell this picture. Make a profit, please. Because this is how I really am, this is exactly how I feel. You nailed it, Rory. I am one fucking gutted animal." Tears were falling down her face, but there was no crying in her voice. "Go ahead, Rory, please. Make something out of me."

Rory looked at her hands. They were shaking, but she couldn't bring herself to move, to speak. It was the dream she'd had so many nights in a row—it was coming at her in flashes now, but it had changed, nights ago, it had shifted and the animal that woke her—the animal she always saw struggling on the hillside, trying desperately to free itself from the path of her house—was Vivian. Vivian on the night Charlie died. She knew this, she sensed it. And Rory remembered feeling that Vivian stood a chance to get free until she paused and looked right at Rory and smiled, a perfectly posed smile-for-the-TV-cameras smile, and then she was gone. And Rory still had not woken. The house still falling.

She was right, of course. Of all the things I had stolen, this was the worst.

Vivian picked the binder of prints up from the desk and she threw it across the room—some prints sliding free of their sleeves—and then the lamp, grabbing it by its stem and slamming it to the floor. Rory heard the green glass shade shatter, but the room had gone dark. The letter, Rory thought, give her the letter from Sarah. She started digging in her backpack again, desperately. The winds were howling outside, rattling the windows in their frames. And then the door opened. "I don't know where the fuck she went." Johnny's voice. "But—"

Wade flicked the switch on the wall and light sprang onto them like theater lights, too clarifying, too obvious. Johnny was in the doorway. Wade had a bottle of tequila in his hand. The lamp was shattered on the floor. Rory and Tomás were behind the desk. Tomás was blinking, as if he'd been hit, his hair still matted from sleep. Rory had her hand in her backpack, her camera hanging across her chest. The letter had been tucked inside the binder. She saw it now, the ocean waves of Sarah's handwriting sliding under the edge of the couch. And Vivian was bent over, racked with sobbing. A piece of green glass was stuck in her foot like a wing. The pictures were scattered across the floor. "Fuck," Rory said.

"*What the fuck* is right," Wade said.

"Here," Tomás said. "Let me help." And he started toward Vivian.

"Don't you fucking touch her." Johnny. Rory saw his hand go to the edge of his belt, to his hip; was he reaching for the gun? Rory put her arm out, stopping Tomás.

Vivian had the shard of glass pinched between her fingers. She turned her head away and pulled, crying out in pain, then a hysterical kind of laughter. "I did it," she said, holding the shard. "I did it."

"And what is this?" Wade was sliding one of the prints with the toe of his shoe. It was Vivian unraveling from the curtains. Naked. "I know that house," he said.

"Of course you do, you stupid fucking prick. You know everything, don't you?" She threw the shard of glass at him and it bounced off his chest. "You know everyone and everything about everybody, including the man who took my brother from me, so you take me to his house?" She was hitting him with open hands, the glass crunching under her sandals. He hadn't taken his eyes off the picture on the floor, as if the image were the only thing that mattered. *"Where are the keys?"* Vivian was demanding, slapping his chest. "Give me the fucking car keys! I'm not fucking staying here with any of you."

"They're in the car," Johnny said.

Wade looked up at Johnny, a rattled, crazy look in his eyes. "What the fuck, Johnny?" The door slapped back. Vivian was already gone, the engine of the Scout turning over, the tires squealing against the asphalt. Wade lunged at the open door, yelling, "That's my fucking truck," the wind swallowing his words, spiraling them up into the trees. "You fucking bitch."

Johnny ran his arm across his nose, looking at Rory. "These are yours?"

A cellar door was opening, everything hidden suddenly pressing into the light.

Tomás was murmuring, "Lo siento, Rory, lo siento."

Johnny bent down and picked up the binder, his shoe pushing the letter deeper under the couch, almost out of view. "I told you," he said. "I had a feeling."

Wade walked over to Rory, and without looking at her he took hold of the straps of her camera, wrapping and tightening them around her throat. "Wade," she said. "Please."

"You've been—" He bent down, picking up one of the proof sheets, dragging Rory with him. "You've been fucking her, haven't you? I tell you to stay off my sister, you don't listen. Then that's not enough? You have to go after Vivian? What kind of fucking voodoo bitch are you? She's no lesbian."

Tomás, Rory would understand later, had picked up the Silver Trophy cup from the end of the desk and brought it down onto Wade's head, so that his grip on her went slack. She fell onto her hands, but then Tomás was pulling her up off the floor and steering her toward the back door, screaming at her to run. Rory heard the blunt crash of Johnny slamming Tomás against the wall, picture frames dropping from their nails.

I briefly thought that I was safe. I had run up the hillside and had made it behind Tomás's house. The air was so thick with dust, I wiped my tongue with the back of my hand and spat in the dirt. That was when I heard, above all the rattling of the trees, the gunshot. I froze, at first, as one does. As if you have to hold very still to know if it is your own heart that will or will not keep beating. Of course, I thought, they've killed Tomás. I didn't doubt that they were capable of that. And then I was running again, sure that I was next. I was running up the fire roads, the path that I had taken months before, looking for ground soft enough to break and bury the fox. There were no houses up there. There was no one I knew. And then there were headlights piercing the ground in front of me, almost as if steering my way, until they were right up on me. It was Tomás's car.

She had turned around to see, to find Tomás in the window, but he wasn't driving and before she could begin to run again, the car came up on her, the lip of the fender meeting her calves, knocking her down. She was on the ground, rocks gouging into her knees as she tried to stand again. Her camera had both broken her fall and knocked the breath from her. Up ahead were the rotund bodies of two water towers. Water towers you could see from the road, from Old Topanga. She had run farther than she realized and she had found traction in the toes of her boots when Wade grabbed the strap of her camera again, leading her by the throat, a dragged dog. He was talking, his words moving on a higher plane, the wind making layers out of the sounds: the scraping of her body over gravel, the quaking of trees and brush, a muffled voice, a cotton-choked, crying voice—Tomás. She wept. *Tomás, help me.* And above all this there was Wade talking to Johnny, having a conversation as if at the table of a restaurant. "They take this leather strap, see, like this."

A belt is ripped clear of its loops.

The thing about trauma is that even after it is over, it is still happening. It is a memory in motion, forever present. I have tried to outrun it, but I am still that girl, and she is me.

And she is holding the straps of her camera and kicking at the ground, trying to get to her feet. Wade hits her in the face and blood fills her mouth; and he is still talking. "They call it a hobbler, cause it keeps the horse from kicking out, right?" Her hands are held to her back and he is lashing them with his belt and she is kicking and kicking, but there is a black sheet in the upper third of her vision, a curtain closing. "Tomás," she says, but her tongue has gone fat in her mouth. "Quit fucking kicking," Johnny says, and he swings his leg back and he lifts her up by the belly and flips her over onto her back, her arms twisting into the knot of the belt, and she sees now the bandanna that has been tied across Tomás's face, muffling him, and Johnny is holding the gun to his head. She turns away and throws up all over her arm and shoulder. "Sick," Johnny says. "Fucking sick."

"That is precisely why neither one of us is gonna touch her," Wade says.

"You're fucking brilliant, Wade." Johnny laughs. "Always get a wetback to do your dirty work."

The sun would be up soon, breaking over the ridge, but Rory could already see clear enough how they had bound Tomás's hands, how they had already won.

It is the kind of wind that rips through the trees, snapping branches away, scurrying trash cans down the road, flinging rocks up from the ground and throwing them back down. All god's creatures wait it out in their dens. Birds root themselves in the densest shrubs, tucking their beaks. And the horses press their faces into the corners of their stalls.

Rory had closed her eyes, willing herself to black out, wishing someone would kill her. She felt the weight of Tomás drop down, the cold metal of the buttons of his jeans on the insides of her calves, his bare skin against her thighs. Someone had torn her underwear away. "Get the fuck in her," Johnny kept saying, panting. He had his hand in her hair, lifting her head, shaking her as if she were a doll whose eyes he could rattle awake. She could hear him, his hand rubbing himself. She felt it on her face. She threw up again.

"You're a sick fuck," Wade said.

"Look who's got the butch tied up and a gun to the spic's head."

They both laughed, sharp, brusque laughter. Someone kicked Tomás, called him a nag, a burro, told him to keep moving. She had stopped struggling. "I think she likes it." She let dirt crawl into her mouth. She felt Tomás's tears pooling at the base of her throat before everything slipped away. Only her body remained.

Tomás. I don't know his last name, Charlie. Maybe it is his mother's, Delgado. Maybe Flores, for Jorge. But in all the years I knew him, I never asked. I called him my friend, but I never knew his full name. He was there when I woke up, wiping my face clean. Crying beside me. I've never felt so many things, the chaos of so many emotions, though I have seen it on thousands of other faces since.

What I wanted was for everything to burn.

The car was gone, of course. It was found weeks later. They'd pushed it off a cliff in Tuna Canyon. It was charred down to the frame. Wade magically disappeared for a while. I didn't look for him, but June tracked us down in Wyoming years later, called to tell me—of all people—that her brother had died. An overdose, she said, not a suicide. Johnny Naughton went to prison, I know that. He was arrested for slashing tires and pouring sand into the gas tanks of protesters who were rallying to keep Malibu beaches accessible to the public. When they fingerprinted him he came up wanted in two separate cases, one of assault, another for armed robbery.

Eventually, Mrs. Keating and her husband, Harold, bought the ranch, believing it was worth rebuilding.

Why do I think you will want to go there? I suppose because you can.

We aren't all given the same choices, Charlie. We aren't all so fortunate.

The gas pan that Johnny had supposedly replaced for Tomás either hadn't been repaired or had cracked again when they drove that car up the fire road. Either way, I saw the dashed line of dripped fuel, the wetness on the earth, as we staggered back to the barn, fighting the winds. I had a cigarette in my mouth, a lighter in my hand, and a singular, wrathful thought in my head. And then there was fire.

ACCORDING TO ARTICLES I've since read, a blue Ford pickup truck was reported near where the blaze began, a truck that they traced to two newly minted firefighters. Men who fell under the scrutiny of a blame-hungry community and were accused of setting the fire so that they could put it out (they'd conveniently had a garden hose in the back of the truck) and go on to be hailed as heroes. One witness came to their defense, saying the power went out seconds before he saw flames, that the high winds had to have downed a power line, dropping a spark into the tinder-dry grass. Years later, those firefighters were acquitted and went on to win a lawsuit against the county for defamation.

Still, investigators ruled the fire had to have been arson.

On the phone, Vivian said to me, "Any one of us could've started that fire."

"But you weren't there. You were home."

"Yeah, I left. Was I supposed to stay? I was hurting, Charlie. And when I got home there were people sleeping on my floor. Friends, supposedly. People who hadn't even called me after my brother died. But a photo shoot? By all means. June was already gone. I went looking for her. There was puke on my kitchen counter. A horror show. It took everything out of me just to kick those people out. I wanted to be left alone. Funny, right?"

"And then you drank some more."

"I did, yeah. Am I supposed to be apologizing to you? I went look-ing for her, you know. When I saw Wade's car was gone again—that he hadn't even come in the house to yell at me, call me names—I knew then. Not what, just something. What was I supposed to do?"

"You could've called the police."

"You haven't been listening," Vivian said.

"So, you called your friend."

She snorted. "He was a better friend than anyone else had been."

I picture McLeod driving up the canyon, his hands gripping the wheel, disbelieving that he has finally given in, comforting himself that this was a truly earnest cry for help, that this time she really needed—she was quite specific—*him*. Only he could help. He lights a cigarette to calm his nerves, this nascent habit of his so blatantly connected to their conversations that with each inhale he can hear her breathing in his ear, a Pavlovian conditioning—no, it is a sickness, his preoccupation with this girl. His hands shake as he steers his aging Peugeot up the canyon roads, the combination of nicotine and curves (perhaps his conscience) making him nauseated. As he crests the hill she cracks her window and drops his cigarette through its narrow opening.

The two firefighters' stories never changed; they'd been driving to the valley to visit a friend when they happened upon the first flames. Their intentions were good, but the fire had been more than they could battle alone.

GUS DROVE STRAIGHT through, only stopping once for gas.

As he climbed the roads into the canyon, the wind was blowing fierce, making a tin can of the trailer behind him.

At the ranch, Sancho was steering the tractor around, finishing the morning feed. A hat on his head to protect his eyes and a bandanna covering his mouth, the dust in the air was that bad.

The office lights were on, but Gus didn't see anyone inside. Robin's car wasn't there yet.

Gus unloaded the mare on his own. "Easy, girl," he kept saying.

He'd thought he would let her run around in the turnout, but she was too fresh, too scatterbrained by the wind, likely to hurt herself. He drew the stall door closed, her bedding lifting up around her in a tiny cyclone.

Of all the people to whom he wanted to make amends—a running list in his mind—it was Sarah Price, the memory of her at least, that he took some comfort in. He thought now of the night in the hospital, what she had said when she leaned down and whispered to him: *We should have known.* There was comfort in the collective *we,* that the blame was not his alone, but there was also comfort in the idea that they could have known, that there was a way of being in the world that could elude disaster, or at least limit its possibility. He'd have given her his life in exchange for her son's. If he could go back, he would have thrown the truck into reverse and blocked the road, blocked the path of the car that he had known was following him. He'd have gotten out of the truck and moved the fox to the side of the road.

At the house there was a black Peugeot in the dirt turnaround, a car he didn't know. Yet another friend of Mona's? But that didn't matter anymore. He was massaging words, trying to find how to say what needed to be said, wanting to be deferential, apologetic, to establish some peace in the house before he told them that he was going back to Little Snake for a while, that he wanted some more time with Joy, though he already suspected he would be staying on for good.

He'd not yet gotten to the door when Vivian Price came running from the house, going for the car. "Gus," she said, knowing who he was. She had on a well-worn T-shirt and jean shorts ripped in half a dozen places, their pockets hanging from the holes.

A man came out behind her, saying, "We can't just barge into someone's house like that." He was wearing tortoiseshell glasses, a clean white pressed shirt tucked into belted trousers, his sleeves rolled up, sweat blooming on his face. The sort of person who seemed innocent enough to cause real trouble.

"Rory isn't here," Vivian said, above the racket of the wind. "I'm worried."

"Can I help you?" Gus said, more concerned right then with this man, his air of thievery.

He offered his hand to Gus. "I'm a friend," he said, "Mickey McLeod. I meant"—he was tripping over his own tongue, shaking his head—"I'm Vivian's teacher. Used to be."

"Gus," Vivian said again. "I have such a bad feeling. I have no idea where she is." She was grabbing Gus's arm. "I thought—I don't know what I was thinking. Wade and Johnny—there were pictures."

"She's been through a lot," McLeod said, like Gus didn't already know.

That's when the first sirens came screaming past.

EIGHTEEN THOUSAND ACRES, nearly four hundred homes, a man who went to save his cat, an older couple whose car didn't start fast enough—a fire that began on the mountain's farthest peak and then went hopscotching over canyons, moving west and north, an unfathomably bright wave gliding down the hills, over to Malibu, igniting new blazes, lapping up homes, and meeting the shore within minutes.

The worst part, Grandad said, wasn't the heat or that it was nearly impossible to breathe, but the fact of the horses.

"There was no outrunning fire like that," Grandad said. "There was nothing we could do but stay and try to save them. We gathered them into one ring—fifty-four horses in this arena-turned-pen. That's all there was to do. Round them up and turn the fire hoses on. We were aiming for the trees, the grasses—whatever would burn the fastest. Trying to wet down a perimeter around us, with our backs turned on these frightened animals. They were so scared. Bodies slicked in sweat, white-lathered, and kicking out, turning on each other in surges of anxiety. The air was so thick with smoke, the heat so hellish. And we had to stop them from jumping out of the ring. It was the safest place that they could be, but every now and then one would jump the railing. Your mama, she never got over that. Wild horses," he said. "They catch the smell of smoke in the distance and they move in the opposite direction. But not horses like those, horses who have only ever known the four walls of their stalls. If that's the only home an animal has ever known, they will run for the barn even when it's the barn that's on fire."

I made the turn up Old Topanga, the creek running alongside the truck. I stopped at the sycamore tree, where Mama said people sometimes left balloons. There is no longer a wall or gates outside the Price estate. Though the house survived the fire, it is a husk in disrepair, sold off after the earthquake in '94.

As I drive on, the spaces between houses widens, allowing for the rock faces that jut from the hillsides, white and pocked as the moon. Every turn is a blind one, every corner unknown, yet somehow familiar to me. And then the road opens and I see the silhouettes of grazing horses on a hillside, the surrounding grasses grown long, the chaparral dense and verdant after a long winter of rains.

I wish I could have come here as a passenger in Mama's car. I wish I were five, or ten, or even fifteen, but I wish we had come here together. I would have put my hand out the window and let it ride the wind, begging her to look, getting her to smile. I would have told her then that none of what happened was her fault. That she could hold my hand and talk to me and that she wouldn't get hurt for loving me.

I would have told you this, Mama, for us both. But chaos, that was what you knew.

I have pulled over to look at the vista that you described to me, the ranch that you loved: the rows of paddocks, the windbreak of cypress trees, the three smooth-planed riding rings, the rebuilt barns, and the corrals, the rock teetering at the edge of the property. All of it held together by the surrounding hills, *like a bowl made of two cupped hands.* It is early July, but the sun is still gentle with its heat. The sweet odor of hay and horses hangs in the air.

I pull down under the wrought-iron archway that still reads LEANING ROCK EQUESTRIAN and park the truck, alongside a car that could very well belong to Robin Sharpe; Mrs. Keating kept her on for continuity's sake. Walking down the driveway, toward the school horse corral, I wonder who might recognize my amber eyes, this brown hair, the sun-thickened freckles over my nose. You wrote that I have my father's eyes. That my height is his, as I have always suspected, but it is also that of a hog farmer, hopefully long dead by now.

Which stories we honor, you said, *that is the difference between being kept and being free.*

When I find him, he is stealing time in the shade, alone, as I so often have, whittling balsa, or maybe oak, with a pocketknife.

When he looks up, I suspect he will have that tic of cordiality— the standard wave, the half-formed smile—that working a ranch demands. I will wait. I won't respond, but after one or maybe three heartbeats, he might ask, "Do I know you?"

"No," I'll say. "But twenty-two years ago, you and Mama, you buried an animal together, a fox, up in the hills." I'll look toward the summit, beyond his house. "She told me you helped her that day, that you held her hand while she said a kind of prayer." I might see recognition in his eyes then, his mouth gently open. "She told me you said a prayer for the little boy, too, that you cried together. You helped her that day and then again, months later. She blamed herself for that fire. And she said you were probably living with a similar kind of guilt."

Mama, these are the things I thought I would say to him, that I would be the first to speak. But standing here now, I see that he has already found the answer to who I am, and each of us is asking, without having to say a single word, that we be allowed to begin again.

ACKNOWLEDGMENTS

I am indebted to Meredith Kaffel Simonoff, my friend and agent, for her unfaltering belief and for always knowing exactly what I need to hear.

Thank you to Nan Graham for championing this book from day one. I am grateful to the entire team at Scribner, especially Roz Lippel, Colin Harrison, Katherine Monaghan, Zoey Cole, Kara Watson, Ashley Gilliam, Sally Howe, Laura Wise, Jaya Miceli, Alexis Minieri, and Emily Mahon. And to my editor, Valerie Steiker, who saw potential in a big, sprawling draft and with profound insight and good humor taught me to trust my voice.

To Louise Jarvis Flynn, for our pact to press on. To the writers who nurtured this book in its earliest days: Olga Zilberbourg, Charles Smith, Cass Pursell, Mari Coates, and Scott Landers, with special thanks to Peg Alford Pursell for all those hours writing side by side. My gratitude to the Tin House Summer Writer's Workshop, the Tomales Bay Workshop, and PAMFA, for time spent in talented company. To Pam Houston—who taught me not to say the same thing twice—thank you, thank you. To Joy Williams, for reading the first rough forty pages and insisting I tell her the rest. To my teachers at the Bennington Writing Seminars, whose wisdom is threaded throughout; thank you, Amy Hempel, Shelia Kohler, Martha Cooley, and Elizabeth Searle. To Julie Orringer, thank you.

To Edan Lepucki, Kara Levy, Lydia Kiesling, and Yael Goldstein. Love, here is my chance to hug you for all eternity!

To the legacy of Francesca Woodman, whose images provided the first spark of this novel. To the authors whose worked informed mine here: Mike Davis, Luis Alberto Urrea, Peter Orner, Francisco Cantu, Darin Strauss, and to Kate Brooks, Deborah Copaken Kogan, and Lynsey Addario, photojournalists and authors of whose work I am in awe. Thank you to the Topanga Historical Society. And to my equestrian family, especially Ayshe Anderson, Gracie Benson, Steph Busley, Heather DeCaluwe, Devin Dunsay, Jennifer Marder Fadoul, Amy DiNoble Farley, Lola Elfman Greene, Carlos Gomez, Kara Kask, Stephanie Middler, Mario Trejo, Emily Kanter Zalewski, and to Corey Walkey, who taught me as much about how to live as she did horses. Thank you to Robert "Shell" Evans for answering my questions about Thoroughbred breeding. To Kimberly Coats and Jonathan "Jock" Boyer of the Boyer YL Ranch in Savery, Wyoming, for their hospitality. To Melissa Cistaro, who is a dream.

To the friends who welcomed me into their spare spaces to write: the Samson-Cowans, the Zink family, and Linda Michel-Cassidy. Thank you to Cathy Garvey Simon—for sustenance and shelter in every form—and Steve Simon, you complete our village.

To Grace McKeaney, for telling me to get back on the horse.

ACKNOWLEDGMENTS

To Mark Milliken, for making California his new home. To John Getz, for bringing out the best in me. To Lynne Benner and Grace Simmons, the missing puzzle pieces found. To Clare Milliken and Hannah Getz, my heart is whole because of each of you. To Emily Meier, my sister in words.

Writing this novel was—in part—an act of figuring out who I might have been if not for various forks in the road and it is because of the love and support of Adam Karsten that I could go back and steer my way out again.

Unfortunately, as I write this, I am sitting in the smoke-thick air of yet another wind-driven fire, because these disasters have and will continue to proliferate. I want to thank the journalists and the advocates who amplify the voices of those who are most profoundly impacted by our rapidly changing climate, and the first responders who risk everything to save lives.

This book is for my family, by any and all definitions of the word, but especially Alida and Markus.

ABOUT THE AUTHOR

KATE MILLIKEN is the author of the 2013 Iowa Short Fiction Award–winning collection of stories, *If I'd Known You Were Coming*. A graduate of the Bennington College Writing Seminars, she has received fellowships from the Vermont Studio Center and the Tin House Summer Workshop. She lives in Northern California with her family. *Kept Animals* is her first novel.